H. S. Cunningham

The Coeruleans

A Vacation Idyll

H. S. Cunningham

The Coeruleans
A Vacation Idyll

ISBN/EAN: 9783337158569

Printed in Europe, USA, Canada, Australia, Japan

Cover: Foto ©Andreas Hilbeck / pixelio.de

More available books at **www.hansebooks.com**

THE CŒRULEANS

A Vacation Idyll

BY

H. S. CUNNINGHAM

AUTHOR OF 'CHRONICLES OF DUSTYPORE,' 'WHEAT AND TARES,'
ETC.

—— to the sessions of sweet, silent thought
I summon up remembrance of things past

London
MACMILLAN AND CO.
AND NEW YORK
1889

TO

H E C

'The idea of her life shall sweetly creep
Into his study of imagination.'

SIMLA, *September* 1886.

CONTENTS

CHAPTER VIII

CHAPTER IX

CHAPTER X

CHAPTER XI

CHAPTER XII

CHAPTER XIII

CHAPTER XIV

CHAPTER XV

CHAPTER XVI

CHAPTER XVII

PAGE

CONTENTS

CHAPTER XVIII

CHAPTER XIX

CHAPTER XX

CHAPTER XXI

CHAPTER XXII

CHAPTER XXIII

CHAPTER XXIV

CHAPTER XXV

CHAPTER XXVI

CHAPTER XXVII

CHAPTER XXVIII

CHAPTER I

CŒRULEA

'O qui me gelidis in vallibus Hæmi
Sistat et ingenti ramorum protegat umbra !'

ENGLISH travellers, and still more English exiles in the east, love the Cœrulean Mountains for their suggestive resemblance to the Surrey Hills. They love them, too, for their blue, transparent atmosphere ; their sweet sylvan vistas ; their woodlands thick with wild roses ; their undulating stretches of sward, where the horseman may gallop as freely as on the Brighton downs. Unlike the gorgeous outlines of the great ranges of the north,— Simla with its wide perspective and snow-clad horizon, Naini-Tal clinging to its precipitous mountain side, or the far-off, awful, chilling majesty of Everest and Kinchinjunga,—the Cœruleans win you by a loveliness which owes much of its fascination to being essentially homely. The unpretentious landscape smiles suggestively of the possibility of hamlets clustering round well-kept mansions, of village spires embosomed in immemorial elms, and comfortable homesteads nestling in

B

some sheltered bend. As you wander over the great uplands, you would scarcely be startled to meet a ruddy English farmer, jogging homeward from the market-town, or a smock-frocked shepherd, sheltering his ewes and lambs from the keen Christmas frost. But you will meet no one—unless, perchance, you come upon a group of startled buffaloes or the tiny-rounded abodes of primitive hillsmen, who have lingered on from a dim legendary past into the modern world, and whose wild shouts to their cattle sound like the cry of Faun or Dryad rather than the articulate utterances of civilised humanity. If you part from your comrades and, as you easily may, miss the landmarks that would guide you home, you will speedily enjoy the unaccustomed sensation of being lost. The path, which just now looked so inviting, turns out to be an impracticable swamp; the woodland behind is tangled and rugged; the track by which you came has suddenly disappeared; the fast-setting afternoon sun is throwing the shadows higher and higher on the mountain's side; a weird howl recalls with disagreeable vividness the exploits of the leopard that is reported in the neighbourhood. Except this all is silent; and the oppressive tranquillity reminds you that, to conventional mankind, solitude, to be quite enjoyable, needs to be shared with some one who will sympathise in its enjoyment and express his sympathy in living words.

Such, at any rate, was the mood of the modern occupants of Cœrulea,—a kindly, sociable race, little given to solitary wanderings or other egoistic, self-inspective practices. Few of them, it may safely be affirmed, ran any risk of getting lost. Rather they clustered in closely-serried groups,—talked and laughed,—loved and quarrelled,—dined and danced,—occupied themselves intensely with each other's affairs, and lived generally in the keenest and completest enjoyment of one another's company. Among the various shortcomings against which the successive Chaplains of Cœrulea felt themselves called, from time to time, to warn their flocks, no one had ever been unreasonable enough to include the sin of unsociability.

Mr. Chichele, who, at the moment when this story opens, guided the fortunes of Cœrulea, was as fond of society as his subjects, but, perhaps, more discriminating in his sociability. He was sometimes condemned as inhospitable by dull people, in whom, with the kindest intentions, he found it impossible to take an interest, and by pretentious ones, to whom his laboured politeness betrayed a lurking touch of sarcasm. Such persons he, no doubt, banished, as often as official etiquette would allow, from banquets at which it was his hobby to collect all that Cœrulea could produce of the best ingredients of agreeable society. For the experience of life had convinced Chichele—by this time middle-aged and philosophic—that an official day ought to be ended by a good dinner, and that good dinners are most enjoyed and best digested when partaken of in the company of agreeable and intelligent women. If they were beautiful, to boot, the effect was still more complete. Soothed by such pleasant influences, Chichele's nature, which froze into a sort of long-enduring apathy under the routine of officialdom and the expositions of secretaries, blossomed into a geniality, which those who shared it, appreciated all the more for its intermittent and fugitive character.

Chief among the alleviations of existence was a pleasant little mountain settlement whither he was wont, as the summer drew on, to betake himself and his surroundings. Here life was, if uneventful, picturesque, and, at any rate, free from many of the ingredients of active boredom. Chichele was something of an artist, and Nature was everywhere around him close at hand and lavish with interesting effects. He was sportsman enough to enjoy an occasional gallop after jackal over the wide upland, sloping gently to the precipitous ghat, which, all along the western confines of Cœrulea, frowns upon the steamy Malabar lowlands, and sheds upon them the swollen torrents of the south-west monsoon. He had plenty of work, and Masterly, his Chief Secretary, brought it all to him in a form, which gave the dullest subject a touch of brightness. Nothing, not even a box full of Cœrulean office papers, could baffle Masterly's diligence or damp his fun. The two men often sat laughing together over the monuments of other people's dulness. Masterly could knock a spark of merriment out of anything, even out of blunders of Cœrulean officials. Mrs. Paragon, also, was a near neighbour and a good one. She was distinguished by an agreeable person, a fine turn of wit, a ready flow of conversation, and a feminine appreciation of the foibles of her neighbours. When, as not unfrequently happened, the two met at Chichele's hospitable board, they generally managed to pass an amusing evening. The amusement was apt to take a more cynical turn on those evenings, when Mr. Montem, who, as president of the Wear and Tear Department, naturally saw a good deal of the seamy side of men and institutions, accepted Mr. Chichele's invitation to a quiet rubber. His gloomy view of life was the wholesome bitter in the salad of which Mrs. Paragon's good humour was the freshness and sweetness, and Chichele relished the one as much as the other.

CHAPTER II

CHICHELE

' It little profits that an idle king,
   By this still hearth, among these barren crags,
   . . . . . . I mete and dole
Unequal laws unto a savage race,
That hoard and sleep and feed, and know not me.

ULYSSES.

WHEN Mr. Chichele accepted the Secretary of State's invitation to become ' Governor of Cœrulea and the Hilly Tracts,' he was labouring under one of those accesses of boredom and disappointment which occasionally drive Englishmen to make essays into the region of the unexpected. Ten years before he would have resented the suggestion as an implied disparagement of pretensions, which justified a higher flight of ambition. He would have sneered at such an appointment as a shelf. Now shelves are excellent things, but one does not like to get on them too early in life. Every man, who has a grain of ' ambition's perilous stuff' in his composition, feels himself, till he is forty, capable of great things, if only luck will bring the opportunity in his way. He sees his contemporaries go on to glory, and he knows, in many instances, that their qualifications for glory are in no way exceptional. Boys, whose Latin verses he used to do for them at school, have blossomed out into Cabinet Ministers, Parliamentary Orators, or brilliant Generals. The fag, whom he used to thrash for carelessness, has become a Queen's Counsel. The pleasant comrade of idle summer afternoons has become an Ambassador. By degrees such a man's ambition grows tamer. He recognises that luck is for the lucky few, and that, besides luck, a great many things go to command success or to make it possible. Audacity, diligence, adroitness, the quick knack of seizing the right occasion and taking Fortune at the turn,—the clear, keen sight that is all the keener for having a narrow area of vision,— the moral levity that glides with happy and unconscious grace over difficulties which bring thoughtful men to grief—all these are ingredients of success, as well as genius, surpassing ability or preter-human energy. The man who does not succeed may console himself with the reflection that it is to the want of these, as much as of nobler claims to greatness, that his failure is attributable. By fifty a man is beginning to grow modest, and to doubt whether, after all, he has not had fully as much as, or even more than, he deserved. Despite such philosophical consolation, however, the life of unsuccessful men has doubtless its reactionary moments of melancholy ; and when a man is dull and melancholy, there is no saying what he will not do.

Chichele's career, so far, had not been fruitful in

great results. He had left Christ Church with no other reputation than that of a popular member of a cultured set, and had betaken himself, by way of completing his education, to reading for the law. A few months in an eminent Conveyancer's chambers had convinced him that his chances of eminence at the Bar were not such as to justify years of uncongenial toil. His patrimony —though too modest to allow of any extravagance—was yet sufficient to enable him to dispense with the questionable advantages of a profession. The influence of a rich, unmarried uncle, whose presumptive heir he was, secured him an easy seat for a Borough, which made but small demands on his energy or his purse. A few dinners, a few visits, still fewer speeches, straight votes with his party, and a large number of local subscriptions, satisfied all the political requirements of his constituency. Meanwhile Chichele drank deep of the pleasures and excitements of society, and formed a large circle of agreeable friends. In course of time he fell in love, or believed that he did so, with a very smart young lady, with whom he had valsed and chatted through half a London season. The smart young lady, on being brought to the test, lost no time in explaining to him that her ambition had a higher flight, and that an agreeable valser is not necessarily an eligible husband for a lady, whose affairs of the heart were in strict subordination to the necessity of providing adequately for the maintenance of a brilliant position in polite society, and the gratification of a large number of expensive tastes. Then Chichele, in a fit of disgust at the heart-

lessness of smart young ladies, had become more indolent
than ever, had renounced conventionality and taken a
plunge into Bohemianism, from which he emerged a
wiser and a sadder man, fettered with the extremely
inconvenient appendage of a wife, whom it was impossible to introduce to his friends, and whose society—
when the first outburst of boyish passion had died
away—he himself found to be entirely insupportable.
His wife was not long in affording him legal justification for an arrangement which secured him—what he
now felt the most paramount of necessities—a home,
which should never be darkened by her presence, and a
circle of friends, in which her name should be never
mentioned except in the bated breath due to a misfortune of the past. Chichele's separation had been a three-
days' gossip in his own set, into which he was speedily
readmitted on the footing—not altogether without its
redeeming comforts—of a man whom it was impossible
to dislike, but equally impossible to marry. But he
was weary of purposeless enjoyment. His conscience
rebelled at the idea of becoming a mere idler. On the
other hand, it was not particularly easy to find anything
to do. Having satisfied himself that he was not in the
running as a future Cabinet Minister, that nobody
thought much about his speeches in Parliament, and
that, somehow, he did not feel inspired to write a book
worth writing, Chichele began to look further a field for
active achievement; and when the opportunity presented itself of reigning over a discernible fraction of
British India, of which he knew about as much as of

the internal economy of Kamschatka, he accepted it, if not with enthusiasm, at any rate with a laudable determination to do the job as well as his resources, moral and physical, would allow him.   He had worked really hard at his task, and had been rewarded by becoming far more interested in it than either he or his friends would have believed it possible that he could be in anything which Parliament recognised as only a far-off colonial detail, and as to which no human being in his London set could affect to possess the most rudimentary knowledge, or to feel the very slightest concern.

Chichele's new post, however, was not without some distinguished associations.   Cœrulea had, from time to time, welcomed a succession of rulers, each of whom had, in his own particular line, a substantial claim to be considered remarkable.   Again and again had one of these heaven-sent despots come sailing sublimely up from the southern horizon, and the official world of Cœrulea had donned its gayest attire and its gravest looks, and honoured with unquestioning alacrity the latest beat of that imperial pulse, which throbbed from the far-off, tiny island of the west.   No one knew exactly why they came; for sometimes, so Fortune willed, an interval occurred; and then the Cœrulean sun still rose and glowed according to precedent: the south-west monsoon still came raging, as usual, over the mountains; the melancholy ocean still heaved and howled on the low Windipatam coast-line; the ships rolled and staggered in the roads; and the huge cargo boats, with their innumerable rowers shouting in wild cadence, came, as heretofore, tumbling and crashing through the surf. Life, in fact, went on as usual; and the more advanced Cœruleans confessed a dawning consciousness that Governors were an expensive superfluity, which, if so Heaven willed, might be spared with something short of a convulsion. Then the new Governor's vessel would appear in the horizon, and with the first applausive whiff of gunpowder, all these anarchic ideas died away; Cœrulea chanted its accustomed welcome, and the new Sovereign was led off,— serene, bland and condescending,—by smiling Secretaries, like a Queen Bee by her attendant males, first to take the oaths of office, and then to be fostered, taught, and managed as his predecessors had been before him. For, from the nature of the case, the Governors of Cœrulea needed a great deal of education and no little management. It was a great thing people felt to get freshness, but freshness has its price, and part of the price was unbounded ignorance. Some of them were accomplished, courtly gentlemen,—learned their lesson with quick intelligence, and practised what they were taught with laudable tact and promptitude,—presided at Missionary Meetings and proposed the bride's health at weddings with affable condescension,—evinced a thrilling interest in female education, shed a ray of fostering benignity on hospitals and zenanas, and stirred the pure depths of female loveliness by a smile which told its happy recipient that Governors, after all, were mortal, compounded of the ordinary ingredients of flesh and blood, and animated by the same genial impulses as thrilled their fellowmen. But others of these imperial emissaries were of less malleable material and of more stubborn wits. There had been, so tradition whispered, Governors who would be taught by no one ; whom Nature had intended, so their outward man asserted, to succeed by muscle and sinew ; but whom Fortune, in one of her playful moods, doomed to be rulers of mankind. The succession of a ruler of this order naturally produced an embarrassing result of independ- ence of judgment, stiff-neckedness of purpose, the vehe- ment self-assertion of one who knew his own will, and intended that others should share that knowledge. Panoplied against conviction, he would impress his personality on Cœrulean affairs with a painful distinct- ness,—would do what he pleased, and in the way he chose to do it, and 'would have his way' in that dis- agreeable fashion in which a resolute man, who goes trampling through a crowd regardless of the wishes and toes of all who are unlucky enough to cross his path, may be said to have it. The reign of chaos would seem about to set in, and the Cœrulean officials would be looking very grave when Providence, tempering the wind to the shorn Cœrulean lambs, would send another Pharaoh to restore order to a convulsed administration and a community quivering with discomfort. Such a saviour of society presented himself in Chichele's im- mediate predecessor. The new ruler was accomplished, erudite, with a wide experience of courts, salons, libraries, and studios. Under him the Cœruleans speedily became aware of the high privileges of their

position. His inaugural address became at once a land-
mark in provincial annals. It was followed by many
others, which explained exhaustively to the Cœruleans
the grandeur of the British Empire, the weight of the
Cœrulean Governor's Crown, the dignity of the Pro-
Consular Office, and the fact—hitherto but scantily
recognised—that it was round the Governor, as around
a sort of sacred omphalos, that the various atoms of
Cœrulean existence were destined to live and move, and
have their being. 'Round me,' he oracularly apprised
his subjects, 'for the future you will all revolve.' 'A
sort of solar system!' whispered a fair member of his
audience, rather awed, 'what does he mean?' 'He
must mean,' suggested Mrs. Paragon, whom nothing could
awe, 'that he intends to give plenty of balls. I hope
that he will honour me with a valse.'

Mrs. Paragon's hopes were disappointed, for the
Saviour of society was not an enthusiastic valser, and
had other and deeper interests than the aspirations of
ball-goers to satisfy. He travelled about his dominions
with a truly heroic zeal; harangued his subjects, and
submitted to be harangued by them on every possible
occasion; piled up masses of invaluable information,
and took an interest in every local product—even the
Cœrulean butterflies—of which he and his Aides-de-
Camp formed an excellent collection. Mr. Chichele,
when he ascended the throne, fell far short of his predecessor's standard both in interest and zeal. He
danced more; he minuted less; he made speeches on the
rarest possible occasions, and then in a manner which

proclaimed at once that he contemplated no oratorical effect. On the whole, his popularity with his subjects was, perhaps, none the fainter for a less pretentious programme and a more human theory of humanity. On the other hand, he now and then achieved, to all appearance unintentionally, a witticism which told the Cœruleans that their ruler was something more than a mere official; and it not unfrequently happened that impostors, social or official, whose fate it was to interview Chichele, left him, after a few searching questions, with a disagreeable impression that the new Governor understood them and their machinations a good deal better than they intended or approved.

CHAPTER III

PRINCE CHARMING

'Embroided was he, as it were a mede,
All full of freshe flowres, white and rede ;
Singing he was, or playing all the day ;
He was as freshe as is the moneth of May ;
Short was his goune, with sleeves long and wide ;
Well coude he sitte on hors and fayre ride ;
He could songs make and wel endite,
Juste and eke dance and wel portraie and write.'

CANTERBURY PILGRIM.

PHILIP AMBROSE was a young gentleman who had always been a source of bewilderment to those who were responsible for his education. There was a sort of caressing familiarity about him, which his father constantly felt to be impertinent, and yet did not know how to check without surliness. An amiability which nothing could ruffle, made any attempt to deal seriously with him seem morose. His time at school had been a disappointment, an anxiety and vexation. All his monthly reports had been in one key, of which Mr. Ambrose was absolutely sick. They all pronounced Philip's abilities excellent, his disposition amiable, and his tastes correct, but his character weak, and his energy fitful and evanescent. 'He wants backbone,' one of his complaining tutors had roughly said, and his father had a cruel conviction that the criticism was just. Every one agreed that he could do much better if he only chose, but then young Ambrose never did choose, and came back from school and college alike with manifold stories of failure, and fluent explanations of his reverses, which were so perfectly satisfactory to his own mind that his father felt it in vain to endeavour to refute them. 'My dear Philip,' he said, bitterly, 'you're like that General whom Napoleon cashiered because he had a perfect genius for scientific disasters.'

'Only,' said Ambrose, with a sweet, pleasant smile, 'dear father, you can't cashier me, unfortunately, and my disasters are not scientific at all, but accidental—I am so frightfully unlucky.'

'Well,' said his father, with a fatigued air, 'I am unlucky myself; perhaps it is hereditary.'

'You are lucky,' said Philip, taking his father's arm with an air of affectionate familiarity, 'in having the most dutiful, exemplary, and admirable son in the world; so now don't scold me any more to-day, there is a dear, good father.'

Philip's shortcomings were rendered all the more provoking by his occasional exhibitions of capacity for better things. He had a good memory for anything that pleased him, a delicate ear for rhythm, a pretty knack of style, a nice perception of the delicate shades of tense and mood, and a reverential love—the only form of reverence, perhaps, that he ever achieved—for

the grand classical beauties, which form the inspiring
sentiment of academic life. His translations of Theo-
critus brought a flush of pleasure into his tutor's cheeks,
and inclined even that austere functionary to condone
the wild irregularity of Philip's attendances at morning
chapel. He won the Newdegate with a Prize Poem,
which, though ornate with conventional plagiarisms,
was admitted even by the stern censorship of Oxford
common-rooms to be extremely pretty. Its subject
was the Girondins, and Philip's description of Madame
Roland, as he recited it to an applauding audience of
undergraduates and young ladies in the Theatre, made
his father, who had come into Oxford for the occasion,
feel a proud and happy man. Many sympathising spirits
understood his pride and joy; and brilliant were the
vaticinations on his behalf uttered by the young prize-
man's guests at the banquet, which he gave that night
in honour of his father and himself. Philip's delight in
his achievement, and his modesty as to its real merits,
were in the best of good taste. 'After all,' his father
thought, as he walked through the silent Oxford streets
back to his hotel, in a happier mood than he often
experienced—'he is a clever fellow, and a nice fellow,
and I ought to be content.' Prize Poems, unhappily,
shed but an evanescent glory, and, despite his niceness
and cleverness, and the nicely-rounded couplets about
Madame Roland, Philip came as badly as ever to grief
in his next examination.

So matters had slid, and as the time for the close
of young Ambrose's college career drew near without

any achievement which promised future result, it became a more and more pressing problem to decide what could be done with so accomplished, irresolute, and unpractical a young gentleman. None of the ordinary professions, it was quite clear, would suit him. The Church would have been a natural refuge for a man of culture, who came of a stock with several good family livings in its gift, and who was lacking in mental and physical vigour; but the Church was, his father felt with some bitterness, out of the question. Philip, whatever else he was vague about, was perfectly clear that he had no vocation for anything theological. His father was a student, and had brought away from college a deep-set reverence for Church history and Church institutions, and a real veneration for Church authority, however difficult it might be to ascertain its origin or define its limits. He had succeeded early to a College Rectory, and had brought to it all a student's tastes and habits. Here he had been for years working, more or less fitfully, at a heap of learned curiosities about the early Councils. He had a project, too, more or less incomplete, of some 'Studies in mysticism,' to which he had devoted many laborious hours of affectionate research. The result was the accumulation of a large amount of somewhat obsolete learning, and of many portraits of characters more remarkable for self-contemplative piety than for practical robustness. He was annoyed and discouraged to find that Philip could not affect to take the slightest interest in his work, and could scarcely speak of it with proper respect.

Once, when Philip was at home for the Long Vacation, his father had proposed to him to read some of the manuscript of his book, and Philip had readily assented, as he assented to everything which cost no immediate exertion or sacrifice. But he was in no hurry to begin the perusal; and when he did, Mr. Ambrose perceived, in a few minutes, that the task was more than Philip's energies could support. He fidgeted over it just as he had been used to fidget in old days, when Mr. Ambrose had insisted on his sitting down in the Library to his holiday task. Before he had read a dozen pages, he got up with a sigh, put a marker into the manuscript, and went out on to the lawn, where Mr. Ambrose found him, an hour later, lying on his back in the shade, smoking a cigar, and enjoying the pleasant ripple of the stream, down to which the garden sloped.

'That's a stiff chapter, father,' Philip said, apologetically, 'about the Council of Cappadocia; it has given me a headache. What fellows those old Popes were—were they not? They stuck at nothing—did they? By Jove! there's a trout rising; shall I go and get my rod, and see if I can make him rise to me? Shall I try that brown moth I had on yesterday, or what?'

'Yes, Philip,' said his father, 'try it;' Philip went for his rod, and Mr. Ambrose retired sadly to his study, put away the discarded manuscript, and did not renew his invitation to Philip to peruse it. Nor did it occur to Philip to ask for it again. He had no turn, it was evident, for Church history.

Equally bootless were his father's attempts to interest

him in the mystics. 'I had always fancied,' Philip
said, when his father told him about his project, 'that
a mystic was the most useless and unintelligible thing
in the world—next to a metaphysician.'

'That,' said Mr. Ambrose, for once betrayed into
showing that he was provoked, 'is because you know
as little about theology as you do about metaphysics.
In my days it was the fashion at Oxford to learn something of both.'

'Well,' said Philip, 'I should like to learn something
about it too.   Read me what you are writing, father.'

'It is St. Bernard,' said his father; and then Mr.
Ambrose read : 'External nature is but the shadow
of God, the soul His image.   The chief, the special
mirror is the rational soul seeking itself. . . . If the
invisible things of God are understood and clearly seen
by the things which have been made, where, I ask,
rather than in His image within us, can be found more
deeply imprinted the traces of the knowledge of Him ?
Whosoever, therefore, thirsteth to see his God, let him
cleanse from every stain his mirror; let him purify his
heart by faith.'

'Now do you think that interesting ?'

'It is beautiful,' said Philip, for a moment sobered
into seriousness.

'You are right,' said his father: 'there is nothing so
beautiful as a pure and elevated soul busying itself
with the noblest and most sacred thoughts : "*ardentissima divini caliginis intuitio.*"   Dear fellow, Life would
be a poor affair without something of that sort in it.

Sometimes, do you know, Philip, I am afraid that you are a heathen,—a pleasure-seeking, pagan, apolaustic Greek.'

'Come, come, father,' said Philip good-naturedly, anxious to ward off a lecture on his own shortcomings; 'don't call a poor fellow bad names. I am a very good Christian, you know, and a very dutiful son. All the same I could not be a mystic if I tried ever so, could I? That is not the way that Nature made me.'

'No,' said his father; 'but I would give my right hand, Philip, to see you for half an hour in earnest about something, mysticism or anything else. You had better go out now and see if you cannot catch another trout.'

Scenes such as these had made it a recognised fact between father and son that Philip could not go into the Church. Mr. Ambrose would have regarded it as an irreverence, his son as a bore. Nor did any other opening present itself as acceptable. Philip himself was completely at a loss, and provoked his father by his serene indifference to the subject, and his light-hearted unconsciousness that it was his business, any more than anybody else's, to decide how he would make a living.

Something, he felt certain, would turn up. Certainty of this kind is only another word for indifference.

Then the Indian Civil Service was suggested, and Philip, after a spell of Mr. Wren, passed a very decent examination, and was numbered among the future officials of Cœrulea. For once he had gained a practical success. His father felt an inward relief that Philip was at last tied down to some definite line of life, and could no longer trifle with existence as if it were a bouquet of roses. Philip accepted his fate without demur, rather enjoyed the vague idea of life in India, and was less unhappy than his father felt that he ought to be at leaving his home.

To Mr. Ambrose, in his heart of hearts, his son's choice of a profession was the crowning disappointment of the long series to which Philip had accustomed him. He had lived on for years in that lonely Rectory, and the one thing that he really cared about was this light-hearted lad, who was going off now, without a pang, to seek his fortune in another hemisphere. He had pictured to himself all sorts of pleasant schemes in which Philip figured as his companion; and now all vanished into air. Philip little suspected the pangs which his adoption of an Indian career was costing his father. He felt no pang himself. He was conscious of a sort of fondness for his home ; but a little of it went a long way. He never had been able to fancy how his father could live on in that dreary house, consorting with stolid farmers, and preaching, Sunday after Sunday, to a handful of boors. It came, he supposed, from his father having been a College Don, and so having learnt to like a sort of half-monastic life.

But Philip had no touch in him of the monk. For him a week of it at a time was as much as he could stand ; so the thought of leaving it fell very far short of agony. Mr. Ambrose, on his part, buried his disap-

pointment deeper and deeper under a calm exterior;
hardened his heart as best he could against a tenderness which he felt to be irrational; and set himself
with Stoical philosophy to endure his son's departure
as he had borne other troubles, each one as it came.
He so far indulged his affectionate mood as to accompany the young adventurer to Paris, and at Paris he
fell in with an old friend, and Philip closed one chapter
of his life with a romantic incident.

CHAPTER IV

VALE! VALE!

THE Hotel Melancthon was a quiet little Parisian establishment, frequented by the countryfolk of Mr. Ambrose's neighbourhood in their visits to the Continent. The host was an enterprising Swiss, the hostess a lady who had, in earlier life, served as a maid in various comfortable English families, and who had managed, on her marriage, to retain and expand her English connection. Hither Mr. Ambrose used to come because he knew the ways of the place and its prices, and was sure of a good bath, an airy room, and a wholesome dinner without ruinous expenditure. Hither, too, came Sir Marmaduke Croft, — baronet, banker, country gentleman, politician, and theologian, — and with him his two maiden sisters and his orphan niece.

What mysterious influence led Sir Marmaduke year by
year to exchange the comforts, pleasures, and dignities
of his home for the vicissitudes of foreign travel, we
shall never know. It was not, presumably, amusement;
for amusement was not one of the forces in life with which
Sir Marmaduke reckoned; and his tours can hardly, in
the most liberal acceptation of the word, have been regarded as amusing. His view of Paris and French life
in general was not that of sympathetic approval. It
presented itself to his mental vision as an irreligious,
expensive place, in which the ill results of Popery,
Sabbath-breaking, republicanism, and other objectionable phases of human error were aggressively displayed.
There were, however, a few fine old faded mansions
which recalled to Sir Marmaduke the gaiety and flirtations of his youth. There were, too, in Paris good little
English societies, where excellent people met from time
to time to raise a feeble protest against the prevailing
enormities, and to proclaim *the truth*, as they modestly
termed their views of morals and theology. At these
functions Sir Marmaduke was accustomed to assist with
a prowess that gave him great satisfaction. But these
performances gave less satisfaction to his companions,
and to his niece Camilla they were occasions of the
acutest suffering. The general feeling of discomfort
and repression, in which she habitually lived, rose at
these moments to absolute effervescence. Camilla's
mental constitution was such as continually to prompt
longings for a bolder flight than her present surroundings
allowed her. Her mother, Sir Marmaduke's youngest

sister, was considered to have been the flighty member
of the family. She defied its traditions of dull decorum,
scandalised her elder sisters by outbursts of ill-regulated
sentiment, and shook the family creed to its very base
by an independence of thought, taste, and action, which
Sir Marmaduke—a man with firm prejudices and a great
deal of fine, old, stupid blood in his veins—could neither
understand nor condone. Her want of self-control had
been at last exhibited, with distressing emphasis, in her decision to marry, against her brother's wishes, a too charming officer of small means and extravagant habits, who
shortly afterwards committed the crowning extravagance
of going off on a campaign and getting killed in his first
engagement. His young widow had, for a year or two,
with her little daughter endured, with what grace she
might, the penance of Sir Marmaduke's grave and re-
proachful charity. From this she presently escaped by
dying herself. Camilla since then had been the guest
of her uncle and the victim of her maiden aunts. The
two worthy ladies had laid their feeble heads together
for the purpose of oppressing her. They discovered,
even in her childhood, the symptoms of hereditary
flightiness, and warned by the mother's example, they
determined to crush it in the bud. Camilla, though she
had now arrived at the mature age of fifteen, was still
untamed. She had proved a reluctant and refractory
pupil in the arts of conventionality. Her sorrows were
mitigated by long intervals of school-life, which, however, had the ill result of making her home seem all the
more unendurable on her return. The general sense

which her surroundings had produced upon her was one
of impending suffocation. There must be a world outside,—Camilla instinctively felt,—beautiful, interesting,
wonderful, alive with every sort of pleasure and excitement. Around himself Sir Marmaduke seemed to
create a sort of moral vacuum of decorous inanities and
unrealities,—an oasis of dulness into which no really
living thought from without could ever find its way,
or could have existed in it for an instant if it did.

At Paris Camilla always experienced this disagreeable sensation with especial acuteness. Here *was* the
world, she knew,—the grand stream of life raging along
only a few yards away,—rapid, sparkling, brilliant, mys-
teriously delightful ; but her uncle's party were safely
moored in a little, dull backwater; no eddy could find
its way to them to disturb the stillness of the pool.
When the regular sight-seeing of the day had been done,
the due quota of churches and picture-galleries inspected, and her uncle was engaged with his home correspondence, and her aunts had retired to repose, there
were still hours when Camilla felt in need of anything
rather than repose, and the quiet hotel began to feel
like a sort of respectable prison. She would have liked
to glide invisibly through the knot of servants who
guarded its portals, and fly out,—she knew not whither,
nor cared, so long as she could indulge a passionate
desire to escape from something she felt to be asphyxiat-
ing her. She longed for a fresh atmosphere, however
boisterous and shaken by whatever storms. Surely
kind Heaven would some day send the refreshing gust

that was to revive her drooping soul and to make real existence begin.

The hoped-for relief presented itself in the form of two unexpected visitors, whom Camilla, coming into the salon one afternoon, in a condition of despair, found calling upon her aunts. She had often seen Mr. Ambrose before at her uncle's, and Philip, too, had occasionally, in his holidays, come with his father on a visit to the 'Vines.' Neither of them had, hitherto, impressed themselves on her mental consciousness with any deeper import than attached to a neighbouring clergyman and a Harrow schoolboy. She now hailed both in the light of deliverers. They came from the outer world, and broke down the sense of isolation which her uncle's society always engendered. Both visitors lost no time in securing their position in Camilla's good graces, which, on the first impression, she had assigned to them. Mr. Ambrose was agreeably gentle and courteous, and treated her with a politeness that Camilla felt very gratifying. Philip's boisterous, restless, irrepressible good humour were a delightful relief. It was like a rush of ozone into a stifling atmosphere. What Camilla especially wanted just now was contact with the outer world, and Philip at once established connection of a most efficient kind. He was enjoying Paris and its pleasures to the full, and described his enjoyment with infectious vivacity. He and his father had been to half the sights of Paris,—amongst the rest to various amusing theatres, each of which Philip described with natural frankness. He had 'crammed' modern languages at Mr. Wren's to good purpose, talked French fluently, and joked, criticised and mimicked with the daring of an experienced Parisian. Even Sir Marmaduke felt himself reduced to playing second-fiddle to this impressive youth. Philip accepted the *rôle* of his instructor without the least hesitation, explained to him his mistakes about the French and their doings, and laughed away the elder ladies' pedantic scruples with an airy politeness that could not be resisted. Camilla, as she listened to his pleasant, eager talk, felt herself almost afloat on the great stream of life.

Both parties were equally well pleased with a fortunate meeting. Sir Marmaduke was tired of haranguing his sisters, and found it a relief to have some other men of the party. It was only natural to go about Paris together; and the fact that Philip was in a few days to disappear on his journey to India and to begin to belong to another world, gave their brief time together, Camilla felt, a strange, melancholy charm, and made it right and natural to waive all ceremony.

'When people go to India, for how long do they go?' she asked.

'Oh,' said her companion lightly, 'twenty or thirty years, I believe.'

Now twenty or thirty years at Camilla's age seems a lifetime. If Philip had been going to start for the moon, the departure could hardly have seemed more absolute. She felt that the idea of it exercised a sort of mysterious influence over herself, and invested the pleasures, partaken in such exceptional circumstances, with something of romantic, half-mournful interest.

The days sped all too quickly away. Every one seemed determined to make them as pleasant as possible. Sir Marmaduke relaxed his accustomed severity of moral tone, and was several degrees less dogmatic and didactic than usual. The two maiden ladies, infected by their brother's mood and encouraged by his example, became absolutely frisky. Mr. Ambrose took the greatest fancy to Camilla. Philip was charming to every one, and used the privileges of his position with grace, dexterity, and a courage which almost took the two Miss Crofts' breath away. The limited range of these ladies' experience had never yet exhibited their august brother in the position of being 'chaffed,' nor would they, antecedently, have regarded such a proceeding as within the scope of human audacity. Philip, however, was quite unawed, joked with Sir Marmaduke quite at his ease, quizzed him with a graceful deference, and carried him off in triumph for a game of pyramids in the billiard-room of the hotel. As for sitting still in the salon all the evening when one was in Paris, the idea, Philip felt, and made all the party feel, was not to be heard of for an instant.

'Let us see what there is to-night at the theatres,' he said, gaily, taking up a newspaper. 'Here is the list—Ambigu Comique—"*Rien n'est sacré*," etc. etc., Palais Royal: *Les escapades de*—hm-hm. That will hardly do—will it, Sir—for the ladies?'

The two Miss Crofts looked at each other as if

expecting some frightful physical cataclysm to follow
upon such unhallowed suggestions.

Sir Marmaduke did not look as if a French farce at
the Palais Royal was likely to suit him any better than
the ladies; but Philip's irrepressible cheerfulness was
in truth somewhat of a relief to the monotony of his
Paris visit, and Sir Marmaduke's spirit rose to the
occasion.

'The Paris stage is a national curiosity and a painful
one,' he said, oracularly. 'Its tone is deplorable—low,
corrupt, debased, infamous.'

Camilla knew what this sort of beginning meant, de-
spaired of the play, and made up her mind for a sermon.

'The days of the great writers,' continued Sir Marmaduke—by this time getting himself into full swing
for a speech—'the days of the great writers, Corneille,
Racine, Molière, when the stage was a real school of
fine manners and refined thought'——

'Are happily not extinct,' cried Philip, cutting short
Sir Marmaduke's oration with an evident impatience
that Camilla shared but dared not to exhibit: 'Look
here, Sir, there is *Polyeucte* at the Comédie Française, and Molière's *Le Mariage Forcé* to follow.
What could you wish for more? Let me go and get
a box for us all.'

The Miss Crofts' hearts began to beat. They had
never been to a French theatre; they had never been
so nearly going as at this moment. The very proximity of such an event was agitating. As for Camilla,
her vehement desire drove her into unusual action.

She seized Sir Marmaduke's hand and added her entreaties to Philip's courageous counsels. Her uncle began to waver.

'I should like Camilla to see some fine acting,' he said, 'and to hear French properly pronounced and spoken. The right use of such a language is a fine art in itself.'

'It is,' said Philip, resolutely. 'Now, Sir, do let me go and order the box.'

Sir Marmaduke was not a man to be hurried. His mind travelled, as he liked to travel himself, with a dignified leisure.

'*Le Mariage Forcé*—dear me,' he said—'I remember having a good laugh over that when I was a boy. We all used to go to the French theatre when I was a young man : all young Englishmen did as part of our education.'

'Yes,' said Philip, 'and that is why English gentle-men talk French so beautifully.'

Camilla, with whom Philip had been taking off Sir Marmaduke's British French, half an hour before, in a highly amusing manner, cast her eyes downward, as if to refuse participation in this piece of audacious hypocrisy. The victory, however, was now nearly won.

'By the way,' Sir Marmaduke said, '*Polyeucte* is all right and proper,—is it not?'

'Right and proper!' cried Philip, with a laugh,— 'why, all the people get converted to Christianity and go to martyrdom in turn,—it is as good as a sermon : don't you remember, Sir?'

'Yes, I remember, of course,' said Sir Marmaduke, with that unscrupulous generosity to himself which people generally exhibit in matters in which their memory is in question. 'Well, Philip, go and get a good box for to-morrow, and we will make a night of it. What do you say, Ambrose?'

'Hurrah!' cried Camilla, clapping her hands in the excitement of so unexpected a victory; while the two Miss Crofts, more self-restrained, performed little silent hurrahs in their own gentle bosoms, and felt that Mr. Philip's influence over their brother was something quite remarkable. Mr. Ambrose readily agreed. Sir Marmaduke, in high good nature with himself for being so good-natured, became positively facetious, quizzed his sisters about old forgotten topics, which brought the blushes into their faded cheeks, and was evidently resolved to recall, so far as might be, the pleasures of his youthful days in Paris.

'We will go and have a dinner at a restaurant. I will be host. Camilla has never dined at a restaurant, and I am heartily sick of the Melancthon cuisine. Ambrose —you will come, will you not? and Philip and I will go this afternoon and order dinner at the Trois Frères. They used to have capital chambertin there in old days.' And so the old gentleman went off, arm in arm with Philip, and came back an hour later, delighted with his companion, having confided to him a host of his juvenile experiences, and actually smoking a cigarette which Philip had given him to try as a new experience.

The Miss Crofts looked on in silent amazement.

They had often been told that they lived in a revolutionary age; but now they felt it.

The next night at the theatre concerns us only in so far as a little incident, which occurred in the course of the evening, and was witnessed by no one but the two parties concerned, converted the mutual liking, which had been growing for some days between Mr. Ambrose and Camilla, into a friendship, which, gathering strength through after-years, became a permanent possession to them both.   After each act they all changed seats, and as the evening went on, it became Philip's turn to sit in front.   On either side sat one of the maiden ladies. Philip, however, was quite lost to their neighbourhood, and, indeed, to everything but the story enacted on the stage, which he watched with intense interest, and applauded at intervals with vehement delight.   Behind him sat his father, to whom, in truth, Sir Marmaduke's hilarious mood had not been very congenial.   The fine dinner at the Trois Frères had been dust and ashes: the choice chambertin had quite failed to raise him out of the melancholy mood which had settled upon him like a gathering cloud, growing but the blacker at every effort to dispel it.   Every one was laughing around him. *Le Mariage Forcé* was exquisitely funny.   Sir Marmaduke had forgotten his dignity, his party, the prospects of the Church,—the crimes of the Communists—his mulct farms—everything, in the unusual sense of intense amusement, and was shaking in hearty guffaws,—the maiden ladies were rippling in gentle cachinnations,— Philip was breaking out into gleeful bursts of laughter

at each new turn in the piece,—meanwhile poor
Ambrose felt his soul growing darker and colder. His
sorrow was taking possession of him. There was the
lad who, with all his shortcomings, was dearer to him
than anything in the world; who had plagued him so
by his weak will and passionate desire for enjoyment;
who had fallen so often and come home to be forgiven
and restored to favour and petted as before; and who
was now leaving his father and his home, practically,
for life, and going, with a light heart, to seek his fortunes
in a world, so strange, unknown, remote,—and all, it
seemed, without a pang. How would he fare, poor
fellow, with no kind, fatherly hand to catch him as he
stumbled, and to help him on his pilgrim's path, so
beset with dangers and temptations? Then Ambrose's
thoughts wandered back to years long past, and showed
him Philip again lying in his cradle, a little smiling,
crooning baby, and a sweet gentle form bending over
him,—the dear companion of the only really happy
hours that Ambrose had ever known. And then he
recalled a dark day when that tender friend, about to
leave him and life for ever, had held his hand in hers,
and bade him be mother as well as father to the child
who was presently to be motherless. All this was a
very familiar train of thought to poor Ambrose. That
last scene had stirred his nature to its inmost depths,
and as it closed, all the colour and taste had faded out
of his existence. Nothing since then had ever seemed
really to touch him. None of the prizes of life had fired
his ambition even if they had come within his reach.

His book—never yet beyond the stage of fragmentary manuscript and half-finished sketches—had grown obsolete before it was born. He had failed in everything, nor had his failures cost him any keen pang of regret. But he had, at any rate, kept his vow to his lost darling. He had loyally, with a pious constancy, put all his heart into doing his very best for Philip. He had grudged him nothing. He had pinched and scraped in order that Philip might have everything in abundance. He had never said an unkind word to him. He had borne from him, again and again, things that were hard to bear. He had forgiven—when to forgive was almost weakness : and now the trust was done, and Philip was to sail away into the mysterious, unknown future, and make his way through life on his own account. In another week he would be gone, and Ambrose would be back in his lonely Rectory,—lonelier, and grayer, and duller than ever.

'I have done my best,—I have loved him,' Ambrose thought sadly to himself, 'and he cares no more about leaving me—not so much as when I sent off Red Hazard the other day, and the poor old chap turned round in his stall and whinnied as I patted him for the last time.' Mr. Ambrose sat in a dark corner of the box, and no one but Camilla had the least idea that he was not enjoying the play as much as the rest of the world. She, too, was not finding the performance as amusing as she felt that she ought. Something was jarring on her nerves. She was feeling sad at Philip's departure,—sad for herself, sad for Philip, and sad for

the sorrow which she knew it must cost his father.
She watched Mr. Ambrose in his reverie with eyes bent
on the stage, but with thoughts evidently far, far away;
and as she watched and pitied, Ambrose, happening to
turn, bent his eyes—by this time dim with tears—
suddenly towards her, met hers, and read in them the
touching story of a kind woman's sympathy. A sudden,
tender impulse seized Camilla. She felt a pang of
compassion. Poor, sad, solitary father! She longed to
comfort him or to share his sorrow. She put her hand
on his as it lay beside her, with a tender, furtive, half-
frightened air of pity. She pressed it for an instant;
it was a moment's act; it was nothing; but its meaning
was lifelong. Many a time in after years did Ambrose,
in hours of solitude and gloom, feel that kindly touch.
The curtain fell presently amidst peals of hilarious
applause. Mr. Ambrose gave Camilla her cloak, and
took care of her through the crowd, with a sort of
paternal tenderness. They walked home together along
the Boulevard, still ablaze with light and gaiety. Philip
was on her other side. Camilla's heart ached for father
and son. 'Good-night, dear,' Mr. Ambrose said to her
in his gentle, pathetic way, as if he were blessing her,
Camilla felt. They had become fast friends.

As the day for his departure came close, Philip grew
increasingly demonstrative in his tenderness. He petted
his father in a hundred little gracious ways. He
accepted the petting that everybody gave him with
amiable appreciativeness. His manner and speeches
had a caressing gentleness. The two Miss Crofts fell

into a melting mood, and watched the opportunity to do Mr. Ambrose or his son some little kindness. They sallied out one morning and bought Philip a cigar-case; Miss Augusta presented it with a blush and a little nervous air, which told that she was really moved. Camilla felt that she had suddenly come upon a chapter of existence that was painfully spirit-stirring. One day Philip insisted on his father coming with him to be photographed.

'We will be done together, dear father, arm in arm, just as we used to like to stroll about the garden at home. It will be a pleasure to have that in India.' So they all went to a famous photographer's, who exercised his best skill in producing a pretty picture of father and son, and did full justice to Philip Ambrose's upright form, comely features, bright aspect, and general picturesque-ness of appearance. 'But, dear old father, how grave you look in it,' Philip exclaimed, when the copies came home. 'One of them is for you,' he said to Camilla, 'and, in return, you must give me one of yourself, please. I shall like to look at it, and remember these pleasant Paris days.'

'I shall like to remember them, too,' said Camilla, with her sweet, serious air, and the exchange was forth-with effected. The whole time seemed to Camilla strangely interesting and romantic, and to justify and even demand proceedings that were not commonplace or conventional. Such meetings, such friendships—so sweet—so soon to end—how full of pathos did life become when stirred by incidents such as these.

Once, as the party walked homeward across the garden of the Tuilleries, Philip and Camilla fell to each other's lot, and Philip began sketching the career which his youthful imagination, enriched by the study of various Indian biographies, suggested as his own. 'At first,' he said, 'you ride about the country and hold trials under big, spreading banian trees. You have a lot of horses, and you fill up your spare time with hunting pigs and tigers, and shooting peacocks and wild deer. Then you distinguish yourself. There is an *émeute*, and you come out strong in the way of calmness and resolution,—or there is a famous dacoit, who is a terror to the neighbourhood. You start off at night with a handful of policemen, ride a hundred miles to his lair, post your little force round it, descend the chimney of the house where he is sleeping, and appear at his bedside. Moral ascendency carries the day. The dacoit surrenders, and you carry him off in triumph. This sort of thing goes on till you become a Lieutenant-Governor or some great swell of that sort.'

'Well,' Camilla had said with great animation, 'I hope you will catch plenty of dacoits and come back a great swell, as you say,—with a great reputation,—a Lieutenant-Governor at least.'

Philip was in a melting mood; and charmed with his companion, he was touched and delighted with her ready enthusiasm. 'Yes,' he said; 'and when I do, I shall come with all my honours and lay them at your feet. That will make them worth having.'

Light words, and lightly said : Philip himself could

not have exactly defined what meaning he attached to them, except that he was very much touched by his charming companion. She was enough of a child to make it permissible to talk fond nonsense to her. His own position, too, justified an affectionate outspokenness. He was a lad without a shilling of his own, except the moderate endowment with which the Indian Civil Service rewards the labours of beginners. One of the compensations of such a lot is that one's love-making is not taken too seriously. Philip thought no more of the scene except as an agreeable incident which had thrown a romantic charm over these few days at Paris. He felt at the moment extremely affectionate and in need of saying something tender. Camilla treasured it up in her recollection, a ray of heavenly light that illumined her dreary existence and filled her girlhood's dream-land with a thousand visions of delight. He would come back, this charming friend, some day—and then—and then—what golden landscapes does fancy draw for young and hopeful hearts.

The excitement and the interest intensified as the inevitable last moment arrived.

'You must come with us to the station,' Philip said to Camilla, 'and keep my poor father's spirits up when he comes back without me.'

'Yes,' said Camilla, 'I should like to come.'

'And I shall like to have you,' Mr. Ambrose said kindly—'my kind and tender little friend.'

And so the three started. At the station Philip became very tearful, threw off all convention, and gave his father a hearty, childish hug with no sort of *mauvaise honte*. How natural that, when it came to Camilla's turn to wish good-bye, in that great busy crowd of total strangers, Philip's brotherly feelings should require something more demonstrative than the frigid hand-shaking of an everyday farewell. 'Give me a kiss, dear, to think about in India—sweet, sweet Camilla!'

Every one was in too great a bustle to notice the little group—Camilla's pretty child-form—as she stood, with the blush still lingering on her cheek, smiling heroically through her tears, unconscious of everything but her present interest—Philip holding his father's hand and trying to encourage him, with the cheerfulness which, even, in the darkest hour, youth has close at hand—Mr. Ambrose, grave with the sorrow of a man old enough to know beforehand what his sorrow will be to him and to feel its weight.

Meanwhile the hubbub roared higher and higher: a belated passenger came panting up, just in time to be hustled into his place : at the next carriage a voluble group of French ladies were indulging in some hysterical good-byes. '*En voiture!*' cried the bustling officials, ruthlessly slamming the carriage-doors, and cutting short a long string of leave-takings. A bell rang, flags waved, the engine gave an admonitory shriek ; the train went clashing and banging out of the station into the darkness beyond, and Mr. Ambrose and Camilla drove back to the Hotel Melancthon with aching hearts.

CHAPTER V

SIR THEOPHILUS PRANCE

'Faites galoper vos agents,
  Extirpez les erreurs funestes ;
Mais, pour Dieu, soyez bonnes gens,
  Et, si vous pouvez, plus modestes.'

IF there was one thorn in the rose of Chichele's official existence which marred its sweetness more than another, it was the troublesome activity of his next-door neighbour, Sir Theophilus Prance. Sir Theophilus was at this time the most conspicuous civilian of his day. He was Governor of the adjoining province, where he had made his presence felt in acts and speeches, which excited the enthusiasm of the populace, and the alarms of the prudent, and which provoked the sneers of cynics like Chichele, who despised alike the popularity and the arts by which it was achieved. His popularity was but one phase of his success, for Sir Theophilus had been immensely successful. He had exhausted the supply of Indian honours while he had still youth enough to be ambitious. He meant to go home and achieve something in England—something more, too, than the respectable interment in the committee-rooms of the India

Office, which bounded the hopes of his less pretentious
compeers.   To preside at charitable meetings, to swell
the mob of second-rate busybodies at a Social Science
Congress, and wait for a seat in Council, was not the
programme which Prance imagined for himself.   He
had resolved on parliamentary life, and instinct and
antecedents alike led him to the camp of advanced
liberalism.   He had been a Liberal all his life.   Liberalism, moreover, was the winning cause, and the winning cause had a charm for Sir Theophilus.   Too busy
to be discerning, and too well satisfied with himself
to be anxious to discern, he had reached middle life
with a touching belief in the formulæ of his party, the
soundness of its principles, and the goal to which they
were tending. If, as it has been asserted, every genius has
a vein of scepticism, and moments of mistrust in its
mission and itself, Sir Theophilus lacked this stamp of
genius ; for his faith in himself was firm, unwavering, and
unembarrassed by scruple, unclouded by doubt.   It was
the sort of faith that can move mountains, and Sir
Theophilus was quite prepared to try it on the Himalayas.   A temperament of this order is more alive to
broad effects than to nice shades of distinction, and
Sir Theophilus, naturally, applied the commonplaces of
English politics, without any of the narrowing reserva-
tions which an English mob-meeting of ordinary intelligence unconsciously takes for granted.   His convictions
were eternal truths, whose applicability, no less than
their verity, was as unquestionable in the East as in
the West, and which needed only vigorous enforce-

ment to achieve demonstration and acceptance. Thus Sir Theophilus not unfrequently found himself in conflict with the fears, tastes, and convictions of those whose temperament shrank from innovation, whose sagacity protested against the peril of experimenting with human nature, or whose experience supplied a practical refutation of theoretic hopes. Such collisions cost him no pang of hesitation, no whisper of self-distrust. It was natural that minds dwarfed in the narrow confines of bureaucracy, reared on the unwholesome dietary of officialdom, should lag behind his flight or refuse to move at all except in an opposite direction. Sir Theophilus went his way, self-satisfied, confident, rejoicing; and he had reason to rejoice. To be certain that one is right, to enjoy an equally absolute conviction that other people are wrong—to be placed by fortune on an eminence, from which one can carry out one's views on a grand scale, amid the plaudits of adherents and the general admiration of the universe, how should not Sir Theophilus accept his splendid *rôle* with thankfulness and pride! So he went from height to height, from one glory to another, till he achieved a sort of provincial deification. Even here, however—such is mortal destiny—there was an *amari aliquid* in the cup of joy—the slave in the Roman triumph, the corpse at the Egyptian feast. Europe and Asia might applaud, and newspapers and deputations exalt the hero of the hour beyond the roll of common men; but his own colleagues and subordinates denied his divinity and ridiculed its assumption as vulgar, political acrobatism; and discriminating friends in England, while vociferously applauding the performer, were, even now, giving him a quiet hint that the interests of his party demanded that the performance, delightful as it was, should come to a close at the earliest possible date.

Sir Theophilus, however, was in no mood to take the hint. He was riding on buoyant waves of popularity, and wafted by breezes, so balmy, so caressing, that the particular direction in which they were bearing him became a matter of indifference. All must be well where all was so pleasant; and Prance, as he perused the well-rounded peroration of his last manifesto on the true basis of power, or the last address which assured him of the undying gratitude of emancipated India for all that he had done for her emancipation, was not to be troubled by the reflection that his secretaries saw through him, that his contemporaries deprecated his reforms as unreal, premature, and dangerous, and that privileged onlookers, such as Chichele, could not be induced to evince the slightest sympathy with his doctrines, or the least approval of his acts.

Chichele, no doubt, found much in Sir Theophilus that was intensely antipathetic. He resented his shallowness, his self-satisfaction, his glib hardihood of thought, his inveterate habit of mistaking hackneyed commonplaces for eternal principles. There are natures, it must be supposed, to which the India of to-day presents itself merely as a convenient arena in which to exercise their political or social hobby-horses,—a *tabula rasa* expressly designed for the inscription of theories or arguments which otherwise might fail to get a hearing in the hurly-burly of English politics. A man, it is felt, may think pretty much what he likes about things so alien, so different, so remote from home experience as the shadowy politics of Asia, and may say what he thinks without risk of too violent refutation. There are other minds, like Chichele's, to whom India, such as a century of English rule has made it, seems so replete with unknown and incalculable influences, with unseen and unpreventible dangers, that anything like confidence about it is the attribute of a fool. A chapter of accidents, among the strangest and most romantic that history records, has resulted in an equilibrium of transcendent forces. It has its own law of stability; once disturbed, it may defy the universe to restore it, and its crash may mean a second chaos. Sir Theophilus never troubled his head about the equilibrium; Chichele never forgot it. Prance's political courage never sank below a cheerful assurance that all would go well with the British Empire and the great Liberal cause; Chichele's never arose above the hope that, as the chapter of lucky accidents was already a long one, one more lucky accident might, when the next emergency arrived, be added to the chapter. Thus it was natural that Chichele's powers of politeness should be sometimes strained to conceal his disapproval of his neighbour's proceedings, and that, in the secret conclaves of the Cœrulean Court, many things were said about Sir Theophilus which that gentleman (who, amongst other opinions, had a very good opinion of himself) would have been excessively surprised to hear.

Chichele was a man of calm temper and measured words : but the mornings on which Prance's speeches appeared in the Cœrulean papers, specially telegraphed, in impressively large type, and enforced by applausive editorials, his equanimity was shaken and his language strong. It was on these occasions that he found Mr. Montem's society especially congenial. Montem's imperturbable cynicism, his sarcastic mood, his disbelief in short cuts, his hard common sense, his contempt for fine phrases and pretty theories—to say nothing of a Junius-like faculty of denunciation—were, Chichele felt, a real comfort. Montem at such times used to blow off the steam of his indignation in highly condensed phrases of vituperation and in official orders, which made the Wear and Tear Department a real scourge to the unfortunate officials who came within its reach. As, from the effects of the south-west monsoon, or some other subtle stimulant of decay, everything wore out in Cœrulea more quickly than it ought, its reach was pretty wide, and Montem, it must be feared, was not a general favourite. In private life, however, his severity was mellowed by good humour and enlivened by a dry wit, and, after a day spent in withering public delinquents, he would come over, tamely enough, to Chichele's little dinners, and sit down to whist with a determined air, as if thankful for a sanctuary into which human imbecility could not intrude, where no reformer could suggest a revolution, and where every blunder avenged itself by immediate exposure and certain retribution, which could be measured in rupees.

One of the ways in which Sir Theophilus Prance gave his neighbour the acutest annoyance was his habit of making his headquarters the rendezvous of all sorts of objectionable tourists, reinforcing them with supplies of congenial information, and then sending them on to Cœrulea with letters of introduction, which Chichele could not ignore without impoliteness, nor act upon without extending his hospitality to guests whose tone he heartily disliked and disapproved. It was part of Sir Theophilus's programme to keep open house and to welcome any sympathising spirit with encouragement and good cheer. The sympathising spirits responded freely to the call, and Prance's residence became a sort of house of call for radicals and revolutionists on the loose in Asia. Here they found the mood, the method, and the material for which they were in search. Here, so rumour whispered, were laid the foundations of many a fair edifice of criticism, theory or denunciation, which shortly established the reputation of a pamphleteer, or ran a lucky magazine into a second edition. Here hints were dropped, which reappeared, a few weeks later, in the form of parliamentary interpellations, each of which imputed a blunder, an oppression, or a job, until the laconic contempt of an under-secretary revealed them in the light of ignorant and silly impertinences. Here amateur administrators qualified themselves to demonstrate the shortsighted apathy of the Government, the cynical cliquism of the Civil Service, the Sybarite habits of idle and overpaid officials, the crushing taxation, the beggared Exchequer, and the generally prostrate and bleeding condition of the country at large. Here young India met silly England, and embraced with the affectionate recklessness of youth. Here it was that Mr. Frontinbras—poet, diplomatist, and incendiary—came to drink the inspiration for a metrical tirade against his country, which some thought blasphemous and others dull, but all admitted to be a tissue of absurdities. Here Sir Joseph Plant, of the Tillage and Manure Inquiry, intoxicated with the heady beverage of Sir Theophilus's talk, and oblivious of the humbler claims of chemicals and rotation crops, broke out into a dissertation on the art of governing India, so consummately foolish, that the Secretary of State, on decency intent and ashamed of so ridiculous a counsellor, buried it, as speedily as might be, with the dull *hic jacet* of a Blue Book. Here Stain, the renegade civilian, rested in his tours of treasonable propaganda, and consulted, *in camera*, with the wire-pullers of disaffection. Prance's headquarters had become, in fact, a large and active *officina* for the manufacture and dissemination of inflammatory material, and more of the inflammatory material than Chichele cared to have found its way to Cœrulea.

Chichele had learnt by experience how the infliction of these visitors could be best endured. He was accustomed, on their arrival, to immure himself in his study on the plea of a severe pressure of public business.

Entrenched behind a barricade of despatches and office-boxes, he awaited the onset; and if ever his guests requested to be put in communication with a judicious cicerone, he was used, with a certain Saturnine pleasure, to hand them over to Mr. Montem. This naturally ruffled Montem, and the result not unfrequently was mutual dissatisfaction. Montem retired from the encounter with protests against the dispensation which brought all the most idiotic travellers to India; his interviewers with the conviction that, of all narrow, bigoted and illiberal bureaucrats, the Head of the Cœrulean Wear and Tear Department was the worst. They came to him with a vague, pleasurable idea that India was a stage, on which 'the great Liberal Cause' was being exhibited in a phase of rapid progress for the edification of Asia and mankind: that freedom of the press was accomplishing its beneficent mission; that public opinion was successfully combating administrative abuses, and trial by jury judicial oppression; that a great nation was rallying for self-assertion; that, with the development of institutions, as near as possible on the model of those in force at Westminster, the future of India, as a prosperous, enlightened, and orderly member of the community of nations was assured. The effect of this sort of thing on Montem's nerves was to create a morbid activity, which discharged itself in electrical discharges of cynicism, and the gloomiest possible prophecies as to the future of mankind at large and India in particular. He would point out that the process of filling some of the oldest bottles in the world with the strong wine of modern civilisation was a highly perilous one alike for bottlers and bottles; it should be done—if it must be done—with extraordinary precautions, like the iron-masks in soda-water manufactories. Chaos being the condition to which all mundane things naturally recur, it was interesting to observe in India the rapid growth of the conditions under which such a recurrence would be inevitable; and, the world being a collection of colossal jokes, no joke could be better than that of an English democracy administering a vast military despotism on the basis of universal equality. Explosions were another great natural and, probably, beneficent law, and it was curious to speculate how soon India would explode. The chances of an explosion were not, Montem went on to observe, rendered more remote by people who went about the country—like children with lighted sticks in a powder magazine—delighted with the brilliancy of their performance and sublimely unconscious of its risks. This sort of thing is not exhilarating, nor, Montem's visitors felt, congenial to radicals in search of aids to radical faith. They went away sadder, if not wiser, men, regretting no doubt that they had quitted for such a stony moor as this the fair mountain pastures where Theophilus had led them, with a shepherd's care, from one agreeable demonstration to another of the safest and best-administered of all possible worlds.

CHAPTER VI

A KINDLY WELCOME

'. . . . In speech, in gait,
In diet, in affections of delight,
In military rules, humours of blood,
He was the mask and glass, copy and book,
That fashioned others.'

Young Ambrose made a better start in India than his father had ventured to hope for him. The disappointing barrenness of his college career had assumed in Mr. Ambrose's mind a deeper tinge of failure from a long list of debts, which had to be disposed of, somehow or other, before the young civilian could be allowed to leave England.

'I am very sorry, dear father,' Philip had said with his usual facile repentance, 'I had no idea that I owed anything like as much. Now I shall earn something, and I will pay you back.'

'No,' said his father, who had an instinctive dread of Philip's good resolutions, 'make no rash promises. You will find it hard enough to live on your pay without any old debts hanging round your neck. You start clear now. Keep out of debt for the future, like a good fellow, and I will forgive you your Oxford follies, and try to forget them.'

The tears sprang to Philip's eyes. 'You are too good to me, dear father; you always have been, and I have been a bad son to you. I know these horrid debts of mine have given you a lot of bother,—haven't they now?'

'I have had to borrow the money,' said his father, wearily, 'and to insure my life. It will make me poorer, of course, and be an inconvenience. However, I must not buy so many books, and I mean to sell Red Hazard. I shall get on very well with Robin and the gig.'

Now Red Hazard was a fine old favourite hunter, on which Mr. Ambrose used to ride about the lanes of his parish, and sometimes, when the hunt was near, would go to the meet, have a chat with the neighbouring squires and farmers, and get a gallop with the hounds. It was, Philip knew, his father's only out-of-door amusement, and it was a great one. The doctors greatly approved it as a main condition of his father's health. A sharp pang of shame and remorse cut him to the heart.

'Sell Red Hazard! no,' he cried, in sincere consternation; 'you shall never do it, father. I would sooner not go to India. Let me borrow the money myself.'

'No, Philip,' said his father, with grave decisiveness; 'that would cost us both a great deal more. You would have to pay high interest; I know you could not do it. All I beg and pray now is that you will keep out of debt, and not come to me again to be set on your legs.'

'Never! never!' cried Philip, and for his first year in India he seemed in a fair way to turn his good resolutions to practical account. He threw himself with eagerness into his new work ; by a spasmodic effort mastered a vernacular language, and passed his examinations early and well. All gave good promise of a brilliant career.

Everything just now looked bright to him. His new home was full of life and colour and picturesque effects. The great wide roads, shaded on either side by grand avenues of primeval-looking trees, whose huge knotted trunks, confusion of sinuous boughs and pendant down-growth of suckers, made each one like the beginning of a small forest in itself,—the endless streams of way-farers trudging into the city,—the bullocks moving deliberately on their task, as if in constant protest against a world where motion was a necessity, or chew-ing a peaceful cud in some dusty halting-place beside the road—the villages nestling thick amid clumps of palms, with innumerable little blackamoors playing in the sand, or trotting by mothers hardly less children than themselves, or scampering into the jungle at the stranger's approach ; outside, the blazing parade-ground, where, morning after morning, the rigid red battalions wheeled and formed, and the horse artillery went rattling by in a dusty whirlwind of its own creation, or roared its harmless thunders to the sleeping world around— the inland lakes where the toil of past generations had

accumulated a precious store, presently to find its way
to the steaming rice-beds—the Englishmen's homes
with their deep verandahs and vast expanse of thatch,
as if shrinking from the cruel glare of the outer world,
—the sea-breeze, which, as the day warmed, came raging
inland with life and refreshment upon its wings,—the
bay, where the sea was heaving and breaking in an
angry surf-line on the shallow shore,—the fishermen,
astride the bare log that serves for boat, riding across
the ridges of the waves as they came homeward with
the spoils of their morning's fishing—all fell on Philip's
young eye with the effect of a fresh and graphic picture.
He was untravelled, and this first bit of travelling was
full of charm.

There were other charms, too, about his new life, of
which Philip presently became aware. He was in the
land of hospitality.

Cœrulean society, with one consent, accorded a
kindly welcome to a newcomer, whose good looks were
an excellent letter of introduction, and whose manners
implied a frank eagerness to please and be pleased.
Mr. Montem forgot his accustomed cynicism in the discovery of a youngster, who took whist seriously and
played a better rubber than he did himself. The
young ladies felt a similar satisfaction in Philip's proficiency at lawn tennis. Chichele found Philip's cheerful, boyish gossip a pleasant reminder of his under-
graduate days. Mrs. Paragon, with a keen eye for
masculine merit, pounced at once on the fortunate
youth,—in the most unblushing manner, threw over

three of her established favourites in his behalf, and rained all her sweetest influences upon her latest protegé. Philip, in common gratitude, was bound to find Mrs. Paragon not the reverse of fascinating, and accepted with alacrity the opportunity of making his first essays in Indian society under the guidance of so accomplished a patroness. The Fates had decided that he was to remain at headquarters for a while; and Mrs. Paragon set all her genial powers at work to make his sojourn in a world of strangers as little melancholy as might be. She gave a *recherché* little dinner, the express *raison d'être* of which was to help Philip to intimacy with the people whom he would like to know, and who would like to know him. She talked this dinner over, beforehand, with Philip, told him about each of the guests, and admonished him as to the directions in which it behoved him to be specially polite.

' I hope you will be duly grateful,' she said; ' I have done the most disinterested thing in the world; I am sending you into dinner with our choicest Cœrulean beauty, Miss Rashleigh, the daughter of our General. When once you have seen her you will have no eyes or thoughts left for any one else. In self-defence I have asked Mr. Montem—I must have some one to talk to me while you and Miss Rashleigh are flirting; for you will have a desperate flirtation; my prophetic eye foresees it even now. You will think her adorable; and so she is: I wish I were a man to flirt with her myself. I believe, though, by your guilty looks, you have begun already.'

Philip, with some blushes, was obliged to confess that he had been to pay his respects at the General's, and had found Mrs. Rashleigh gracious and the young lady as charming as Mrs. Paragon described her.

'Well,' said Mrs. Paragon, 'if I allow you to take her in to dinner, you must promise me not to devote yourself to her for the rest of the evening. Talk to Mr. Chichele about politics or art, or the last new book you have read—I never read anything myself, I must tell you, life is too short and books are too long—or ask the General about the battle of Ahmednugger, where he got his Victoria Cross; or get that little crosspatch, Montem, to snarl to you about the last batch of Globe-Trotters who have invaded his domain. You cannot afford to go about the world simply amusing yourself. You see I am a businesslike woman.'

'I see you are a very kind one,' Philip said, with effusion, for Mrs. Paragon's interest in his fortunes, and zeal to promote them, gave him a new and most agreeable sensation. No woman had ever before troubled her head about him or his affairs; and what flattery is more seductive than that unspoken form of it, which bids the happy recipient understand that he is watched by sympathetic eyes—that his failure or success, is a matter of importance to another besides himself. Philip, as he looked at his bright, kindly companion, beaming with high spirits, at the same time busy with plans to make things pleasant for him, began to think that he should like India very much indeed.

Mrs. Paragon's dinner convinced Philip that she was

not only a good-natured friend, but an admirable hostess. Expert in all the arts by which mankind can be enslaved, this was the art she understood the best, and practised with the most effect. Her guests always came to her with the peace-giving assurance of an excellent dinner and congenial company. In such a mood men are easily pleased, so that half Mrs. Paragon's battle was won before the action commenced. Her table was small, and no power on earth would have induced her to enlarge it; but round it flowed a stream of pleasant talk which the vivacious mistress of the feast kept ever at the proper pitch of effervescence, and guided, with a fine dexterity, in the direction where most amusement would be had. Dinners occupy so considerable a fraction of human existence that it is strange that so many people go through a dyspeptic existence without an effort to improve them. 'Talk to me,' Talleyrand said, 'of a pleasure which comes every day and lasts for an hour.' Mrs. Paragon's dinner lasted just an hour, but that hour was one of pure enjoyment, checkered by no *contretemps*, prolonged by no delay, dimmed by no possibility of failure. If Mrs. Paragon was frivolous, she was never ill-natured, and on this occasion she was sweetness itself. Philip had never experienced anything of the sort before, and it all came to him with the charm of a new sensation. Mrs. Paragon let him clearly understand the entertainment was for him.

'Come a few minutes before dinner,' she had said, 'so that we may have a little chat;' and so eight o'clock had hardly done striking before Philip arrived,

well pleased at his privileged position, and found the
enchantress arrayed in artistic simplicity — putting the
final touches to a little trophy of fruit and flowers that
was to grace the centre of the banquet.

'Not too high to talk across, or look across, you see,'
she said; 'I hate dining in solitude, shut off from my
opposite neighbour by a wilderness of flowers or a barricade of silver. Nothing pleases me so much as the
human face divine. I shall see how you behave, and
mind, I allow no *tête-à-têtes* at dinner. There are the
people coming. What distracting punctuality! I must
fly to the drawing-room. You may follow in a minute,
and remember about the General and Ahmednugger.'

Mrs. Paragon, in providing an agreeable companion
for Philip, had not been forgetful of herself. Chichele
took her into dinner, and left her with little leisure to
listen to any one else. On her other side was Mr. Caro,
a devoted adherent, who, she knew, would be more than
compensated for not having a lady to himself by being
allowed to come and sit by her. Mrs. Paragon considered Caro indispensable to the success of her entertainments, and Caro did his best to maintain his prestige
as an agreeable necessity. He seemed, his friendly
critics were accustomed to tell him, to have walked,
ready made, in typical completeness, out of an American
novel. There was the same high finish, the same air of
exaggerated culture, the same gentle, innocent amative-
ness, copious but well controlled—the same comfortable
cynicism, the same sense of having seen through everything, ascertained its delusiveness, and acquiesced with

cheerfulness in the discovery. His tolerance was unbounded, for it was co-extensive with his indifference.
He was, however, a severe critic of champagne, an
unflinching dogmatist on whist, entertained deep convictions as to the right way of dressing ortolans, and
rose to absolute enthusiasm about Circassian mats and
old Indian pottery. From these sublime topics he con-
descended, in intervals of weakness, to the duties of life
and the problems of humanity. The human problem,
in which he just now took most interest, was his
hostess.

Montem, who was a great recluse, and regarded the
social amusements of life as amongst its heaviest burthens,
had, for a wonder, been inveigled to a ball the night
before, and was naturally the object of some gentle
satire on Mrs. Paragon's part for this lapse into
frivolity.

'I am glad you came to look at us, if nothing
more,' she said. 'A ball would be an interesting study,
I suppose, if one had time to philosophise.'

'But why philosophise when one can valse?' said
Caro.

'Ah, but,' said Montem, 'some of us can't valse, and
are driven to look on. For my part I improved my
opportunity. The astronomer De Vico, I was reading
somewhere, made 10,000 observations of the rotation
of Venus, and lengthened its period by twenty-two
seconds. I shall soon be in a position to contribute a
like discovery to the planetary science of Cœrulean
society.'

'And,' said Mrs. Paragon, appropriating her share of the compliment without hesitation, 'how fast do I go?'

'You!' said Montem, one of whose foibles it was to humour Mrs. Paragon's taste for homage, and to lavish on her the politeness he refused to the rest of the species—

' "You move
Too fast for science, not too slow for love"—

just the right pace, I am convinced, to make you a delightful partner. I looked on with envy, and only wished that I were two-and-twenty and knew how to dance.'

'I shall be delighted to teach you,' said Mrs. Paragon; 'you shall come away with the ladies after dinner, and Miss Rashleigh will play to us, while I initiate you into the mysteries of the art. I object to men's standing about at balls, doing nothing themselves, and criticising other people's dresses and behaviour.'

'You are safe from me as far as the dresses are concerned,' said Mr. Montem; 'I know nothing about them and I hear too much. The modern Novel, especially the American one, is always full of fashion-plates— the ambrosial dresses that fitted like gloves, and all that sort of thing.'

'Naturally,' said Mrs. Paragon. 'It is most important that they should : it is a great feature of modern life.'

'Of course,' Chichele put in. 'The survival of the fittest means the survival of the woman whose dress fits her the best. That is the way that women rule the world.'

'Yes,' said Montem, 'by enslaving themselves, which they love to do. That was an acute remark of somebody or other's, that women don't care for freedom, but must have form. The Chinese lady has laid her feet heroically on the altar of convention. Feminine Europe emulates her self-devotion.'

'But, do you know,' said Mrs. Paragon, 'that there are 180,000 more unmarried women in England than there are bachelors to marry them? What is to become of them?'

'I can think of nothing,' said Chichele, 'except allowing the 1000 richest men in England to have 180 wives apiece. It would add a charm to wealth, and modern wealth—your Mackays and that sort of person—requires a new field. I suppose 180 wives—each with an account at Madame Elise's—would make an impression on the resources even of an American millionaire who has "struck oil," had a "boom" in hogs, or a ring in a silver lode.'

'But, only think,' said Mrs. Paragon, who seemed much impressed with the idea, and spoke now with the air of a person exhibiting an unquestionable mathematical demonstration, '180,000 of them! that makes the odds 180,000 to 1 that no woman ever gets an offer! What a comfort to have got safe to the paradise of matrimony against such fearful odds! My dear Miss Rashleigh, what do you think of your chance?'

'It is something,' said Miss Rashleigh, 'to have 179,999 companions in misery. If nothing but polygamy will save us, I submit to the inevitable.'

'But,' said Montem, 'I return to my charge, women think too much about dress and nonsense generally. Every woman should have an object.'

'I agree,' said Mrs. Paragon, 'but no woman should *be* one. That is just the point; and then, think of our education! Just look at me!'

'Delightful mandate,' said Montem. 'For my part, I am dead against education. I had an examination for a clerkship in my office yesterday, and found a young gentleman, who was under the impression that "romans de cape et d'épée" was French for "Romans from head to foot."'

'An excellent translation!' cried Chichele. 'I hope you gave him the appointment. It is no worse than the radicals in England, who fancy that, when Tory gentlemen talk about striking "pro aris et focis," they mean their hares and foxes.'

'But that is what they *do* mean,' said Montem, 'as Sydney Smith said, a long while ago, "God save the Queen" means "God save my country seat, my town house, my precious rents, my balance at my bankers, my seat in Parliament, and a great many other comfortable things with which no patriot could conveniently dispense."'

'But, talking of pretty dresses, now,' said Mrs. Paragon, instinctively apprehensive of an approach to serious conversation, 'what did you think of Miss Aureous?'

Miss Aureous was the daughter of a distinguished tourist, who had recently been exploring Cœrulea; she was a topic of general interest. Her toilettes were by acclamation admitted to be incomparable; but public opinion was divided as to her good looks. Mr. Chichele liked to tease Mrs. Paragon by his uncompromising championship.

'She is a most beautiful young woman,' he now said, with authority.

'A beauty, of course,' said his companion, 'but how common!'

'Common!' cried Chichele; 'I wish they were commoner! What a lovely smile!'

'A maid-of-all-work smile,' suggested the other.

'It is a very pretty maid at any rate,' said Caro, 'which is something.'

'It is all jealousy,' said Montem; 'that is another feminine failing, if one is to be candid.'

'And being candid is a masculine failing,' said Mrs. Paragon, who was just a shade ruffled by the extravagance of Chichele's partisanship of a woman she disliked, 'and not always a pleasant one.'

'But you like us candid, do you not?' asked Montem.

'Sugar-candied,' said Mrs. Paragon, recovering her equanimity, and leaving a sweet smile behind her as she rose to carry off the ladies to the drawing-room.

Mrs. Paragon, as during dinner she looked at Ambrose across the flowers, had found no reason to be dissatisfied with the results of her admonitions. He paid his homage to Miss Rashleigh with discreet reserve, and showed as little inclination as she did to fall out of the current of the general conversation. Miss Rashleigh greatly liked amusement, and all the gentlemen, Chichele among the rest, were prepared to amuse her. Her smile was so bright, her laughter so gay, that even Montem was glad to be able to provoke it. Philip went home that night with the conviction that his lines had fallen in pleasant places, and that Mrs. Paragon and Miss Rashleigh were, each in her own way, among the most delightful women he had ever known.

CHAPTER VII

DESCENSUS AVERNI

"I can get no remedy against this consumption of the purse: borrowing only lingers and lingers it out, but the disease is incurable."

As the months went on, Philip was moved from one post to another with a rapidity which implied that the dispensers of patronage regarded him as a promising recipient of their favours. In fact, he was very pleasing; above the average in ability; and Harrow and Christ Church had turned him out with an air of distinction and a keen polish of culture which contrasted, much to his advantage, with the commonplace ruggedness and unpretentious diligence of many of those with whom he found himself consorted. From the first he was a marked man; and high officials, ever on the look-out for any sign of exceptional ability, soon gave him the chance of showing of what metal he was made. Ambrose had naturally an eye for style, and without conscious effort wrote his reports and statements with the ease and neatness of an Oxford Essay. He got on capitally with his subordinates, who were at

once won by his ready affability and impressed by his
magnificent ways. The native gentry found him
courteous, accessible, and a gentleman. Even those
whom he was constrained to disoblige, recognised that
he was a good-natured fellow, who had no touch of the
rough swagger of office, and whose natural tendency
was the reverse of tyrannical. His native friends, with
the sensitive intuition of Orientals, recognised in him—
what is always a delightful discovery—the possible
perpetrator of a job,—not a job in any criminal sense,
but that kindly, gracious exercise of personal interest
in one's behalf, the consciousness of which helps to
lend a sense of calm and comfort to existence. Ambrose was evidently a Sahib, from whom such pleasant
influences would be apt to emanate, and whom, accordingly, it was expedient and—so kind Heaven willed—
not difficult to conciliate. So Philip soon had a little
court of smiling, obsequious admirers who gave him to
understand, in terms of pleasant flattery and by a
judicious deference, that his highness's pleasure was
law, and his highness's favour the great object of their
existence. His highness felt this a congenial and
agreeable condition of affairs. Ambrose had a natural
turn for good-natured despotism,—for having his own
way, and for pleasing others when to do so did not
interfere with his own gratification. It was right,
everybody said, for an English official to be influential
—and here was influence in a practical and pleasurable form. Muggins and M'Trant, two uncouth north
countrymen who had passed in the same examination

as Ambrose—and, it so happened, a good many places above him—showed no such happy aptitude. Philip laid this flattering unction to his soul in grasping the situation. They toiled at their work in a way that their ornamental and gifted companion felt to be really servile. They went about, looking like mechanics, in shabby, old clothes and outrageously hideous sun-hats, presenting nothing to the world that was in the slightest degree impressive. Their appearance at the lawn-tennis court and reading-room,—where the polite society of Philip's first station assembled in the evenings for exercise and conversation, and where he was conspicuous by his good looks, smart clothes, and general magnificence,—was really a disgrace. Magnificence, however, cannot, even in Cœrulea, be achieved for nothing; and Ambrose speedily found that the few hundred rupees, with which a grateful Government rewarded his services at the end of the month, proved an income which was wholly inadequate to the necessities of the case as he understood them. If a man is to receive native gentlemen with becoming dignity, and to impress and influence European society around him, he must have a decent house and a decent cook, and a few dozen of wines, such as a gentleman need not be afraid to drink himself or ashamed to set before his friends. The exigencies of the occasion demanded also a brand of fine cigars and their liberal consumption. One of the duties of a district officer was, everybody acknowledged, to be constantly in the saddle; and three-saddle horses were the very least that a con-

scientious view of his obligations in this respect allowed
Philip to regard as an adequate equipment.   He picked
up a couple of good Australians at not much over
£100 apiece, and a nice little Arab, which did well
enough for hacking about the station and lending to
any young lady who happened to be in need of it, and
who, by way of acknowledgment of his good nature,
would allow Philip to accompany her in her morning
rides.   This little Arab was in constant request.   The
supply of young ladies in need of early exercise, at
other people's expense, proved to be unfailing.   Philip,
too, was so good-natured about it and dispensed his
favours with such agreeable modesty, that many of the
fair recipients considered that they were doing him a
favour when they rode his horses and occupied his
time.   Philip's bill to Abdoolah, the Arab Dealer, was,
however, a long one.   Nothing, so he assured his father,
could be a greater mistake than to fancy that India was
a country where horses were to be had for the asking ;
and yet it would never do not to have a good stable.
Muggins and M'Trant might go shambling about the
district on their shabby ponies, with their clumsy shoes
and their trousers halfway to their knees, just as they
might hob-a-nob over their whisky-toddy in the humble
bungalow, which they shared for the sake of economy,
and which, with its dusty garden-path, camp equipage,
and camels,— its great bare whitewashed walls, its
tables littered with office memoranda, Civil Procedure
Codes, and Administration Reports, — its passages
beset with clerks and moonshees, squatting in every

available corner, filled Philip's æsthetic soul with absolute horror. A gentleman's horse should be a gentleman, and his house an abode where ladies may come for five-o'clock tea without incongruity,—where Generals may be regaled without a loss of dignity, and where the business-side of life may be kept duly subservient to the tastes of a cultured and refined society. So Philip's drawing-room speedily became one of the prettiest places in his Station ; and society, which always rejoices in every new form of gratuitous entertainment, congratulated itself on the advent of a young official, so alive to the duties of the position, and so ready to perform them with magnificent indifference to the pecuniary results of the performance. Everybody speedily recognised the fact that Ambrose kept an open house, and rushed to the conclusion that he was possessed of private means. A large number of his friends showed the greatest alacrity in enjoying the *recherchés* dinners which Ambrose and his Major Domo concocted for their benefit. The fairest hands in Cœrulea often wrote the *menus*, and oracular mouths pronounced Philip Ambrose's Perrier Jouet the best champagne that had been tasted in the Station for many a day. What with horses, champagne, elegant five-o'clock teas, and well-considered dinners, Ambrose found himself, before two years were past, not only at the end of his resources, but—what was of more immediate importance—at the end of the accommodation which the local European bank was disposed to afford. He had no alternative but to confide his embarrassments to a portly native gentleman, who had been bowing and scraping in his verandah, on every possible occasion, for a twelvemonth, and who now, with more obsequiousness than ever, made Ambrose feel that he conferred a favour instead of receiving one, when, in exchange for his note of hand, he allowed the trifling sum of Rs.10,000 to be placed to his credit at his bankers.

As Ambrose arrived at the bank for the completion of this little transaction, he met M'Trant, who was coming away with a rueful face.

'Are you going to remit to England?' he asked; 'Exchange is down again, and likely to be worse, the Manager says: I have to send £20 a month to my people at home, and, by Jove, it costs me more each time I do it.'

Ambrose said that at present, luckily, he had no occasion to remit money to England, and went into the bank with a heavier heart than usual, and with something almost approaching to a pang in his conscience. There was something, after all, he acknowledged to himself, to be said for men like M'Trant, despite their hirsute ponies, shabby clothes, and nondescript manners. His searchings of conscience, however, whatever they might have been, were cut short by the practical necessity of hurrying home, inasmuch as Mrs. Rashleigh and her pretty daughter were coming to have tea, and to admire some lovely bits of old Indian pottery, which Ambrose—already a judicious and daring virtuoso—had picked up the week before in the bazaar.

CHAPTER VIII

AN ENTANGLEMENT

Polonius. —   'I do know,
When the blood burns, how prodigal the soul
Lends the tongue vows: these blazes, daughter,
Giving more light than heat—extinct in both,
Even in their promise, as it is a making,
You must not take for fire.'

THERE are, it has been well observed, a great many ways of being the loveliest girl in the world. There are transcendent beauties whose very pre-eminence in loveliness strikes a sort of moral chill. We admire them as we do some distant snow-summit, set about with impracticable precipices, dark ravines, and chilling glaciers. They rise in superb isolation, far, far beyond the reach of ordinary humanity. Here and there some adventurous Alpine-Club man may try to invade the august precinct and scale the dizzy height, and comes back, humbled, footsore, and benumbed, even if he escapes without actual catastrophe. To the generality of mortals they are about as interesting as the top of Monte Rosa. There is, happily for mankind, another and more genial order of feminine perfection,—the

charm which appeals less to respectful admiration than
to the warm pulses of sympathetic interest—a beauty
which wears its honours with affability and graciousness
not too high for human hearts or human attainments,—
which is ready for intimacy, which invites friendship,
and accepts the ready homage of mankind with a cordial
and appreciative frankness.

It was in this latter, agreeable view that Cœrulean
mankind recognised Miss Rashleigh as the most charming of her sex. She was greatly admired, and the
admiration, which she aroused, was not only well
deserved but ungrudged. No one, not even Mrs. Paragon, who had a great faculty for satirical comment, and
who, with the natural instinct of self-preservation,
might have been expected to use her gift for the depreciation of a dangerous newcomer,—not even the two
Miss Scratchlys who, under the embittering effects of
neglect and years, had hardened into a mood incompatible with goodwill either towards man or woman,—
nay, not even their mother, a well-known female Tartar
of the most uncompromising order :—no one, in short,
had a word to say against Miss Rashleigh. She had
come out, two years before, to join her parents in India.
Her father, the General in Command of one of the
Cœrulean Divisions, was a soldier of many campaigns
and much well-earned renown. The manly expanse of
his wide chest scarcely gave room for the glittering
array of medals which commemorated a long list of
successes or of actions which deserved success. General
Rashleigh was justly proud of his country and his pro-

fession,—the regiment he had often led to action, his honours, and himself. But he had felt that, with his daughter's arrival, a new splendour and new delight had broken into his existence. His feelings were speedily shared by the rest of the community. Miss Rashleigh's presence vibrated with an agreeable pulsation through the Cœrulean body corporate. Her English beauty, fresh from its island home, her radiant expression, young and credulous of joy, her air of courage, her cordial manners, her ready appreciation of all the pleasant aspects of existence established her at once as an acknowledged Queen of society. Her ascendency had been undisputed. Votaries in abundance had been anxious to assure her of her position, in their thoughts at any rate, as the paragon of womankind ; but none of them had, in the slightest degree, come near her heart, or even aroused her interest. All men pronounced her adorable, but none of them found adoration, except when practised at the most respectful distance, at all an easy task. What Miss Rashleigh wanted was, not adoration, but amusement ; and the men with whom she came in contact, speedily discovered that, if they wished their offerings to be acceptable, the incense burnt at her shrine must be as highly spiced as possible with this latter ingredient.

With the exception of a fugitive affection for one of her cousins when she was quite a little girl, Florence Rashleigh was inexperienced in the cares and joys of love, nor did she feel in the least impatient for the arrival of this sentimental stage of existence. She was perfectly happy with her father, who petted her as so charming a daughter deserved to be petted. Her mother was equally indulgent, still more sympathetic,—shielded her from the fatigues of society,—banished, unbeknown to her, its less agreeable elements, and guided her course with dexterity, none the less sedulous for being unobtrusive, through the shoals and shallows which, even in the microcosm of an Indian Station, beset a handsome girl's existence. Her father, who had been a notable pigsticker in his younger days, was still a gallant rider; and Florence found riding with him—when her riding had ceased to be a topic of paternal criticism—a most delightful way of beginning the day. When on field days she accompanied him to the parade-ground, a thrill of admiration pervaded the staff, melted the sturdy sergeants and corporals, and flashed, like an agreeable electric shock, through the ranks. By general admission she lent lustre to the scene, and inspired each martial bosom with chivalrous devotion. It was natural that every one should wish to make love to her. The difficulty in doing so arose, not from any active or conscious resistance on her part, but because the mood, in which such things are possible, was wholly absent. It was hopeless to be sentimental with one whose gaiety was never overcast, whose merriment never knew a cloud, and who found the whole of life amusing. Some of the disappointed ones disparaged her as heartless ; only the utterly reckless denounced her as a flirt. Miss Rashleigh was no flirt, she was simply enjoying life and the many pleasures and excitements which it brought to her.

It was inevitable that Philip Ambrose, keenly susceptible to every form of attraction and promptly obedient to its impulses, should, at an early date, be numbered among the other adorers. He had succeeded conspicuously in making himself agreeable. He tempted the General with quiet dinners and a well-assorted rubber, which his own proficiency rendered especially interesting. He laid siege to Mrs. Rashleigh's gentle soul with five-o'clock tea-parties, at which flowers, fruit, and a little music added new charms to a refined repast. With the young lady herself he had established relations of the pleasantest familiarity. Perhaps the obvious absence of any designs upon her recommended him; perhaps his unreflecting good nature was congenial; perhaps the simple explanation was that he was young, good-looking, an accomplished valser, and generally a charming fellow; or, perhaps, it was that, from some subtle sympathy, Miss Rashleigh experienced a sudden access of brilliancy in her own conversation when Ambrose was her companion. He struck a chord in a key in which she found it easy and agreeable to perform. Florence considered her parents to be perfect in every respect but one; they cared not a whit for books and all that a love for books implies. Miss Rashleigh was often in want of a congenial volume. This want Ambrose was ready to supply. He read everything, told her of all the best novels, the most interesting reviews, busied himself in procuring whatever book she had a fancy to read, and was always ready to discuss it with discriminating vivacity. He had brought her

Daniel Deronda, when that interesting study in female vagaries first delighted society.

'I don't care a straw for Gwendoline,' he said, as they discussed the story afterwards; 'she is a commonplace, selfish beauty, dressed up in a halo of metaphysics.'

'But,' said Florence, 'I am certain that you would have found her irresistible. Fancy yourself now with a charming creature, dressed with romantic elegance, majestic, miserable, confiding, stretching her beautiful tapering fingers, in fresh, exquisite lavender gloves, towards you, praying for guidance, and hinting at interesting confessions, all the while throwing unutterable glances out of her slanting eyes.'

'I should have begun a vehement flirtation on the spot,' said Philip, 'of course. I suppose it was his strength in refusing to do that which gave Deronda his ascendency over her.'

'Yes,' said Florence, 'and his being a Jew. The true genius must always have a strain of Semitic blood in him, somehow or other. But for my part, I should have snapped my fingers at Deronda. I don't like George Eliot's dreamy young men near well enough to think of being fascinated by them.'

'And,' said the other, 'when the beautiful Miss Rashleigh has found the world's apple turn to bitter dust, into whose ear will the confidence be poured?'

'I shall not, at any rate, choose you for a confessor,' answered his companion; 'I should suffer in silence. Not that I mean to suffer; I don't intend my apple to be dust. It is a lovely, rosy pippin, full of delicious juice to the very core. I love it, rind, pips, and everything.'

'Dissembler!' cried Ambrose, 'I dare say you have some corroding disappointment already of which your heart is aching to disburthen itself. Every woman of sentiment is broken-hearted before twenty.'

'I leave you to pick up the bits of mine,' cried Florence, airily, 'and make what you can of them.'

'Interesting employment!' said Ambrose; 'but fragments will not do for me, I like broken hearts as little as you do. They should be fresh, strong, complete, and without a flaw, like mine.'

'How uninteresting!' cried Florence; 'sometimes, Mr. Ambrose, you make me think that I dislike you very much.'

'And I,' answered her companion, 'always find you adorable; what an unfair world we live in.'

Young Ambrose was not alone in finding Miss Rashleigh's society an exhilarating relief from the commonplace of existence. Mr. Chichele did all that judicious flattery could do to turn her head. But then, as he observed in flattering her, hers was a character that nothing could spoil. Armed with this comfortable assurance, Mr. Chichele felt no scruple in behaving to her in a manner which would have given good ground for vanity, if Florence had had any material in her composition which flattery could set aflame. The admiration of so critical, experienced, exacting a connoisseur was, in truth, a great compliment, and it was a compliment

which might be safely accepted. No fact could be
better established as an article of social faith in
Cœrulea than that Chichele was not a marrying man.
His past was wrapped in mystery, but it was certain
that he had burnt his fingers in marriage, and regarded
the institution with suspicion and dislike as a delusion
and a snare—

> ' He wedded a French dancing girl
> And had his heart danced over in return,

some one had said of his matrimonial misadventure.
At any rate he had no thought of repeating the experiment in his own person. Marriage was a general
necessity for obvious reasons, and might even be pleasant for certain people and at certain times of life.
But then there are many necessary and pleasant things
which it is well to leave to other people to enjoy.
Chichele was a cautious talker, but he occasionally let
fall observations which were felt to be extremely
cynical, and some of his most cynical sayings had been
about the happiness of his married friends. He chose,
it was obvious, to figure in the world as a person with
whom it would be absolutely fatuous to associate
the notion of conjugal felicity. Many people, many
mothers, had felt inwardly what a pity it was that, as
Mr. Chichele was so nice, it should never occur to him
to share his niceness with some dear, faithful companion
for life. But all had recognised the stern fact that he
never would entertain such a wish, and had accepted
his solitary condition as settled in the immutable

decrees of fate.　This was a state of things which suited Miss Rashleigh exactly.　Mr. Chichele was immeasurably the best company of any one in her circle of acquaintance.　He knew the world, he knew political life, he knew society, and he had culled from each a rich crop of shrewd judgments and curious recollections. He had been friends with a great many interesting women—whom Florence only knew of as great ladies of the world.　It was not in human nature not to be gratified by finding oneself among the number of women whom he considered interesting.　Chichele now made Florence understand with great distinctness his desire to be 'friends' with her, and she accepted the proffered friendship with unhesitating alacrity.　He brought her the very things she wanted, and he brought them in just the way she liked—a way which safeguarded kindness from awkward complications and robbed intimacy of its possible dangers.　It was an immense comfort, Miss Rashleigh told herself, to have a friend whose kindnesses need not be suspected of masking a battery of sentiment, and with whom one might be confidential without the risk of his becoming inconveniently confidential in return.　If any one had proposed to her, and she had felt in difficulty, Chichele would, after her parents, have been the first person to whom she would have looked for counsel. Chichele accepted the *rôle* which she assigned to him with unquestioning cheerfulness, and seasoned his amusing stories with a great deal of excellent advice. It had not hitherto occurred to Florence that she might

ever need to ask his opinion about Philip Ambrose.
None the less when, some months later, the *Cœrulean
Gazette* announced that Mr. Philip Ambrose had obtained six months' leave from a date which was start-
lingly close at hand, Florence Rashleigh became suddenly
conscious of a feeling about the matter that was something different from the absolute indifference with which
she regarded the comings and goings of mankind at large.
The appearance of such a feeling took her by surprise
and challenged inquiry. Why was it that she cared?
Florence asked herself this question, and the ingenious sprites which hover in the inner consciousness of each of us—the ready ministrants of self-
deception—assured her, at once, that it was but natural
to regret even the temporary absence of one whose
high spirits, good nature, and vivacity gave a zest
to life wherever his presence happened to make itself
felt.

A little further reflection satisfied Florence, who was
honesty itself, even in her self-communings, that she
was not, in truth, as serenely indifferent to Philip
Ambrose as she had imagined. After all he was in-
finitely nicer than nine-tenths of the men whom she
came across. He had a natural refinement, and did
not, as many men did, on the first approach to familiarity, betray fatal faults of taste, fatal barriers to
any approach to real intimacy. If she and Philip
sometimes sparred in conversation, it was because they
had enough in common to make it worth while to
explore their differences. Anyhow she felt a decided

interest in him and his fortunes. He had described to her his adventures in Paris, and had shown her the picture of Camilla, which had greatly taken her fancy. 'That,' he had said, ' is the little girl who wished me good-bye in the station at Paris ; is not she pretty ?' 'It is a most sweet, touching face,' Florence had said, and, being a vehement matchmaker for every one but herself, she forthwith had sketched out mentally a romantic project that Ambrose should, some day or other, go home and marry this pretty child-friend. And now Ambrose was to go home forthwith, and Florence admitted to herself that the prospect of his departure, and of his possibly resumed adoration of his child - friend in England, was not altogether without its mixture of melancholy to her. His absence would make a blank, which would not easily be filled, in her little world. Ambrose, too, began to grow sentimental as the time approached ; and as soon as he discovered it, encouraged the growing sentiment in his own mind with fostering care. Florence's quieter and gentler mood struck him as extremely touching. A pang of regret shot through his heart, not an agonising pang,—perhaps even it was slightly pleasurable, but still craving expression. What is one to say to a charming woman whom one is about to leave, and who holds out little distress signals of regret at one's departure? Philip solved the difficulty by becoming extremely tender; and tenderness was so natural a mood to him that he never felt more at ease than when he was indulging it. So, somewhat unawares, they had lapsed into a far more serious and affectionate mood than they had ever hitherto contemplated as possible.

One morning—it was amongst the last two or three which remained before his departure—Philip had joined Florence and her father in their ride, and the General being deep in business talk with one of his officers, the two had ridden some way homewards *tête-à-tête*.

Last things, last rides with charming women among the rest, have always a touch of melancholy. Philip felt this with great acuteness as he watched his beautiful companion and saw that she, too, was feeling it. Her accustomed joyousness was pervaded with the subtle aroma of a pensive mood. The truth was that Florence was rather sad. She had enjoyed many pleasant things in Ambrose's company, and his companionship, she now realised, had formed a large part of their pleasantness. For weeks past he had been exactly in the mood in which she liked him best,—a bright, gentle naturalness, which half-amused, half-touched her by its confidential *naïveté*. She had sometimes pictured him to herself as a Faun, a charming creature, with natural grace and brightness provided, possibly, with a slightly inadequate supply of soul. Now the Faun was going back to his native woods, and it was natural that he should be pleased to go ; but he was leaving his forest companions, the familiar faces of to-day and yesterday, and breaking off the pleasant routine of existence. So the Faun was sad, and made no secret of his sadness. Florence would have scarcely been surprised if he had sat down under one of the huge spreading trees under which they were riding, taken out his pan-pipes, and breathed to the forest deities a strain of half-animal distress. But Philip was not Faun enough for that. His emotions were never inarticulate.

'Do you know,' he now said, 'the nearer I get to this journey to England the less I seem to like it. I have more than half a mind to give it up. Yet I want to see my father badly. I have been away from him for an age, and he is lonely without me. He lives all alone, you know.'

'No wonder you are in a hurry to get to him,' Florence said; 'India is a cruel country to fathers like yours, is it not?'

'It is a cruel country to us all,' said Philip, bitterly; 'it is the land of regrets—the desolate kingdom of separations—we live in a scramble : one is always being torn from the people one likes the best. It is scarcely worth making friends, is it, only to leave them?'

'Don't say that,' said his companion; 'we are all sorry to lose you now, and we shall welcome you back. What is to become of my father's whist, meanwhile, it is dreadful to think. We shall have to ask Mr. Masterly, who is always revoking.'

'But will *you* miss me,' asked Philip, turning round in his saddle, and looking straight at his companion with sudden earnestness.

'Excessively,' said Florence; 'I never play lawn tennis so well as when I have you for my partner. By the way, who will take care of your lawn while you are away? Shall I watch over it?'

'You don't understand me in the least,' said Ambrose; 'cannot you see that I am really very unhappy; I thought that women saw everything.'

'I should not have thought that you were so very unhappy,' said his companion; 'you ought not to be: you will have the great joy of seeing your father again. You will have a charming time in England and enjoy everything immensely. All the same, as I said, we shall be missing you dreadfully here, and it will be only fair if, among all your pleasures, you regret your Indian friends a little.'

'I shall regret leaving you, but not a little,' answered Ambrose; 'go where I will, I shall never find a more delightful friend. I shall be for ever wishing myself back in Cœrulea again with you. To be with you, to see you, to hear your voice, is all I want—all that I care for in the world. No other pleasure is like it, or could be. I have found it out to my cost, now that I am about to lose it—to lose you. That is why I hate this horrid journey to England. Tell me to give it up, and make me the happiest fellow in the world.'

Philip thought that Miss Rashleigh had never looked more absolutely enchanting than when, on coming to the close of this avowal, he looked up and met her fine, tender, courageous glance, startled as she was by a sudden shock and confronted by an immediate embarrassment. Her face had in it a great deal of latent nobility, which only needed occasion to rush to light.

She was now, he could see, nerving herself to master a surprise and to face with composure a trying ordeal.

His outburst had been almost as great a surprise to himself as it was to her. He had frequently, of late, felt prompted to say something extremely affectionate to Miss Rashleigh, but prudence had immediately insisted that this something should be as vague as was compatible with the necessary degree of strength. His money troubles, which were a mere inconvenience to a bachelor, would look very different and very much more serious when confronted with the additional embarrassment of a wife. Nor was it probable that they could ever be settled except with the assistance of a wife who should be, not only charming, but opulent. In the abstract Philip was determined not to marry for several years to come, and then to marry money ; in the concrete he adored Miss Rashleigh. The conflicting impulses had whirled him, a helpless victim, to an unintended result.

And now the die was cast. Ambrose's fate, so far as it depended on himself, was sealed. The strong current had caught him : resistance was impossible, nor did he wish to resist. Why resist ? Why not rather revel in it to the full, and taste the full ecstasy of the one supreme moment of existence, let the rest be what it might ? 'At a touch I yield : let the great river bear me to the deep.' Philip's feelings, by this time, were quite beyond the control of sober discretion, and were carrying him rapidly on to the wild tempestuous sea. What his fate would be there he was in no mood for considering.

Florence, he could see, was moved. Her gay preparedness of speech was gone. Her courage was shaken,

her bright composure had given way to a nervous embarrassment. On such fragile materials love builds its
silly hopes.

'Tell me to give it up,' he said; 'but I have no need
to be told. I am determined not to go. Yours or not
yours, happy or wretched, I cannot bear to leave you.
Whatever your decision, I shall stay.'

Florence had now had time to collect her scattered
senses and decide on the reply which it behoved her to
make.

'You must not do that, Mr. Ambrose,' she said, 'or
you will forfeit my friendship for ever; and, please
now, to say no more on the subject. You are speaking
strongly, wildly, on the spur of the moment, I am convinced, not of settled design. For my part, I must tell
you frankly that your words have been an unwelcome
surprise, and that I cannot imagine myself ever feeling
for you as you have spoken to me. Till to-day I have
never thought of you but as a pleasant friend; nor, I
believe, can you have thought otherwise of me. We
will remain as friends, if you please. I like you,
as you know. If our friendship is to last, you must
promise me never again to talk to me like this.'

'Never!' cried Philip, 'that's a long word. How
can you tell what you may feel hereafter?'

'Well!' said Florence, catching at the first chance to
bring matters to a close; 'never, at any rate, till you
return from England. You are going home. Go, free
as air. When you come back, we can see how matters
stand between us.'

'But I am going for six months,' cried Ambrose.

'I know,' said Florence; 'for six months, then, silence! and remember you are free.   We are both free.'

'Six months or six hundred,' cried Ambrose; 'I shall never think of you but as the perfection of womankind. Only give me leave to stay.'

'No,' said Florence, by this time again quite mistress of herself and of the situation, 'I tell you to go—and, remember, you are free, and I am free.'

CHAPTER IX

A WOUNDED HEART

'Methinks I feel this youth's perfections
With an invisible and subtle strength,
To creep in at my eyes.'

FLORENCE'S answer to her lover had been, like herself,
honest and courageous. She had told Ambrose the
exact truth as to her feelings about him; she had not
concealed her liking for him or underrated it; she had
warned him that her liking was not love nor likely to
become so. On the other hand, she had not bidden
him to despair, or forbidden him to renew his request
if, after six months in England, he was still of the
same mind. In this Miss Rashleigh had shown her
courage—a courage, however, that was full of danger to
herself, and of hope for any man who really loved her.
Such a concession, construed by the insight of true devotion, would mean that the battle was more than half-
won, and victory already assured. Her rejection of him
had lacked the decisiveness of indifference or dislike,
still, when Florence came to think over the interview
with her lover in cold blood, she was less and less favour-

ably impressed with his behaviour. It had been too spasmodic, too abruptly intense, too wanting in self-restraint, too suggestive of a suddenly-kindled and fugitive passion. It had wanted the true ring of real earnest devotion. She told her mother of it with a light heart, and treated it with an indifference that satisfied Mrs. Rashleigh that no harm had been done, and that no danger was to be feared. She contented herself with saying that Philip had behaved very foolishly, and hinting that his dismissal might well have been more absolute.

'I would have sent him about his business for good and all, dear, and taken good care that nothing of the kind should occur again. That sort of love-making is one form of impertinence.'

'Poor fellow!' Florence said, 'that would have been needlessly cruel. He is so impulsive, you know, mother, and I should have been sorry to hurt him. After all, I rather like him, you know.'

'It would have done him no harm,' her mother said, decisively; 'he had no business to speak as he did.'

Florence knew that this was so. She knew that she had been right to keep herself free; yet freedom is not always happiness, and Florence was far from happy. Philip's kindly, unconscious mirthfulness, his irrepressible good humour, his unstudied, gentle manner had made a deeper impression than she had at first suspected; and the impression grew deeper and deeper every day. In some moods she wondered how she had ever had the heart, the nerve, to let him go, and thought to herself that if he had come within her reach again, she must have kept him at whatever risk of future misfortune. Then common sense would assert its reign, and Florence scorned herself for a foolish fancy, and resolved to be as heart-whole as ever.

Philip by this time was halfway across the Indian Ocean on his homeward journey, and was spending long dreamy afternoons in siestas in which Florence's image figured only as one of a host of pleasant recollections of a world which was every day fading faster from his thoughts. Europe, England, home, with all their thousand interests and delights, were already in full and exclusive possession of his mind. He was free, and freedom seemed fraught with a host of delightful possibilities. India and Indian things, even Indian people, seemed merging into the indistinctness which is the prelude of oblivion.

His relations towards Miss Rashleigh were conveniently vague, and his feelings, if still those of affectionate remembrance, were obscured by an overgrowth of young and radiant hopes and more immediate claims on his attention. No sort of tie, so a well-disciplined and courteous conscience assured him, bound him to the young lady, who had declined his proffered devotion, and disbelieved his protestations of eternal fidelity. If he was free, whose fault was that? Florence, it was certain, was less tender-hearted than himself; and it might even be a form of judicious self-protection against the melancholy of disappointment if her rejected lover took full advantage of any compensatory alleviation that kind, tender eyes and sympathetic hearts in England might be ready to afford. In plain words, Philip had, before he reached the Mediterranean, determined with himself that, if kind Fortune brought a flirtation in his way he would make the most of her kindness. Now Fortune, though proverbially fickle, is almost invariably kind to good-looking Youth when thus prepared to welcome her largess.

Meanwhile, the seed so carefully sown was growing apace in the fine soil of Florence's heart. It grew and grew until she acknowledged to herself, with a sort of remorseful indignation at her own weakness, that it had become the master-thought, and threw all other influences into the background.

' Vulnus alit venis et cæco carpitur igni.'

Life somehow had grown darker—pleasure had lost its zest. Everything seemed worse, commoner, less interesting. Now that Philip was no longer present to remind her of his slightness, it was so easy to forget it, and to remember only that he was mirthful, charming, and devoted. In a man's absence, imagination so soon begins to idealise him, to throw his shortcomings into the shade, to set his attractions in a striking light— to make him what friendship would wish him to be. *Les absents ont toujours tort*, the proverb says : but the pleasant companion who has left us is the victim of no such injustice. Rather he benefits by an indulgent obliviousness of all about him, for which oblivion is desirable. It is not with material beauties alone that

distance lends enchantment to the view. And indeed,
without being in love with young Ambrose, one may
admit that Cœrulean society, and especially that fraction
of it which formed the atmosphere of Florence's daily
life, was the duller for the want of his presence. Miss
Rashleigh, at any rate, found it very dull indeed, and
cheered herself with hazy visions in the mind's far
horizon—a rosy dawn, lovely as Aurora's self, when
Apollo would rise again from the orient wave and come
to glorify her world again. Alas, when Apollo reappeared
—so the cruel fates had willed—it was under circumstances not calculated to give her the least satisfaction !

Florence's predicament could not for long pass un-
observed. The kindly General found the companion
of his rides changed ; he could not tell how, but
decidedly changed. She was as devoted, as anxious
to please him, as prompt to read his wishes and wants,
as ready in her sweet, filial solicitude as ever. But
her mirthfulness had fled ; the bright, unconscious joy
of life was no longer there. Her face, as she rode
beside him, wore some other look than that which of
yore spoke of high animal spirits and keen natural
enjoyment in her gallop. She looked grave ; she looked
even sad. The General, in great perturbation, confided
his observations to Mrs. Rashleigh, and his alarm
increased when Mrs. Rashleigh admitted that she, too,
was aware that something was the matter. These two
tender hearts, linked in a common love, shrank and
shuddered, sensitive to the approach of evil, at the bare
thought of sorrow coming near the child they both

adored. The situation became critical. All were more affectionate than ever; no one spoke of it, but each of the three secretly felt, by a subtle instinct, that a secret sorrow had overclouded that bright and happy home.

How happy that home had been! The General and his wife belonged to that favoured class of married people who continue lovers to the end. His old age was as chivalrous, as ardent, as devoted as his youth had been, to the dear companion, who had followed his fortunes through good times and bad. They had travelled together for many a year in rough places and smooth; together they had borne the blows of fate; they had enjoyed the bright and the dark hours of life in company till the one could scarcely think of pleasure or pain, except as shared by the other. There had been some dark days of disappointment, suspense, and deadly anxiety—what soldier's wife escapes them? Now the good times had come, and good things, and, best of all the good things—the daughter who, two years before, had arrived from England, with a long-cherished store of affection, to be the crowning joy, the charm and ornament of the closing scene of their Indian career. And the charm had been as sweet in realisation as in Hope's fondest day-dream. Neither of them had known how delightful it would be. Again and again their good fortune would take them by surprise. The General's manly heart would throb, now and again, with a sudden rush of pleasure, as Florence—fresh, joyous, beautiful—went sailing along on her Arab by his side, witching the world with noble horsemanship and charming every

eye with the radiance of exulting youth. Mrs. Rashleigh's eyes would sometimes fill with unbidden tears
of love and gratitude as she watched the sweet child
of their youth, whom it had sometimes seemed to break
her heart to part with, restored to her at last, the
crowning blessing of a blest existence. Their common
joy had bound these true and faithful hearts closer than
ever; and now they were confronted by a common
trouble. That Florence was not as happy as she had
been—as she ought to be—was an idea which, the
General found, put all his stoicism to the rout at
once; and as he buckled and strapped on his uni-
form for the morning's parade he inwardly admitted
that, put what courageous face upon it he would, a
reverse in this direction would mean not only defeat
but disaster. Like a good soldier as he was, he determined to do his best to obviate defeat.

Florence's outspokenness on the subject to her
mother had been unembarrassed, and her assurance that
her heart was disengaged so obviously sincere, that the
conjecture that she might possibly be mistaken had not
suggested itself to Mrs. Rashleigh as a possible explanation of her new-found melancholy. The two were on
far too good terms for reticence on either side. Florence
was anxious to disburthen herself of her trouble, and,
one day, her mother with gentle compulsion forced the
secret from her.

'Florence, dear,' she said, laying her hand kindly
on hers and looking straight at her, 'you have something on your mind.'

'Yes,' Florence answered, 'and something I am heartily ashamed of. I have been **weak**, mother. I *am* weak and I am behaving like a fool. I cannot get that foolish Philip Ambrose out of my thoughts. I don't love him. I don't respect him. I don't wish to marry him; all the same it hurts me to have lost him; sometimes I let myself think I really do love him. That is what has been making me miserable. Do you despise me very much? What will my father think? I know that I despise myself.'

'There is no need to do that, dear,' said her mother, 'only I beg and pray you, dear Florence, not to play with day-dreams. Your decision was assuredly right. We all feel alike about Philip Ambrose. You yourself think him weak and unstable; he would never make you happy; you will not go on thinking about him— will you? Promise.'

'I tell you what, mother,' Florence replied, evading a pledge which she may have doubted her ability to keep, 'I think men are very horrid, and I don't feel at all inclined to have anything to do with any of them. Why can they not let one alone? How happy we three are together! As for my foolish fancy I mean to laugh it away and be ten times gayer than ever.'

And gayer than ever in society Florence forthwith became. The old colonels found her even more affable and more amusing than they had believed. Mr. Chichele made no secret of his admiration, pronounced her the best company in Cœrulea, and threw over his friend Mrs. Paragon without the least compunction

whenever he got the chance of a chat with Miss
Rashleigh. The subalterns, to a boy, burnt incense
at a respectful distance; no one who was not in the
secret had a suspicion but that Florence was still the
gayest, brightest, most whole-hearted of her sex. Meanwhile the secret trouble grew none the less troublesome
for being recognised by those who had to bear it. The
General growled out a hearty execration under his
grisly moustache, when Mrs. Rashleigh explained the
nature of their daughter's trouble. 'I always told you,'
he said, 'that that fellow was no good ; he has no
backbone—he has no principle—he has no strength.
It was dishonourable to speak to Florence as he did. I
wish to goodness I had never played whist with him.
He is confoundedly pleasant and all that sort of thing,
but you will see, Maria, he'll come to awful grief some
day and break the heart of the woman who is unlucky
enough to marry him.' With this grim vaticination the
General was constrained, *faute de mieux*, to console
himself in a crisis which, he began to fear, did not admit
of any consolation.

CHAPTER X

MR. MONTEM LOSES HIS TEMPER

Lucius—   ' His enemies confess
The virtues of humanity are Cæsar's.'

Cato—' Curse on his virtues ! They've undone his country ;
Such popular humanity is treason.'

Miss Rashleigh was not the only person to whom
Philip's departure implied a serious diminution of
enjoyment—Mr. Montem was another sufferer. That
gentleman's exterior, as exhibited to mankind at large,
was of an irritable, unconciliatory and aggressive order,
not unfitly symbolised by the quills upon the fretful
porcupine. Deep hidden, however, below—deep as the
recesses of the terrestrial globe, at which fortunate
explorers 'strike' gold or petroleum—were smouldering
fires of wit, and a copious supply of that agreeable
ingredient known to moralists as the milk of human
kindness. Both qualities needed only a congenial touch
to spring to the surface, and Ambrose, with his usual
good luck, appealed effectually to each. Montem had
grown really fond of him; and, whenever he got the
chance, would carry him off from the whist-table to a

tête-à-tête dinner—not, it must be confessed, of the most *recherché* order,—where, under the mellowing influences of whisky and soda-water, the old Scotchman would blossom into a genial mood, and produce all his treasures of wide reading, subtle thought and humorous analysis of character, for the edification of his guest ; and then the two would have a fine time of it.   Philip found Montem's racy talk an agreeable change from the frivolous chatter of ball-rooms and band-stands, or the dreary round of military gossip.   One may have enough even of pretty young ladies : and, as for the army, Philip used to say, it is as great a puzzle as the Athanasian creed : the only thing that is certain about it is that every man has a grievance which he wants to tell you.   Montem's grievances were of a less personal and more interesting order ; and they were enforced with a picturesque extravagance —now fun, now pathos, now prejudice, now serious conviction,—but in every case alike, full of character. Philip made an excellent listener, and differed just often enough to stir the acids and alkalis of his instructor's talk into continual effervescence.   Much good advice had Montem given him on his approaching visit to England.

'Young man,' he said, 'let me give you a hint. When you get home,—as you value peace and quiet and a kindly welcome by your friends,—let nothing tempt you to say a word about India—not one word.   Polite people will ask you about it, but that is only to please you.   Do not answer them.   They cannot bear it.   Take my word. You are a *revenant*, you know ; and well-bred and judicious *revenants* say as little as possible about the place they have come from.'

'Especially,' said Philip, 'when it happens to be a hot one; but I thought that India was rather the fashion.'

'The India of sentiment and nonsense,' said Montem, 'is, and always will be the fashion—the India that Burke flooded with bombast, and Macaulay with antithesis—the India that Stain writes pamphlets about, and Frontinbras sonnets—the India that never was, and never will be, except in foolish heads. The English are a curious race. They hate intellectual exertion, and they like to have their passions roused. Consequently they hate alike the effort which serious thought costs, and the many-sided, hesitating results to which it leads. Hence comes the sensational method, with vivid outline and strongly-marked effects, which involve no thought, and generate plenty of passion. You remember Thucydides's dictum about the little trouble that the Athenian οἵ πόλλοι took to find the truth. The English οἵ πόλλοι like exertion just as little. They *will not* take the trouble to learn, and, in consequence, they are always making colossal blunders; and the blunders are growing more and more colossal every year. Sometimes, as I sit in my office and watch the wear and tear of things in general, I feel a horrid conviction that the English national character has suffered with the rest, and begins to show signs of dilapidation.'

'Of course,' said Caro, who came in at this moment, and at once took up his accustomed *rôle* of capping Montem's cynicisms. 'It ought to be allowed for in

the national accounts, if they were properly kept—
"depreciation of moral rolling stock," at so much per
cent.   Only, what Chancellor of Exchequer would venture to gauge it?'

'Look at the nation's behaviour about Egypt,' continued Montem; 'was it not suggestive of decrepi-
tude? a want of fixed purpose—an incapacity for sustained effort—a degrading mixture of levity, violence
and irresolution?'

'That was the fault of their rulers,' said Caro; 'each
one trying to catch the nation's whim and set his sails
by it.   No nation could undergo such a process of petting and escape the natural infirmities of a spoilt child.'

'Please listen to this,' said Montem, taking up a
Review from the table.   'Hear the great apostle of
Radicalism on its agreeable consequences.   "Does the
excitement of democracy," he asks, "weaken the stability
of national character?   By setting up a highly increased
molecular activity does it disturb, not merely con-
servative respect for institutions, but for coherence and
continuity of opinion and sentiment in the character of
the individual himself?   Is there a fluidity of character
in modern democratic societies which contrasts not
altogether favourably with the strong solid types of
old?   Are Englishmen becoming less like Romans and
more like chattering Greeks?'

'Yes,' said his companion; 'and the worst Greeks
are those who will chatter about India.   But talking of
fluid characters and chattering Greeks, Frontinbras is
coming presently to call on you, with an introduction

from Mr. Chichele; I shall escape while I can, and leave you to convert him if you can.'

'Convert him!' cried Montem, making a wry face at the impending infliction, '"Though thou shalt bray a fool in a mortar, yet shall he not depart from his folly."'

'Excellent text,' said Caro. 'That, I suppose, is why I never see Frontinbras without thinking of braying. Farewell, Philosopher, till whist-time this afternoon. I must be off.'

'And I will come with you,' said Ambrose; 'I have a particular engagement.'

'You have a particular aversion for garrulous blockheads,' said Montem, 'and so have I. If Chichele keeps sending his revolutionary visitors on to me, I intend to resign my appointment, and leave Cœrulean wear and tear to go to the devil as they please.'

Presently Frontinbras arrived, keen on interviewing a Cœrulean character, and determined—thanks to Chichele's admonitions—to be as little offensive as he could. Montem, on his part, bent himself, in the true spirit of Christian resignation, to receive the Governor's guest with all due politeness. For a while all went on smoothly, till the smoothness of the interview imperceptibly threw both parties off their guard. Frontinbras began to air some of the foolish things which he had heard at Sir Theophilus's Court; and, unluckily, quoted one of Montem's pet aversions in support of them.

'He is a man, you will admit, of great experience,' he said, throwing a tone of assurance into the speech, which ruffled the unnatural calm of Montem's equanimity with a sudden gust of displeasure,—'a man of great and varied experience.'

'He is,' said Montem; 'but then ill-judging experience is the very deuce. The experience of stupid or careless people is merely an intense form of misunderstanding. It means that they have collected a number of misperceived facts in support of a blundering conclusion. As George Eliot says somewhere, "Experience cackles far oftener than she lays a live egg." Of the two I prefer ignorance as absolute as your own.'

'Do you?' said Frontinbras, who by this time was beginning to feel decidedly less amiable than when the interview began; 'and I suppose you think just as little of Sir Theophilus, to whom I was indebted for the introduction. Tell me frankly.'

'I will,' said Montem, 'with pleasure. Prance is the worst of the lot. There is no man in India, as I judge whose vanity, shallowness, and want of political foresight has done more to impede useful work for the present or laid up greater difficulties for the future.'

'I have heard that sort of thing before,' said Frontinbras; 'I should be glad to learn what it seriously means.'

'I will tell you,' said Montem. 'He could not set the Thames on fire at home, so he is trying his hand on the Ganges, Burampootra, and the rest of them.'

'Drop metaphor!' cried Frontinbras, by this time well on towards being in a passion. 'What is it that makes all you Indian conservatives so bitter against him?'

'Because,' said Montem, who had now forgotten

politeness in the necessity of being forcible,—'because he has seized the most dangerous points in a dangerous position, and used them for self-glorification. India just now is full of explosive materials—restlessness, envy, race-jealousy, class-animosity—a vast, half-educated class, with just little knowledge enough to be a dangerous thing and to feel at a loss what to do with its newly-found powers. Prance has appealed to all in behalf of himself and his party; and, what is worst of all, appealed in a way that has put all his countrymen against him. He postures as the friend of freedom. He is really the apostle of disorder. He has convinced himself, in truth's despite, that white is black and black is white, and he appeals to young India to prove it. The solemn truth remains that they are remarkably unlike, but Sir Theophilus cannot or will not see it. He found the task of quiet, rational government in India difficult. He and his admirers are doing their best to make it impossible.'

'You seem to think us all very dangerous characters,' said Frontinbras.

'Not dangerous,' answered Montem, with amusement twinkling in his eye, for he knew that it was Frontinbras's foible to be considered dangerous, and was resolved not to indulge it. 'If you were dangerous, the Governor would have to deport you, and, if you objected to deportation, to imprison you.'

'Imprison me!' cried Frontinbras, by this time in a white heat of indignation, 'and without a trial?'

'Without a trial,' said Montem, with an exasperating composure, 'by a *lettre de cachet*. We have them here, you know. It is one of the many advantages of a military despotism.'

'It is one of the infamies that we are determined to efface,' cried the other; 'Englishmen have no business with military despotisms.'

'Except that they happen to own the largest in the world,' said his companion.

'But you do not want it to last for ever, I suppose,' cried Frontinbras.

'It will last none too long,' said the other, with an earnest tone that struck even Frontinbras as impressive; 'and, meanwhile, it has converted the biggest bear-garden the world has ever seen into an orderly and, as things go, fairly prosperous community. Remove it, and you will have the bear-garden back in a twelve-month, and an invader, pouring once again through the Afghan passes, within a decade.'

Frontinbras shook his wild locks, and was trembling with excitement. Had he not that very morning been constructing a forcible stanza comparing India to a crucified slave, with brutal soldiery around, and ribald persecutors gibing at his pangs? 'Our whole views are antipathetic,' he said. 'Have you no hopes for India, for mankind ?'

'I have,' said the other, 'perhaps as high ones as your own,—so high that I think their accomplishment is well worth the toil and patience which several generations of unconspicuous Englishmen have loyally contributed towards their accomplishment,—so high that I resent the levity, the hardihood, the sensationalism that risks all for its gratification. You hasty gentlemen have not leisure to understand the complications of the case. You prescribe before you have diagnosed; you must have sensationalism, and India is full of sensational effects. But you indulge yourselves at a heavy cost. You force the hand of the administrators of a country, where an administrative mistake means calamity to millions; you obscure the daylight of common sense with will-o'-the-wisps that tempt to disaster. You give form and substance to floating folly; you instil baseless discontents and vain hopes; you rally the scattered germs of disaffection, and try to bring them to a head; you would ruin the Government if you could. It is a proof of its strength and of its reliance on the good sense of the community against the feelings to which you appeal that the Government can afford to let you and your fellow-fanatics to go where you will and say what you please.'

'Still,' said Frontinbras, who was well accustomed to having strong things said to him, and rather liked it, 'if you had your way, you would deport me?'

'No,' said Montem; 'I would imprison you.'

'Then I had better be going while I can,' replied his companion; 'you may have a *lettre de cachet* about you; who knows?'

'No such luck,' said Montem, good-naturedly; 'but have a cigar before you go; you will find this a good one.'

That evening a well-assorted circle at Chichele's table listened with sympathising amusement to the narrative of all that poor Montem had been through, in the cause of hospitality on the one hand and truth on the other.

'There is one plain, prosaic question,' Chichele observed, 'to which no apostle of India's regeneration has ever yet given a satisfactory answer. If India, in order to be regenerated, is to dispense with British rule, who is to guarantee the repayment of the two hundred millions sterling which Englishmen have lent India to make railways and canals with? It is vulgar perhaps to ask it, but, from a business point of view, it is important.'

'And who, if it comes to that,' said Montem, 'will give back to the English all they have sacrificed for the country—our wasted lives?'

'And,' added Caro emphatically, 'our enfeebled livers:' and as he had just been restricted by a stern committee of doctors to a penitential diet of toast and gruel, and was unable, in consequence, on the present occasion, to enfeeble his own any further by rash experiments on Chichele's excellent cuisine, he was, no doubt, in a position to speak feelingly as to this particular form of contribution to the welfare of his Aryan first cousins.

CHAPTER XI

GATHER YOUR ROSES WHILE YE MAY

'We figure to ourselves
The thing we like, and then we build it up,
As chance will have it, on the rock or sand ;
For Thought is tired of wandering o'er the world,
And home-bound Fancy runs her bark ashore.'

FIVE years had passed away since Philip left his home, and, except on rare occasions on which Mr. Ambrose paid a visit at her uncle's, Camilla had heard nothing of the man who had so deeply impressed her. Even when he came, Mr. Ambrose was not particularly communicative as to his son's fortunes. Philip, he said, was a shockingly bad correspondent; and life in India, it might be supposed, did not supply material for many amusing letters. 'Anyhow, I cannot say that Philip's letters are either numerous or amusing. However, he is all right, and keeping well, which is the great thing; and he is getting on, I suppose, for he has been moved from Moldipettiah to Mustipollium, a much grander station; and he is now, he tells me, what they call a "Joint."'

This sort of information was, naturally, not at all

such as that for which Camilla's ardent imagination
craved. A romantic young woman cannot satisfy her
flights of fancy by dreaming of her lover as translated
from one unknown, unpronounceable place to another,
and being described as if he was so much meat. The
expression meant, she supposed, that, in some mysterious way or other, Philip formed a humble member of the
body corporate of Indian officialdom. But what an arid
fact ! What honey is to be sucked by the liveliest fancy
from such a flower as that ?   Meanwhile Camilla was
rapidly growing out of a picturesque girl into a woman
of beauty, strength, and character. Her mind was
forming; she had learnt to formulate her girlish instincts
with distinct convictions and views. The narrowness
of her uncle's world had become an accepted fact, and
she bore it more quietly because she understood it
better. She recognised it as essentially intolerable,
despicable, and to be escaped from at the first opportunity. She knew now, by actual experience, a little of
the vast world without,—the great river of human life
rushing along; of the realms of science, art, thought,
and feeling; the wild dreams—the grand discoveries;
the grave doubts that swayed mankind; the theories
with which men's minds were busy, the hopes and
fears which stirred them,—for all which topics those
around her cared as much as for the social economy of
Timbuctoo. In this discouraging and uncongenial
surrounding Camilla lived alone. She had always
cherished a grand ideal : she took life seriously; regarded
it with deep interest, as of a sort of awful significance

to every one; she felt its issues to be supremely important, the difference between its various possibilities so tremendous: on the one hand, such lofty, beautiful eminences, serene and pure, and bathed in heaven's own light; on the other such abyssmal depths of dulness and turpitude: on the one hand such wild, free flights amid celestial pleasures; on the other, such enslavement amid narrow, soul-destroying, enervating vacuity. Between these alternatives she had made her choice with a passionate, eager decisiveness; she vowed to herself that her life should be something worth living—something pure, good, elevated and refined. These were her vehement cravings as soon as she began to think at all; and she had never wavered in their pursuit. This sort of self-culture had given her a certain exquisiteness of mind, which bespoke itself in her appearance and manner. It gave her on the one hand, an uncompromising dislike of all that militated against, or even fell short of her standard—a sort of moral daintiness: on the other hand, it invested her with all the strength which comes from a fixed purpose and a will ever bent towards one set of noble objects. Camilla was never distracted, never dissipated, never without an object. She moved onwards towards her end, sometimes, no doubt, with stumbling feet, sometimes with halting and uncertain steps—but with her gaze on the goal she had imagined for herself. The Beautiful Mountains were for ever in her horizon, fair with celestial beauty, the object of her pilgrimage. This settled purpose gave her a fine disdain, perhaps too little concealed, for all things petty, mean, unreal, or unrefined; she cherished a vehement repugnance to every sort of sham. The lightnings of sarcasm played about her finely chiselled lips, and she, not unfrequently, produced the impression of unintentionally withering the object of her disapproval with polished bolts of scornful wit. Her uncle had on various occasions had reason to remark that Camilla's tongue was a great deal too sharp, and that sarcasm was one of the last qualities for which a well-educated young lady ought to desire to be remarkable.

'Now Camilla,' Sir Marmaduke confided to his sister, in his sham oracular fashion, 'is distinctly sarcastic.' Camilla had some excuse for being occasionally sarcastic. Her uncle's conversation produced on her nerves the effect which the *Autocrat of the Breakfast Table* describes so feelingly as wrought upon himself by a dull discourse; it stirred a hundred mental currents into inconvenient activity. 'If,' says that ingenious writer, 'you ever saw a crow with a king-bird after him, you will get an image of a dull speaker and lively listener. The bird in sable plumage flaps heavily along his straightforward course, while the other sails around him, over him, under him, leaves him, comes back again, tweaks out a black feather, shoots away once more, never losing sight of him, and finally reaches the crow's perch at the same time the crow does; having cut a perfect labyrinth of loops and knots and spirals, while the slow fowl was painfully working from one end of his straight line to another.'

This simile describes exactly the action of Sir Marmaduke's conversation on Camilla's nervous system, and the sort of road by which their minds travelled. Sir Marmaduke's journeyed slowly, cautiously, complacently, along a well-beaten road of conventional commonplace; well pleased with his sagacity in discovering it, with his progress upon it, and perfectly assured as to his destination. It was impossible not to listen to him; Camilla had often tried that resource; it was equally impossible to listen without an access of nervous fatigue and exhaustion. While Sir Marmaduke trudged complacently along, scattering commonplaces as he went, Camilla's eager thoughts were stimulated into unnatural restlessness; they touched him every now and then, and rebounded into the empyrean: they returned from the airy void, took a look at the honest pedestrian, and were off again, soaring out of sight. Hodgson, the head keeper, endeavouring with whip and whistle to inspire sobriety into a couple of young pointers, wild with escape from the durance of the kennel, was not less capable of emulating their movements, or more in the dark as to their delight, than was this worthy banker as to the aspirations, interests, and pangs of tedium which stirred the bosom of his mercurial niece.

She knew his stories, and the exact point at which the joke—that horrid thrice-told joke—would explode. She knew his arguments; she knew his demonstrations, which he ordered out just as he ordered out his carriage whenever wanted. Even her Aunt Augusta flinched sometimes, and gave a little sigh of fatigue as her brother began. To Camilla it was maddening; she would fly away, lock herself up in her bedroom, and there breathe the awful revelation to the respectable ancestors, who gazed at her from its walls, that her uncle was a bore. There are men, it has been well said, with whom it weakens you more to talk for an hour than would a day's fasting. Camilla had frequently to experience this sense of prostration. Her outbursts were only the flutterings of a spirit in prison, beating against the bars of a too narrow cage, and expectant of the hour of deliverance. In the background of her character, and lighting up her lofty aspirations with a gentle radiance, was a large store of tender romance. This was her true self; it recoiled, like some sensitive plant, from the rude contact of the outer world. Her uncle's rough, unsympathising touch inspired her with a real terror— the terror which gentle creatures feel at strength which can neither pity nor understand. Thus Camilla frequently seemed proud when she was really only frightened, and fastidious merely because she tried the things and persons about her by a high standard of refinement. If, as her uncle sometimes reprovingly observed, she thought nothing good enough for her, it was less from a too-exacting critical habit than because the ideal, which she instinctively followed, was something very good indeed.

Youthful idealism must rest its tired wing on a concrete ideal, and in Camilla's imagination her sudden friendship with Philip Ambrose lived as something exceptionally charming. The sweet memory of those few happy days in Paris—their mysterious charm—the deep impression they had made upon her; that last scene—that farewell kiss—had been stored up in her thoughts, like some treasure, laid away in a secret drawer under lock and key, and guarded jealously from the general gaze, to which one goes, every now and then, to feast the eye and be assured of its loveliness. Camilla had often repaired to her secret drawer, and had found her treasure safe and sound and delightful as ever. Those days had been different from all other days, that friend from other friends. Each scene, each word almost seemed to live—graced, vivified with some imperishable charm in her recollection. No colour faded from the picture as years went on—the weary years of dulness, commonplace, and hollowness. There lay for her the possibility of bliss ; there was the man whom she could fancy herself trusting, loving, idolising. Was it a dream—a half-remembered, half-imagined phantasm ? or would that enchanting vision again shape itself into flesh and blood ? Would Perseus arrive, strike off Andromeda's chains, and carry her off to liberty and love ? The courageous credulity of youth breathed a confident reply. The sombre atmosphere of Camilla's real existence lit up with a great brightness of hope and joy, and the gloomy realities around her died away or glowed into brightness, like some sombre landscape irradiated with the glow of a summer morning.

So Camilla lived in a phantom-land of her own creation—a land of noble ideals which she had fashioned for herself. She had had several lovers; one, the young rector of the parish, a cadet of a great county family, whose suit Camilla's aunts—half-terrified at their own audacity—furtively abetted; and one, a neighbouring squire, who used to be constantly riding over to see Sir Marmaduke on business, or to walk with him through the home coverts. They were both, as the two Miss Crofts confided regretfully to one another, nice men—gentlemen, good, attractive—in every way eligible. Alas, alas! Camilla would elect neither. The first thought of it, directly it dawned upon her mind, convinced her of its impossibility. Her aunts' mild persuasions, her uncle's unconcealed displeasure — and Sir Marmaduke had no need to speak in order to make Camilla understand that he was very much displeased with her indeed—produced no effect but to convert indifference into aversion. Pastor Aristæus, as Camilla irreverently described the clergyman, retired, despairing, to his flock, and consulted the Miss Crofts no more about his Sunday School and evening classes—that Sunday School in which, with artless craft, he had beguiled Camilla into teaching a little smiling row of rustics, and whither he had watched her—with what admiring eyes!—coming in her pony-carriage, on Sunday afternoons, across the park and along the sweet-scented country lane, his heart beating at the thought of a happy moment when he would meet her at the porch, and see her standing—charming apparition to clerical vision!—among her curtseying and smiling disciples. The youthful squire, too, had received his dismissal and gone his way, and came no more to ask Sir Marmaduke's advice about drainage schemes or kill his pheasants. Both lovers disappeared.

'This is trifling with life,' Camilla's elder aunt informed, her reproachfully.

'What?' Camilla had cried, with a sudden outspokenness very unusual to her, 'Trifling with life to decline to marry a man I don't care twopence about! Come, Aunt Augusta, do you really mean that? If you do, thank you, I care a great deal too much about my life to trifle with it by doing anything of the sort.'

Aunt Augusta, who was at heart extremely sentimental, was forced to admit the cogency of the reply, and to content herself with reminding her niece, with a sigh, that people, who do not gather their roses while they may, are in danger of not being able to gather them at all.

'Yes, but,' said Camilla, with a pretty blush, 'let me wait till the roses come—the true rose, the rose I really love; then, Aunt Augusta, you will see me gather it fast enough.'

At last it seemed that the real rose was about to make its appearance. Mr. Ambrose came over one day to lunch, and told them that he had received a telegram from Philip, the day before, to say that he had got six months' holiday, and was already on his road to England. Camilla's heart went pit-a-pat, and she was conscious of a vehement effort to conceal the agitation that the announcement had occasioned.

'You remember my boy, Philip, your old friend,'

Mr. Ambrose said to her, ' and the pleasant time we had in Paris ? '

'To be sure,' said Camilla, trying, with but scant success, to look as if nothing had happened, and with a crimson cheek signalling her consciousness of failure. ' What fun we had ; and how M. Got did make us all laugh ! '

M. Got, indeed ! As if the most brilliant performance that ever yet took place at the Comédie Française weighed for a feather in the balance against the painfully interesting drama which was at that moment enacting itself in Camilla's tender heart; and as if the little hypocrite had not, even then, formed her deep design, and did not, the moment luncheon was over, carry off the unsuspecting Mr. Ambrose to look at her flowers, and from the flowers to walk about with her, in kindly confabulation, in the pleasant, shady terrace under the cedars, for a good half hour, during which Philip's father poured into her sympathetic ear many tender confidences about the much-beloved son, whom he was to have with him again so soon, and many pleasant stories of Philip's childhood and youth, such as a loving father might be pardoned for treasuring up in his recollection and imparting to a congenial listener, as Camilla always proved. These two were always sworn friends. She behaved to him with a pretty filial respect, and Mr. Ambrose had, no doubt, often reflected how great a charm a daughter-in-law, such as Camilla, would lend to life. He returned now, all the better for his walk. Camilla, too, came in flushed with hope and joy, such as her aunts had never before seen in her face, usually so calm, often so sombre and unimpassioned. The long, dull, cold winter was over, the golden summer had come. The rose of Camilla's existence—the incomparable rose—was at last about to bloom !

CHAPTER XII

THE TRUE ROSE

'—Thoughts and dreams and sighs—
Wishes and tears—poor Fancy's followers.'

THE next few weeks proved a trying period to Camilla. She was the prey of a great excitement, which no one around her shared, whose existence no one suspected, or could be allowed to suspect—a great hope, a great fear,—perhaps supreme felicity, possibly a cruel disappointment. Camilla did not try to conceal from herself that Philip Ambrose's arrival must mean something of vital importance to her. She had often thought of it, in the far distance, as a turning-point in her existence; and now the crisis was too near for comfort or tranquillity. She began to realise of what slender materials her castle in the air was built. It had been a daydream—vague, charming, unsubstantial, fair with whatever colours imagination chose to paint it. It had now to be reckoned with, face to face, as a solid fact of actual, waking life. The proximity was distressing, and, though Camilla was courageous, alarming. The harsh, hard light of day was beginning to pour on to the fair

edifice of moonlight romance. It is one thing to play
with an idea in some remote region of might be or might
have been. It is another, and a far less agreeable one,
to confront it in midway, bring it to exact account, and
.to be brought to exact account by it. Camilla, the soul
of truthfulness, was obliged to admit to her own conscience that she had been romancing. But what is the
good of such an admission? Would it make the impending event less eventful? Would it assuage her
anxiety? Would it calm her nerves, which, every day,
stood in more need of composure? Would it save her
from agitation, unrest, fear? Camilla began to feel that
the tranquillity of her uncle's house,—the commonplace
routine of life, was not, after all, without its advantages.
It was dull, uninteresting, uninspiring; but it was safe;
and there are moments when to be safe becomes a transcendent consideration—when, like Falstaff, one feels
that one would give all fame for a pot of beer and
safety. Camilla had often deplored and despised the
tame home-brew of her circumscribed existence. But
now it seemed a somewhat ambrosial beverage. In
short, she was getting into a regular fright. Then the
news came that Philip had actually arrived, and
was already with his father, only a dozen miles away;
and Camilla became more frightened than ever.

After a few days father and son came over to the
Vines to call upon Sir Marmaduke and his sisters.
Camilla was speedily relieved of one part of her
anxieties. Her childish impressions had not been
wrong. Philip was as charming as he had seemed to

her at Paris; he was more charming than ever. His
good looks had improved. The years in India had
turned his boyish pink and white to a manly bronze.
He was stronger and manlier. His active life had given
him, Camilla could see, a certain courageous, outspoken,
off-hand demeanour, which was very much to her taste.
He had an air of success, an air of command, which she
felt to be impressive. Philip, his father said, had been
representing British rule over a tract as big as an English
county. Ruling people for their own good was one of
the employments which Camilla felt to be deserving of
pursuit, really worthy of the dignity of man—one of the
few things in the world which it was really worth while
to do. It was the work of high natures and an imperial race. Camilla invested Philip with this imperial
glamour. Then Philip was not only very imperial in
manner, but he was delightfully kind and courteous.
He behaved to Sir Marmaduke with a gracious deference,
which had no touch of obsequiousness. He was evidently
petting his father to his heart's delight. The two Miss
Crofts felt just the same half-terrified, half-pleased
amusement at his proceedings that they had experienced
in Paris, but could not withstand his ingratiating politeness. His behaviour to Camilla made her conscious at
once of the admiration she inspired. She knew instinctively that to him she was beautiful, transcendent,
adorable. He had remembered her all these years and
amid all those far-off, mysterious scenes—her, the little
girl whom he had half-played with, half-petted for a
few days at Paris. He had cherished the recollection

of those happy days as she had cherished it. She had never forgotten him; she had never wavered in her feeling about that recollection. Philip too, she felt, had never wavered; presently he began to talk about their meeting in Paris, and his recollection was as fresh and vivid as Camilla's own. He had remembered his friends, too, in a substantial way, for he had presents for every one—a handsome cane for Sir Marmaduke cut from Muddipollium forests, with an iron ferule from the Muddipollium iron-works, and a top of gold that once had lain buried in Muddipollium quartz.

'Iron and gold!' cried Sir Marmaduke, greatly flattered by this act of attention.

'Yes, sir,' said Philip, cheerfully, 'it is the land of Ophir, you know; we have gold and iron and virgin forests, and water power enough for the mills of twenty Manchesters. All it wants is development, and that's what we are doing for it—we're developing it.'

'Ah,' said Sir Marmaduke, airing his new possession with great satisfaction, 'development—that's a good business, Philip, and just what a young fellow, like you, should be about.' Camilla, for once, fully concurred with her uncle. And then there were two soft, white shawls for the Miss Crofts, into which the gentle ladies nestled peacefully at once, and declared that they had never known perfect comfort till then. There was, too, a pretty necklace of rough turquoises, strung on a barbaric string, for Camilla,—beautiful, rugged, and full of local colour of its far-off home. Philip gave it to her with such kindly, respectful, affectionate courtesy, that the act and the gift became inscribed in her thoughts with the sacredness of chivalrous romance. She carried it off presently to her room, and wept over it some happy tears of pleasurable sentiment, and appeared, wearing it, that evening,—so bright and blushing and radiant,—that the Miss Crofts exchanged furtive glances, and began to guess the cause of Camilla's sudden excitement. The roses, indeed, were blooming thick about her. The fated hour had struck, the long-enchanted sleep of dulness closed, the deliverer was at hand who should bid her awake to liberty and joy and life.

Fortune smiled upon her, for nothing would satisfy Sir Marmaduke but that Philip should pay them a visit at the Vines, and have some partridge shooting. Philip was delighted to come, and enjoyed his holiday with an intensity of pleasure for which five years' exile in Indian jungles is, no doubt, one of the best of all possible prescriptions. It was exquisite September weather, and everything at the Vines seemed to Philip delightfully redolent of the well-ordered peace and plenty of an English harvest time. Sir Marmaduke listened with amused satisfaction to his bursts of unaffected delight at all the accustomed sights and sounds of an English autumn. The truth is that, when you have been about the world and seen how ninety-nine-hundredths of mankind are housed, an old English country-house, with its trim gardens and lawns, its immemorial trees and wide-stretching park, with the village nestling at its gates,—the moss-grown church where lord and peasant have worshipped for a thousand years, strikes one as an extraordinary achievement in the way of beauty, magnificence, and comfort. It combines so many and such contrasting charms. There is grandeur without parade, profusion without waste, dignity without ostentation. The present seems linked by so many outward and visible signs to the past. There is an air of well-ordered, temperate life—of refined economy—of cultivated and pure enjoyment—of days bound each to each by natural piety—a sort of exquisite propriety everywhere manifest. So, at least, thought Philip, as he drove up to the Vines, and saw its red gables showing faintly through the elms, and compared it with the tumble-down or half-finished palaces, the ruined gardens, the tawdry splendour, the ramshackle finery, the ragged rabble of untidy attendants and prancing horses of the magnates with whom he had had, of late, to do. Then came some delightful days; mornings with Sir Marmaduke in dewy, fragrant turnip fields, or the new-reaped corn-stubbles, where the barley shocks still stood uncarried, and the partridges were lying thick among them. 'These turnips,' he declared, drawing a long breath, 'are the best thing I have smelt for an age. We have no good smells in India.' And then, at the right place, there would be lunch, and the ladies would come out and join them; and Sir Marmaduke, having walked enough, and busied with matters at the farm, Philip did not care to go on shooting alone, and would send guns and dogs and keepers away, and sit chatting with his companions in the shade till, soon, the afternoon was old and the evening rays came slanting through the woodland. And then, as the two Miss Crofts could never pass a cottage without going in for a chat, Camilla and Philip would saunter on, homeward, through shady lanes and by cool water-meadows, and so reach the postern gate and the path that led across the park to the terrace of old cedars that skirted the gardens and lawn.

'This avenue,' Camilla said, as they watched the sun's last rays lighting up bough and stem with a golden glory, 'is my pet haunt. It always makes me think of an idea I read somewhere of venerable trees that seem to be pronouncing a benediction, "Grace, mercy, and peace be with you."'

'I feel as if they were,' said her companion; 'I shall always remember them as dear and sacred friends, who stood over me and gave me a blessing in some of the happiest moments of my life.'

Alas that such happy moments should fly so fast! Autumn was already come, and winter near at hand. Before the spring buds were out Philip would be back again in India, and these golden hours only a recollection!

Some natures, though affectionate and even loving, find it difficult to make love. With others, when a charming woman is their companion, the difficulty is not to make it. Philip's difficulty had always been of this last order. The sentiment of delighted homage, which the prevailing deity of the moment inspired, was always strong enough to make anything easier than reticence. It seemed so natural, so pleasant, so inevitable to feel tender and to express one's feelings. Accordingly the various young ladies who had inspired him with this emotion were speedily apprised of its existence, if not in actual language of the tongue, yet by those more subtle, but equally efficacious means of communication with which Nature has provided us. Philip had no taste for solitude. When he admired, he desired that the object of his admiration should know his feelings and should sympathise in them. He was affectionately communicative, and the natural frankness with which his communications were made won him, no doubt, many friends. No one, however, of the many charming women who had impressed him, had ever made so strong an impression as Camilla. It was, perhaps, owing to this fact that Philip's wooing proceeded less smoothly than Camilla's friendly attitude and the warmth of his own feelings might have seemed to justify. He was quite sure that he had never known a woman so deserving of homage, so refined, so charming, so exquisite in taste, so noble in mind. But then this exquisite taste might easily be shocked—this nobility had something that rather awed one. Philip was conscious of being mentally and morally on his very best behaviour when in Camilla's society. How could he have ever dared to kiss her at the Paris station? Should he ever dare to repeat that agreeable performance? Philip's courage, however, rose with the difficulty of his task, and so did his admiration for its object. For once in his life he experienced the sensation of feeling something more than he dared to express; and this

unaccustomed sensation added an intense glow to the
fever-heat of his sentiments.   He had never felt frightened at a woman before.   Camilla, though sweetness
itself to him, made him feel afraid, doubtful of himself,
doubtful of his success, doubtful whether he deserved
to succeed.   So despondency beset him.   Then Camilla
would come into the room, so radiant with tender
beauty; she moved about the task of the moment
with so exquisite a dignity.   If she put on a garden-
hat, and went for a stroll on the terrace with her
uncle, was ever a garden-hat worn with such a grace?
Did ever woman walk with a more nymph-like air,
or show a prettier foot as she stept across the dewy
lawn?   Was there ever so charming a flush of youth,
health, and beauty as shone on her face as she came
in at the breakfast-room window with her hands full
of freshly-gathered flowers?   Then she made tea—
with what an ineffable charm did she officiate at that
sacred domestic rite!   Philip felt it a sort of privilege to put to his lips the cup which she had filled.
He was, in fact, very far gone in love; and as
love has been, ever since the days of Ovid, an affair
full of anxious fear, Philip became very much afraid,
and being constitutionally unfit to bear any burthen
alone, poured the tale of his love and his anxieties into
his father's friendly ear.   Mr. Ambrose received the
communication with more cordial pleasure than Philip
had ever known him evince at any previous event in
his career—more even than when Philip had won the
Newdegate prize poem in his Oxford days.

'My dear fellow,' he said, 'I am delighted to hear of your wish, and I trust with all my heart you may succeed. She is as good and charming a girl as I have ever known. If you could get her, it would be the making of you. But you must take care. What a pity your time is so short.'

'I don't think the time signifies, father; we know each other very well. My conviction is that she has made up her mind already, but then I can't feel sure which way she has decided.'

Had Camilla made up her mind? So far, at any rate, that she felt a vehement desire that Philip should not bring matters to a crisis between them by an actual declaration, and a distressing apprehension that he would. She liked him very much; she would have grieved to lose him. His pleasant courtesy, his friendship, his devotion were very charming. He brought a great brightness into her life; he inspired existence with a strong, delightful excitement; he was very agreeable; but still the thought would suggest itself that he was not the ideal of her day-dreams. There were feelings and beliefs in Camilla's mind which were a great deal to her, to which he seemed to be an utter stranger, unable to make any response. He seemed to take lightly matters which to her seemed very serious— sacred. He passed over with an easy, cynical indifference topics which weighed heavily upon her as great problems demanding solution. Her view of the world invested it with a sort of mysterious sanctity— a stage where not to play one's part well and nobly

was to miss the very object of existence ; and Camilla's
'well and nobly' meant a great deal—self-sacrifice,
self-abnegation, efforts on a grand scale to enrich mankind and ennoble human life. George Eliot's exquisite
profession of faith was to her a sort of daily aspiration,
to part with which would be to part with all which made
life worth having—

> 'May I reach
> That purest Heaven, to be to other souls
> The cup of strength in some great agony,
> Enkindle generous ardour, feed pure love,
> Beget the smiles that have no cruelty,
> Be the sweet presence of a good diffused,
> And in diffusion ever more intense,
> So shall I join the choir invisible,
> Whose music is the gladness of the world !'

This was the kind of aspiration that stirred the
inmost depths of Camilla's soul, and made the ordinary
lives of the men and women she came across—the
dull, frigid, heartless ceremonies of social politeness,
the cold, rough struggle of London society, the absurd
little pomp of her uncle's house—seem to her an almost
intolerable travesty of what life was meant to be.
This was her true self to which the true sharer of her
heart would make appeal; these were the vague, blind
longings and cravings to which he would give form and
substance and definite aim. But nothing in Philip's
character tended at all in this direction. She could
not by any effort of idealising fancy invest him with
those qualities of head or heart with which her sweetest,
highest aspirations had affinity. His aims for humanity
were circumscribed to the tiny atom of it which circled

round himself, his own pleasures, interest, and success; and especially his own pleasures. The world appeared to be to him merely an 'I writ large,' and the 'I' was a creature of selfish good nature and aimless self-gratification. He spoke of India as a place where, amid a great many millions of very abject creatures, whose condition—the growth of centuries—it was as impossible to improve as to alter their colour, a man had to make his way and, if possible, his fortune as speedily as possible. Camilla had been horrified at some pitiable stories, which she had read somewhere, of the tragedies of an Indian famine. Such things, Philip explained glibly to her, were inevitable, quite inevitable, with a vast agricultural population, living, to begin with, at a level which an English pauper would regard as starvation, with scarcely any railways or roads, and a harvest dependent on a highly variable season. The mortality, vast in numbers—as everything in the East is—was comparatively insignificant—and, anyhow, it was but the effort of Nature to get rid of a redundant population. It was a necessity; it was even an advantage. There was a struggle for existence in which the fittest survived; the feeble ones, naturally, according to Nature's stern but beneficent law, succumbed. Such explanations struck a chill into Camilla's very soul; she consoled herself as best she could, still shuddering, with the reflection that men's theories were often much harder than their hearts. Still the man, whom one could really love, the ideal lover, would stand in need of no such apologies. On the whole she very much hoped that Philip would not propose, and became, every day, more apprehensive that he would; and, while Camilla was still dealing with it, in her thoughts, as an approaching danger, the crisis came upon her; and Philip was added to the list of Camilla's unsuccessful suitors.

Her refusal, however, cost her more than she had anticipated. All the more because she found it extremely difficult to formulate in any language, that did not seem ridiculous and high flown, the reason of her decision. She did not attempt to conceal her liking for him. Philip must never, never doubt her friendship, her warm friendship, but——

The reasons why she stopped there were too subtle for expression. They sounded absurd, directly she tried to put them into words. They would seem monstrous to any one who could not understand them. Philip, she felt sure, would never have understood them. What man, ardently in love with a lovely girl, who confessed to, nay, herself professed her friendship, would understand being refused because his aspirations were not high enough, his views about life insufficiently serious, and the political economy of his explanation of Indian famines too coldly scientific? You had only to say it to feel how unnatural it was. Still Camilla felt instinctively certain that she was right, and with many tender expressions of regard and wishes for his happiness, and many affectionate heart-searching compunctions, bound Philip down not to mention the subject again before his departure to India. Then her compunctions became more grievous than ever. Poor Ambrose was dreadfully grieved, but accepted her decision with a touching humility. 'I know,' he said, 'I am not a quarter good enough for you. What fellow could be? but, for all that, I love you with all my heart. It is a dreadful disappointment—a dreadful grief.'

'It is a grief to me too,' Camilla said, by this time in a very melting mood, and anxious to bear her share in her lover's troubles—'but it is inevitable, believe me. You must think of me always as your friend.'

'A dear, sweet, cruel, hard-hearted friend,' Philip said, with a sad smile. 'If you would only have had me, with all my shortcomings, I would have tried to deserve you.'

He was gone; and Camilla's day-dream had ended. She was awake; the rose had faded, ungathered. She was alone again with the stern facts of life; and very stern and sad they looked.

CHAPTER XIII

CHÂTEAU QUI PARLE

'She is a woman—therefore to be won.'

ONE of those stern facts was that Camilla would have, in a few days, to meet Philip's father, who was coming over to the Vines on some county business with her uncle. Now Mr. Ambrose touched a very tender spot in Camilla's heart. He was, in one way, her greatest friend. She always found it easy to be confidential with him. He had often talked to her about his books, and the pure and lofty natures with which they had made him familiar. Once, when she had driven over to the Rectory with her uncle, who, as a College visitor, was bound once a year to inspect the church, Mr. Ambrose had taken her into his study and left her there, awhile, happy in a wilderness of books, where every volume and title filled Camilla's thirsty soul with rapture.

'What a charming room,' she said, when he returned from the inspection, and found Camilla with a flush of pleasure on her cheek, busy with an open volume; 'and what delightful companions. I have been reading

Marcus Aurelius. Here is a pretty bit!' And then Camilla read aloud—an art in which she, unconsciously, excelled :

'"Men seek retirement in country-houses, at the seaside, on the mountains ; and you have, yourself, as much fondness for such places as another. Still there is no proof of originality in that ; for the privilege is yours of retiring into yourself whensoever you please—into that little farm of your own mind, where a silence so profound may be enjoyed."'

'Ah,' said Mr. Ambrose, 'that little farm, my dear, is what we all have to guard from profane intrusion. Take care of yours and till it well ; it is a sacred soil. You shall take the volume with you, Camilla, if you like ; and take this one too—St. Bonaventura's *Journey of the Soul to God.* He too, like Marcus Aurelius, loved "the sacred silence" where none but holy sounds are ever heard. You will find my mark at all my favourite passages. See, here is one which I will give you to think about next time you are alone and in a serious mood :

'"The perfection of recollection is for a man to be so absorbed in God as to forget all else, and himself also, and sweetly to rest in God—every sound of mutable thoughts and affections being hushed."'

Camilla had gone home that afternoon in a happy, peaceful frame of mind. A new window had been opened to her mental vision, with a delightful, serene vista. Henceforward Mr. Ambrose became her guide, friend, and father-confessor. He lent her many a dear volume —his faithful companion from College onward—and Camilla found in them and in him the congenial nutri-

ment which fed her natural mood and taste. They met
but rarely; but Camilla felt a sort of peaceful confidence in his protecting care and thoughtful, sympa
thetic counsels. She had been more open to him than
to any one in the world: and now there was a topic on
which any confidence between them would be extremely
embarrassing.

Mr. Ambrose came, sure enough, on the appointed
day, and Camilla could see at once that he was greatly
distressed. He looked older, grayer, and more careworn.
Camilla had always thought him rather pathetic—a
gentle, dignified, refined nature, bearing the troubles of
life with a patience which scarcely fell short of heroism.
These troubles had been many, and now she had
added to them, she could see, a more than ordinarily
grievous one. He took it, as she had known he would,
as a gentleman should meet a reverse. He was politer,
gentler, kinder to her than ever, in a way that smote
Camilla to the heart. She could not bear the thought
that she had grieved him. What a wretch she was so
to wound this kind and tender friend! She felt very
much grieved. She could not, at any rate, let him go
away without a word. 'I will come with you, Mr.
Ambrose, if you will let me,' she said, as he was taking leave of them, 'and walk home across the fields.'

Mr. Ambrose was delighted to take her. It was a
comfort to be alone with him, yet it was alarming, for,
of course, there must be an explanation of what Camilla
most shrank from explaining, if indeed it was not really
inexplicable. They tried to talk commonplaces; the

attempt completely failed.　At last in her perturbation she plunged, with the courage of despair, into the dreaded topic.

'I am so very sorry,' she said; 'you are not angry with me, are you?'

'Angry? my dear Camilla,' Mr. Ambrose said; 'what an idea!　But I am sorry—very, very sorry for Philip's sake, and my own.　I own that I should have liked you for a daughter-in-law, dearly.　I have always wished and hoped that it might some day come about.　I was rejoiced when I found that Philip's wishes and hopes were the same as mine.　Poor fellow—you would have been the saving of him.　However——'

They had reached the postern gate, and Mr. Ambrose pulled up his horse.　Here Camilla was to leave him. She could not speak; her heart was aching.　Mr. Ambrose gave her one of his pathetic smiles.　She loved this kind, tender friend, whom she had wounded so badly. She loved Philip, too, after a fashion.　Why was she rejecting the gift of these kind, generous hearts?　Her will was wavering.　Her heart gave a jump at the thought that she might, by a word, turn all this sadness into joy.　The two looked at each other, and tears were in the eyes of each.

'You are very good to me,' was all that she could say, 'and you may pity me, for I am very unhappy too.'

'Well,' said Mr. Ambrose, with a dismal smile, 'then we are all unhappy together; for there is Philip breaking his heart about you at the Rectory, and I mind

it for him, poor fellow, as much as he does for himself.
How I wish you liked him.'

'But I *do* like him very much indeed,' Camilla said,
with vehemence; 'I told him so. He is a friend—a
great friend. Why cannot he be content with that?'

'Why?' cried Mr. Ambrose, with more animation
than Camilla had ever before known him to exhibit:
'because, my dear, he loves you; wait, Camilla, till you
love some one yourself, and then see whether friendship
will content you.'

Mr. Ambrose sat watching while Camilla let herself
through the postern gate and waved him good-bye. As
she turned to walk homewards he could see that she
was in tears. Then he drove away, somewhat comforted
in soul, and reflecting that Philip's chance was not,
perhaps, after all, so desperate as he had feared.

Camilla had not long to wait before she began to feel
that friendship between such friends as Philip and herself is but a very poor affair. She missed him dreadfully. The house seemed sunk in gloom and silence.
The days, with no chance of a visit from him, were
appallingly long. The half-pleasurable, half-painful excitement was gone, and gone with it, Camilla found to
her cost, all that gave zest to life. She began to doubt
the justice of her decision. Was her estimate of Philip
a fair one? Suppose that, after all, her theories of
existence were but the fantastic dreams of theorists,
mystics, and recluses, and the shock, which Philip's
speeches sometimes gave her, only the necessary consequence of contact of the visionary with the real?

Might not his way of talking and feeling about things be the natural language of men immersed in practical work, and too busy about it to think about their thoughts and feelings. She had found in Saint Bernard a passage in which the human soul was described as a mirror, in which he, who would see God in it, must keep pure from every speck or stain, and unobscured by any breath of unholiness. But were not such conceptions the morbid dreams of the monastic cell—the hysterical cravings of half-crazy fanatics, scourged, starved, and frightened into a saintly frenzy? Had not human beings—had not active young Englishmen, at any rate,—full of health, strength, and daring, with nerves and muscles of the soundest possible order, something else to do in life than to sit polishing the mirrors of their own self-consciousness, and waiting, like an ecstatic nun, for beatific revelation? And, as soldiers in the field talk lightly of death, was it not natural that busy men, grappling hourly with practical emergencies, and familiar with horrors, should use less dainty phrases, should even think less daintily about them than those whose lives were stirred by no such excitements, no such rude, useful, necessary work? Philip might have spoken with an almost brutal levity of an Indian famine, but he had acted admirably. There had been quoted in the *Times* a 'Resolution' from an Indian Gazette, in which his good deeds were set forth by a grateful Government in no faltering terms. Sir Marmaduke read it out at breakfast. The famine had been in charge of Sir Optimus Maximus, and he had made it historical ; and amongst

other topics, which engaged his historic muse, was the
admirable zeal and disinterested self-devotion, with
which the officials concerned, and Philip amongst the
rest, had busied themselves in camp and hospital and
many a far, outlying, squalid hamlet, in combating the
dreadful foe. Sir Optimus possessed a rich official
paint-pot, and wielded a lavish brush. Each officer
received his daub of rose-colour. Mr. Ambrose's hospital arrangements were especially commended, as
sensible, effectual, humane. 'The warmest thanks of
Government are due to this officer for the untiring zeal,
wise foresight, and administrative capacity, which he
evinced throughout a long succession of difficulties and
anxieties, and which rendered his famine camp, despite
all its inevitable sadness, a bright spot amid the surrounding gloom.'

So the Resolution ran on in streams of grateful
panegyric. The fact was that Philip Ambrose and a
lot of young fellows, finding themselves suddenly transformed into almoners-general and poor-law inspectors
for a country half the size of England, had set themselves, with a good will, to meet the emergency as best
they might. Philip had ridden his fine Australian
horses fifty miles a day on inspection tours, had laid out
famine camps, organised food depôts, and distributed rice,
with the enjoyment that a vigorous lad feels in a piece
of important work, and quite unconscious of achieving
anything heroic till Sir Optimus's Resolution informed
him of the fact. Camilla now read the glowing phrases
with a beating heart. This was the man, whose love,

so generously proffered, she was rejecting; and for what reason that was not too fantastic for expression? Mr. Ambrose, her old and faithful and sympathising friend, who knew Philip better than any one, saw no reason, evidently; for he urged her to accept him. On the other hand, an obstinate, quiet voice, in Camilla's innermost soul, sounded clear and unmistakable, and counselled refusal. Camilla began to feel desperate,— as if all power of decision were deserting her. Meanwhile she was supremely miserable. The days were slipping fast away. In a few weeks Philip was to start for India, and then the mistake, if mistake it was, would be irreparable. At last, in her despair, she consulted her Aunt Augusta.

Aunt Augusta, under her composed exterior, was a sentimentalist. She had, in her youthful days, had a desperate affair with a penniless curate, in which all her own happiness had been shipwrecked, and of which, even now, she sometimes thought with an aching heart. She had been right on that occasion and her advisers wrong; for life had been cold and dull and gray to her ever since. She felt about all such subjects with a sort of terror at the pain they may occasion. Camilla found her kind and sympathetic.

'He is a very nice fellow, dear,' she said.

'I know that only too well,' said Camilla bitterly, 'but that is not the same thing as marrying him. Do you think I should be happy?'

'You are very unhappy now,' said her aunt.

'Yes,' said Camilla; 'I know that too—as deplorably

miserable as any one could be, and I have been getting worse every hour since I refused him.'

Aunt Augusta sat looking at her for an instant, awed by a sense of responsibility. Camilla met her look with another of helpless expectancy. Then the die was cast.

'My dear child,' said her aunt, 'sit down here and write to him to come to you at once. You are thoroughly in love with him, but you are frightened.'

Camilla burst into tears. 'I believe you are right, Aunt Augusta,' she said; 'I love him—I know it to my cost—but I am dreadfully frightened.'

So Camilla's fate was sealed; she wrote the letter, there and then, with a trembling hand. Aunt Augusta, greatly impressed with the solemnity of the crisis, and, her match-making propensity mastering all thoughts of prudence,—took charge of it, and, as a precaution against any further wavering, sped it, forthwith, on its way. Camilla stood at the window with a beating heart, and watched the groom go galloping across the park, carrying her fate with him. A dreadful terror seized her, which all Aunt Augusta's exhortations could not allay. She would have recalled the messenger even now, had it been possible.

'Be a little courageous, dear,' said her gentle consoler; 'why should you be frightened?'

'Frightened!' cried Camilla, shivering and pale with excitement, 'I am indeed. Don't you see that I am an arrant coward? Do *all* women go through this sort of thing before they are engaged?'

'Yes,' said Aunt Augusta, firmly, for she felt that it was no moment to stick at trifles, 'they *all* do ; you will be as happy as possible when once you have seen him.'

And so it proved. Philip, in the course of a few hours, arrived, and speedily put all Camilla's doubts and fears to flight. He played his part as accepted lover with a confident, yet respectful joyousness, which infected Camilla with a sudden fit of high spirits. His tenderness was so natural and gay ; his mood was so congenial ; his admiration so heartfelt, that any further hesitation would have seemed a sort of treason. Camilla forgot her coyness, and, in a sudden rush of sentiment, told him all he needed to make him the happiest of mortals. After all, it is delightful to be worshipped, and Philip was an excellent worshipper. Camilla felt remorseful for her doubts, and showed her repentance in a sweet, tender contrition. There was no longer any room for doubt. A happy pair of lovers, they strolled about the garden in a sort of enchantment, and came back to the prosaic realities of life (and dinner at eight o'clock was a solemn reality at the Vines, which nothing short of an earthquake could have disarranged) with the air of favoured beings, to whom the celestial aspect of existence had been suddenly revealed.

'Well ?' said Aunt Augusta, as Camilla came into her room, radiant and serene, as she had never seemed before.

'It is more than well,' said Camilla, with an air of rapt fervour ; 'he is all that I could wish. Why did I ever hesitate ? You were my good genius, Aunt

Augusta, when you put these foolish doubts to flight.
How can I ever be grateful enough to you?'

Philip rode home that night in a sort of ecstasy.
The silent meadows through which his path lay were
enchanted ground. The moonlight seemed a flood of
magic radiance. It was no common night—no common
world. Life was transformed and glorified. Camilla's
sweet, refined nature had inspired him with something
higher, purer, more serious than he had ever known
before. 'To have loved her,' it was said once of a
charming woman, 'is a liberal education.' To love
Camilla, to be loved by her, to be the happy master of
that noble heart, to read its thoughts, to be admitted to
its sacred shrine, was, Philip felt now, a revelation of
undreamed-of delights—of unimagined heights, where
privileged spirits move in finer air than that which
ordinary mortals breathe.

Mr. Ambrose came over the next morning with
Philip, and added to the general rejoicing. Camilla
could not have believed that he could look so radiant.

'My dear, dear Camilla,' he said, holding her hand
with an air of paternal benediction, 'you have made
me very happy.'

'And I too am happy,' Camilla said, giving him a
filial kiss—'and I shall have a very dear father-in-
law.'

CHAPTER XIV

LAST DAYS IN ENGLAND

PHILIP'S return to India was drawing near, too near to admit of any question as to Camilla's accompanying him. Even if it could have been delayed, Camilla felt a great disinclination to be hurried from her home and her English life. It was decided in a family conclave that she should follow in the course of the winter, as soon as the business arrangements could be completed and some desirable companions for the journey found. Meanwhile, it was but natural that the young lovers should make the most of the days which still remained before their first separation. These days were very charming, and the charm spread beyond the two people immediately concerned.

Mr. Ambrose had grown quite young again, and lived the days of his courtship once more in his sympathetic appreciation of Philip's good fortune. He had never

been gay since the dark hour that closed his own
married life ; but now a great happiness had befallen
him exactly at the point of his being where feeling was
most acute, and his heart was light. Father and son
strolled arm in arm about the Rectory garden, descanting
on Camilla's character and singing her praises, like a
pair of shepherds in an eclogue. Philip learnt now that
his father—ascetic as he looked—had once been a lover.
He had been in depths of despair at Philip's rejection ; he
was now as elated as the young lover himself. Philip had
brought him Camilla's portrait, which was to be their parting gift, and which, placed on an easel in the study among
all the sombre books and faded Oxford prints, seemed
to light up all around it with a ray of youth and joy.

'She is beautiful, dear Phil,' his father exclaimed as
he stood admiringly before it, 'and it is the best sort of
beauty, the fitting shrine of the beautiful soul within ;
what sweet eyes, and what a noble brow—

> ' " Dilated nostril, full of youth,
>   And forehead royal with the truth." '

'And what courage, father,' said Phil, delighted at
his father's congenial mood. 'Richmond has caught
that well, has he not ?—

> ' "Courage was cast about her like a dress
>   Of solemn comeliness ;
>   A gathered mind and an untroubled face
>   Did give her dangers grace."

Camilla has a pretty hand, too, the prettiest I ever saw.
I wish it was in the picture.'

Mr. Ambrose's thoughts at that moment were busy

with other topics than Camilla's hand. He turned to
Philip with a sudden gravity; the tears were in his
eyes: 'Dear Phil,' he said, 'you have been very fortunate. May God help you to deserve your good fortune.'

At the Vines Philip's high spirits and joyous love-
making spread a sort of brightness over the dull, old
house and its commonplace inmates. By a fortunate
instinct he did and said exactly the right thing—the
nice thing, on each occasion, to each person concerned.
The result was that he was a general favourite. Sir
Marmaduke's disapproval of the alliance, which at first
was pretty emphatic, had been neutralised by Aunt
Augusta's judicious diplomacy, and by his own conviction—the result of previous experience on similar occasions—that Camilla, in such matters, was fanciful,
determined and unamenable to the ordinary influences
by which well-regulated young ladies may be supposed
to guide their decisions at this critical stage of their
career. How it should come about that any woman,
out of Bedlam, should prefer a young Indian official,
with the certainty of expatriation and the probability of
impaired health and great many other drawbacks and
discomforts, to a comfortable country gentleman, with a
fine park within a dozen miles of her home, or a well-
connected clergyman, who had already got a good living,
and might, very likely, ultimately become a dean—was
one of those mysteries before which Sir Marmaduke's
intellect fairly broke down, and which made him think
that there must be something radically wrong in the
condition of society, when such blunders could be made.

On the other hand, Sir Marmaduke rather dreaded an encounter with Camilla's sharp wit, and knew that he was powerless to convince her. 'Are you quite sure that she has made up her mind?' he asked his sister.

'I am absolutely positive,' said Miss Augusta—who had now taken the engagement under her special protection, and was committing herself more and more deeply to its success—'and I trust, Marmaduke, that you will say nothing to distress her.'

'I shall tell her what I think,' Sir Marmaduke said, decisively; and so he did, with the unpleasing sensation that he might just as well have been addressing one of the marble statues in the hall. Camilla's nerves were brought up to a high pitch; she was entirely unimpressed by her uncle's dark picture of the disadvantages of an Indian husband.

'I love him, Uncle Marmaduke,' she said, 'and I love India, beggary, illness, and everything else that loving him involves. I would go with him to the end of the world. Pray, say no more.'

She held her uncle's hand; the tears stood in her eyes; her lip trembled with excitement; she looked the very embodiment of courage and devotion. How oppose such a mood as this with the cowardly suggestions of worldly wisdom? Sir Marmaduke felt his defeat, and was obliged to content himself with deploring that such a high-spirited girl should be so entirely irrational.

'She looked like a young martyr,' he told his sister afterwards, 'and talked like a fool. She must have her way, I suppose, as her mother did before her.'

Sir Marmaduke eased his conscience by resolving to be very firm and exacting in the matter of Camilla's settlement. People were continually asking him to be their trustee, and he determined that all his experience should be now devoted to safeguarding this wilful young lady's future by every expedient that human ingenuity could devise.

One awful morning Philip was summoned to Sir Marmaduke's study,—a dread-inspiring chamber, with a portrait of Sir Marmaduke's father, as M. H. of the Vine Hunt, on one side, and a statue of Mr. Pitt, turning up his nose at the enemies of his country, on the other; and here he found the worthy baronet and Mr. Greaves, the family solicitor, drawn up in conclave for the interview. Mr. Greaves, a thin, shrewd old gentleman, profoundly versed in the affairs of the Croft family, and devoted to its interests, had come down from London for the occasion, and treated it with the solemnity of an affair of State. He congratulated Philip with ceremonious courtesy on the prospective alliance, and was greatly interested in Camilla's fortunes. 'Dear me,' he said, 'I remember drawing her mother's marriage-settlement more than twenty years ago. We discussed it in this very room—do you recollect, Sir Marmaduke?'

'Perfectly,' said the other, with the air of a man with whom family events were far too important to be forgotten, and whose standard of what was befitting could not easily be moved; 'and I am sure I hope this affair may turn out more happily than that did.'

'Well, sir,' said Philip, trying desperately to resist

Sir Marmaduke's melancholy tone, 'I am not likely to get killed in battle, am I?'

'I am sure I don't know,' said Sir Marmaduke, equally determined to shut out any ray of consolation; 'in India, I am told, the civilians have frequently to attend military expeditions, and even to lead them; but let us get to business, Mr. Greaves, if you please.'

Philip had been feeling more and more abject ever since the interview began, and was now completely prostrated by having to confess that he had no immediate possessions to settle on his wife. He was entitled to some £10,000 at his father's death, and his father had promised to allow him £300 a year as long as he held his living. Besides this, Philip had a good appointment, and if anything befell him, his widow would have a pension. 'Humph!' said Mr. Greaves, and Philip felt his annihilation to be complete. Sir Marmaduke looked stern. The Master of the Hunt seemed to be frowning at him from the middle of the hounds, as if he would like to lay his hunting-whip across his shoulders; Mr. Pitt's nose was higher in the air than ever. At this stage of the proceedings, however, Sir Marmaduke gave Philip the agreeable information that Camilla was something of an heiress. Her mother's property had been judiciously nursed into a comfortable little fortune. Sir Marmaduke had watched over the investments, in which he had placed his niece's little store, and took a personal satisfaction in its growth. As a banker, he knew of all the good things that were going, and some of them had proved to be very good indeed. Then, one of Camilla's great-aunts had left her a legacy, which had swelled the total of her patrimony, and had grown, with the rest, under Sir Marmaduke's fostering skill. Sir Marmaduke, however, with Mr. Greaves to abet him, now felt it due to the occasion to raise objections and contemplate various remote contingencies and embarrassments with an anxiety which appeared to Philip very unnecessary. 'In the event of your predeceasing your wife and leaving a family,' suggested the solicitor with ruthless bluntness, 'and your father (as he may very likely wish to do on account of failing health or fifty other things) resigning his living, what would be Mrs. Ambrose's position?'

Philip had not contemplated this adverse conjunction of events, and felt completely unable to suggest any proper expedient by which it could be met. 'That is a very unlikely thing to happen,' he feebly remarked.

'My dear young gentleman,' said Mr. Greaves, with a provoking air of superior sagacity, 'when you are as old as I am, you will know that it is just the unlikely things that always happen, and, in any case, the use of a settlement, as Sir Marmaduke well knows, is to provide for the unlikely things. Don't you remember the story of poor Lord O'Rush, who stopped in the middle of making his will to go to lunch, and fell over a step and broke his neck as he was walking from his study to the dining-room?'

'Good heavens!' cried Philip, 'Mr. Greaves, don't tell such fearful stories—you make one quite nervous.

I do not intend to break my neck, at any rate, I can tell you.'

'Possibly not,' said the solicitor; 'nor, I presume, did Lord O'Rush. All the same, this is a serious matter, and I don't see how it is to be got over.'

It was got over at last by Philip's suggesting that his father's covenant should not be contingent on his retaining his living. Mr. Ambrose, he was positive, would agree to this. Mr. Greaves was constrained to admit, with some reluctance, that if this were so, Camilla's future might be regarded as moderately well safeguarded against absolute destitution. And then Sir Marmaduke announced that he intended to give his niece £2000, to be put into settlement with the rest. At last Philip escaped, with a great sense of relief, to the drawing-room, where Camilla was awaiting him.

'It is all over, thank goodness,' he said. 'Everything is all right, and we are to be as rich as Crœsus; but, Camilla dear, what a dreadful sort of personage a family solicitor is—his mind's eye occupied with all sort of horrible possibilities. Let us go into the garden and forget him and them amongst the flowers.'

'Poor fellow,' said Camilla, 'you look tired to death. I am tired too. I have had a dreadful morning over my village-hospital accounts—why is it, alas! that all good deeds involve so much arithmetic? Come under the cedars, and you shall lie on the grass while I finish *Elaine* to you.'

'Delightful!' cried Philip; and so the happy lovers

strolled across the lawn, and reached their favourite haunt, and soon forgot their troubles and fatigues in the happy oblivion of propitious love-making. All this part of the business Philip did to perfection ; Camilla could not doubt, at any rate, that, whatever might be his other imperfections, her lover was excessively in love.

Philip had not, however, even now arrived at the last of Mr. Greaves's persecutions. That gentleman, it soon became apparent, was far from satisfied, and took a most gloomy view of Camilla's intended alliance. The whole thing, he felt, was rash and inexpedient. His firm were not accustomed to draw settlements in which the prospective husband settled nothing but promises and contingencies, and in which the accidents of life in India had to be taken into account. It was not like Sir Marmaduke's usual good sense to have allowed such an alliance for his ward. Camilla ought to have found a home in one of the county families. He went over to the Rectory and talked about the marriage in terms which Mr. Ambrose, who, in his quiet way, stood immensely on his dignity, felt to be covertly disrespectful. Greaves, he found, had been to the India Office and made all sorts of impertinent inquiries about Philip's position, pay, and future pension, as if Mr. Ambrose's word were not enough. When, some weeks later, Mr. Greaves came down to the Vines with the settlement, his dissatisfaction was apparent even to Sir Marmaduke, and excited his alarm.

‘ What is it you do not like, Greaves ?’ he asked, confidentially.

'Well, sir,' said the solicitor, 'I go by instinct, and I instinctively doubt young Mr. Ambrose. He looks weak, and is a wretched man of business. He knows nothing about his own affairs, such of them as there are to know. I feel pretty confident that he is in debt, and he will die in debt—men with that sort of expression always do.'

Mr. Greaves's warnings, however, came too late. Sir Marmaduke was as much annoyed at an arrangement which he had approved being called in question as Mr. Ambrose had been at the suggested disparagement of his son.

'Suppose now,' Mr. Greaves said, in his cheerful way, ' he dies in some remote spot—Masulipatam, you know, or Chandernagore, or that style of place—with no friends at hand, and with a number of outstanding bills, what a position Mrs. Ambrose and her family might be in! We ought to have provided for it, Sir Marmaduke.'

'Come, come, Greaves,' Sir Marmaduke had answered testily, ' the thing is settled now, and it will do well enough.'

All the same he hinted his anxieties to Mr. Ambrose, and Mr. Ambrose to his son.

'What is it that they want?' cried Philip in a passion. 'I tell you what I will do, father. I will insure my life the moment I get back to India.'

'That is a good notion, Philip,' said his father; ' I wish you would. I really can do nothing more for you. Go and tell Sir Marmaduke at once what you mean to do.'

CHAPTER XV

SINCLAIR

'I have lived
As he lives, who through perilous paths must pass,—
And lifelong trials, striving to keep down
The brute within him—born of too much strength
And sloth and vacuous days—by difficult toils,
Labours endured, and hard-fought fights with ill;
Now vanquished, now triumphant; and sometimes,
In intervals of too long labour finding
His nature grown too strong for him, falls prone —
Awhile, a helpless prey—then once again
Rises and spurns his chains and fares anew
Along the perilous ways.'

An escort was found for Camilla in time to give her the benefit of such approach to cold weather as Cœrulea enjoys—in time, too, to initiate her into the horrors of the overcrowded vessels, which, as winter approaches, carry out to India a multitude of officials rejoining their appointments, of wives rejoining their husbands, and of tourists, who in the course of the ensuing three months intend to master for themselves, by ocular inspection, the various problems of Indian administration. Camilla was not inspirited by her surroundings. She tried in vain to find them picturesque or interesting. A considerable portion of her fellow-passengers bore the stamp of shabbiness ; others were objectionably smart. Several young ladies lost no time in establishing flirtations of a vulgar order ; several married women followed, or, perhaps, set them the example. The Brandons, under whose protection Camilla was travelling, were not much of a resource. Colonel Brandon was a heavy, worn, dull man, whose twenty years as a police officer had left him apparently with few ideas about India, except that it was a supreme misfortune to have to return to it. Mrs. Brandon was gentle and depressed, with occasional flashes of rather dreary amusement at her own misfortunes. Her appearance told a tale of hot seasons in the plains, of frequent ill-health and of generally enfeebled powers, on which life was continually making overdrafts in the way of uncongenial effort. Her existence had been too hard, too busy, too hopeless, to allow of any of Camilla's high-flown ideas of self-improvement or embellishment. Her heart was aching now for the boys and girls, whose school arrangements were an unfailing source of perplexity, and the dearly-beloved youngest born, whom the doctors had said was just too old to confront India in safety, and from whom, for the first time, her mother had been obliged to separate. She shared Camilla's cabin, and soon became confidential. Her revelations were not of an exhilarating order. Life had to her little that was bright. They were dreadfully poor, she told her companion ; her husband's chances of promotion had been, for years, fading away, as one by one the opportunities arrived and passed without result. They were heartsick with disappointment, and had determined, with a rather sad stoicism, to hope no more. Their income was barely enough to cover the school bills at home and the current expenses of Indian life. Every month the fall of Exchange was making them sensibly poorer. One of the girls was delicate, and required constant care and every sort of luxury. She ought to have been wintering at Cannes. It was heartbreaking to be obliged to leave her in a shabby comfortless home, in a chill English suburb. As Charles Lamb said, it is not only the classes known as 'poor' that have to 'drag' their children up, instead of bringing them up, as richer folk can afford to do. Camilla felt all this very depressing, dingy, and incompatible with any theory of life which could be regarded as tolerably adequate. Such lives seemed to her merely one long, degrading struggle with poverty. She was quite relieved to see that Mrs. Brandon cheered up considerably in public, chatted away with vivacity in a daily enlarging circle of acquaintance, did not scorn a valse when occasion offered, and was roused into actual enthusiasm by the private theatricals which some enterprising young travellers extemporised on the quarter-deck. On the whole, she gave Camilla the idea of a rougher, sterner, more work-a-day life, than any with which she had as yet come in contact in the safe, sheltered confines of the Vines—a life whose rough and smooth aspects had alike to be accepted—whose duties, often onerous and unattractive, had, as a matter of course, to be dis-

charged,—whose pleasures must be accepted for what
they were worth, and made the best of. The idea of
any fortunate, brilliant event coming their way, or of
life leaving room for any heroic achievement, did not
fall within the range of Colonel Brandon's wildest flights
of fancy. What a dreary ambition! What a life, unlit
by other hopes than these! Those flights seldom
ranged beyond the chance of acting for a while in the
appointment of some more fortunate compeer, or the
delightful possibility of becoming a head-jailer in
England. These good people's story struck Camilla
rather sadly. It was like that of some humble member
of a theatrical company, not aspiring to, hardly wishing
for, a lucrative or conspicuous *rôle*, but earning his
wages by a conscientious performance of an ungrateful
and almost unnoticed part. Camilla began to recognise
that life in her uncle's comfortable house was, however
dull, a luxurious affair, fenced round from the rude
world outside — different from the stern, laborious
struggle with the prosaic and often ignoble difficulties
which beset the existence of ninety-nine hundredths
of mankind. She consoled herself with the reflection
that the life, at the threshold of which she now stood,
was, at any rate, extremely real, and with the hope,
which the facts of the case rendered not irrational, that
her future husband might be one of the happy few for
whom fortune had some especial prize in store. A
more solid ground of comfort was that, for better fate
or worse, she would now, in a few weeks, be with the
man she loved.

The Brandons soon found acquaintances on board; people whom they had known before, or whom they knew about, or with whom similarity of employments, common friends or common anxieties, presently furnished an adequate supply of topics for the sort of conversation that is possible in the hurly-burly of a crowded deck. None of them seemed to Camilla in the faintest degree interesting, with a single exception. One day Mrs. Brandon introduced her to a Major Sinclair, who was on his way to join his regiment at a Cœrulean station.

'I am sure I don't know if you will like him,' Mrs. Brandon told Camilla beforehand; 'I do not like him much myself. He is too intense for my taste, and takes everything too tremendously in earnest. But he is a firstrate soldier, they say, and, moreover, a great reader. He will talk to you about books as much as you please. He will be a comfort to you on this stupid voyage.'

And so Camilla found him. He proved an invaluable ingredient in the mild composition of the little temporary world in which, for the next month, she was to live. He had been five years in India and was now returning, not in the best of spirits, Camilla could see, after a year's furlough at home. He and Camilla not unfrequently found themselves companions for a portion of those interminable evenings, which the deities who govern that portion of man's destiny have decreed that everybody shall spend in the twilight of a badly-lighted deck.

Friendships grow quickly on board ship, and before the voyage was nearly over Camilla found that she had glided into great intimacy with her new-found friend. Sinclair was extremely sympathetic. He looked at the world from much the same standpoint as her own. His theory of life was her own too, only tamed by actual experience—a struggle to ennoble it, to rise above its temptations, to trample down everything that could degrade, to seek high aims. It was impossible to resist so good a claim to her regard. Nor did Camilla feel inclined to resist, for she was very much impressed.

Sinclair left on her mind the idea of a more intense character than any she had hitherto met. There was a laboured calmness about him which bespoke an habitual effort at control and compression, and a systematically maintained mastery over feelings, tastes, and passions which were capable of a desperate struggle for mastery. His temper loomed in sight, every now and then, just enough to assert a vigorous existence and to admit accustomed subjection. His opinions were clear, definite, unqualified; standing, clear, and hard, in the sunshine, with none of the hazy atmosphere of indistinctness which gives some minds a convenient intellectual chiaroscuro. His likes and dislikes, especially the latter, were of the most vehement order.

'Talking to him,' said Mrs. Brandon, 'is like being in a gale at sea: his talk exhausts one by its very strength. Other men seem like silver paper to his granite; but then silver paper is the best for wrapping such smallwares as mine. Major Sinclair is absolutely granitic.'

Camilla, however, liked the granite, and she found that Sinclair, if he had a giant's strength, had no wish to make a giantlike use of it. He was always delighted to talk to her, and on whatever subject she chose to start; he broke off from his books—of which he appeared to have an endless supply on hand—with cheerful readiness whenever the chance of doing anything for her, or with her, presented itself. He took her out of the crowd for long walks on the upper deck; he devoted his afternoons to teaching her whist, not the gentle, guileless, and somewhat fatiguing struggle which her aunts and uncle waged through quiet evenings at the Vines, but the profound and exact system of tactics which Cambridge mathematicians have elaborated for a later generation. Camilla soon recognised the dignity of the newly revealed science, and became extremely interested in understanding Sinclair's instructions and applying them.

'They are,' he said, 'the nearest approach, hitherto discovered by mankind, to eternal principles; anyhow, they are essential to the salvation of whist, if it is to be saved from degenerating into a dull pastime for babies.'

'It is incurring a grave, moral responsibility to play at all,' said Camilla; 'happily I now know my leads, so that I am safe from one set of heresies; but my conscience is not yet alive to the call for trumps.'

It was not into the laws of Cavendish alone that Sinclair found it an interesting employment to initiate his new companion. He was no sooner assured of her fellow-feeling on some points than he seemed possessed by a vehement desire to command her sympathy on all. Camilla found that any difference of opinion between them appeared to give him real concern. He took a great deal of trouble to convince her that they did not really disagree, and was quite uneasy till their agreement was clearly made out. Confidence once established, Camilla found a daily increasing interest in exploring her companion, and in conquering his reluctance to talk about himself. She discovered in him a vigorous impersonation of the commonplace, but by no means common, creed, in which doing one's duty is the main article of faith and the inspiring sentiment.

Fame, success, enjoyment, happiness, all seemed—as she understood Sinclair's modest and unconscious self-delineation—matters for which he had no ardent aspiration. They were accidents which befell some men, as did wealth, high birth, good health, good looks or any other piece of good luck; but they were no objects for serious desire, far less active effort. To perform his appointed task with a scrupulous and conscientious exactness, to get through life without some dreadful shortcoming, to sacrifice whatever was necessary for its performance, to die in the last ditch or on the last barricade—such was Sinclair's ideal of felicity; no other view of life could render it endurable, or reconcile one to its innumerable vicissitudes. Camilla found his theory of life a graver one than any she had hitherto confronted in real life. That its prizes fell often to unworthy recipients gave him no pang of envy, no feeling even of annoyance. It was the natural order of things;

and the success of most was too dearly bought to create any feeling but one of surprise that they should think it worth its cost. To a great extent it was a lottery. One lad, loyal, able, brave as a lion, with all the making of a great commander in him, gets knocked over in his first engagement, or dies of sunstroke the day before the battle. Another fellow arrives at the right moment, has the good luck to keep his head clear of the cannon balls, and finds himself a few weeks later figuring in gazettes, and be-praised and be-medalled and be-lettered into fame.

'You know what Othello says of reputation,—"an idle and most false imposition, oft got without merit and lost without deserving." The only sensible thing is not to care two straws whether it comes or goes.'

'But,' said Camilla, 'what about the last infirmity of noble minds?'

'That means, or ought to mean,' said Sinclair, 'that it is the last infirmity which a really noble nature ought to have.'

'What!' cried Camilla; 'you would not have men without ambition surely?'

'It comes to few of us,' said Sinclair, 'to have a chance of indulging it. Everybody must like the good things on which ambition feeds, but one is much better without them. Take public life, for instance, full of delightful interest and excitement, of course; but just look at the sacrifices which it involves—the surrender of leisure, independence, individuality, all that makes life worth having. Look at its struggles, its degradations, its disappointments, and, worst of all, its rewards. Fancy working hard at it for twenty years to find oneself a burthen to one's party, politely ignored by one's friends, edged out of a Cabinet, shelved with a convenient sinecure, or banished to a colonial governorship. What a way of spending life!'

'Ah,' said Camilla, 'that is for the unsuccessful only; but then, of course, one is determined to succeed.'

'Yes,' said her companion, by this time warming into his defence of indifferentism; 'and if you do, is not success, often, the worst misfortune of all? Has not the function of statesmanship been reduced, as Matthew Arnold says, to "the cult of the jumping cat"? and is not the most successful statesman he who has the keenest instinct of the way she means to jump, and most encourages her in jumping. Has not the greatest statesman of the day laid it down as a political axiom that the most important duty of a leader is to ascertain the average opinions of his party, and largely to give effect to them?'

'That is from the point of view of self-preservation,' said Camilla, who had learnt from her uncle, at any rate, to be somewhat of a politician. 'A Government has got to keep itself in existence, you know, like anything else.'

'Yes,' said Sinclair; 'but from the other points of view,—honour, justice, reason and the common weal. Are they all to be sacrificed to a degraded opportunism? Fancy, now, being admired for half a century as the greatest politician of one's day, and ending it all by breaking one's party to pieces in an abortive attempt to dismember one's country, with half your countrymen doubting your sanity, and the other half your rectitude.'

'That,' said Camilla with a laugh, 'must have happened to some statesman of antiquity,—anyhow, I am for ambition. "A crust of bread and liberty" is all very well; I have always had an idea that, notwithstanding its perils, the town mouse had the best of it after all.'

Nor did Sinclair, Camilla found, show a weaker front to the pleasures of life than its ambitions.

'Pleasant things are pleasant of course,' he said; 'but most people make too much fuss about them, exalt them to a philosophy or a religion. I think they are a very poor religion. I suppose it is very prosaic, something wanting in my nature, but that is how they strike me. I see that many things have a charm, a reality, a meaning for other men which they have not for me. Beauty is one of them — in art, in literature, in our mode of life. I cannot worship it. I cannot understand how a man can satisfy himself by making it the end of life, by filling existence with prettinesses, by surrounding himself with elegant trifles, by providing a continuous succession of artistic effects, a series of exquisite sensations. I don't venture to decry such men — very likely they are higher, more refined natures; but I cannot understand them.'

'But,' said Camilla, 'was not the love of the beautiful the chief light of the world till Christianity eclipsed it, or, rather, supplied a new standard of beauty?'

'Yes, and that is why I can least of all understand the æstheticism of people and natures that have drunk the strong drink of Christianity—with its solemn view of man's being, its awful depths, its dreadful menaces, its enrapturing hopes, its saints and martyrs. It seems to me a sort of pitiful falling away—a sinking to a lower level. Existence is to me a grave, rather a grim affair, where each one has his load of duty to carry. One can carry it, if one tries,—with more or less success, probably less. One is always making the most hideous mistakes, the most deplorable failures; the great thing is to try to do one's best. Whether it is pretty or not, seems beside the question. This view is Puritanism, I sup-pose, but the Puritans had a good deal to say for themselves: at any rate I am one myself. The world is too old for the child-play of the Greeks—the broken toys of a Greek nursery, lovely though they be. It can only be done by resolutely shutting one's eyes to the real world around one—its atrocities, its miseries, its dreadful, cruel wrongs—its trampling on the weak—its gross impudent frauds—its rapid passage into the un-pierceable gloom beyond. How can one stand in the midst of such things and be thinking merely of whether one's own little speck is beautiful or no? It is like the naturalist at Paris who went on arranging butter-flies in his studio all through the reign of terror. I would rather have been out with the fighters on the barricades.'

'Ah,' said Camilla, 'you love excitement; you have a weak point, you see, like the rest of us.'

'Yes,' said Sinclair, 'I will confess to that common failing of Englishmen. The moments when I have been excited have been the most delightful of my life. But then the excitement must be a strong one, something that really stirs a man's blood.'

'Storming barricades, for instance,' said Camilla; 'not the discovery of a new butterfly. That is why you chose to be a soldier, I suppose?'

'It is a reason why I have never regretted my choice of a soldier's life, notwithstanding its vexations, its pedantries, its disappointments. You are unlucky, out here, if you do not get a campaign sooner or later, and then all your doubts about your profession disappear. You drink a stronger wine of life than any that can be had elsewhere, and it makes all other drink seem very poor stuff. I was in a charge once, and a half-hour's fight; it was called a skirmish of cavalry, and history has never deigned even to name it, but I would not have lost that half-hour for a lifetime of quiet existence.'

'But after all,' Camilla said, 'that sort of excitement is only a sort of moral dram-drinking.'

'Yes,' said Sinclair, 'but it is a dram one gets so seldom that there is no risk of its hurting one, and when you taste it, it is nectar.'

CHAPTER XVI

AT SEA

> 'Some unborn sorrow, ripe in fortune's womb,
> Is coming to me, and my inward soul
> With nothing trembles . . .
> I cannot but be sad.'

CAMILLA now came to appreciate the truth that, when once we leave the safeguarded barriers of home behind us, our intimacies and friendships depend on other forces than our own free will. Forcible as circumstances always are, they are nowhere more irresistible than in the close-packed microcosm of a ship. Camilla had started on the voyage with the desire and the prospect of a quiet—in one sense a solitary—month. She was longing for solitude. She had passed through a great deal of late, much that was agitating: she had come to a momentous decision, and she wanted to be alone with her own thoughts, and to realise to herself, in undisturbed reflection, the meaning of what she had done, and what she was about to do. There were many scenes, many conversations, which she desired to recall; and where could the process of recollection be better conducted than in the enforced idleness and monotony of sea-life and in the solitude of a crowd of strangers? And all around her were completely strange, as strange as people of another world. The Brandons made no advance to familiarity, nor did Camilla feel inclined to be familiar. Mrs. Brandon, on further acquaintance, revealed nothing that could serve as a common ground for thought or feeling. She was a weary, hopeless woman, scrambling through a fatiguing existence as best she could, with poverty always at her elbow, and the cares of each day more than each day's strength sufficed to meet. Her protests against her lot were not without a touch of somewhat dreary humour; but her flashes of fun were few and far between. Her thought never travelled beyond the petty interests of a life that was only saved from being ignoble by the sturdy fortitude with which it was endured. So far as interesting Camilla, or being interested in the things for which Camilla really cared, she was no more than any other of the crowd of unknown beings with whom she was sharing a month's captivity. With no one else had Camilla even a speaking acquaintance. So, for some days, when she started on her journey, she had felt, and was glad to feel, very much alone. Then Sinclair had appeared on the scene, and Camilla, before many days were over, was conscious that she was understood, appreciated, impressed, in a manner which defied indifference and brought her sense of isolation to a sudden close. Sinclair's strongly marked personality could not be ignored : nor would the current of Camilla's thoughts run on unstirred by the ideas he called to light and the

moods which he excited.   Camilla had, at first, resented
the sort of influence he began to exert upon her, and
tried to repel it: but Sinclair, quite unconscious of her
efforts, was not to be repelled.   Of what use was it to try
to conceal from oneself the fact that he had a hundred
things to tell her that she cared to hear—feelings
to express which stirred a sympathetic pulse—tastes
which were common property—convictions which, once
uttered, gave the speaker the privileges of a common
faith ?

Thus, before the Indian Ocean was nearly crossed,
Camilla found herself sliding, insensibly, into an
intimacy with Sinclair, more real, serious, and far-
reaching than any she had ever yet formed with any
one, except, perhaps, Mr. Ambrose ; and her confidences
with him were rather such as are breathed by a disciple
into the ear of a spiritual father than the free intercourse of mind with mind.   With Philip her intercourse
had been too brief, too agitating, too passion-stirred to
allow of analysis or even of thorough knowledge.   She
knew but one aspect of his character—the bright,
effusive, mirthful, affectionate, sentimental side.   It was
a sweet, gentle, lovable aspect.   What was the rest of
him like ?   She had still to find out.   But Sinclair, as
they sat and chatted through the long evenings, made
her feel his whole range of sentiment and belief stamp-
ing itself forcibly upon her own mind.   He had nothing
to conceal, nor would any form of concealment have
been compatible with his notion of the rational ends of
human intercourse.   He bore her along with him on

the strong current of his own convictions. His theory of life was hard, rugged, even distressing; yet it had a pathos and a sort of solemnity of its own which sank deep into Camilla's soul. Here, at any rate, was a man who was walking on the heights, unattracted by vulgar aims, unimpeded by vulgar infirmities, stirred, not by enthusiasm—for enthusiastic Sinclair never was—but by a noble instinct and moral chivalry, which was to him a sort of religion. He opened to her an altogether new horizon of thought about the strange country which was to be her future home. 'Read all you can get hold of about Buddhism,' he said; 'the story of the grandest effort of mankind towards the spiritual, the sublime: it is, to say the least of it, the step-sister, if indeed it is not the mother, of Christianity. That has revolutionised the western world—has it not? and given it whatever of nobility it possesses. Well, Buddhism did the same for India and the East. The story of Sakia-mooni is a foreshadowing,—too close in its resemblance to admit of any explanation but relationship,—to that sacred life which we in Europe venerate as divine. It is a beautiful life, inspired by the same tender compassion for the miseries of mankind that has carried Christianity—like a ray of heavenly light—to so many millions of aching hearts. But it is dying as religions do. Perhaps it has reached the stage when, as they say, an expiring creed is like the setting sun; its rays can no longer give warmth, but only create forms of beauty.'

'Do all religions die then?' asked Camilla.

'A great many have died, that is certain,' said her companion. 'One may stand in a Buddhist temple—only not ruined, because it is cut in solid rock—and wonder who the men were who prayed and fasted, chanted solemn litanies, or, in the solitude of the monk's cell, tried to come to terms with conscience two thousand years ago. All has gone but the solid rock itself. Do you remember Matthew Arnold's dirge ?—

' "The sea of faith
Was once, too, at the full, and round earth's shore
Lay like the folds of a bright girdle furled :
   But now I only hear
Its melancholy, long, withdrawing roar,
   Retreating to the breath
Of the night wind down the vast edges drear
   And naked shingles of the world." '

'How dreary!' said Camilla; 'but there are sweeter and more inspiring sounds, surely, than that to the ear that is attuned to hear them. There are some tides still, are there not, which run full and strong. Men must have a living creed.'

'Would you like to hear a fine one?' said Sinclair, taking up the volume which lay beside him. 'I was reading it when we began to talk. It is as grand as St. Athanasius', and a great deal easier to understand.'

Yes,' said Camilla, 'let me hear it.'

'It is poetry,' Sinclair said, 'but none the worse for that;' and then he began :

' " We stand on a mountain pass, in the midst of whirling snow and blinding mist, through which we get glimpses, now and then, of paths which may be deceptive. If we stand still we shall be frozen to death. If we take the wrong road we shall be dashed to pieces. We do not certainly know whether there is any right one. What must we do ? 'Be strong and very courageous.' Act for the best, hope for the best, and take what comes. Above all, let us dream no dreams and tell no lies, but go our way, wherever it may lead, with our eyes open and our heads erect. If death ends all, we cannot meet it better. If not, let us enter whatever may be the next scene, like honest men, with no sophistry in our hearts and no masks on our faces." '

'That is very impressive,' said Camilla; 'it is like the old Norseman's idea of life being the bird that comes into the bright hall from the stormy night outside, flutters an instant in the light, and disappears again into the darkness. But I object to your description of it as a creed—it is rather the half-desperate courage of a man who has to live without one.'

'At any rate he believes in the mountains, the snow-storm and the precipices,' said her companion, 'and that is something—and more than many men achieve, in the way of belief, nowadays.'

'Well,' said Camilla, 'I am thankful to travel by a lower road and a safer one. A kind hand leads me through some peaceful valleys, and I fancy I sometimes catch glimpses of the white presences of the immortals on the mountain side. Life is full of delightful possibilities, surely.'

'Yes,' said the other, 'but look at its horrid disappointments—its dreadful failures, and what they mean in the way of suffering and degradation. Who could be enthusiastic about it ?'

'Ah,' said Camilla, 'that is it—you have no enthusiasm, Mr. Sinclair; you are a pessimist of the worst order.'

Sinclair must have been in particularly bad spirits that day. 'Yes,' he said, 'I am a pessimist, so far, that I do not regard life as particularly worth living, or the world and its prospects as brilliant enough to kindle any very ardent hopes. It seems to me a gallery of more or less disastrous mistakes; and one is so liable to make mistakes, and bad ones, that it is an escape to have done with life before their occurrence. It is like riding a bad horse out hunting in a difficult country—a fall, sooner or later, is inevitable; why should one make the experiment?'

'Don't frighten me, please,' said Camilla; 'I am on the brink of one such experiment myself. I am going to be married.'

'I know,' said Sinclair, turning pale as he spoke, and with a set look in his face which Camilla had already learnt to interpret as the signal of some unusual effort at self-restraint; 'pray Heaven it may be one of the successful experiments.'

'Of course,' said Camilla; 'I intend it to be a splendid success.'

'I hope and trust, indeed, that it will,' said the other.

Sinclair's face wore a grave, determined look—the look, Camilla fancied, of a man whose composure is not rest but repression, and whose mental eye is saddened by the prospect of troubles to come. It was a sad look and grave, and brought no ray of encouragement to her anxious soul. She dreaded—she almost hated him, as one hates the prophets of evil. Sinclair said no more, nor, much as she longed for it, did his companion dare to bid him divulge his gloomy thoughts.

As the days went by, Camilla became conscious that this reticence weighed increasingly upon her spirits. It was a refusal to be sympathetic exactly where sympathy was most needed and could best have been given.

It was disappointing to her, and, in her apprehensive mood, seemed somewhat ominous that, though their intimacy had reached a very confidential stage, Sinclair never volunteered an observation on her impending marriage—could not, even, be led to do so. She stood greatly in need of reinforcement, such as his sympathising approval would have supplied. She knew, necessarily, but little of her future husband—of his character so much only as could be discerned in the commerce of society and the treacherous mirage of a courtship; of his daily life, work, and habits, as near as possible nothing. It would have been a relief if Sinclair would have said something about him which would ratify her judgment—some expression of friendship or esteem— some story, some act, something upon which her willing fancy might build its edifice of hope. Sinclair knew Philip perfectly, and even had lived in the same house. But, beyond this, he was resolutely silent, and would not take Camilla's hints to be communicative. Rather, her sensitive ear seemed to detect a settled intention to satisfy the requirements of courtesy without saying anything that could gratify her inquisitiveness or throw a ray of light on the common object of their thoughts.

Philip, he said, was a great favourite, and had now
justified his reputation as the luckiest fellow in the
world. He had such a pretty drawing-room and such
lovely old china. This was not the sort of thing of
which Camilla stood in need, or that it was natural for
Sinclair to say on such an occasion, or, indeed, to say at
all. Why should the thought of Philip suggest a refer-
ence to pretty drawing-rooms and choice pottery? Why
were Sinclair's communications on the subject so obviously artificial? Why did they come to so abrupt a
close? Camilla felt it depressing and not a little
alarming. She tried to delude herself with the explanation that, perhaps, this was the sort of thing that
happened when one was married, and that Sinclair
would have regarded a compliment to her future
husband as an impertinence to herself. But no: the
explanation, Camilla knew well enough, would not
do. It was not a question of compliment. It was a
matter of life or death. She wanted to be assured that
the man to whom she had given her heart, her happiness, her life, was deemed by those who knew him
worthy of the trust. This was what she craved for—
and on this Sinclair, who seemed generally to read her
wishes almost before they were conceived, could not be
induced to throw a ray of light.

CHAPTER XVII

CAMILLA'S BIRTHDAY

'L'amour fait tout excuser; mais il faut être bien sur qu'il y a de l'amour.'

SINCLAIR's silence was not without a cause, though not exactly the cause which Camilla's fears suggested. It was not so much his knowledge of Philip's antecedents that made it difficult for him to speak, as his consciousness of what was going on within himself. He knew various things about poor Phil which would have gone far to disillusionise his future wife, if she cherished any illusions about him as approaching a lofty ideal of moral perfection. He had in his desk, at that very time, an I.O.U. for sundry thousands of rupees, which Ambrose had given him before his departure for England by way of temporary settlement of an old standing debt. Philip, a year or two before, had been ordered to a station as Sinclair was leaving it, and, with his accustomed magnificence, had offered to take his house, horses, and household belongings off his hands.

'You are not in a hurry about the money, I daresay?' he had added, lightly.

'No,' Sinclair had said; 'I am in no hurry; pay me just when you please.'

Philip had taken full advantage of the accorded delay—an advantage which, as the weeks and months rolled by, and the opportunity of paying the debt never presented itself, had often made Philip feel uncomfortable and ashamed. Somehow, whenever he had been on the verge of accomplishing the feat, some untoward accident intervened to stave off accomplishment. Now it was a creditor, whose forbearance was less proof against impatience than Sinclair's, and whose impatience would make itself disagreeably perceptible in ways to which Sinclair would never resort: now it was an alluring investment, in which one might well hope to turn an honest penny by a judicious courage in immediate outlay: now a run of bad luck at cards or a rash bet: now a new horse, a tempting carriage, a lovely set of engravings, or choice books, happening as bad luck would have it, to be going at the moment for cash, and which Philip could not bring himself to do without,—had swept away the sum with which he had meant to set himself straight with Sinclair. So a year had passed, and when Sinclair had gone to England and had asked for the money, Philip had been constrained, with shame and confusion, to confess his inability to pay, and to give his creditor this wretched I.O.U. by way of assuring future liquidation. What business, Sinclair had asked himself, had Philip to be going holiday-making to England with such a debt unpaid? Still more, what busi ness had he to marry while that and other debts, of which pretty persistent rumours were floating about Cœrulean society, were hanging about his neck? It would have been easy enough, however, to ignore all these as well as other indications of Philip's frailty and to give him whatever support, in his future wife's esteem, might be derived from a generous acknowledgment of his good points. But the problem that was beginning to force itself on Sinclair's mind was less simple, and its solution was replete with embarrassing struggles and alternatives. That problem was, What is the duty of a punctilious man of honour when he discovers that he is falling, or perhaps has fallen, in love with a woman, whose faith is pledged to another, that other being, from the necessities of the case, absent and unable to protect his own interests? Sinclair's creed, his tastes, his temperament, his sturdy habit of self-control, of choosing, when in doubt, the least agreeable course of conduct—all conspired to give a clear, concise reply. He must turn from the idea, conscience said, as from any of the pleasant temptations to meanness, self-indulgence, and dishonour with which life abounds. The woman who was his temptation now was as good as married. She was alone; she was defenceless; the man, to whom her love was given and whose presence would have been her best protection, was, through no fault of his, absent. She was at that critical stage when doubt and fear must ever be close at hand. Could it be right to play upon such doubts and fears to one's own advantage? Supposing Camilla was induced to change her mind, would not the act be one which cynics were used to quote as a typical instance of woman's frail purpose and varying mood? Supposing the positions to be reversed, and Ambrose to have done to him what he was now tempted to do to Ambrose; what would he have felt? No. Honour, conscience, and chivalry pronounced it impossible.

It is so easy to say impossible; but when the impossible thing happens to be one's heart's desire, the one particular atom of the universe which makes the difference between joy and woe, between life being a dreary void— flat, dull, unprofitable, as Hamlet found it—or a dream of rapture, ablaze with unimagined delights—then one scrutinises the impossibility with more minuteness; and differences begin to be discernible. A woman's engagement, after all, is no vow, especially her engagement to a man who courts her for a few weeks in the course of a holiday run to England. She knows—she can know—next to nothing of him. Is she not entitled to whatever additional knowledge Fortune may bring within her reach before the irretrievable step is taken and her doom finally sealed? If there be cause for doubt, by what law is one bound to conceal it? nay, rather, is not concealment the cowardly act of an accomplice? 'Ambrose,' said the inward voice, 'will never make her happy, and you know it. In moral, intellectual fibre, in taste and tone, in earnestness of purpose, in purity of character, above all, in delicacy of conscience, she is worlds above him : she will discover her mistake, her fatal mistake, when it is too late. Can it be wrong, is it not rather a sacred duty to undeceive her, while disillusion can bring something besides regret and misery? Why stand by, like a fool and coward, with folded hands, and see her happiness and your own shipwrecked? Serious questions indeed, and difficult to answer, except in the way that Sinclair wished with a vehemence that rendered all calm reasoning impossible. He could only turn fiercely away from the delightful seduction. He would never be a poacher. The prize was Ambrose's, worthy or not, and Sinclair resolved that his should never be the hand to snatch it enviously away. Camilla had made her choice, and one could, after all, only conjecture as to the causes by which that choice was influenced. She had never given him the least pretext to intrude within that region of her thoughts. What right had he to do so? His intimacy, he resolved, should go no farther.

So Sinclair resolved; and having resolved, became forthwith convinced of the futility of his resolution. The very consciousness of it left no room in his mind for any other thought. He went sternly to his cabin and got out a huge treatise on Modern Siege Operations, which he had destined to be the *pièce de résistance* of his voyage, but which, somehow, till now had remained uncut. It was one thing to cut the pages with a determined hand; another to re-establish the serene passivity of mind, when the intellect will play its part and each function of the brain work harmoniously to the desired result. Where this is not,—when the soul's citadel is in disorder, what dust and ashes do the materials of thought become; what a mockery the attempt to bid intellect perform its accustomed duties. Sinclair plunged heroically into the law of trajectories, and forced his way from formula to formula, from one dreary exposition to another, and only realised, in doing so, how bootless is the attempt to make the mind work as if it were a mechanical instrument, regardless of its environment of flesh and blood, of nerves and tissues, of hopes that stimulate and passions that consume. A man may fill his eye's retina with engineer's diagrams and the serried millions of the mathematician's art; but the mind's eye, who shall dictate what it shall see, what visions shall brighten it with rapture or dim it with misery? So Sinclair found now, as he sat through weary hours, furious with his own weakness, and read or seemed to read. In vain he bent himself to his book, and forced his attention to the page, continually growing more and more unmeaning. It was in vain: one face—why lie to oneself any longer about it?—one dear, sweet face shone through it all—one voice was the only sound that Sinclair cared to hear—one look, one word from her, his very soul was longing for it with an intensity which only burnt the hotter for every attempt to ignore it. He shut up his book with a groan; and as he shut it Mrs. Brandon's voice from overhead summoned him to come on deck and join her party.

'Pray come and talk to us,' she said, as he joined them, 'and help us through this dreary afternoon.'

Camilla looked up from her book with the kindest, brightest smile of welcome. No suspicion of Sinclair's predicament had, it was obvious, crossed her mind. She made no secret of her pleasure at his arrival; why should she?

'Yes,' she said, closing her book; 'I have had enough—too much of the Renaissance for to-day. Mrs. Brandon and I both want badly to be amused; and why have you been deserting us all day?'

'Deserting you?' said Sinclair, in consternation at the prompt discovery of his intention, 'no, indeed; but I have been deserting my profession shamefully of late, thanks to too pleasant companions. Look at this portentous volume which I have vowed to finish before we reach India—all but the first dozen pages uncut.'

'Well,' said Mrs. Brandon, 'you chose a bad day to begin, for you must know that we are keeping high holiday to-day, and want it to be as pleasant as possible.'

Camilla was in her brightest, most joyous mood. Sinclair had never seen her looking so serene, so satisfied and hopeful—so bright with that most efficacious of female embellishments, the certainty of being loved.

'Yes,' she said, 'it is my birthday, and I want you to wish me joy. I have had a very happy day—a letter and a beautiful present, and I am in the best of spirits.' And with this Camilla showed a little Indian gem that sparkled at her neck, and told him how it had been in the captain's custody since Aden, and how she had found it on her pillow that morning, on waking, with the letter—a pleasant surprise. 'So, you see,' she said, 'I have a right to be in good spirits, have I not? and

that my friends should wish me many happy returns of
a day as bright as this one.'

'And I do,' said Sinclair, valiantly rising to the
occasion, 'wish you all joy from the bottom of my
heart. Well, how are we to celebrate the day as it
deserves?'

'By a rubber,' said Mrs. Brandon, who never lost a
chance of her favourite amusement. 'Go and wake
my lazy Colonel, who is asleep there in the easy
chair.'

'Yes,' said Camilla, who, fancying that Sinclair was
in bad spirits, wanted to be especially kind to him,
'and we will be partners, if you please, Major Sinclair,
and retrieve our yesterday's defeat.'

Sinclair's resolutions had been heroic, and Fortune,
to reward his heroism, decreed that it should be his
fate, after dinner, to take Camilla for a walk, and to sit
by her side, in a sort of enchantment, through a long
evening, on the outskirts of an amateur concert, the
charms of which were not lessened by a little distance
—a distance sufficient to allow of subdued conversation
without discourtesy to the performers. Camilla was
joyful, longing for sympathy, and in a more than
usually courageous mood.

'I want you to be very nice to me to-night,' she said,
'and to say exactly the sort of things I want to hear—
to make the day perfect. Talk to me about my future
life.'

'And your future husband,' said Sinclair, determined
to go through the business heroically. 'That is what

you really mean, is it not? Well, now let us see. He is one of the best liked men in India, and a general favourite. You will find yourself in the midst of friends.'

'That will be nice,' said Camilla; 'go on in that way, please.'

'But I can only tell you what you know,' said her companion. 'He is very bright and clever, of course—you know that.'

'Yes,' said Camilla; 'everybody, I believe, thinks him that.'

'Yes,' said Sinclair, 'and very charming in society. You are not the first young lady who has thought him adorable.'

'I dare say not,' cried Camilla, mentally rejoicing in the plenitude of her own good fortune; 'and now to reward you for being so nice, I will show you something that came this morning in my letter: would you like to see his photograph?'

'Immensely,' said Sinclair, only too glad to purchase Camilla's approval at any price. 'Well, he looks rather adorable, I admit. What business has a man to be so picturesque, I should like to know! But he is a fortunate fellow, as I always say.'

'And deserves his good fortune,' cried Camilla, gleefully.

'No,' said Sinclair, firmly; 'I will not say that, even to please you. No man, in my opinion, could do that; but it is something to be fortunate—deserve it or no.'

'Well,' cried Camilla, in the best of spirits, 'I maintain that he deserves it; I ought to know, ought I not? My letter this morning was a treasure.'

Phil's birthday epistle had, in fact, been a very pretty bit of love-making—as bright and natural and full of affectionate nonsense as any young woman could wish to have it. The historic muse shall not desecrate it by revelation to any other eyes than those for which it was intended. Suffice it to say that Camilla had stolen down to her cabin, more than once in the course of that happy day, to reassure herself, by reperusal, of its delightfulness, and had wept some happy tears of joy and gratitude over each loving phrase. It had been indeed a golden day. Sinclair would have been worse than a churl if he had marred its golden perfection, or his dear companion's joyful mood, by a single unsympathetic word.

CHAPTER XVIII

A CRISIS

THE confidences of that day, which Camilla, in her hour
of joy, entrusted to Sinclair's unwilling ear, made a sensible difference in their relations. Camilla showed no
wish to recede from the intimacy which such confidences
implied. She felt Sinclair to be her friend, and evidently
wished him to consider himself such. She trusted his
judgment ; she appealed to him for advice ; she relied
on his opinion. Having once broken the ice about her
engagement, she naturally talked much of the subject of
which her thoughts were full, of the man who was now
the master of her heart. Their greater intimacy convinced Sinclair that Camilla was thoroughly in love
with Philip Ambrose. It was equally clear that she
was altogether in the dark as to his real character.
Sinclair had by this time convinced himself that it
would be a cruel act of disloyalty to leave her unde-

ceived; none the less was he certain that she would resent the disillusion : she would regard the hand that brought it as an enemy's. Nor would Sinclair be able to conceal from her any more than from himself the mixed character of his motives. He was anything but a disinterested adviser, on the contrary, the advice was of the supremest personal interest to himself. He was firmly resolved on the enterprise, but it was a desperate venture, a forlorn hope. He would speak, but his words would, a persistent instinct forewarned him, lead to certain disaster. This sweet, gentle creature, who, with the confidence of an innocent mind, was pressing her friendship on him and asking for his, was capable, he felt certain, of a very different mood; and that mood would reveal itself the moment that she felt her love called in question, her loyalty assailed, her ideal of honour endangered. So Sinclair grew very much afraid, and, as courageous men do when fear besets them, rushed blindly to his fate. The opportunity presented itself a night or two before their journey's end. There had been a group of idlers on the upper deck, watching the great volumes of phosphoric light go streaming by. One by one the onlookers had departed, and the two found themselves alone. Camilla, too, rose to go, but Sinclair stopped her. 'Stay,' he said, 'I have something to tell you, and I can conceal it no longer. I fear saying it as I have never feared anything before, because I am risking your esteem.'

'No,' said Camilla; 'I feel no fear of that—what is your confession about? I feel confident that you can tell me nothing of yourself that will endanger our friendship.'

'But it does endanger our friendship,' said the other; 'it will probably ruin it. I am going to ask you to do what the world will condemn and society deride—what you will, at first, think wrong—what *is* wrong, except for the higher, special reasons which make it right, of which we must judge for ourselves.' Camilla rose from her chair with a gesture of terrified surprise. The colour had left her cheeks. Then she turned as if to confront a suddenly disclosed foe. 'I dare say,' Sinclair went on, 'that you will resent it as a blunder and an insult. You will condemn it as a crime. But here is the truth. I love you from the bottom of my heart. I would die to serve you. I know your character. I know that I could make you happy. I *will* make you happy if you will give me the chance. More—I know what a tremendous thing it is to say, and I say it advisedly—I will save you from unhappiness—from certain misery and disappointment. Believe me; trust me; I claim the right by the law which bids us claim our highest good, regardless of less sacred obligations, regardless of the casual, ignorant opinion of society, regardless of pain to others, regardless of everything but the passionate necessity, such as I now feel, to have you as my own.'

Camilla felt a chill terror taking possession of her soul, and darkness settling thick upon her. Here was this strong man, shaken to his very heart's core by emotion, speaking with a positiveness—a decisive, im-

perative tone, which implied full knowledge of the facts
—asserting his claim in a way which carried a sort of
conviction of its justice—laying an injunction upon
her with an authority which seemed to trample down
resistance.   She felt a sort of cowardly instinct that, if
he went on, Sinclair would convince her against her
reason, her will, her very vow.   The step, to which he
was urging her, was one which had never crossed her
mind as possible, as conceivable : it was base, her conscience told her—weak, faithless, despicable—humiliating even to have thought of, degrading, repulsive, when
actually urged for her acceptance.   She had given
Philip Ambrose all the treasure of her heart ; she had
consecrated her love with tender vows and the pledge of
mutual devotion.   She was her betrothed's, and he was
hers, in the sight of Heaven, and no law, no rite could
bind them by a more indissoluble tie.   What meant
these threats of unhappiness with which Sinclair sought
to terrify her into compliance with a dishonourable
request ?   Unhappiness indeed ?   Where for her was
peace and happiness to be found but with the man who
was master—unquestioned master—of her heart?   Abandon him ? abandon the vows, the prayers, the conse-
cration of body and soul, the dreams of bliss, in which,
far more than in her outward surroundings, she had for
months past been living—the bliss now almost within
her grasp ?   What madman was it that breathed the
monstrous suggestion to her ear?

'You were right, Major Sinclair,' she said, 'in one
thing; I resent your proposal as an insult—the greatest,

the worst that could be offered to me—an invitation to
degrade myself by an act of perfidy to the man whose
love is all I care for in the world. Our friendship—it
can never have deserved the name—is at an end. I
beg you leave me.'

'I can never leave you,' said Sinclair; 'do what you
will, I shall claim you as mine by a higher right than
any that can be urged by society or forged by law—the
right of a nature like mine, which finds a nature which
he can understand, with every movement of which he
can sympathise, whose aspirations are his, which is his
—as you are mine—by the supreme right of absolute
devotion. Whatever becomes of you and of me—I shall
worship you with my dying breath.'

'I am defenceless,' said the other. 'You might spare
me. How can you bear to ask me to break faith?'

'It is no breach of faith,' said Sinclair, 'to do what
I ask you—no breach to recall a promise made blindly
in the dark, in ignorance of the truth, in ignorance of
what your promise means, and of the man to whom
you made it. Recall it, for God's sake, while yet you
can. I bid you do it. Be the responsibility mine.
I am certain I am right.'

'And I,' said Camilla, 'am certain that you are
wrong. I know not, nor care to know, the meaning of
the disparagement that you are cruel, cowardly enough
to insinuate against an absent man—my husband, as
he is in the sight of God though not in yours. Be his
faults what they may, he is mine for better or worse,
and I am his; I am certain of his love, and he of mine.

Your threats and hints but make me long for the moment when he will be at hand to protect me from outrage.'

Camilla's cruel words were cutting into Sinclair's very soul, but he gave no sign of suffering.

'As you prize your own happiness and mine,' he said, in tones of solemn persistency—'as you care to save your life from ruin and mine from misery, think of it but till to-morrow. Give me one night to hope. By the God above us, who sees our hearts and knows if I am speaking true, I conjure you to let me save you. Think of it but till to-morrow.'

'I will harbour no such mad and guilty thought for an instant,' cried Camilla; 'why persist in tormenting me? I implore you to leave me.'

'God help us both, then,' said Sinclair in a solemn tone that lived in Camilla's ear for ever after.

He was gone. Camilla was alone. She sat on the now deserted deck in the silence of the night and tried to rally her forces, mental and spiritual, after that dreadful encounter with the passion-shattered, imploring man who had just left her. She had repelled him with indignation; she had laughed to scorn alike his entreaties and his threats; and she had been right. Still his strong will and impassioned earnestness had told upon her. She was still trembling with excitement; but, as the excitement died away, there loomed in the horizon a dreadful misgiving—an agonising doubt. What was it that Sinclair knew about her future husband that made him so certain, that gave

such alarming distinctness to his threats?   He was no
random talker, Camilla knew full well.   What meant
that vehement, positive prediction of unhappiness?
What had meant, all through the voyage, his persistent
refusal to respond to her invitation to enlighten her as
to Philip's character?   It meant something, she had
always known.   Now the fact was staring her in the
face.   Sinclair was certain that she would be miserable,
and his opinion was one which, but an hour ago, she
valued almost beyond any one's in the world.   It has
a terrifying thought; her vehement resistance to it was
really terror.   She knew that she had pronounced the
doom of Sinclair's happiness.   An awful misgiving shot,
with a sudden pang, into her mind, whether she had
not pronounced her own.

CHAPTER XIX

GOLDEN DAYS

> ' Ah, the joyous days
> Of innocence, when Love was Queen in Heaven,
> And Nature unreproved!   Break they there still,
> Those azure circles on a golden shore ?
> Smiles there no glade upon the older Earth
> When, spite of all,—gray wisdom and new gods—
> Young lovers dream within each other's arms,
> Silent, by shadowy grove, or sunlit sea ? '

ONE morning the state of things on deck bespoke an impending break in the monotony to which, for some weeks past, Camilla and her fellow-voyagers had been growing accustomed.   For several days an unusual painting, cleaning, and furbishing-up had been in progress.   Now the hatchways were opened, donkey-engines were plying their noisy task, and huge piles of cargo and baggage were emerging from the cavernous depths below.   A new excitement stirred the little community from its habitual attitude of languid endurance.   The ship went on, ploughing its way through a tranquil sea, but tranquillity no longer reigned among its denizens, least of all in Camilla's mind.   Tedious as the voyage had been, its tedium seemed, in her present agitated mood, a welcome refuge from the excitements and anxieties of such an arrival as hers would be. She had longed for it; yet she could not bring herself to feel about it otherwise than as somewhat formidable. It was becoming alarmingly near, and Camilla's soul was never proof against alarms. As the day wore on, telescopes were in request, and before noon it was announced from the look-out overhead that land was in sight. That dull horizon, which for so long had been a sort of unmeaning limit to the field of vision, suddenly became full of the keenest interest. In another hour the low Cœrulean coast rose slowly into sight, and Camilla's heart gave a bound as the outlines of her future home began to reveal themselves distinctly. She had always felt a nervous apprehension of meetings, however little really formidable; but now what a meeting awaited her! The change from a lover in one hemisphere to a husband in another was a tremendous transition. What woman was it that first summoned courage for such an undertaking? Whose was the first audacious soul that dared it? Did not love itself, the most timid of entities, shudder at the proximity of such an ordeal? A world of strange people, and strange sights; all the familiar surroundings of existence separated by an ocean's width; every trace of home obliterated—a new world, and—a new life—and, newest and most terrific of all sensations—a husband. The man to whom a woman's love is promised should be ever close at hand to reassure her that she has promised aright. It was months since Camilla had seen Philip Ambrose, and in those months the old misgivings had sometimes haunted her. They gathered strength as time went on, and the final moment, when her decision would become irretrievable, was now close at hand. The terrible scene with Sinclair, bravely and promptly as she had met it so far as his advances were concerned, had left a deep impression, and would not be so summarily dismissed from Camilla's thoughts. It was terrifying to have her original doubts reinforced by Sinclair's certainties ; and with what certainty, what terrible decisiveness, he had assured her that her present step would be an irreparable blunder. With what imperative earnestness he had urged upon her a step which, strong as was his personal interest in it, he would not, Camilla felt conscious, have counselled without a positive conviction of its justice and wisdom. What did Sinclair know or believe, that made him confident of his right to advise Camilla to break off her engagement ? She had dismissed him summarily ; but it was not so easy to dismiss the anxious questionings which his conduct had suggested. She had bound him to silence, and she knew that her wish in this respect would be law. There was a still, small voice, however, that would not be silenced, and which whispered that his warning was a wise one. So Camilla stood at the vessel's side and watched. The coast was growing clearer ; the dingy, low-lying buildings of Windipatam were distinguishable ; quaintly-rigged sailing vessels began to hover around ; the vessel rolled and pitched in

the long ground-swell : presently the engines stopped ;
a little horde of native boats settled, like a flock of sea-
birds, around the arrested leviathan.   In another minute
Philip came pushing his way through the crowd.   His
eager, joyous look and tender greeting put all Camilla's
doubts to flight.

Then began a period during which Camilla seemed
to herself, then and afterwards, half-dazed with excitement.   She was too frightened and agitated to collect
her thoughts—to gauge her feelings, to review her
position, to recede from it, even if she had wished to do
so.   All that could be done was to go on as boldly, or
at least with as little exhibition of cowardice, as the
nature of the case allowed.   She retained, in after times,
a dreadful recollection of a crowd of strange faces, of
innumerable introductions, of the solemn moment when
her husband and she pledged their mutual vows before
God and man ; of the toast with which Mr. Chichele,
who acted for the occasion as her guardian, bade them
God speed on their journey that day begun.   It was a
comfort when it was all over, and Camilla found herself
at the end of her journeyings and of her excitements, in
her own house and alone with her husband.   One of
her life's ideals had shaped itself into actual existence.
The rose was plucked.   Her lot was chosen : henceforward doubt or fear would be not only a folly but a
crime.

Nor was there any room for doubt or fear in Camilla's
happy soul.   Joy, hope, and courage lit it up with a
serene radiance.   She was tired in mind and body ; she

had passed through a long period of excitement, disturbance, moral and physical fatigue. At last she was at
rest, blissful rest—rest too perfect for its blissfulness to
be questioned. She had felt, all her life, an ardent longing for happiness ; now happiness of an intenser order
had come to her, and Camilla met it with joyful gratitude and gaiety of heart. How should she not be gay ?

A load had been lifted from her spirits, always till
now weighed down by adverse surroundings. She had
her heart's desire—desired, in vague, fond expectation,
through patient years of waiting. She had loved some
one in thought, and had endowed him with all lovable
qualities from the rich treasure-house of her generous
and ardent mind. Now the well-beloved one sat at her
side—a living reality—and told her with sweet words
and tender acts that her gift of love had not been
lavished on an unworthy recipient.

Philip made a perfect lover. He was greatly in
love ; and nothing was easier, more natural, more delightful than to let his love bespeak itself in what
utterances it would. His mood attuned itself instinctively, by a natural tact, to that in which his wife would
wish him to be. He knew the things which pleased
her, and those were the things, just now, that pleased
him most, and about which alone he cared to think and
feel. So Camilla found him delightfully congenial and
sympathetic,—set up her little domestic altar of hero-
worship, and, in half-ecstatic adoration, bowed her
sweet, pure brow before it. She brought to it many a
votive gift and fragrant offering of pious incense.

Along with all her lofty theories, and the sacred glamour with which she invested every phase of life— love and marriage amongst the rest—there was in Camilla's temperament a fine, warm, joyous pulse of womanhood, which swayed her with a sudden emotion, and spoke with clear, spontaneous accents when the promptings of reason were indistinct.

The female angel, as seen among mankind, must, in order to be perfect, have in her a strong vein of humanity, and lapse occasionally from the angelic. Camilla felt this human pulse beat strong and fast. Once she might have theorised about Philip and criticised him ; but she was a woman ; and an instinct more cogent than any theory, clearer than any critical faculty, now told her how dearly she loved him.

'You were right, indeed, dearest father,' she wrote to Mr. Ambrose, 'and counselled me well. My life's gratitude is yours for that wise counsel. I am very, very happy.'—'And so,' added her husband's hand, 'and so is Phil—a thousand times happier than he ever hoped to be—a million times happier than he deserves.'

Philip gave the letter back to his wife with its affectionate postscript.

'There,' he said, 'that will gladden the dear old father's heart. Now let us go out and sit in the shade, and you shall read to me, Camilla ; we are both in the mood for it. Here is Julia's pretty speech in the *Two Gentlemen of Verona*—you would act it to perfection.'

And so Camilla read :

> ' "The more thou damm'st it up, the more it burns,
>   The current that with gentle murmur glides,
>   Thou know'st, being stopped, impatiently doth rage ;
>   But when his fair course is not hindered,
>   He makes sweet music with the enamell'd stones,
>   Giving a gentle kiss to every sedge
>   He overtaketh in his pilgrimage :
>   And so by many winding nooks he strays,
>   With willing sport, to the wild ocean.
>   Then let me go, and hinder not my course :
>   I'll be as patient as a gentle stream
>   And make a pastime of each weary step,
>   Till the last step has brought me to my love,
>   And there I'll rest, as after much turmoil,
>   A blessed soul doth in Elysium."

'I feel very tired,' said Camilla, as she shut up the book and leant back, with closed eyes, against the tree behind her, 'and this is very restful. I believe I am myself in a sort of Elysium.'

So the golden days floated smoothly away, each with its own new joy. But Camilla's honeymoon, enchanting as she felt it to be, was not destined to pass without that touch of imperfection from which not even the most perfect chapters of human life are exempt. A single disagreeable incident—and that almost too unsubstantial to be reckoned an incident at all—passed like a cloud across its summer sky and marred the completeness of its charm in Camilla's recollection. One afternoon, weary with a long morning's ride, she lay reading on the sofa. More exhausted than she knew, she closed her book, and was presently asleep. What demon of disorder is it that rules the chaos of our sleeping hours and shapes the fierce chemistry of our dreams, as De Quincey calls it, to absurd, incongruous, shocking results? Of what unsuspected materials are they compounded? From what dark corner of memory do they spring? Be the cause what it might, Camilla had a horrid dream, and one that nothing which had consciously passed in her mind of late could at all explain. For long she had never thought of Sinclair. The excitement of her new life, its real happiness, had driven from her mind alike the misgivings of the voyage and the event which had given those misgivings their acutest form. In the circle of her present thoughts and wishes there was no space for him. She wished it to be so; she rejoiced that it was so. She had banished him effectually from among the topics of her daily thought. She had resolved to forget him, and she had achieved her resolution. Yet he entered now and sat beside her, as so often on board ship. His presence blotted out all that had subsequently happened. Her husband, her marriage, her married life, her married happiness—disappeared into the limbo of the indistinct—effaced, as it were, by a more vivid presence. Sinclair sat beside her once more, and was speaking in low, impassioned terms, imploring, warning, commanding her. His face was solemn with the pathos of earnestness. His frame was shaken with passion; his voice trembled; his words were the same as they had been before, terrifying in their vehemence—the vehemence of an impassioned seer, who seeks in vain to warn his hearers against the doom, revealed to his eye, but hidden from theirs. And this time Camilla's power of will was gone; she strove to speak, but no word would come in obedience to her effort. Sinclair approached her, stood by her—earnest, solemn, pathetic as ever.

'Recall it, for God's sake,' he seemed to say, 'I implore you, while you can. I bid you do it. Be the responsibility mine. I am certain I am right.'

Still Camilla could neither speak nor move. Sinclair stretched his hand to take hers. He touched her, and the spell was broken. Camilla started back with a scream, and awoke shuddering, wretched, exhausted with her journey to the land of dreams. Philip came running in from the next room. He found his wife fevered—agitated—labouring, evidently, under some strong excitement. Camilla looked at him, still half in terror. Never had she seemed so tender, so appealing, so in need of help. She took his hand fondly.

'I have had such a dreadful dream,' she said ; 'bring your book, dear, and sit by me. I am afraid to be alone.'

Philip brought his book and read her a story. But Camilla, as she lay and listened, or seemed to listen, was haunted by the phantasm of her morning's dream, and puzzled herself with disagreeable conjectures as to the cause and meaning of the visionary intruder upon the sacred isolation of her honeymoon.

CHAPTER XX

SIR THEOPHILUS IN DIFFICULTIES

'Shephards of people have need know the Calendars of Tempests,
which are commonly greatest when things grow to equality; as natural
tempests are greatest about the æquinoctia.'

WHILE thus the course of married love was flowing
pleasantly along with Philip Ambrose and his bride,
Sir Theophilus Prance's political horizon had been
growing menacingly dark. His triumphal chariot's
wheels were driving heavily. Like other objects of
too impulsive devotion, young India had been growing
inconveniently exacting. The glib phrases, which at
one time had delighted audience and speaker alike,
had ceased to charm. Prance had read in Bacon that
'the politic and artificial nourishing of hopes' is a good
antidote against the power of discontentments; and he
had found the specific to be effectual. He had led his
willing flock from one pleasant pasture of expectancy
to another; each prospect had been more delightful
than the last. All had gone well, so long as the sheep
were contented with the faint enjoyments of anticipation; while they would browse where they were told,

and shepherd and flock were agreed as to the still waters by which they should wander and the heights which it was desirable for them to scale. But then had come a day when roseate prospects would no longer suffice—when the sheep showed a temper, a taste, and a decided intention of their own, and sorely perturbed their kind shepherd by a certain waywardness of conduct for which he was entirely unprepared.

Pledges, like curses, come home to roost, and Sir Theophilus's pledges had been numerous and strong, and refused to get on their perch and sit quiet, as a well-regulated domestic fowl should. On the contrary, they asserted their claims with an insistance which could neither be circumvented nor ignored. Sir Theophilus felt that the world was not going as it should— as it would have gone, had he had the disposing of it. Several pretty theories had dissolved in the rude, garish light of practical experience. Several panaceas had proved ineffectual : Expectations had been dashed ; Hope itself had ceased to be hopeful; common disappointments had ended in mutual recriminations. The free press, whose praises Prance had been wont to proclaim so confidently as an inexhaustible source of national beatitude, had revealed itself in an unexpected light as the uncompromising assailant of its panegyrist whenever it chanced to be his fate—as it now not unfrequently was—to cross the good pleasure of the writer. Upon no topic had Sir Theophilus dilated with greater enthusiasm than on the value of public meetings as a means of political education, and us, at once, demonstrating and forming the popular will. It was in this robust school, he had often told admiring audiences, that Englishmen had learnt the lessons of freedom and the arts by which freedom is maintained. Acting on these suggestive observations, the youth of the province—the noisy, the restless, the possessors of a grievance or the champions of a cause—organised assemblies, at which nothing was wanting in numbers, rhetoric, or unanimity that could make a public meeting all that an enthusiast would wish to have it. Much was said on these occasions that Sir Theophilus excessively disapproved; but the first hint of disapproval would, he well knew, be the signal for still more outspoken expressions. In former days the fact of his disapproval would have been a cogent influence to guide opinion in an opposite direction; now it merely lent zest to the enjoyment incidental to a startling theory or a paradoxical conclusion. The wise, sober, influential men of other days, whose example and advice were always available on the side of order, had lost their hold upon a generation which had broken with the past and its traditions of moderation and good sense. Sir Theophilus still floated on a wave of popularity; but he knew the frailty of the power which held him there, and the fickleness of the allies on whose help he was driven to depend. For men of weight, he was disagreeably conscious—Native and European alike—were holding aloof from him. He had welcomed isolation, when isolation meant a monopoly of Fortune's shining hour—when he stood alone because none shared the

compliments, the caresses, the laudatory extravagances
which graced him as the popular favourite. Solitude
was less agreeable when there might be graver business
on hand than the exchange of mutual congratulations—
less agreeable, and, possibly, less safe. So poor Sir
Theophilus, it may be believed, was not without his
anxieties; nor were they likely to be lessened by the consideration that ambition's journey, like the path across
some Alpine slope, leads, not unfrequently, to a crisis,
at which advance is perilous and retreat impossible.

Camilla soon learnt that the India of real life is
something very different from that figured in Prance's
speeches or the magazine articles, in which his visitors
recorded their impressions—something very different,
and which appealed far more effectually to her imagination, interest, and conscience. She found herself, for
the first time, in a community where every one was
hard at work—work which formed part, however insignificant, of a beneficent enterprise. The nobility of the
task seemed to throw a sort of moral grandeur over
lives that might otherwise have been commonplace and
even ignoble in their dulness. Unconscious as many
of them were of the process, it infused an earnestness, a
reality, a purposeful steadiness of aim, into the character
of the men who took part in it. Mr. Chichele she
found—despite his air of polished calm—to be tremendously interested in his work. Mr. Montem, with
whom Camilla speedily formed a hearty friendship, hid
under his rough exterior and biting phrases a serious
concern for the wellbeing of the silent millions around

him, and a real kindliness to those of them who crossed
his path, which—greatly as he would have resented the
description—amounted to very substantial philanthropy.

'You are fond of books,' he said to her one day.
'If you would like to visit a curious library—the most
interesting, I suspect, that you have ever been in—
come with me to-morrow, and see what a native gentleman can be and can do. He is a great friend of mine.
I have a prophet's chamber in his house, where he lets
me take refuge from the world.'

Camilla was delighted at the proposal. Next day
accordingly they went; and, leaving the trim Cœrulean
roads and bustling, smoky bazaars behind them, drove
away out into the silent country, and across long
stretches of level rice-fields and multitudinous, clustering villages, and came at last to where, by the shores
of a historical river, a grand old devotee of learning
has accumulated the precious outcome of a lifetime of
skilful, diligent and generous research. Their venerable
host—standing like a patriarch with sons and grandsons
around him—blind with age, and his steps guided by
a filial hand, met them at the door, and welcomed them
with a courtesy which realised all that Camilla had
ever fancied of Oriental grace. He responded promptly
to Camilla's enthusiasm—told how, year by year, and
decade by decade, the work of accretion had gone
steadily on; and summoned from the strongholds, where
they lay immured, many a curious volume and precious
Buddhist manuscript, which his zeal, as a collector, had
gathered from the treasure-rooms of Benares or Cashmir,

or the monasteries of far Thibet. The old bibliophile knew all their histories, and laid a loving hand— Camilla fancied—on each, as he described it. Presently he deputed to a son the duty of guiding his visitors through the long galleries, where thousands of volumes, on whose pages—so the contrariety of Fate had willed—his eye might never rest, stood ready for the first comer—his gift, a noble one surely, to his country. Camilla roamed from room to room with ever-increasing pleasure, and insisted at last on exploring the prophet's chamber, to which Montem, who was an indefatigable student, was accustomed to retire on occasions of any more than usually important literary business.

'Here,' he said, 'I am within reach of every book that I can possibly want, and out of the reach of troublesome people who may possibly want me. My good host is himself enough of a bookworm to know the value of a safe retreat ; and this is a pleasant one, to boot, is it not ?'

By this time they stood on the terrace, and watched the great river below them, ablaze now with the sudden glories of the setting sun. The moon was high overhead, and, even while they sat and watched, the day had died, and a flood of moonlight as it fell on the wide expanse of water, and country craft floating swiftly down the tide, and the darkening shore beyond, lit up all with a softer glory.

'I like this scene, and this place,' Camilla said, with vehemence, 'better than anything I have seen in India.

It is all delightful—the people and the place. I must come myself, if I may, some day, and make my " retreat " here. It would do one real good after too long a spell of common life. Even now it refreshes me, and the thought of it will always be refreshing. For my part, I could die happy, if I had created such a little oasis as this, for the benefit of weary pilgrims in times to come.'

As they travelled home in the moonlight, under long half-illuminated arcades of over-branching trees, Montem discoursed to his companion, much to her edification, on the scene which they had been witnessing, and the significance of it, and many other like scenes, which, he told her, lie open in India to the understanding eye.

'The worst of it is,' he said, 'that most of us are too hard at work, and have neither leisure nor imagination, nor perhaps a prompt sympathy for feelings other than our own. The problem in India is as strange as ever nation was called upon to solve. The very newest, strongest wine is being put into some of the oldest bottles in the world. Her connection with us has poured the fierce light of modern European civilisation— if civilisation is the proper word for it—on an old-world *régime*—and venerable shrine and crumbling tower, and sacred rite, and family custom—all are tottering alike. To tell the young Hindu that we are not attacking his religion is true in one sense, but delusive in another. We create an atmosphere in which it cannot breathe. We asphyxiate it with science. We cannot help ourselves. We have no choice between that and leaving gross ignorance supreme with its train of monstrosities. The rising generation is caught into the full swirl of the tide—the chaos of thrones and altars—which we call modern Europe. They are impressible, and are, naturally, very much impressed. A crisis is all too likely—the dangerous crisis of transition. What we have to do is to let the patient face it under as favourable conditions as may be—with order, goodwill, reverence, self-restraint—all other good things of the sort working in his favour, to keep the political atmosphere pure and fresh ; above all, to prevent the generation of political gases—Sir Theophilus and others—which can end only in an explosion. Do you remember that grim toast in the *Vision of Sin ?*—

> ' " Drink to lofty hopes that cool,
>   Visions of the perfect state :
>   Drink we now the Public Fool,
>   Frantic love and frantic hate. —"

Dashed hopes and vain dreams of ideal perfection—the unreal love that sours quickly into hate—imaginary cures for equally imaginary grievances—all these, Mrs. Ambrose, form dangerous political material; and the public fool, who is always ready to turn them to the best account, is one of the most influential personages in the world. He has ruined some great states and dismembered others ; he endangers all. Let us hope that he may not prove his efficiency upon the British Râj.'

Camilla had thoroughly enjoyed the expedition and the talk. It was not often, however, that she could inveigle any of her companions into so serious a mood, and she learnt by experience that, when she had more than one of them at a time upon her hands, the attempt was desperate. There was a sort of mutual encouragement in frivolity which, even if it amused her at the time, Camilla secretly condemned as below the mark. Montem and Caro, she was vexed to find, produced an especially impracticable combination; each of them, when alone with her, gave occasional glimpses of more interesting qualities than they chose to reveal to mankind at large; but together they were mere steel and flint, and produced nothing but sparks. It was currently believed in Cœrulean circles that, when these two got by themselves and encouraged each other in daring flights of speculation, they 'made hay,' so to speak, of many of the generally received opinions of society in a manner which—like a dynamite explosion—made one shudder to think of even at a distance. Mrs. Rashleigh, despite Montem's serviceable wisdom at her hospital committee and Caro's devotion in writing its reports, was beset by an awful misgiving that these two conspirators would blow the world to pieces if ever their views should chance to pass beyond the stage of theory. To Sir Theophilus, however, and his disciples they presented a front of unalloyed conservatism. Many were the witticisms, of which in their secret conclaves his blunders and misfortunes were the butt, and fervent the unction with which Montem was accustomed to point to the stern, retributive justice with which popular impatience was now requiting his unscrupulous bids for popularity.

CHAPTER XXI

THE LITTLE RIFT

DOUBTS and fears are as unwelcome in love as they are
in theology, and as inevitable. The soul that defends
its portals against their inroad becomes, from the very
effort of the combat, only the more intensely conscious
of their presence and their force; temporary victory is
merely the prelude of completer ultimate defeat. The
besieging force may experience a check, but only to
renew the attack with greater numbers and a heavier
cannonade. Sometimes the enemy feigns abandonment,
and, like the Greeks before Troy, seems to have retired;
the unwary custodians are no sooner off their guard than
the assault becomes more determined, more terrific than
ever. How fortunate those peaceful natures, whose
serenity is broken by no such unwelcome visitant: how
fortunate—and how rare. Denounce such fears and
doubts as the judicious moralist may, how many lately-
wedded pairs are happy enough to pass through the
early stages of their new existence without the intima-

tion that some such perilous intruders are hovering near. There may be natures so exquisitely attuned, from the outset, to a complete harmony—whose every fibre, moral and intellectual, so exactly fits that greater intimacy reveals no possibility of dissonance in taste or judgment,—to whom each new unfolding of character discloses only a fuller revelation of perfect sympathy of taste. But they are, it must be surmised, a favoured few. There must be some compensation for such exceptional good luck. It may be that such people, as Madame de Staël suggested, have no immortality. Bliss so superhuman can be enjoyed but once.

To the majority of mankind the earlier months of married life are, it may be supposed, marked by the discovery of some hidden incongruities, uncongenialities, by disappointments, possibly even—as the glamour of love's rosy morning sobers into the commonplace illumination of day—some disillusions.

Camilla, at any rate, had not been many months married before she was forced to admit that some phases of her husband's character were unquestionably unheroic. As the course of daily life ran on, some serious divergence of taste and feeling would, from time to time, force itself into notice. One of these had been as to Philip's debts, about which Camilla, despite her husband's reticence, gradually came to know, and which she was quite unable to take as airily as he did. The idea of being in debt, as a predicament which could actually beset oneself, was one which Camilla found it difficult to realise. Wealth, more than sufficient for

the sober splendours of her uncle's house, comfortably
panoplied by prudent settlements against misfortune or
a chance lapse into extravagance, and capable of being
replenished, on emergency, from various recondite but
inexhaustible sources of supply—had been one of the
incidents of Camilla's youth which she had sometimes
felt oppressively dull.   Nothing short of the repudiation
of the National Debt could have disturbed the financial
equilibrium at the Vines.   Sir Marmaduke, in the
wildest flights of his somewhat narrow imagination, had
never dreamed of such a disturbance as coming within
the area of human possibilities.   When he informed his
sisters, as he occasionally used at Christmas-time, that
he was dreadfully poor, the announcement was understood to mean nothing more than that his share of the
bank's earnings had been a fraction less substantial
than usual, or that the home farm, on which it was Sir
Marmaduke's hobby to waste the edge of his balance on
expensive essays in amateur farming, was costing him
this year a few hundred pounds more than last.   He
was never in debt; and, never having been tempted in
that direction, was accustomed to speak with grave
severity of people who were.   Camilla had frequently
heard him lay down the proposition with all the
emphasis due to a financial discovery, that the simple
specific for keeping out of debt was to live resolutely
well within one's income and leave a wide margin for
accident.   Upon nations, classes, or individuals, who
did not practise this wholesome rule, he poured out the
vials of a righteous wrath; Camilla had been early im-

pressed with the folly and sinfulness of living on other people's money, and trusting to to-morrow to make good the extravagance of to-day. Her allowance had been ample. The nearest approach to a money trouble that she or her aunts ever accomplished, was the adjustment of rival claims on their charity, which expeditions to the neighbouring cottages brought to light. Philip's hazy, muddled accounts and unsettled bills filled her with shame and discomfort, which her husband quite failed to appreciate. All young fellows, he explained with airy indifference, run a little into debt during their first few years of India. Now that he was married, it was different, of course; they were economising tremendously, and it would all be right.

Camilla was far from being reassured. She saw clearly that Philip did not in the least know how he stood, and had not the courage to look. It was so easy to let things slide. To his wife it was insufferable, and her feelings and his on the subject sometimes came into open collision in a way which especially provoked him. He had been searching everywhere for a horse for her, and had at last found one which he considered perfection. One of Philip's soldier friends had lent his first charger to Camilla for a month, while he went on leave, and now wanted to sell him. Camilla had been delighted with him—as well she might be—for 'Marquess' was a fine Australian thoroughbred, with strong indications of his Arab sire, an angelic temper, and the fine manners engendered by the discipline of a regimental riding-school and his military experiences of the parade ground. Philip had never seen his wife in higher spirits or more radiant than on her return from her first gallop on her new possession.

'There is all the difference between pretty good and very good,' she cried, as she stroked Marquess's tapering nose and fine open nostril approvingly—'and you are a perfect darling.'

Since then Camilla and the Marquess had become increasingly affectionate—an affection stimulated on Camilla's part by carrots, lumps of sugar, and other votive offerings, and testified on his by a welcoming whinny at his mistress's approach. Now, however, Camilla quite declined her husband's gift, and was resolute that Marquess should go back to his owner. Philip protested in vain.

'We shall never get such a chance again,' he pleaded; 'you like the horse—he is dirt cheap—it would be an economy to buy him. You will be ill, Camilla, if you don't ride. Please consent.'

'No, thank you, Philip,' his wife had said, 'I can ride one of the ponies; I like a pony, and I hate being in debt.'

'I hope you will agree, dear,' Philip said; 'I wish particularly to give him to you.'

'I would much rather not have it,' answered Camilla; 'please do not press me; I should feel it dishonest.'

Philip flushed red, and had an angry word trembling on his lips. But Camilla's sweet, serious look disarmed him. She was evidently speaking from conviction, and such a woman's convictions must be right. She spoke with an earnest decisiveness, which, Philip felt, meant something more than a mere matter of taste. It was in vain to urge the point any farther, and Marquess went back to the barracks. This was an aspect of indebtedness on which Philip had never reckoned; and it was, he felt bitterly, a particularly disagreeable one.

Another source of disagreement had been Philip's habit of playing at whist for somewhat high stakes, and the consequent addition to his income. There was a Club whist-account, which was sent round every month to its members, with the total result of the month's whist. To some members this represented pretty often a ·formidable minus quantity; but in Ambrose's case the paper came invariably accompanied by sundry cheques, which tangibly represented the superiority of his play to that of his companions. These adventitious additions to his income were very welcome to poor Ambrose, who was always in straits as to money, with an unascertained burthen of outstanding debts, and a balance at his banker's, as often as not on the wrong side of the account. When money is a necessity, its absence makes itself felt with distressing distinctness, however naturally indifferent a man may be to its possession. Philip resented his impecuniousness, as he resented every disagreeable sensation, as one of the degrading details of life, which had to be ignored. He would have liked to live in a world in which such sordid considerations had no place; but, the world being what it was, he caught at the first chance of escape with an avidity too ardent to be discriminating or compunctious. These chance supplies gave an immediate relief; they were fairly earned, and the effort of earning them was one which Philip felt to be within the limits of the achievable. There was something pleasurable, he felt, in such success. He had devoted some trouble to mastering the theory of scientific whist, and a great many afternoons and evenings to acquiring perfect familiarity with its practice; and he now reaped the reward. Was it his fault if a glance at the cards, as they fell, told him a hundred things which the gross vision of observers, less acute or less instructed than himself, failed to perceive? Was there not a sort of moral fitness in the dispensation that stupid, old dunderheads, who played an utterly obsolete game, or brainless lads, who were too idle to read their Cavendish, who barely knew their leads, and played on in defiance of every rule, and in serene unconsciousness of signals clear as daylight, should lose their money, when it was their fate to be confronted with an accomplished antagonist? At any rate Ambrose pocketed the proceeds of his victories with a great deal of satisfaction, and frequently swelled the amount by a judicious bet. To his wife these additions to their income, when she came to understand them, wore a very different aspect. She had brought from her home an old-fashioned prejudice against playing for money at all; but playing for money, when the play invariably had one result, seemed to her sensitive conscience a sort of degradation, which hardly differed from that of card-sharpers and pick-pockets. How could it be right for a man of honour to live by his wits on the unskilfulness or bad luck of his neighbours? How could a gentleman endure to touch the proceeds of his friends' mistakes or misfortunes? There was something to be said for playing for money in order to enhance the excitement of the game, if people considered excitement necessary to its enjoyment. But to treat the money as the end in view, even as an end in view, seemed to Camilla a base perversion of the objects for which gentlemen frequented each other's society. She had read of a saying of Mr. Wilberforce in his young days that winning at play was even more odious than losing, and that was her own sentiment on the point. Philip's glee over his winnings filled her with a sense of humiliation.

At last silence became no longer possible—the smouldering fire broke out into flame. Camilla had never before distinctly objected to anything that her husband did. She felt her heart beating now, and knew that she turned pale as she spoke.

'Philip,' she said, 'have you no scruples about all this money?'

'Scruples?' said her husband, in a tone of great surprise, 'no, why should I? Scruples? what about?'

'About winning other people's money, who don't happen to be as good players as yourself. I cannot fancy liking it.'

'Cannot you?' said Philip, more provoked than Camilla had ever yet seen him. 'It is quite simple. They would win mine if only they knew how—it is all fair play, you know.'

'Of course,' said Camilla, 'except the essential unfairness of a fight between strength and weakness. It
is like the duels one reads about where one man is a
better shot than the other.'

'They need not play unless they please,' Philip said,
very indignant at the implied disparagement of his proceedings; 'and, if they choose to play, they take their
chance. If they cannot afford to lose, they ought not
to play.'

'Some of them cannot afford to lose, and ought not
to play, as we know,' said Camilla. 'If they are weak
and foolish enough to do so, why need you be an
accomplice?'

'How am I an accomplice?' said Philip. 'I don't
want them to play, and I could not stop their playing
if I tried.'

'No,' said Camilla, 'and I could not stop your playing if I tried; all the same I do not like it. Perhaps
I am quite wrong, but one cannot help one's dislikes,
can one?'

Camilla sat at the table, her hand playing with one
of the obnoxious cheques. It was an exquisite hand,
delicately chiselled, nervous, sensitive; it touched
things with a fastidious, half-shrinking touch, as if
—as Philip had often told her laughingly—scarcely
anything in life was quite good enough to touch. She
now pushed the bit of paper from her with an unconscious gesture of refined scorn, most of which, Philip
felt a disagreeable consciousness, was really intended
for himself. His wife, he began to know, thought some

things about him despicable. She was really pushing him from the sanctuary of her devotion.

As the months went by, and the excitement of her new life died away, Camilla found herself not in the best of spirits. She was very homesick. The parting from her English home had cost her more than she had expected. Her uncle and aunts had been very tender to her, as the time for her departure approached, and had felt it, she knew, a real misfortune to themselves. Aunt Augusta had on several occasions quite broken down while the preparations for India were on hand— had clasped Camilla in a tender, tearful embrace, and in vain summoned all her gentle heroism to conceal the pang which the prospect of the separation cost her. Camilla longed for another of those tender kisses—for another taste of that loving companionship. She had made light of it once, in all the insolent light-heartedness of youth. She regretted it now, in her new world of strangers, with remorse and self-reproach. Her married life was giving her less happiness than she had hoped. She had been reduced more than once to consoling herself with the familiar medicament of unhappy lovers, the theory that the first years of married life are the least enjoyable. But it was a depressing remedy even to acknowledge that her happiness was incomplete. Her husband was affectionate, caressing, with words and acts of devotion, always ready at her service ; but, somehow, he had not dominated her character as she had hoped that he would, and felt that a husband ought. She was more than ever without a guide ; she trod with

an anxious timorous step in the strange path in which
her lot was cast. She often felt terribly alone. On the
whole, Camilla had been disappointed, and, in some
ways, was not the better for her disappointment. Her
bright, sweet, noble dreams of life had been rudely dispelled.   Her husband's careless irreverent hand had
shattered some delightful ideals which had lighted up
all her youth with a sort of sacred glory, and which she
had prized as amongst her dearest mental possessions.
She could think of them now only with a gloomy bitterness of regret—as of some priceless shattered treasure :
they belonged to another world—an Eden before the
fall—which was hers no more. The fine things that
people said about the world and human destiny, and—
worst illusion of all—marriage, how much too fine they
were for actual life. How could they ever have been
realities to her? And yet in them for years she had
lived and moved and had her being—a being nobler,
sweeter, holier than any now within her reach. So
Camilla, it may be believed, was far from happy. She
had gathered her rose, and its fragrance was not as
charming as her imagination had depicted it. It had,
too, some thorns which, every now and then, pierced
her with a sudden pang that made her blood run cold.
Such shocks, coming when she least expected, destroyed
all sense of peace. She had discovered, thus early, that
life is made up, to a large extent, of disillusions.

As one thing after another showed her husband in
a humiliating light, she felt an icy something growing
at her heart. Were her first forebodings right, was her

instinctive fear just? The idea was too dreadful to be allowed to come into existence. She shut her eyes to it and turned away. She saw it no more, but she well knew that it was there—the dreadful conviction that her idol was no true divinity. Philip, she could not refuse to see, had an element of slightness. He was the slave of moods ; he yielded at the first compulsion ; he was systematically self-indulgent, incapable of sustained effort or determined resistance. For one thing, Camilla had not been long in discovering that, if she was mistress of his heart—the supreme object of his adoration—her rights were shared with various subordinate deities. The main sacrifices were hers, indeed ; but little streams of incense were often floating away in other directions. Her husband had a tender and capacious heart, and when he found himself in the society of a pleasant woman, abandoned himself to pleasing and being pleased with a completeness which Camilla felt to be disrespectful—disloyal to herself. It hurt her, and she was too proud to show her suffering, and suffering endured in silence sinks deep. Philip seemed quite unconscious of disloyalty, and described each new enthusiasm to her with a frankness which convinced his wife that it would be a hopeless task to make him understand her feelings about it. 'They are all interesting, all charming,' she said to him one day with a slightly contemptuous good-nature ; 'the curious thing is that there are so many of them.' There were other discoveries, however, which tended more seriously to disenchantment. One of these was that her main

romance about Philip was, unfortunately, not borne out
by the real facts of the case.

She had once in a confidential moment told Mrs.
Brandon the story of her engagement,—of Philip's
sudden affection for her—of his five years' devotion
and faithful allegiance. Philip had never, it is true,
vouched for this in so many words ; but it had always
been taken for granted between them. Camilla herself
had never wavered ; and the belief that Philip had been
equally constant was very precious to her. Fidelity of
that kind might well be set in the balance against many
apparent symptoms of fickleness or levity. And now
that agreeable illusion was destroyed. Mrs. Brandon
had listened to her story with an air of wondering
amusement which politeness did not enable her to conceal. There was something in the background which
spoilt the story or made it absurd. Presently Camilla
discovered what the something was. Her husband had
passed through a long series of flirtations. This was
all that Mrs. Brandon would tell her; and this she
could, with a contemptuous forgiveness, have condoned.
But there was something more. Miss Rashleigh, to
whom she had, at first sight, taken an immense fancy,
had received her advances towards friendship with an
embarrassment which Camilla could not understand.
'What is Miss Rashleigh's story?' she had asked her
husband. 'Her story?' Philip said with some embarrassment; 'has she a story?' 'She is beautiful and
romantic, and so probably has one.' Camilla looked at
him with a fearless, honest, searching glance which

Philip always felt to be painfully scrutinising. 'She was a friend of mine,' he added. 'A great friend?' 'Yes,' Philip had said, 'a great friend. You are not going to quarrel with me, Camilla, for every pretty woman whom I admired in my bachelor days? Your rights had not begun then, you know.' 'No,' Camilla said, mentally taking down her husband from the pedestal on which her fancy had placed him for adoration; 'my rights had not begun. I had forgotten. Let bygones be bygones.'

'My dear,' Mrs. Brandon had said, when Camilla asked her about it, 'I really know nothing, except that the greatest flirts make the best husbands, and that men proverbially return to their first loves. Be that your consolation.'

Camilla, however, felt anything but consoled, and began, unknown to herself, to cherish a little spot in her heart where resentment and contempt were not unknown.

CHAPTER XXII

LADY MIRANDA

'This is such a creature,
Would she begin a sect, might quench the zeal
Of all professors else, make proselytes
Of whom she but bid follow.'

WHATEVER were his other shortcomings, Philip managed
to live well up to his reputation for brilliancy and success. His abilities and agreeableness were carrying
him well to the front. Before their first year in India
had expired, Mr. Chichele had selected him as one of his
secretaries. The post was one of much honour and glory,
and of higher emolument, and it involved the attractive
duty of accompanying Chichele to the mountain home,
from which, during the long Cœrulean summer, he
guided the fortunes of his little kingdom. Here Chichele
found his existence supportable, when he could surround
himself with a small atmosphere of congenial society;
and this year Fortune had been especially kind to him.

For one thing, he had the Ambroses, who were established in a hill-cottage not half a furlong away, and, of
necessity, enjoyed the privilege of almost forming part

of his own household. Mr. Chichele, whose good fortune it was to know what was good, had speedily recognised that his new secretary's wife was something very good indeed. He had, too, a houseful of pleasant guests from England. The most notable of these had an official justification. Mr. Brownlow, the head partner in the firm of Brownlow, Mattock and Co., the eminent Railway Contractors, had come, at the Government's special request, to ascertain for himself the possibility of a system of light railways, which Chichele was convinced would be the making of the province. Mr. Brownlow was Chichele's old friend. They had been at Christ Church together ; together they made their first appearance in London drawing-rooms ; together they had become Members of Parliament, and their intimacy had deepened in their first common essays in public life. Then their courses had diverged. Brownlow had been caught into the mäelstrom of a colossal business ; his thoughts and time were occupied by the inquiries and calculations incidental to railway enterprises on a huge scale. He was tremendously busy, and tremendously rich,—and business and riches alike made his life one of rough activity. His lines were cast among active, shrewd, business men, who differed by an entire hemisphere in thought and culture from the little, polished, half-bookish, half-pleasure-seeking *coterie* of his Christ Church days. Various undertakings in different parts of the world had given him a cosmopolitan experience : he had visited California for one railway project : he had lived for a year or two in Egypt while carrying out another: he had been the guest of a Roumelian Prince in arranging a third. The results of his enterprises had embodied themselves in agreeable manifestations of substantial wealth. He had a mansion in Queen's Gate, a moor in Sutherland, a villa at San Remo, and a steam-yacht, in which Chichele had spent many a pleasant holiday. He had, too,—nor was this important addition wanting on the present occasion—a very charming wife.

Lady Miranda would have been a valuable acquisition to any society in which good spirits, good nature, and good looks were valued at their proper worth. She was a great talker, and was never seen to more advantage than in the full flow of animated conversation. The daughter of a Liberal peer, she had worked out for herself, in a recklessly ardent fashion, the logical consequences of the liberal doctrines which formed the political atmosphere of her home. Her insight was quickened, and her belief intensified by a ready, eager sensibility to the suffering and injustice she everywhere saw around her. In such moments she felt herself a revolutionist, and it was only because her husband assured her that, in this sense, he was a revolutionist too, that any practicable *concordat* had been established between them. Her only complaint against him was, that he was sometimes in the habit of displaying levity and cynicism on subjects as to which she saw clearly, and felt intensely; and that, on the whole, he did not take her as seriously as she took herself. It tried Miranda sometimes, when she was becoming particularly eloquent and felt particularly in earnest, that her husband should go into fits of laughter, take her to his arms in a sudden fit of delighted fondness and declare her the most terrible woman in existence. Such behaviour was almost degrading. It was some consolation that Mr. Brownlow atoned for these occasional shortcomings by letting her spend as much money as she liked on a long list of projects for the regeneration of mankind, in which Lady Miranda took a personal interest and entertained a firm belief. She at one time had serious misgivings as to the lawfulness of her own expenditure, and had felt a hankering after socialistic communism. Here, however, her husband had stood firm, and had succeeded in convincing her, by the rules of political economy, that the world would not be regenerated by socialistic contrivances of artificial equality, and that the best interests of commerce and so of mankind, were promoted by the free employment of wealth, in its ordinary courses, by those who happened to possess it. Miranda, accordingly, much to her relief, discovered that an ardent sympathy with distressed humanity, and a resolute determination to alleviate it, were not inconsistent with the ownership of a great number of lovely dresses, and with a generally wild expenditure on bonnets, gloves, lace, and other feminine paraphernalia, which she herself would have been inclined to condemn as profligately profuse, until reinforced by her husband's comforting assurance that it was all right, and the best way in which a portion of her allowance could be spent. The consequence was,

that Lady Miranda was as well dressed as Mr. Worth
could make her, or as any young lady of the day could
wish to be ; and that as she had no bad eye for artistic
effect, the general impression which she conveyed to the
human vision was one of an extremely agreeable kind.
She thirsted for information, guidance and help, and
she found a surprisingly large number of men ready
with any one of the three in any quantity she wished.

Yet Miranda's philosophy was more than idle talk
or self-indulgent theory.   It bore a rich crop of energetic kindness toward any form of suffering which came
within her range.   There were poor people in wretched,
grimy London homes, to whom she had made her way
with an unsuspected revelation of sympathy, help, and
encouragement, and who—as Miranda listened to their
troubles with tender, beaming eyes and thoughtful
suggestions of help—learnt for the first time the
meaning of the touch of nature that makes the whole
world kin.   It was in no fashionable freak that Miranda would go off, day after day, for long afternoons,
to homes where her accustomed visit was, she well
knew, awaited with all an invalid's anxiety, by some
poor creature, slowly fading to her end, or by some
fever-wasted child, weary of its long captivity.   She
had a little ' Home,' where a few convalescents, translated from the grimy crowd of London alleys, were
wooed back to health and life amid flowers and sweet
country sights and sounds and the pure breezes of the
Surrey Hills.   They came for a few days or weeks,—
poor waifs and strays from the great sea of misery out-

side. Miranda's kind heart ached to see them go away again, often she knew too well to what sort of homes and life. Few started, we may believe, on that rough journey without some substantial help from that kind hand. All took with them the precious memory of an experienced kindness. Many a poor wizened child,—old already with the grim experience of pauper life,—carried away to other scenes,—to squalid, comfortless lodging, the filthy rag-beclouded alley,—the dirty, angry mother,—the tipsy father whose heavy hand or boot it was well to elude,—the public-house, with its blasts of infamy surging through the half-opened door,—carried back to these dreary scenes a sort of celestial, dream-like remembrance of the sweet, beautiful lady, who had come to sit by his bedside, ready with sympathy and love, irradiating all about her with her tenderness, courage and hope. So it was that when Lady Miranda talked about the troubles of the world, she used no idle phrase, but spoke, out of the fulness of her heart, of things into which she had a practical insight, and about which she felt with passionate acuteness.

Chichele knew Lady Miranda only through their common friends. He felt it a serious responsibility to receive as his guest a young lady who was at once a politician, a philanthropist, and the fashion. His responsibilities would have weighed on him more heavily but that he let a large portion fall on Camilla's shoulders. He was satisfied that the two would be great friends ; satisfied too, that, however wide might be Lady Miranda's field of choice, she could nowhere have found a

rarer nature than Camilla's. Increased familiarity had
only enhanced the respect and admiration with which
she had, from the first, inspired him. He was more
than ever impressed by her refinement, her sweet, grave
dignity, her thoughtfulness on things worth thinking
about, her clear, keen sense, perhaps her occasional bursts
of satire. 'She is delightful,' he told Lady Miranda.
'One of the few things in life I am really proud of, is
that I believe I have at last earned the right to call her
my friend.'

CHAPTER XXIII

MIRANDA CONFRONTS THE BUREAUCRACY

'I have a pattern on my nail,
And I will carve the world fresh after it.'

LADY MIRANDA lost no time in ascertaining for herself the justice of Mr. Chichele's eulogium. She had been, in truth, in need of a confidante—in how great need she had not realised till she found, almost in her first moments of intercourse with Mrs. Ambrose, how sensible a relief it was to have a kindred woman's soul with which to commune. She had been living for weeks past among men; and the female spirit needs, it may be believed, for its complete comfort and wellbeing, some ministration from one of its own more sympathetic sex. Anyhow, when the two ladies found themselves comfortably established in the bay-window of Mrs. Ambrose's drawing-room, Miranda's spirits experienced an immediate expansion; and both of them discovered that they had a hundred things to say to one another, for which, for some time past, no proper listener had been forthcoming.

Miranda had been at first more impressed than altogether pleased by Mr. Chichele. She could see that he was cultured, thoughtful, and on the whole, deserving to be liked. But his attitude towards her had not been satisfactory. She was feeling extremely interested in her life, and especially this Indian chapter of it. She wanted to be businesslike, serious, practical; but Chichele treated her rather as an ornamental appendage to the man of business than as having, conceivably, any real business of her own. It never occurred to him, she could see, to regard her as a working member of the party. Her society, it soon became apparent, was to him an agreeable relaxation from long mornings spent with her husband and the engineers and secretaries over blue books, maps, surveys, and estimates. Chichele had, in truth, come in for rather more than he bargained for when he committed himself to the championship of a project of light mountain railways in Cœrulea. An enterprising chief-engineer had satisfied him, in a lucid memorandum, that the lines which were to scale the Cœrulean hillsides at several points would pay at least five per cent. A discriminating critic at the India Office had set himself to demonstrate that they would certainly fall short of paying three. There had been despatches and counter-despatches and resolutions and memoranda. There was a tremendous disputation as to the proper gauge. The critic at the India Office proved troublesome and pertinacious; Chichele had become bored, and his faith in his chief-engineer waxed faint; his zeal for the development of the Cœrulean tea-plantations died down. More than once he had been tempted to wish the whole project at Jericho. Why, whispered Indolence, take a deal of worry about a scheme which was certain to be troublesome and might be disastrous, and which nobody of any importance seemed anxious to see realised?   Mr. Brownlow, however, with a fine, vigorous, businesslike habit, kept Chichele's flagging energies up to the mark, and would not hear of surrender.   Very likely, he explained, the people at the India Office are right.   It was that fellow Gibson, the under-secretary, picking holes as usual: those permanent secretaries are the very mischief. But the line might be taken by an easier gradient. There was a gap in the Cœrulean Mountains of which, unaccountably, no advantage had been taken.   How, the deuce, had it been overlooked?   Then the bridges, as designed, were a great deal stronger than they need be, and the estimates for sleepers were absurdly extravagant.

'We'll have them from Norway, you know,' he said, enthusiastically.

'All right,' said Chichele, by this time growing dreadfully tired, 'have them from Norway.'

'Or,' said Brownlow, getting fresher as he went on, 'why not try pot-sleepers?'

'Very well,' said Chichele; 'I have no objection to try pot-sleepers.'

'But they won't do for the steep gradients, you know,' continued his persecutor.

'The deuce they won't,' responded his victim, spasmodically attempting to follow the vibrations of Brownlow's thoughts.   'What are we to have for the steep gradients, then?'

Then the chief-engineer would come forward with a new alternative and the secretary with a fresh objection, and Chichele would ruefully think what a fool he had been not to leave well alone, and the Cœrulean light railway project in the limbo of unattempted possibilities. All this sort of thing involved long mornings of hard work; and Chichele used to come out to lunch with his forehead all in wrinkles, his hair tumbled about, and looking the picture of fatigue and despair. It was, no doubt, very refreshing to him at such times to find Lady Miranda in the drawing-room, looking fresh and radiant and charming, and ready to talk and be talked to about other matters than pot-sleepers and gradients. So Chichele indulged his own mood in treating her as an agreeable child, or, worse still,—as she fancied,—a pretty *objet de luxe*, in which his millionaire friend could afford to indulge, and of which he, for the time being, was to get part of the benefit. This was really unendurable. She resented it with a secret indignation. It checked all real confidence. She was longing to confide to him her literary projects, as to which several clever men—real authors in England— had given her advice and help. Only two nights before they left London the catholic-minded editor of a fashionable magazine, imprisoned with a mob of other pleasure-seeking captives on a crowded staircase, had heard about the Brownlows' intended tour, and had immediately pressed Lady Miranda to give his readers the benefit of her first impressions of the East.

'But,' Lady Miranda had said, with a sweet air of

diffidence that would have melted the sternest editor's heart, ' I have never written a magazine-article in my life, and I have not the slightest idea how I should set about it. I very much doubt if I could do it if I tried.'

'And I,' the editor had answered gallantly, 'am perfectly certain that you would do it, as you do everything else, Lady Miranda, to perfection ; so now you must not disappoint me.'

Miranda had cherished this compliment, and the delightful idea of possibly becoming an authoress had grown upon her till she had ceased to regard it as unattainable. Gradually she had come to contemplate an even grander flight—a book of travels which, if not as ambitious as Lady Brassey's famous yachting adventures, might yet convey some of the thoughts and feelings which were seething in her own mind, to mankind at large. Her husband, when she confided the project to him, had treated it as a joke—a capital joke, which, like many of his wife's fancies, would cost him a good deal of money, and give him much more than the money's worth of amusement. Miranda dared not, at this stage, encounter his unsympathetic merriment by further disclosures. None the less she needed guidance and help. She would have liked to make a confidant of Chichele ; but just as the moment for confidence seemed to be arriving, his calm, gray eye would light up with a look of suppressed mirth, which suggested the dreadful possibility that she might be making a goose of herself.

Another ground of disappointment to Miranda had been, that she was finding everything less uncivilised, characteristic, and picturesque than she had hoped that India would prove to be. Her surroundings were agreeable and luxurious; but agreeable luxury was not exactly what Lady Miranda had hoped to encounter in the East. She had looked forward to something decidedly unconventional. Now the utmost unconventionality that Chichele could achieve for her was a picnic on the top of a tame mountain, in a fine tent, furnished with a smart array of sofas and armchairs, and thronged by a little army of redcoated attendants, who differed from London footmen only in being black and wearing turbans. After all, one might, as far as anything exciting or unusual was involved, just as well be lunching at Richmond. Everything was beautifully done, Lady Miranda acknowledged; but it was not India; it was not worth leaving home and coming seven thousand miles to see—it was not business, she informed her husband in a serious way, which sent him into one of his provoking fits of laughter.

'No, Miranda,' he said, 'it is not business; it is amusement of the choicest and most pronounced order, and it would be all spoilt without you. Chichele, as a man of taste, naturally finds you charming, and has already commenced a flirtation. You are a perfect adept at that particular form of communion between two sympathising souls. You will get on delightfully together; he will give you floods of information about India and Indian statecraft. In return you will open your eyes at him in the charming way you do when you are really interested, and he will be well repaid.'

'Mocker!' Miranda had said. 'He is as bad as the rest of you, I suppose: all men are frivolous at heart; it is women who are serious, if we could only get a chance.'

'Well,' said Brownlow, 'all I mean is that Chichele is naturally delighted to have a smart young lady devoting herself to amusing him.'

'Pray do not call me smart,' said Miranda, 'it is a word I detest.'

'It cannot be helped,' said her husband. 'You are extremely smart, my dear Miranda; it is one of your innumerable strong points.'

'I suppose next,' said Miranda, who by this time was half-inclined to lose her temper, 'you will accuse me of being a professional beauty.'

'No,' said Brownlow, 'that profession is out of fashion, happily; but I accuse you, and my heart convicts you, of being the most charming woman in the world, and I condemn you to a kiss.'

'All men are hopelessly frivolous,' cried Miranda, as the sentence was being carried out, ' and you, George, as bad as the rest of them.'

Before many days, however, Lady Miranda got the chance for which she was sighing; for Chichele, an adept in the art of agreeableness, especially where a woman was concerned, was not long in discovering the direction in which his guest's ambition pointed, and in making up his mind that the most acceptable form of politeness

to Lady Miranda would be to take her excessively
in earnest. He listened with grave interest to her
account of the literary projects of which her brain was
full. There lay on her writing-table, at this moment,
a precious, beautifully-bound volume, locked with a
gold padlock from the profane eye. Its name had
been already suggested by a clever young Oxonian who
wrote for the *Times*, and Lady Miranda had grown
quite fond of it in anticipation. To her mind's eye the
title,

Anglo-India:

A Study in Black and White,

BY

LADY M. B.

was delightfully effective. She had intended at first to
put her name in full, but against this her husband
had protested. 'Black, white, and Brownlow,' he had
cried, with irreverent laughter. 'That would never do,
Miranda;' and Miranda's ingenuity had discovered no
other way of surmounting the difficulty but the employment of initials. She consoled herself with the reflection that her friends would have no difficulty in dis-
tinguishing her personality, and would soon publish the
interesting secret to mankind at large. Her volume,
even in its present embryonic stage, was a welcome
relief to many pent-up feelings which clamoured for
utterance. Lady Miranda had great sympathy for the
masses everywhere, and the masses of India especially
fired her philanthropy. She pictured them to herself,

patient, inscrutable, the slaves of an old-world superstition and a modern bureaucracy. She had been with her father and her husband to public meetings in England, and had trembled with excitement at the denunciations poured out on the selfishness, meanness and rapacity of the ruling and wealthy classes. When Mr. Bright described the government of England as a gigantic system of outdoor relief for the aristocracy, she had thought of all her own uncles, cousins, and friends, who were recipients of that relief, and had almost sighed for a revolution.

'My dear Miranda,' her husband had replied to one of her outbursts, 'you are perfectly prepared to make a holocaust of all your relations, and stand alone in a family desert of your own manufacture. Your zeal is absolutely terrifying.'

Naturally, when Miranda found herself face to face with the greatest bureaucracy in existence, she was deeply impressed with the situation. Already her precious diary had received several outpourings of her overburthened soul—not tamed and fashioned, as Miranda felt that they must be before they met the cruel critic's eye, but fresh and wild as the thoughts rushed from their fountain-head. 'I have been a week in India,' the latest entry ran, 'and I already feel certain that I shall find this country extremely interesting. Its very name fills me with a sort of delightful thrill—so old, so vast, so oppressed. All these millions of poor people, and all without the barest rights of humanity. A narrow bureaucracy, as cruel and stupid as such things always are. What a field for the philanthropist and the reformer! My taste for revolution has received a fearful stimulus. George, who differs from me in almost everything, agrees, at least in this, that here almost everything remains to be done. I almost tremble with excitement at the idea, that here I am, face to face with a great military despotism: and that it is a despotism everything around forbids us for a moment to forget. The obsequiousness of the servants and the crowds of servile creatures who stand waiting one's beck and call, contented and submissive, speak of slavery or something next door to it. When I drove with Mr. Chichele this evening, his state was really regal. Can it be right for any man in this age to live like a prince in the *Arabian Nights*, heralded by outriders, surrounded by silent ministrants who anticipate his every whim, hurry at a signal on his behests, fan him while he eats, and stand behind him at dinner with a fan ready to brush away the too presumptuous fly that threatens to desecrate his imperial person! To me it seems simply dreadful.'

Lady Miranda had not screwed up her courage to submit these confidential utterances even to her husband's eye. She began to feel more and more at her ease in indoctrinating Chichele with esoteric views to much the same effect. None the less it was consoling to find in Camilla a companion of a kindred spirit, whose tastes were completely sympathetic with her own on other and less sublime topics than the wrongs of India or the regeneration of mankind.

Lady Miranda's great advantage in acquiring information was that she looked so charming when she was receiving it. Hence it was that, in addition to Mr. Chichele, she found herself surrounded by many zealous instructors. Mr. Montem volunteered a general survey of the machinery of the administration : an ambitious under-secretary initiated her into the mysteries of the Permanent Settlement. General Rashleigh abandoned his rubber in order to explain to her the strategy of the Afghan frontier question, and showed her on the map the exact places where the first battles with the Russians would be fought. Her beautiful violet eyes opened wider and wider, and her lips—Cupid's very home—parted with such a delightful expression of wonder and curiosity that each new preceptor, as he was added to the ever-increasing list, admitted to himself that it was well worth while to talk seriously to her; and to talk seriously to her was easy enough, for almost everything interested Lady Miranda, and a great many things not only interested but touched her.

CHAPTER XXIV

THE WIDENING BREACH

> ' When love begins to sicken and decay,
>   It useth an enforced ceremony :
>   There are no tricks in plain and simple faith.'

AN acute observer of society has recorded the solemn
fact, attested by a hundred calamitous alliances, that it
takes longer to learn to live on rational terms with a
woman than to fancy that one adores her. Philip had
succeeded admirably in the task of adoration. To walk
about the cedar avenue at the Vines in a half-frenzy of
hope, anxiety, or disappointment ; to let his imagination
run riot in embellishing his mistress with a thousand
delightful attributes ; to lie on his back in the grass with
half-closed eyes ; to recall her tones and let her dear
image fashion itself to his mental vision in a sort of inward rapture ; to assure her, when at last she consented
to listen, that she was the dearest, sweetest, noblest
of beings, and Phil's one hope and joy to live and die
her slave—how easy it had been, how pleasant, and,
alas, how brief ! Why is not existence made up of such
enchanting emotional vicissitudes ? Philip had now

realised his ideal in human flesh and blood, and the question was no longer of idolising one's mistress, but of living comfortably with one's wife. The problem was how to please and satisfy her without too extravagant a consumption of nerve and tissue, or too complete a renunciation of one's own personal pleasures and satisfactions. Being the husband of the most perfect woman in the world involves, Philip began early to discover, a considerable moral strain. Camilla's lofty ideas about life were difficult to live up to. She took everything with an earnestness which her husband felt to be incompatible with any real comfort in existence. Life, if it is not to be martyrdom, is a succession of compromises,—compromises between what is ideally right and what is practically achievable by mortals—between duty and pleasure—between the aspirations of the spirit and the weakness of the flesh,—between things that ought, theoretically, to be said, suffered, or done, on the one hand, and a man's natural inclination towards comfort, ease, and a little excusable self-indulgence, on the other. Now it was one aspect of Camilla's perfection that she was essentially uncompromising. Her clear insight and natural candour dispelled the comfortable, soft chiaroscuro in which things lose their exact outline, and the difference between things—between right and wrong, for instance, true and false, honest and dishonest —becomes conveniently indistinct. Many parts of Phil Ambrose's career needed, he was well aware, the benefit of this protecting obscurity, and were susceptible, in certain lights, of an unflattering construction. He had a disagreeable consciousness that his wife's clear judgment could not be imposed upon, nor her conscience beguiled into deflecting by the thousandth part of a hair's-breadth from the strictest possible standard of what was true, honourable or just. What was life worth to her but to try to ennoble it—to raise its aims—to triumph over its pettinesses—to perform its obligations with a chivalrous generosity? But how to reconcile such a theory of existence with the practical exigencies of a man whose means fall short of his requirements, whose affairs have been getting themselves for years into a more hopeless muddle, and who can make both ends meet only by shifts and contrivances, which the plea of necessity might excuse, but which a too nice scrupulosity would certainly condemn. And then married life, with its ineffable happiness, brought also some serious restrictions. Philip had been accustomed, for instance, to drop into the Club, on his way from office, for an hour or two's serious whist with a select company of advanced connoisseurs. The fact that his wife was awaiting him, weary with the monotony of a long solitary day, was a troublesome interference with this bachelor pleasure. Is a man, because he adores his wife, to lie, like a tamed Hercules, with his head in Omphale's lap, and deny himself the ordinary pleasures of his sex? Might not both purposes be served if Camilla met him an hour later at the Band, by which time Phil's rubber could be conveniently achieved? And if, sometimes, the chances of the game made Phil a little late, were not accidents like this just the sort of delinquencies which the familiarity of married life would excuse, the liberties which husbands, who adored their wives, could venture to take?   Once or twice on such occasions he had found Camilla sitting by herself with a look of sadness, which her kind and cheerful greeting could not conceal.   Why was it, Philip wondered, that she could not, as other wives did, join one of the many throngs of talkers, who were beguiling the interval till their lord's arrival with a brisk flow of station gossip?   And then there were houses where Philip had been wont to go—Mrs. Paragon's, for instance,—and where he had, in old days, passed many a pleasant hour and received many a kindness, and where he was still as welcome as ever.   Was he to renounce them now?   And if he stayed chatting on, beguiled by Mrs. Paragon's bright flow of talk, ready repartee and cheery manners, was this a matter of which the wife, for whose sake he had curtailed so many pleasures, had any reason to complain as a grievance, even in thought?   Camilla, Philip knew well enough, would never say a word, however real the grievance; but had she a right to feel it one?   There were other possibilities besides that of Camilla's feeling dull when he occasionally deserted her, which gave Philip uneasiness.   One of these was the possibility of being seen through, and morally brought to book in a manner too businesslike to be convenient.   Camilla had a vigorous common sense and the insight that belongs to perfect integrity of mind.   Her judgment played no tricks with itself, nor could any trick be easily played with it.   Her code of honour and duty was as clear written as it was severe. She was a difficult person—not to deceive, indeed,—that would have been more than Philip could have admitted to himself among possible necessities— but to leave with a partial knowledge of the facts, or with an incorrect idea of their bearing on the case. She had, too,—and this was no agreeable discovery,—a fine touch of scorn for things which might be more reason- ably condoned as excusable infirmities than lashed with satire or pointed at with the unfeeling finger of con- tempt. There were things that people did, and not bad people either, with which Camilla could never be induced to hold fellowship; as well expect her to plunge her beautiful hands into a cauldron of pitch. But how would it be if Philip were ever driven to admit such things as among the alternatives open to himself, to be accepted, perforce, in lieu of something still more disagreeable? Camilla, in such a case, could neither be hoodwinked nor conciliated. She would recognise it— she would feel its full significance. It would be a stain, and the stain would hurt her like a wound. Would she —indeed, could she—forgive the hand that inflicted it?

One such troublesome affair had, indeed, already passed the stage of possibility, and began to assert itself, with disagreeable emphasis, in Ambrose's thoughts, as a fact which it would have been pleasant, if possible, to cancel from the record of one's doings. The Mudda- pollium Mine project had long figured in Philip's day- dreams as an agreeable panacea for his financial maladies. It was quite certain that there was stuff in the scheme to make a dozen fortunes, if only it could be utilised with discretion, and if the fitting opportunity would but present itself. The opportunity had arrived in the form of an Australian gentleman, whom Mr. Palaveram Chetty one morning brought with him to Ambrose's study. This gentleman had great mining experience, and was thoroughly versed in the arts by which embryonic companies are fostered into actual existence. It did not occur to Ambrose—or if the thought occurred, the Australian's magnificent manner at once rebuked it as ill-judged—that it was remarkable that this gentleman's experience should have inclined him to quit its proper scene in Australia and to embark on the unknown seas of Cœrulean speculation. Nor did the Chetty think it necessary to mention that his visitor, despite his magnificent way of talking about money, had found it convenient to resort to his well-filled money-chests for a supply of ready-cash. The Australian, however, whose fresh complexion and splendid physique could hardly belong to any but an honest character, was a man of business, and came at once to the point. Australia, as a field of lucrative enterprise, was, he said, used up. Cœrulea had a virgin soil. He was satisfied that its resources were unequalled, and on this he speedily put Ambrose's mind at ease by specimens which he had just collected on the spot, the purport of which discovery he set forth in glowing terms, as revealing a golden harvest to whoever should be lucky enough to reap it. Philip's heart began to beat as the Australian described the fortunes which had been made in ventures not half so promising as this.

A stream of wealth flowing in upon one spontaneously, in amounts practically immeasurable,—whose blood is not stirred by the idea? and to a man with profuse tastes, large necessities, narrow means and considerable embarrassments, what a great relief it suggests, what numberless vistas of pleasure open upon the delighted imagination, fired with the golden vision! While Ambrose's fancies were at boiling-point, the Chetty and his friend revealed their scheme. The strictest secrecy must be observed; a concession must be obtained from the Rajah to whom the land belonged; then a company must be formed, and then Ambrose's fortune would be made. How much were the concessionaries to charge the public for their invaluable bargain? It was for Ambrose to say. The company was to be brought out in London and India simultaneously. The Australian gentleman was to arrange the details. Ambrose's name, for obvious reasons, was never to appear; but he was to lend his aid to promote the concession and to expedite any transactions in which the infant company came into contact with the Government; and for these services was to be entitled to a handsome share of the promotion money when subscribed. One other small service Ambrose's visitors begged him to perform as his contribution to the scheme. 'We want you,' Mr. Palaveram said, with an ingratiating smile, 'to write the Prospectus. Your Highness' style is incomparable, and will do justice to the theme. We are poor drudges, and would spoil Paradise itself in attempting to describe it. Here are all the facts; they need only your Highness' master-touch to convince the very unbelievers. Write it for us, and the success of the company is a certainty.' So Philip's ready pen had described the coming glories of the Muddapollium Mine—the unequivocal evidence of the precious ore, the abundant water-power, the unfailing supply of labour, the virgin forests, where fuel could be had for the taking, the neighbouring railway which the Government was already designing, and which would waft the treasures of Muddapollium to the coast. Philip's researches into currency, though not profound, enabled him to refer to the injuries which the scarcity of gold had brought upon mankind, and the blessings which the discovery of a new supply had, on various occasions, conferred on the world's commerce, depressed by an appreciating coinage. One of these fortunate discoveries seemed now, the Prospectus majestically observed, once more to be likely to revive the flagging industries of Europe and to knock off the fetters in which trade had been so long coerced. The Muddapollium gold-fields were destined to repeat for mankind the inestimable boon of Australia and California. So the Prospectus got written, the company floated off, and Ambrose felt that wealth was almost within his grasp. The reflection was highly agreeable; the only drawback was the necessity for secrecy, and the consciousness that Camilla, if she knew of the wealth, would strongly disapprove of the means by which it came.

CHAPTER XXV

A HILLSIDE ENCOUNTER

‘ Tantæ ne animis cælestibus iræ ? ’

PHILIP'S life, though stirred by a pleasurable excitement and bright in its outer aspects, was not without its secret misgivings. Nor were these relieved by the behaviour of his friends. The Rashleighs had, obviously, determined that it was most consistent with their dignity to ignore all that had passed between Philip and their daughter. They received him with a cordiality as ostentatious as he speedily found it to be unreal. No true friendship, it was clear, could any longer exist. The General shirked him, and repelled his advances with haughty politeness. Mrs. Rashleigh, with whom he had found it so easy to chatter in old days, had not a word to say to him, nor he to her. They *knew*, it was clear enough, and though not choosing to show it, condemned and despised him. Miss Rashleigh was kinder, more forgiving, more considerate ; but was not her kindness a little contemptuous? She betrayed not the slightest symptom of regret or annoyance, and met him with her accustomed cordiality; but Philip speedily became alive to the fact that he was being kept at a distance, and that no renewal of intimacy was to be allowed. Chichele, too, who, for some time, had not been very nice to Philip, was now less nice than ever. The most courteous of mankind, and with an old-fashioned chivalry of manner towards women, he treated Camilla with a sort of homage. Nothing was too good for her; on the other hand, he gave Philip to understand by sundry unmistakable hints that many things were too good for *him*, and amongst others, his wife. Ambrose began to feel himself, where from temperament he most disliked to be, out in the cold.

Perhaps it was this sense of being out in the cold that quickened into energetic life a feeling which, for months past, had been lurking in Philip's thoughts, in a fugitive, shamefaced, apologetic fashion, but which now began to assert itself with courageous obtrusiveness. It concealed itself at first, as bad thoughts are apt to do, under the garb of a virtue, if indeed, with some natures, it be a virtue to repent. Philip, when he found Miss Rashleigh not at all inclined to reproach him, had begun, with great vehemence, to reproach himself. He had treated her shamefully, he knew—and she knew; and the consciousness that he had acted badly to her was stimulated by horrid self-questionings as to whether he had acted most wisely for himself,—most advantageously for that all-important aggregate of enjoyment, which it was Ambrose's supreme concern in life to make as large as possible and to protect from every risk of

curtailment. Miss Rashleigh, it was certain, was a
most beautiful creature, bright, frank, natural, prompt
to forget and forgive, amusing, and easy to amuse.
Ambrose remembered having felt gayer, more unre-
strained, more completely at his ease with her than he
was ever able now to feel with his wife. Her standard
of taste and morals was not so severe nor so inflexible
as Camilla's. She was readier for a joke and less exacting as to its quality. She took life less gravely. There
was a punctiliousness about Camilla's mind which
was sometimes burthensome,—which narrowed the area
within which mirth could play at ease and the point of
vision from which things could be looked at. Florence
Rashleigh fell greatly short of Camilla in knowledge
and power of thought ; but, then, are knowledge and
power of thought the attributes which conduce most
to perfection in a wife,—to the ease, comfort and
happiness of a husband? Camilla's very perfection of
character was capable, in some moods, of being felt as a
defect. 'She is all fault,' the poet has written, 'who
hath no fault at all.' A man does not want to be continually confronted with unattainable virtues,—to be
reminded, by contrast with his nearest companion, of
his own shortcomings and infirmities. Miss Rashleigh,
on the other hand, made no pretensions to faultlessness :
did not this render her charms all the more endearing
to frail humanity? She ignored the past with a completeness for which Philip felt intensely grateful. Such
a faculty of oblivion was a delightful characteristic in a
world in which many things have to be ignored. Her

beauty was more striking, more impressive, more seductive, more loveable than ever: and she was as generous as beautiful. Other people's behaviour to Philip conveyed a subtle sensation of reproach; but Miss Rashleigh's good-nature was spontaneous, unstudied, suggestive of no *arrière pensée*. She was devoted to Camilla, and evidently intended to be friends with Philip. How could any man of sensibility fail to be touched by such an intention? Philip was profoundly touched and began to feel a passionate desire to set himself completely right with his old love,—to tell her how much of the old love was still alive. And, day by day, he began to be more and more conscious how very much alive it was. Before long the opportunity arrived; and Philip, whose opportunities in such matters were never wasted, spoke out from the fulness of his soul. The chances of a hunting morning, on the mountain side, left them, for a few minutes, close to one another and alone.

'I want to thank you,' Philip said, 'for all your kindness and your generosity to my wife and to me. I had no claim to your help; quite the reverse; but you have helped, more than any one, to reconcile her to our Indian exile.'

'I have to thank you,' said Florence, 'for the greatest friendship I have ever made, and the one that I prize most in the world. Indeed, I never knew what friendship was till Mrs. Ambrose came to teach me. You may well be happy.'

'I should be very happy,' said Philip, 'if I knew that you had really forgiven me.'

' Then,' said Miss Rashleigh, with a cheerful sincerity,
' you may be more than happy, for I do not consider that
I have anything to forgive. You did exactly what I told
you. You see how wise it was to determine to be free.'

' Was it ?' said Philip. ' You were saved from the
risk of a very bad husband at any rate, for I believe I
make a wretched one.'

' You will make a wretched one,' said Miss Rashleigh,
still quite declining to take the conversation seriously,
' if you go about confessing your shortcomings to other
ladies, particularly ladies whom you adore or have
adored. Not that I believe that there are any shortcomings. I am confident that you are perfection.'

' Oh no, I am not,' said Philip, vexed at his companion's banter; ' nor do you, or any one else think me
so ; but a mass of imperfections, which are always
bringing me to grief.'

' Bringing you to grief ?' said Florence, scanning the
hillside for some one to rescue her from her companion's inconvenient seriousness ; ' you are, by universal consent, the most fortunate of mankind, and your
last stroke of good fortune has been the best of all.
Ah ! there are the hounds coming out of the Shola.
Let us gallop on.'

' Stop,' said Philip ; ' do not laugh at me—you would
not if you knew. I have come to grief this time for
good and all. I have behaved to you, I know, like a
weak fool as I was. I could not help it. I am weak
as water and I cannot make myself strong by wishing ;
but I have deep feelings and strong ; and the strongest

and deepest is for you; and I am the most wretched fellow alive. Now what do you think of me?'

'I will tell you what I think,' said Florence, turning to her companion, her face bloodless, and her eyes flashing with excitement,—'I think you a traitor. You were a traitor to me. Now you are a traitor—a ten times worse traitor—to another. I will speak to you openly, Mr. Ambrose, as your friend—as your wife's friend. She is a sweet, noble nature, the highest I have ever known; too good for me; too good for you, or for almost any man : you have had the supreme good fortune to get her : deserve your good fortune ; worship her as you ought; devote yourself, heart and soul, to being what her husband ought to be ; breathe the pure air of her thoughts ; let her high aims and pure tastes be yours ; and you have indeed happiness—unusual happiness—unattainable to most,—before you. Fail to do this—behave as you have just behaved to me—play with each passing mood as it comes—yield to each liking which besets you—say the sort of things that you have said to me—say them to other women who do not love and revere your wife as I do—and you will come to grief indeed and dishonour too!'

She was gone, and Philip was left alone to bear his rebuff as best he might. It was a cruel blow. He was in a tender mood and in dire need of a little petting. He would have liked Miss Rashleigh to forgive and pet him, and allow him the privileges of confidential repentance and absolution. He pitied himself immensely, and wanted Miss Rashleigh to join in the pity and to

look at his case from the point of view from which it
was pitiable and not disgraceful. Why had she been
so inexorable, so harsh? She had turned and smitten
him, like an angel in a holy wrath—stern, unforgiving, .
unpitying, contemptuous. She had never forgiven
him, then, after all; her kindness had been the mere
simulated goodwill that it was necessary to show to
Camilla's husband, however undeserving, for fear of
hurting her. Why was existence,—which was intended,
surely, to be a smooth and bright affair,—replete with
such embarrassing complications, such mortifying discoveries, such humiliating results? Why should the
accidents of life place a girl like Florence Rashleigh,
with all her beauty, interest and charm, so hopelessly
beyond one's reach? Why, when one sorely needs a
sympathising and indulgent consoler, should fate present one with a cold, stern, unflinching monitress?
Why, when one is in a penitential mood, should one
not be absolved?

Florence by this time had disappeared over the
mountain ridge. She was gone, and gone in anger, and
the last bright spot on Phil's horizon had grown dark
and cold.

CHAPTER XXVI

LADIES IN COUNCIL

'All round my room my silent servants wait—
My friends in every season, bright and dim ;
Angels and seraphim
Come down and murmur to me, sweet and low,
And spirits of the sky all come and go.'

ONE of the results, perhaps—with the exception of his debts—the most solid result of Philip's Oxford career, had been a judiciously assorted collection of extremely well-bound books. There are volumes, the publishers' catalogues tell us, which no gentleman's library should be without; and Philip, in accepting the dictum in a generous spirit, had added to it the expensive corollary that a good book deserves the finest coat which the binder's art can give it. The idea of parting with these treasures, at the time when his father parted with Red Hazard, had suggested itself to Philip's mind among other possible expedients, but had been promptly dismissed as unpractical and irrationally romantic. Second-hand books, he reminded himself, always fetch a wretched price ; and then, was he not just starting for India, where a good library would be amongst the few possible alleviations of existence? The consequence was that Philip Ambrose's library accompanied him to Cœrulea, and his house was now well stocked with this delightful order of furniture. The beautiful volumes rose high on the library walls, overflowed into the drawing-room, established themselves in force on three sides of the dining-room, lined the staircase recesses, and effected a permanent foothold on the landing-place. Camilla had found their number, their variety, their splendour, among the chief attractions of her new home. She had always been an eager reader, and agreed with her husband in thinking a pleasant book all the pleasanter for exquisite type, fine paper, and a *recherché* binding. 'There are grand books,' she used to say, 'like grand ladies, that ought to dress grandly in Russian leather and gilt edges.' Camilla's taste for good print and smart bindings, however, was but a foible. Her passion was for reading, and the long days, while her husband was away at office, gave plenty of opportunities for indulging it. One morning, when Lady Miranda came across for her accustomed after-breakfast chat, she found her friend deep in the study of a sombre-coated octavo volume; and, as she bent over her, resting her hand on Camilla's shoulder, she read the heading of the page, ere the other had closed it.

'What grave book is my dear Penserosa so busy about? The Republic! If it is anything republican or revolutionary I shall probably like it. You shall read to me while I try to make a sketch of that dear corner of your garden.'

'It is not revolutionary at all,' Camilla said, with a

laugh; 'it is the purest, oldest conservatism possible—
as old as Plato.'

'Plato!' cried Miranda, 'what an odd book for any
woman to read—to have leisure to read! I wish I had!
For my part I never read a word of anything except
parliamentary speeches, the last popular novel, and my
favourite poems. Life is not long enough.'

'Ah, but you see,' said Camilla, 'Cœrulean life is
long, and the art of Cœrulean housekeeping—so much, at
least, as I can attain to—is extremely short; so I have
taken to the classics, and I make my husband teach me
Greek in the evenings. Meanwhile I have become an
enthusiastic Platonist. It is all so pure, so serene, so
exquisitely good—the loveliest poetry, surely, that ever
mind conceived. One breathes another atmosphere from
that of common life, like that of the enchanting solitudes of some solemn mountain height. I always feel
as if one ought to come down from it to life again, like
Moses from the mountain, with the glory still upon one.
Just listen, now, while I read you this.' And then
Camilla read in grave, impassioned tones:

' " From the souls of those who have once gazed on celestial truth
or beauty, the remembrance can never be effaced. Like some divine
inspiration the glories of this other world possess and haunt them;
and it is because their souls are ever struggling upwards and
fluttering like a bird that longs to soar heavenwards, and because they
are rapt in contemplation and careless of earthly matters, that the
world calls the philosopher, the lover, and the poet mad. For the
earthly copies of justice, or temperance, or any of the higher qualities,
are seen but through a glass dimly, and few are those who can discern
the reality by looking at the shadow. And thus the sight of any
earthly beauty in face or form thrills the genuine lover with unutterable awe and amazement, because it recalls the memory of the celestial

beauty seen by him once within the sphere of celestial being. The divine wings of his soul are warmed and glow with desire, and he lives in a sort of ecstasy and shudders with the 'misgiving of a former world.'"

'Is not that beautiful?' said Camilla, as she closed the book and turned to her companion, herself seemingly infected with something of the ecstasy of which she was reading. 'Does it not carry one to a height from which all common things seem mean and coarse? Does not one seem

> ' "To have seen white presences upon the hills,
> To have heard the voices of the eternal Gods?" '

'Too grand a height for me,' said Miranda; 'for my part, the beauties of the world—such enchanting beauty as we see from your window here—need no such sublime explanation. Are you philosopher, lover, or poet, Camilla, that you take so high a flight? As for me, you know, I am before all things a woman of the world and a politician.'

'Ah, but,' said Camilla, bent on the conversion of her friend, ' it is just about politics that I like Plato best. Here is one of my favourite passages. Let me just read it to you, and see if it does not make you in love with conservatism :

' "They, who belong to this small class, have tasted how sweet and blessed a possession philosophy is, and have also seen and been satisfied of the madness of the multitude, and known that there is no one who ever acts honestly in the administration of states, nor any helper, who will save any one, who maintains the cause of the just. Such a saviour would be like a man who has fallen among wild beasts, unable to join in the wickedness of his friends, and would have to throw away his life before he had done any good to himself or others. And he reflects upon all this and holds his peace, and does his own business. He is like one who retires under the shelter of a wall in the storm of dust and sleet which the driving wind hurries along ; and when he sees the rest of mankind full of wickedness, he is content if only he can lead his own life, and be pure from evil or unrighteousness, and depart in peace and goodwill, with bright hopes.''

' Well,' said Camilla, as she came to an end, 'what do you think of it ?'

' " To be pure from evil, and depart in peace and good-will, with bright hopes,"' said her companion; 'that would be well indeed ! But as for the general idea, I don't like it. It is the philosophy of a Quietist. I like the wind and the dust and human beings, bad as they may be : not that they are so bad. I know a great many excellent ones, the poorest some of the best. But as I said, I am a woman of the world, and worldly. I love politics and philanthropy, and have a hankering after revolutions.

' Well,' said Camilla, 'for my part, I hate wind and dust cordially, and am ready to betake myself, with ignominious gratitude, to the kind shelter of the wall. I admit I am a coward and frightened to death at the very idea of a revolution.'

'You would not be if you could see the poor as I have seen them,' said Miranda ; 'the dreadful, sordid misery—the hopelessness, the degradation, the absence of everything that makes life worth living, or fit to live. When one talks of liking revolutions, one means that anything is better than sitting still, as people do con-tentedly, in the midst of all that sort of thing, calling it the best of all possible worlds and never moving a little finger to mend it. Those are the kind of people I should like to revolutionise.'

'So far we are all revolutionists,' said Camilla; 'but then, will the poor be better for mob-rule, for having their own blind, ignorant way, and being led about by the first impostor who knows how to tickle their fancy or arouse their passions?   They say they are worse off in New York than London.   Now that we have got this beloved Plato, let me read you one passage more—it is about the Sophists, who, he says, "act as keepers to the many-headed monster of a people, understanding its habits and humouring its caprices, calling what it fancies good, and what it dislikes bad. . . . And Phil)-sophy herself," he continues, "is left desolate, and a crowd of vulgar interlopers leave their proper trade and rush in, like escaped prisoners into a sanctuary, and profane the temple of Truth."   Now, is not that a good sketch of your radical politician, racking his brains for a cry to rouse the mob with, or a "great movement of popular opinion" to carry his party through the blunders of a session?'

'You are a Tory, dear Camilla, of the bluest dye,' Miranda said, 'and deserve to live under a despot.'

'At any rate,' said Camilla, 'I am well content to be a woman and to live out of the hurly-burly; under the protection of the wall, in fact.   The best things in life seem to have been discovered a long while ago, and our progress only takes us farther and farther away from them; the world goes from bad to worse.'

'What do you mean by the best things?' asked Miranda, aghast at her companion's pessimism.

'I mean the noblest thoughts,' said Camilla; 'has

any one improved on the Hindoo sages? read their grand hymns—their poems—pure, serene, sublime—and see what men in India were ages ago, and look at what they are now, and talk to me of progress? No; I have begun to think the world a bad business, too bad to be enthusiastic about.'

'It has its disappointments, of course,' said Miranda.

'Ah!' said her companion, 'that is the keynote of the whole—Disappointment. It is the end of hope, aspiration, endeavour; it rounds the little life of each one, and the doings of the great world itself. All the good things, the bright things, come but to that; they all seem to get spoilt—such is the doom of man—by man's own crime and folly. Look at Christianity itself, breaking like a ray from heaven into that wretched, cruel, *blasé* suffering Roman world, and carrying the idea of heavenly calm, felicity, rapture, to the poor souls who lay in its abysses. They hoped then, those happy people, and with good reason clung to their blessed hope through fire and sword and fiendish torture—and how has it turned out? Has it been a success, or a dreary, dreadful failure? Cruel, wicked wretches, debasing it to their own hideous level; Calvin with his demon-god, and the infants a span long creeping on the floor of hell; Rome with her atheist Popes, and blood-stained hands and impudent miracle-mongering—and the poor you were talking about; just look at what one reads of them in London; can Pagan life have been worse?'

'Yes,' said Miranda, 'I believe it was worse, a

hundred times, crueller, fiercer, more animal-like. You
would scarcely call Christianity a failure if you could
be where I have been, and seen how good, how noble,
how refined many poor people are—how patiently they
suffer, how bravely they die. And which is best—your
grand philosophy, too much shocked at everything to be
of any use? or mine, which is to mend the present and
hope for the future? How can you be happy with such
a creed?'

'I am not happy,' said Camilla ; 'very much the reverse. I have had my disappointment like the rest of
the world; or, perhaps, when I spoke of the world, I
meant myself.'

'You shall not be disappointed this time,' said
Miranda, 'if you will let me be your friend. I cannot
bear to think of you unhappy.'

'I am sure of that,' said Camilla, as she drew her
companion to her with a tender embrace. 'It is horrid
of me to let my melancholy mood cast a shade across
your bright sky. I began by hoping too much, I suppose; and now I feel grieved that life will not fashion
itself into the sort of thing I longed for. Somehow it
seems in vain to aspire. Do you remember the lines
about St. Peter in *Aurora Leigh?*

> ' " After our first girding of the loins
>   In youth's fine linen and fine broidery,
>   To run up hill and meet the rising sun,
>   We are apt to sit tired, patient as a fool,
>   While others gird us with the violent bands
>   Of social figments, feints, and formalisms,
>   Reversing our straight nature, lifting up
>   Our base needs, keeping down our lofty thoughts,

Head downwards on the cross-sticks of the world.
Yet He can pluck us from that shameful cross.
God, set our feet low and our foreheads high,
And show us how a man was made to walk."'

'And how a noble woman was made to walk!' cried Miranda. 'Sometimes, dear Camilla, when we stumble the most and the path seems steepest, is it not that we are on a loftier height than usual, farther from earth and nearer to the stars ?

' "Though now he serve me stumblingly, the hour
Is nigh, when I shall lead him into light."'

That evening Lady Miranda discussed the Ambroses with her husband. Brownlow had dressed them up in the rosy light of an ideally prosperous and happy marriage, and was loud in his praise of the career which led naturally to such a pleasant form of life. He was charmed with Camilla, and took her husband on trust as deserving his good luck. The best of the Indian service, he observed, is that it makes it possible for young men and women to marry while they ought, and enjoy themselves and each other while they are capable of enjoyment.

'Enjoyment!' cried Miranda; 'my dear George, you know nothing about it; you men can never see. Mrs. Ambrose is one of the most unhappy women that I have ever known; and, if I mistake not, has got a husband who has broken her heart, or is on the high-road to break it.'

CHAPTER XXVII

A LAND OF AFTERNOON

DESPITE his imperial surroundings, Chichele proved a
ready proselyte to Lady Miranda's revolutionary creed.
He found, in truth, that talking to her was what he did
best and liked best to do.   Brownlow declared that he
surrendered his convictions with disgraceful compliance
in the railway committee, in order to get away and
gossip with her in the drawing-room, or take her for
long rides to all his favourite points of view.   Mr.
Chichele, on his part, had a great eye for scenery, and
knew of a dozen lovely vantage-posts from which the
surrounding country could be admired with the best
effect.   Lady Miranda found, on hers, that cantering
Mr. Chichele's ponies over the long stretches of smooth
turf, up the long valleys, or across the high Cœrulean
table-lands, was an employment exactly congenial to
her tastes.   They used to come all of a sudden on the
sweetest little sylvan nooks, from which the wide
prospect, bathed in the rich blue atmosphere of an

Indian afternoon, could be surveyed in coolness and at ease. The Cœrulean woodlands creep in the most endearing fashion along the valley sides, and afford a hundred tempting situations to those who love to worship Nature in her gentlest aspect and at a modest shrine. At some one of these pleasant halting-places it would generally happen that a little troop of Chichele's scarlet folk would be found busy extemporising a primitive fireplace and an al-fresco five o'clock tea. Hither, by degrees, the scattered members of the party would assemble to chat for half an hour in the shade, and to refresh themselves in the course of the long afternoon's ride. Miranda naturally fell often to the companionship of their host, and neither of them felt at all inclined to grumble at the arrangement. Lady Miranda soon began to feel at her ease and to become increasingly confidential.

'This is a favourite haunt of mine,' Chichele said one day, as he threw down the reins on the neck of his Arab, who stood with upturned head and dilated nostril enjoying the prospect and breeze apparently as much as did his master. It was indeed enchanting. They had reached the brow of a commanding height. Behind them lay the jungle from which they had just emerged, ablaze with wild roses, and its cool, shady depths speaking of infinite refreshment to arid souls. Before them the mountains fell rapidly towards the plain, a tumbled sea of palm and bamboo and tangling creepers. Each ravine and hollow, each bend in the mountains' side, stood out clear and sharp in the bright crystal air.

Over all, the coming twilight shed a purple haze. Miranda's face glowed with pleasure.

'This is delightful,' she cried. 'Let us rest here and enjoy it at peace.'

'Let us, by all means,' said Chichele, getting off his horse and going to help Miranda down from hers. 'Where in the world could half an hour be spent to better purpose on such an afternoon as this?'

Before, however, they had time to establish themselves, Brownlow came trotting on his cob, with a brisk, resolute air, and map in hand. He pointed to a distant headland which he had been reconnoitring.

'Look here, Chichele,' he said; 'we will bring the line up that opposite hillside, and get to our obligatory point through that convenient gap.'

'This comes of having railway projects,' said Chichele. 'Lady Miranda and I were abandoning ourselves to the picturesque.'

'And this comes of marrying eminent contractors,' said Miranda. 'All one's ideas about mountains are merged in visions of running trains up and down their sides.'

'And a very good vision too,' said Brownlow, with good-natured authority. 'A good railway is an improvement to any mountain. Its curves are always lovely. It emphasises the wildness of the scene, and it enables ten times as many people to see it. Now let us have a cup of tea, and then, Chichele, I shall insist upon your coming to the headland and judging for yourself. I am getting quite in love with this line.'

'A horrid form of conjugal infidelity!' cried Miranda; 'and meanwhile I am head over ears in love with this view, and I must positively have a sketch of it before I move. Mr. Chichele was just going to show me how to mix my colours so as to catch this heavenly blue.'

'Come, Brownlow,' said Chichele; 'do for goodness' sake sit down here in the shade and behave like a Christian. You can light your pipe if you please, and enjoy the reflection that this pretty place where we sit will very likely in a year or two—thanks to you—be a noisy railway siding, with porters, ticket-collectors, personally conducted excursion trains full of Cook's tourists, and pleasant things of that sort.'

'No,' said Miranda; 'I protest against such sacrilege, even in imagination. Be a little romantic, George, for once, and inspired by the occasion. Don't you see Puck and Titania under the ferns there and the nymphs and fairies dancing down that pretty glen?'

'Nymphs and fairies, indeed!' said her husband cheerfully, proceeding to light his pipe; 'but you have forgotten, Miranda, that you are a politician on the look-out for new convictions or for proofs of old ones. You must not be too picturesque.'

'A politician?' said Chichele, 'then I shall get Lady Miranda to bring me up to date. My politics have grown frightfully rusty with my exile here.'

'She will like nothing so well,' said Brownlow. 'Now, Miranda, there is a chance for you. You have a passion for proselytism. Chichele's conscience has been fallow for ever so long, and you can sow what sort of seed you please, and have a crop just to your own fancy.'

'Yes, I should like that,' Miranda said; 'politics are what one really cares about, are they not? But what are you, Mr. Chichele? A Liberal?'

'Well,' said Chichele, 'I was supposed to be one when I was in the House—a weak-backed one. What I should be, or what I should be called now, who can tell; but, pray, what are you?'

'I?' said Miranda, opening her beautiful azure eyes with a grave look which Chichele thought extremely pretty; 'has my husband never told you? I am a Revolutionist—a Red of the most anarchic and implacable order.'

'I must double my sentries,' said Chichele, 'and order up a detachment of detectives. You stop short of dynamite, I hope.'

'Just short of that,' said Miranda, with a dreamy hesitation, as if parting reluctantly with some favourite project of annihilation; 'and in Russia where they insult and flog beautiful young women, you know ——'

'We never insult or flog beautiful young women here,' said Chichele. 'You may feel perfectly safe, but I am bound to forbid your getting up any revolutions in my bit of India. I hope you will excuse me; but here in India, you know, we have no politics but to serve the Queen and keep the country in order.'

'So I should have thought,' said Miranda; 'but when we were staying with Sir Theophilus Prance the other day, we were surprised to find that he knew all about the elections, was thoroughly posted up in the gossip of his county, had read all the addresses, and, in fact, seemed to be making a speech to us himself, just as if we were constituents. Did he not, George ?'

'He did,' said Brownlow, 'and a dull one it was. One does not come to India to hear stale radicalism. One wants to get at something local.'

'Ah,' said Chichele, 'but then Prance is not local; he is for the universe. And he is nursing a constituency, and, I imagine, spends his mornings addressing his supporters before a looking-glass. He was, no doubt, delighted to get an audience.'

The Brownlows, having witnessed the performance on the spot, had shared the disillusion which befalls those inquisitive natures who everywhere want to go behind the scenes. They had seen the ropes, the pulleys, the canvas palaces, the dirty scene-shifters, the pearl-powder and the rouge. With regard to Sir Theophilus, they both agreed, as with summer's eve—'twas the distance lent enchantment to the view. Chichele did not even admire him at a distance, and when the Brownlows hinted disparagement of their late host, was not at all inclined to interfere on his behalf.

'I say, Brownlow,' he cried, 'do you remember Bacon's essay on the greatness of kingdoms and estates, that we used to be so fond of, and the story about Themistocles ? Themistocles, I must tell you, Lady Miranda, being asked to oblige the party with a tune, answered, as we should consider, somewhat sententiously, that he could not fiddle but could make a small town into a great city. On which text Bacon preaches an excellent sermon. Brownlow and I used to know it by heart in our Oxford days, when we studied politics as a science. Let me see how my memory serves me. "If," says the wise old gentleman, " a true survey be taken of counsellors and statesmen, there will be found, though rarely, those who can make a small state great and yet cannot fiddle. As, on the other hand, there will be found a great many that can fiddle very cunningly, but yet are so far from being able to make a small state great, as their gifts be the other way, to bring a great and flourishing estate to ruin and decay. And certainly those degenerate arts and shifts, whereby many counsellors and governors gain both favour with their masters and estimation with the vulgar, deserve no better name than fiddling, being things rather pleasing for the time and graceful in themselves only, than tending to the weal and advancement of the State which they serve." Now,' continued Chichele, 'Sir Theophilus is always fiddling, always playing popular tunes, like Paganini, on a single string. I confess, when this sort of performance takes place in high places, I begin to think that things look dangerous. I don't like his tunes or his touch.'

'Well,' said Brownlow, tapping out the remains of his pipe and preparing for a move, 'I don't mind admitting that I did not much like his fiddling either. English platform radicalism does not seem proper in India,—it's like wearing a frock-coat and a tall hat in the sun, you know. But, seriously now, do you think a man like Prance can be really dangerous?'

'I think him about as dangerous,' said Chichele, 'as a child running about in a powder magazine with a lighted candle. He may set nothing on fire; he may escape a catastrophe, but no one can say that he will. Our business in India involves the feat of putting the very newest, strongest, highly alcoholised of modern wines into some of the oldest bottles in the world without their bursting. Surely it can only be done by the gentlest handling. Prance and his set seem to court an explosion, and to think it would not signify. We have got two hundred or three hundred millions of people here upon our hands, stirred by all sorts of fears, tastes, and pre-judices, of which we know next to nothing, and liable to impulses as difficult to judge as a sub-oceanic current. Englishmen, when they talk about India, seem to forget all this, and fling about their fireworks just as if such a thing as a mutiny never occurred to their imagination.'

'A mutiny!' cried Lady Miranda; 'but that is a thing of the past.'

'I hope so,' said Chichele; 'but the afternoon is waning, and Brownlow is becoming impatient; let us be moving homeward.'

As they rode back, Chichele informed Lady Miranda that their party next day would be enlarged. 'My chief-secretary, Masterly, comes back from leave to-morrow,' he said. 'He is immensely clever, has read every-thing that ever was written, and will be enchanted to talk to you about India as often as you please.'

CHAPTER XXVIII

MASTERLY

'Your reasons at dinner have been sharp and sententious; pleasant without scurrility, witty without affectation, audacious without imprudency, learned without opinion, and strange without heresy.'

MASTERLY, at first sight, wore an erratic, artistic, unconventional look, which suggested rather the idea of a rising academician than a risen official. He was a very clever fellow, but had never conquered the mystery of tying his handkerchief in the conventional bow, or of getting his clothes to behave like those of the rest of civilised mankind. His manner was nervous, sudden, apprehensive, like those of some wild forest creature; and, in fact, he was continually apprehensive of dull people who were in the habit of trying to buttonhole him, and of pertinacious instigators to official jobbery. Long training had taught him how to tame his features to inexpressive quiescence, but nothing could prevent the tell-tale flashes of his eye, or the twitches of his nervous lips, that bespoke the presence of a latent electricity. His forehead was Socratic, and a close inspection showed that, despite a general air of uncouth force,

Nature had completed him with the most delicate finishing touches. His lips and chin were chiselled to an almost feminine refinement. His hair, defiant of the prim, hard lines which civilisation dictates, fell about his temples in clusters fine as a woman's. His large, nervous, well-moulded hand, tapered into long, pliant fingers, typical of dexterous vigour. No one who critically examined his physique would have found it difficult to understand how it was that he had won in a canter every intellectual race for which he had been entered at school and college. 'He looks delightfully clever,' Lady Miranda said; 'and I am certain I shall be charmed with him.'

'I am not at all sure of that,' Chichele replied; and when, later in the evening, Chichele brought him to be introduced, Lady Miranda soon began to share his apprehension. There was, however, an impressive air of restless capacity about him which attracted her immensely. They soon fell to serious talk.

'Mr. Chichele has promised that you will tell me all I want to know about India.'

'All I know!' exclaimed Masterly; 'I am afraid you would not like that at all. I know too much.'

'Oh, but,' said Lady Miranda, 'I am longing to hear about it. India, I must tell you, has always been my dream; it is so intensely picturesque.'

'Ah!' said Masterly, with an incisive air, which his enemies considered his most offensive attribute; 'but you must get rid of that illusion at once, if you please, Lady Miranda. India is picturesque, just as the little towns you see from the Mediterranean are picturesque, because there is nothing so squalid, so hideous, so tumble-down, so vilely prosaic, that distance will not lend it a touch of enchantment. India is just the same —well enough to look at through a haze of Burke or Macaulay's rhetoric, but if you really examine it, it is one of the dullest, most tedious, unpicturesque affairs you can conceive. Every Englishman begins to learn about India from Macaulay's Essays (which, you know, are a tissue of falsehoods), and goes on with Burke's speeches, which for exaggeration, bombast, mock pomposity, solemnity, violence, and unfairness are unapproachable.'

'Then,' said Lady Miranda, 'you mean seriously that I must leave off liking Burke. Don't you like him?'

'I like him,' said Masterly, 'because he gave vigorous expression to one of our few national virtues, hatred of the French character—hating a Frenchman like the devil, you know, as Nelson put it—which I hope we all do ; but, as for Burke's speeches about India, why, the very people at the time could not stand them, and used to go away to dinner while he went on refining and inveighing and piling up fine situations. As for any one liking them now, I always think of Hamlet's robustious, periwig-pated fellow tearing a passion to tatters, and fancy I hear the rattle of the tin dagger with which he performed his mock suicide on the floor of the House of Commons.'

'Well,' said Lady Miranda, 'I have a great deal to unlearn, I see. All the same, I feel a sneaking fondness for some of the fine phrases you denounce. There is a beautiful one my husband was reading me this morning, about "the cries of India being carried on the wings of the monsoon."'

'The wings of the monsoon!' said Masterly, waving his long fingers with an air of lively scepticism; 'if Burke had known what a bother and anxiety the monsoon is to us, he would not have talked so glibly about it.'

'Then,' said Lady Miranda, with an air of resignation, 'are all officials as matter-of-fact as you are?'

'Yes,' said Masterly, 'all the good ones; you may find a little poetry and romance in the lower ranks of the service, but it soon wears off. The first thing they do with us is to spoil us. I got spoilt quickly, luckily for me. It was a cruel process. I wrote a lovely style when I was a boy,—vehement, violent, extravagant, infectious, in fact quite like Burke; but it is all gone, alas! The great thing is, to write as if you were ordering a pair of gloves.'

'But I write a very vehement, violent, impetuous style about *my* gloves, I can assure you,' said Lady Miranda, 'if they are not exactly what I like.'

'You know the story about the ambitious young civilian and the East Indian Director. They were always signing minutes and committing jobs—not such jobs as the Secretary of State commits nowadays, but still pretty bad ones. Well, the ambitious boy, who had just been jobbed into a writership, and meant to make the best of it, asked the old gentleman "What style the Directors liked?"'

'"My dear young friend,"' said the old gentleman,

—can't you fancy him wiping his gold spectacles or pulling down his buff waistcoat as he said it—'" the style as we likes is the humdrum."'

'Well,' said Lady Miranda, 'the style as I likes is the humdrum, so there we are agreed; that is to be the style of my book, Mr. Masterly.'

Masterly, whose wide capacities embraced an appreciation of pretty women, as well as of the other good things of life, had already begun to think that his companion was a remarkably intelligent young lady and well worth enticing into a long conversation. 'But you don't look in the least humdrum,' he said. 'I am afraid you could not be it.'

'Nor do you,' said Lady Miranda, 'but I am, all the same; you see I have had to spoil my style, like you, to suit the subject. Now go on telling me why Indian affairs are such a bore.'

'They are a bore,' said Masterly, 'because they are such a frightful muddle : India is like a *salle à manger* after a big *table d'hôte*; one is always having to sweep away the crumbs left by preceding diners; and I don't like sweeping away crumbs. One would like a virgin soil to operate upon—an island in the Ægean or somewhere, with nothing but groves and fountains and dryads.'

Miranda felt that this sort of thing would not do at all.

This was the kind of nonsense that men liked to talk to her, and which she especially resented when she was wanting to be serious.

'That does not sound at all humdrum,' she said,

'and I don't understand you in the least. The older
a country is, the more interesting, surely, it must be.
What can be duller than those virgin soils one hears
about in new colonies—so many hundred thousand
square miles, with no scenery but posts and rails, and
no incidents but steam-ploughs and elevators?'

'Delightful simplicity!' cried Masterly; 'that would
be the country to be Chief-secretary in! What an
Arcadian existence! Here, on the contrary, everything
is complicated into such a frightful entanglement that it
takes a lifetime to understand it—more than a lifetime.
I will give you an instance. Lord Cornwallis was determined to pass the Permanent Settlement and have done
with it—to clear up the frightful mess which, in one way
or another, had come about between landlord and tenant.
Mr. Shore, the well-informed, humdrum official, implored
him to hold his hand, and assured him he did not know
half enough about it to take any final step. Lord Cornwallis's answer showed that he was so heartily sick of
the subject, so despairing of getting at the bottom of it,
that he had made up his mind desperately to have done
with it once for all, *coute qui coute*. Now, we know
to our cost that Mr. Shore was right, and Lord Cornwallis wrong; and the result of the mistake has been
the deuce and all for the Indian finances, for millions
of tenants and for us poor officials, who have to deal
with it a hundred years later.'

'But,' said Lady Miranda, 'you forget that I accept
your doctrine, and have forsworn the picturesque. I
shall not put anything in my book about the monsoon

except that it usually begins in June, and I shall
cut out a beautiful sentence about twenty centuries
looking down on us from the Himalayas. But, Mr.
Masterly, what a sacrifice! and what a book mine will
be. Who will read it? Who will publish it, I should
like to know? I tell you what; I will call it "The
Seamy Side of India," or something of that sort——'

'Or "The Sighs of a Secretary,"' said Masterly;
'that has a romantic sound about it, which would be
impressive.'

'And now,' said Lady Miranda, who wanted to come
to business, 'about this information which you were to
give me. You have not told me anything except that
India is a bore—that is not a suggestive view, is it?'

'Information!' cried Masterly, 'I shall be delighted
to give you any amount you like. It is a perfect drug.
When you have finished your book, send it to me, and
I will have the necessary statistics filled in by the
people in my office. Will you have them in tables at
the end, or put in as footnotes as the topics occur?'

Masterly asked this question with an air of *bona fides*,
which Lady Miranda felt to be extremely impertinent.

'No!' she cried, in dismay; 'that is not at all what
I want. I must have the statistics for myself, and
then when I have marked, learnt, and inwardly digested
them, and formed my views, I shall then work them all
in myself, you know.'

'But surely that method won't do,' said her companion. 'I will show it in a minute. Here we are in
August; you will stay here a month——'

'Six weeks,' said Lady Miranda.

'Ah,' said Masterly, 'another fortnight! that makes a difference; but even out of these six weeks you will devote a large portion to amusement, to riding with Mr. Chichele and discussing pretty views; a large portion to sight-seeing, pure and simple; a large portion to correspondence, a large portion to reading the English papers. What is the residue of your six weeks, available for making up your mind as to two hundred and fifty millions of human beings about whom you know as much as about the wrong side of the moon? No, no; my plan is the right one, you may depend upon it. Put down your impressions, your feelings, your conclusions—the first thing that everybody tells you; they are sure to be fresh, picturesque, and quite as true as any one else's. Then I will get you out the statistics to match.'

'No, thank you,' said Lady Miranda in indignation. 'If I cannot have my information before I write my book, I will not have it at all.'

'Surely,' said Masterly, 'that is unreasonable, and shows, if I may say so, a wrong view of the use and meaning of figures. What are statistics? Groups of figures so arranged as to demonstrate some theory or other which you wish to establish. You shake them up, you know, like a kaleidoscope, till you get them into the particular shape you want. How can I give you statistics till I know what you want them for? I always know what Mr. Chichele wants *his* for. You must really give me some clue.'

Masterly looked at Lady Miranda with a point-

blank, resolute, self-assured look which he put on with
men who came to him for appointments and had to be
made to understand why they could not have them.
This look generally produced conviction, or, what did as
well, prostration. He now paused for a reply. Lady
Miranda was a woman of resource and accustomed to
succeed, and was neither prostrated nor convinced.

'Well,' she said, 'you shall have your way. I will
send you a piece of my book as soon as it is finished—"A
chapter on Secretaries, and how to manage a Bureau."'

'Or,' said Masterly, 'call it "A chapter on Bureaux, and
how to manage a Secretary." Of course, Lady Miranda,
you shall have whatever you want, when you like it
and as you like it. But now there is something that *I*
want. I hear your songs are delightful. I am longing
to hear you. You must really sing to us.'

'But you must promise to sing to *me*,' said Lady
Miranda, 'and then it is a bargain.'

'I hope,' said Chichele, as he wished Lady Miranda
good-night, 'that you found your companion agreeable;
how did you like him?'

'I am not quite sure that I like him,' said Miranda;
'he is rather impracticable, and, like you all, very
frivolous. He tells me that he is humdrum, but I had
great difficulty in making him become practicable and
talk like a reasonable being. However, I have asked
him to come for a ride with me to-morrow.'

'Then,' said Chichele, 'I prophesy that he will soon
become as practicable as you please.'

CHAPTER XXIX

MASTERLY BECOMES PRACTICABLE

' Ingenium ingens
Inculto latet hoc sub corpore.'

Masterly came the next afternoon for his ride in a less amenable mood than ever. The artist in him was supreme. He would talk of nothing but music, and he was full of Lady Miranda's songs the night before.

' They were delightful!' he cried, ' really delightful—that lovely air from *Faust*, what is its name? I have been dreaming about it all last night. What a genius Gounod is! is he not? And my dear old friend *Rend 'il sereno*. Why does no one sing Handel nowadays? and that nocturne of Chopin you played! It was a gem. Ah, Lady Miranda, when one hears airs like that, one feels that music is the one thing really worth caring about in life, really worth troubling about! Tell me, where did you learn your art? I feel it desecration to talk about anything but music to you. Now we have a nice long afternoon before us. I will take you a charming, quiet ride where no one can interrupt us, and you must talk about music to me or sing to me all the time.'

Miranda felt very much discouraged, but it was hopeless to struggle against what was evidently an overpowering mood. The only chance was to lure her companion to more serious themes. It was not without its element of charm, moreover, to find that she had had so appreciative and sympathetic a listener; and Masterly speedily convinced her that he was entitled to criticise with the authority of an accomplished connoisseur. She soon found that he knew a great deal on all musical topics, and spoke about them with a discriminating decisiveness that showed that his taste—his likings and dislikings—was something very real to him. Lady Miranda found herself—in spite of her disappointment and her own intentions in another direction—becoming very much interested, and began to resign herself to her fate with the reflection that the afternoon, if profitless from the business point of view, was likely to prove very agreeable.

'I should like to come and have some musical mornings with you. I have a charming scheme—I will tell you what we will do. We will appropriate some of Mr. Chichele's fiddlers and a violoncello, and have a real, serious time with the old masters. I have heard no Beethoven for an age. What is the Sonata with the wild scherzo that begins like this?' and Masterly hummed the air, and Lady Miranda discovered that his ear was true to a nicety and his voice a plaintive tenor that sounded delicate and melodious.

'Ah,' she said, 'you sing, I see!' And when they got home it turned out that Masterly could sing, if not with a finished exactness, yet with perfect sense of musical effect, and, at any rate, quite well enough to be an agreeable partner in a duet. And then Lady Miranda's portfolios abounded in many charming duets, which were explored, practised, and performed for the benefit of the performers and of Chichele and his guests.

This common taste in music naturally led the way to mutual confidences in other directions, and Lady Miranda found the task of exploring Masterly at once easy and agreeable. Masterly entirely threw off the artificial air of cynicism which he had worn the night before, and allowed all the blossoms of his nature to expand in a way that Lady Miranda felt to be deeply gratifying. He responded at once to her lead into book-talk, and, to her surprise, knew more about all the latest publications in England than she did herself, or than even the more cultured of those among whom she lived. Her husband had been a great reader in his way; but his busy life left him little leisure for anything but the *Times*, the most talked-of review of the month, and any novel which she considered good enough to recommend to him. For poetry Mr. Brownlow had but an unsympathetic tolerance; Browning he condemned as an unintelligible farrago of crude thoughts and obscure language, which it was an impertinence to palm off as art on the credulity of mankind. Swinburne was violent, silly, extravagant rhapsody. Tennyson not violent enough, and growing washier every year.

'Chichele and I,' he said, 'used to think a great

deal of it when we were cultivating conservatism and æstheticism at Oxford, and the *Princess*, I admit, was a pretty skit.'

'A what!' exclaimed Lady Miranda in horror; 'the songs in the *Princess* a skit? Well, George, what next?'

'Well, Miranda,' replied Brownlow, 'it was a skit, you know, at women's rights and girl-graduates and all that sort of thing; and now we have got the real thing, notwithstanding.'

'You must remember that I was a girl-graduate myself, and only left college to marry the most prosaic of mankind. I wish I had stayed and become a mistress of arts.'

'You are perfection as you are,' said her husband; 'but you will never convince me that poetry is anything but rhetoric with a jingle, and rhetoric anything but unhealthy prose.'

'Stop, stop!' cried Miranda in despair; 'it is profanation. Here, George, is Sir T. Brassey's *Work and Wages of the Labouring Classes* for you. Will that do? —as healthy and prosaic as you please.'

'If you had got two thousand labourers all wanting their wages on Saturday nights, as I often have, you would learn that there is some poetry in that too,' said her husband; and so their discussion would end, and Lady Miranda would admit to herself that poetry was not in her husband's line, and was not a good thing to talk about to him.

But now Masterly, having brought her to a lovely

valley and a woodland which was one great tangle of wildflowers, and every branch half-hidden with orchids and ferns, and the mountain side beyond alive with waving grasses and flecked with passing clouds and the afternoon shadows—burst out, of his own accord, into a Wordsworthian rhapsody.

'I have christened this place the Daffodils,' he said. 'It always comes into my head when I am here. What a pretty picture it is !—

> ' "I wandered lonely as a cloud
>   That floats on high o'er vales and hills,
> When all at once I saw a crowd,
>   A crowd of golden daffodils,
> Beside the lake, beneath the trees,
>   Fluttering and dancing in the breeze.
>
> ' "The waves beside them danced, but they
>   Outdid the sparkling waves in glee ;
> A poet could not but be gay
>   In such a jocund company ;
> I gazed and gazed, but little thought
> What wealth the show to me had brought.
>
> ' "For oft when on my couch I lie,
>   For vacant or for pensive mood,
> They flash upon that inward eye
>   That is the bliss of solitude ;
> And then my heart with pleasure fills,
> And dances with the daffodils." '

Lady Miranda broke into an exclamation of delight as the recital closed. 'You love Wordsworth, then ?' her companion said. 'How wise a devotion ! that best physician of weary souls :

> ' " He found us when the Age had bound
>   Our souls in its benumbing round ;

> He spoke, and loosed our souls in tears;
> He laid us, as we lay at birth,
> On the cool, flowery lap of earth,
> Smiles broke from us, and we had ease;
> The hills were round us, and the breeze
> Went o'er the sun-lit fields again;
> Our foreheads felt the wind and rain,
> Our youth returned——"

and then, you know, he was sometimes actually inspired.'

Masterly's tongue was loosed, and the rich storehouse of memory, from which nothing that he liked seemed ever to fade, poured out, at the touch of a kindred soul, its hidden treasures of delight. Masterly seemed to know everything by heart, and to love all Miranda's chosen passages with a discerning devotion, which sent him up at once many steps in her esteem.

'Ah!' he said, as they rode on, '"That inward eye that is the bliss of solitude"—one has plenty of use for that in India, Lady Miranda, I can tell you. Woe to the wretch who has it not, and sees nothing but a world of dull surroundings.'

'But,' said his companion, 'your life does not look to me at all dull. I think I should like it. It is so delightfully free.'

Masterly turned upon her with a sudden earnestness as unlike as possible to his usual tone of persiflage.

'Yes,' he said; 'free as the desert,—"the desolate freedom of the wild jackass,"—freedom from the people you care about, the things you are interested in, the places you love—freedom from everything but what can be tied up in red tape and put in a despatch-box—freedom which is free in the same way that the Roman's solitude was peace.'

'You have disliked India, then, very much sometimes?' said his companion ; 'what a dreadful description !'

'I love these lonely highlands,' said Masterly, lost apparently to all but the scene around him, 'with the monsoon rushing over them with its precious burthen for the famished, parched plains below. There is poetry in it, is there not? But you should see an Indian plain the week before the rains begin to know how poetical they are.· Evelyn's song is a prayer to the south-west monsoon :

> ' " O diviner Air ;
> Through the heat, the drouth, the dust, the glare,
> Far from out the west in shadowing showers,
> Over all the meadows baked and bare,
> Making fresh and fair
> All the bowers and the flowers—
> Fainting flowers, faded bowers—
> Over all this weary world of ours
> Breathe diviner Air." '

Masterly had taken off his hat to have full enjoyment of the breeze that was tossing his hair into wilder disarray than usual. His eye had lit up with animation ; his face was bright with power, tenderness, pathos. His voice, as he recited, trembled with feeling. Lady Miranda felt that for once, in a cold world of commonplace, she had·hit upon a vein of true romance, and forgot her desire to be instructed in the keener enjoyment of being charmed. Masterly was, she felt, a kindred spirit with whom it would be natural to be

confidential about more interesting topics than the
Indian politics.

'Look,' said Masterly at last, as a black mass of
cloud came rolling over the mountain side and blotting
out all the sweet glory of the afternoon :

' " Far along the world-wide whisper of the south wind rushing warm,
With the standards of the people ploughing thro' the thunder-storm,
And the nation's airy navies grappling in the central blue——" '

'Yes !' cried Lady Miranda, by this time in the highest
spirits at having thoroughly enjoyed her afternoon—
'yes, here they come, and we shall have the results of
the battle upon us in another minute. Let us gallop
homewards while we can.'

'Well,' said Chichele, as, half an hour later, he
helped her down from her pony, dripping with the
heavy downpour of a mountain shower, 'how did you
get on ?   Was he practicable ?'

'Most practicable and most delightful,' said Miranda,
'and the least humdrum person I have ever met.'

CHAPTER XXX

MRS. PARAGON'S TRIUMPH

'Ros. What think you of falling in love?

'Cel. Marry, I prithee, do, to make sport withal; but love no man in good earnest; nor no further in sport neither than with safety of a pure blush thou mayest in honour come off again.'

As You Like It.

CHICHELE always felt himself well off when he had Mrs. Paragon and the Rashleighs to dinner, especially when, as not unfrequently happened, Mrs. Rashleigh was not well enough to come, and Chichele, accordingly, escaped the responsibility of entertaining her. This was one of the social obligations for which Chichele felt himself perfectly inadequate. She was a nice, excellent, ladylike woman, but Chichele found her difficult to talk to. His attempts at conversation used to die away like abortive fireworks, and he used to sit in despairing silence, enviously watching the flow of talk around him, and wondering what the deuce he should say next. Providence, which tempers the wind to the shorn lamb, came to the aid of Chichele in the shape of a convalescent home for Europeans, on which Mrs. Rashleigh and Chichele's views entirely harmonised, and about which the lady was delighted to talk for ever. Chichele used to say that this home had been *his* saving, if nobody else's. But with Mrs. Paragon and Miss Rashleigh Chichele found himself in no danger of needing congenial topics of conversation. Mrs. Paragon was a chatterbox of the first water. She brought with her the freshest piece of gossip, the last *bon mot* achieved in Cœrulean circles, Masterly's newest witticism, the last wave of rumour from Simla. Always fully primed with interesting material—longing to let it off,—good-natured, high-spirited, and vivacious—her pretty person set off to the best possible advantage in a series of well-considered toilettes—her presence was generally admitted to add lustre to the entertainments at which she appeared. Chichele, at any rate, very much liked to have her as a guest.

He had with good reason great confidence in Mrs. Paragon's resources in the way of devising amusements for his guests. 'You must really come and stay with me,' he had said, directly he had heard of the Brownlows' intended visit, 'and keep everything straight for me. Without you I shall get into some frightful confusion, I am certain.' Mrs. Paragon was only too delighted to come : she arrived, at the proper moment, with several bullock-loads of boxes, full of pretty dresses, and devoted herself with praiseworthy alacrity to keeping the house in order and all the guests comfortable and well pleased. She assisted the A. D. C.'s in arranging the parties, settled who should be asked, and who should take whom into dinner, inspected and criticised the *ménus*,

had long and confidential communications with Chichele
and the major-domo, and,—all her duties decently fulfilled,
—used to come down to dinner, the picture of innocent
freshness, looking as if no weightier anxieties than those
of her own ambrosial toilette had engaged her thoughts.
In public she retired gracefully into the background,
after discharging satisfactorily all these important and
responsible functions. As Chichele said, she was a
woman of unusual tact; and it was to her ear that he first
entrusted a project of amusement, which had shaped
itself vaguely in his mind, but as to the feasibility of
which he felt grave misgivings. This was to carry off
the entire party to a lovely glen some twenty miles away,
among the mountains, where the scenery was wilder, the
solitude more complete, and life more unconventional
than at his mountain headquarters.

'Here,' said Chichele, 'we will take our ease. Lady
Miranda can write up her journal, and you ladies, who
are so fond of discussion, may have a symposium and
settle all the mysteries of existence to your heart's
content without the least risk of doing anybody any
harm. You may sit, like the angels in Milton, "upon a
hill retired—in thoughts more elevate, and reason high
of Providence, foreknowledge, will, and fate—fixed fate,
free will"—your own sweet wills, that is, and the fixed
fate of your husbands, and anything else you please.
Then, when you are tired of discussion and have convinced one another, we will all tell stories in turn like
the people in the *Decameron*, only that our stories will
all be proper ones, of course.'

'Delightful,' said Mrs. Paragon; 'I have a charming story that I am dying to tell already. We will consider it settled, and the A.D.C.'s and I will arrange the details to-morrow.'

'You will have to get round Masterly,' Chichele said; 'I am sure I don't know if he will allow me to go. He will say it is impossible, and he is awfully immovable, you know. I don't envy you the job.'

'Pour être difficile la tâche n'est que plus glorieuse,' said Mrs. Paragon, with a pleasant assurance of her powers of carrying her way; 'you will see I shall manage him.' And she was as good as her word.

Next morning Mrs. Paragon found Masterly alone in the breakfast-room before the rest of the party had assembled, and confided to him with a gleeful audacity the project which she and Mr. Chichele had concocted the night before. 'We are going on an expedition to the Upper Ranges for a week. We shall leave dull care, debts, duty, dotage, dearly beloved darlings of husbands, and all the other troublesome Ds. behind us, and amuse each other for a week with talking philosophy and looking at the world, like St. Simon Stylites, from a pinnacle.'

'And, amongst the other Ds., how about despatch-boxes and determined demons of Secretaries ?' asked Masterly.

'Of course *you* are to come,' said his companion; 'we could not possibly do without you—you, and as many clerks and red boxes as you please.'

'My dear Mrs. Paragon,' said Masterly, 'it is simply out of the question. I can't possibly come, nor can Mr. Chichele; what can he have been dreaming of ?'

'Of fair women,' said Mrs. Paragon, 'and other nice persuasive things. Now, Mr. Masterly, don't be disagreeable, please—but come, like a good creature.'

'A good creature! Mrs. Paragon,' cried the other, taking off his spectacles and wiping them with an air of determination; 'don't good creature me. Weave your spells for amiable, enthusiastic weaklings like Ambrose. But, seriously, it is out of the question. Neither of us can go. Mr. Chichele is in frightful arrears as it is— about ten big things all wanting immediate disposal. I can't get a stroke of work out of him.'

'You are a perfect tyrant; we will incite him to rebellion—go we must and shall.'

'Temptress!' cried Masterly, throwing himself into an attitude of deprecation:

> ' "Thou hast metamorphosed me,
> Made me forget my studies, lose my time,
> War with good counsel (the Governor-General's), set the world at
>   naught,
> Made wit with musings weak,"

and generally played the deuce with me. No; I can't and won't. This very morning the Government of India has been telegraphing for an answer about our Hills railway.'

'Telegraph back to say that you have gone to the hills to look at it.'

'Sir Theophilus Prance's project is waiting for ours. He will be very angry.'

'Sir Theophilus Prance!' said Mrs. Paragon, with a seductive pout; 'tell him you have called a mass meeting to consider it, and mean to settle the question of its advisability by universal suffrage of Cœrulean peasants. But come now, do *please*, there's a good creature.'

'Will you promise to call me a good creature every day?' said her companion.

'Twice a day, three times a day, and all day long,' said the enchantress; 'only come.'

'Well,' said Masterly, 'it is very wrong; I shall be as dull as ditch water and as cross as two sticks.'

'Only come,' said the triumphant Mrs. Paragon, 'and I will keep you as sweet as sugar; and then, I must tell you, the whole thing is to be very intellectual.'

'Intellectual!' cried Masterly; 'then I certainly won't come.'

'Yes,' said Mrs. Paragon, recalling the terms of Chichele's invitation with a wild inaccuracy, which was her especial forte; 'we are to sit on a hill retired, and discuss fate, foreknowledge, and free trade, like the people in Milton.'

It was Mrs. Paragon's foible to appropriate every phrase which pleased her ear, without in the least understanding it, and her fate, accordingly, to achieve blunders which would have done honour to Mrs. Malaprop. Her friends took these occasional slips as a matter of course.

'Ah!' said Masterly, 'suggestive topics indeed! all the same free trade had not been invented when Milton's fallen angels had their symposia.'

'But lovely woman had,' said Mrs. Paragon, with a

blush at her mistake, which more than atoned for it.
'Anyhow, we are to have a small, private debating
Society all to ourselves, and as I regard argument as my
forte, I look forward to it immensely. I am burning
to convince you.'

'The logic of beauty is always irresistible,' said
Masterly; 'I suppose you must have your way.'

'You are a dear creature,' said Mrs. Paragon, radiant
with success; and then the rest of the party came in
to breakfast.

'That is *once*,' said Masterly, as he took his seat by
Mrs. Paragon; 'remember it is to be three times a
day for the next fortnight.'

Mrs. Paragon beamed him a whole volume of 'dear
creatures' out of her sweet blue eyes, and settled herself to breakfast with the agreeable sensation of having
already done a very good day's work.

CHAPTER XXXI

A HILL CONCLAVE

IIE has consented!' Mrs. Paragon, blushing joyously, informed Chichele, as, a minute or two afterwards, he came in and took the vacant seat beside her; 'now talk to me about diplomacy!'

'Venus Victrix!' said Chichele, 'I had no idea he was so weak-minded. What is this, Masterly, that you and Mrs. Paragon have been plotting against my vows of diligence? When a man's own secretary betrays him into picnics, Lady Miranda, what is the good of one's vows of assiduity? My dear Masterly, I had no idea you were so unprincipled.'

'The woman that thou gavest me, sir,' said Masterly; 'when a governor, Lady Miranda, besets his secretary's path with lovely woman, what is the good of one's well-known devotion to duty and determination of character? I confess to being completely demoralised.'

'Not at all,' said Mrs. Paragon; 'self-surrender is the keystone of morality. Besides, as I told you, we are to be extremely industrious, and settle all the great unsettled questions of the day, sitting on a hill retired, like the people in *Paradise Lost*.'

'But I bar theology,' said Brownlow, who came in from the garden with a volume under his arm; 'please to remember that a theological discussion is fit employment only for fallen spirits in torment——'

'Or a Scotchman in his kirk,' said Chichele,—'though, by the way, that comes, so far as I am concerned, to pretty much the same thing.'

'Just let me read you,' said Brownlow, 'a good story I came upon in my Lecky this morning. Once upon a time, you must know, in the reign of George the Second, there was a Mr. Francis Hutchinson, who was Professor of Moral Philosophy somewhere or other, and had a turn for liberal ideas. Well, in his youth the unfortunate man came home for a holiday and was invited to occupy his father's pulpit, and, naturally, threw his audience into moral convulsions. "Your silly son Frank," one of the elders said, "has fash'd a' the congregation wi' his idle cackle; for he has been babbling this 'oor aboot a gude and benevolent God, and that the souls of the heathen themselves will gang to heaven if they follow the licht of their ain consciences. Not a word does the daft boy ken, speer, nor say, aboot the gude comfortable doctrines of election, reprobation, original sin and faith. Hoot man, awa' with sic a fellow."

'Gude comfortable doctrines, indeed!' cried Chichele. 'Well, we'll have none of them at Devi Shola, except, perhaps, a little original sin to season our virtue, and preserve it from the flatness of monotony.'

'And one point of faith,' said Masterly, 'which shall be *totius mundi ac ecclesiæ:* we all believe devoutly in Mrs. Paragon. But what tremendous fellows those Scotchmen are. I have a good story about one. He was boasting that Scotch apples were far superior to American.'

'Come, come!' some one said, 'you don't really mean to say that!'

'I do,' said the Scotchman, 'but I must premeese that I like them soor and hard.'

'Ah!' said Chichele, 'and that is how they like their theology too, "soor and hard." I remember, the last time I was in Scotland, asking a comely young housewife, who was petting her baby with a tender air, what was the difference between her religion and that of half a dozen conventicles which, along with the public-houses, monopolised the main street of the village. "There's just nae difference, that I ken on," she said good-naturedly, "except that we shall be saved and they will be damned." But about this expedition to the Shola, I shall insist on real hard work. Lady Miranda will be busy with her book and her sketching, and will, no doubt, require Masterly's continuous assistance. So I shall have all his work to do as well as my own. Besides, I am going to read Dante with Miss Rashleigh. But we must have some regular discussions. Mrs. Paragon has already promised me a speech.'

'Yes, and I am polishing it up in private,' said Mrs. Paragon; 'my peroration will be lovely—prepare for rapture.'

'I do not suppose we shall be touched, even by Mrs. Paragon,' said Masterly; 'not even her persuasive lips will melt our unromantic hearts—ours is an iron age. A century ago people were far more demonstrative. I was reading, somewhere, the other day, that when Sheridan finished his speech on the Begum charge, he was greeted by all his friends throwing themselves on his neck in raptures of joy, and Burke caught him in his arms as he sat down.'

'Well,' said Mrs. Paragon, 'I wonder whether any one will catch me in their arms when I sit down at the conclusion of my speech. Mr. Ambrose, I know I may depend on you, *faute de mieux*. But what a phlegmatic age ours is! and why is everybody so horribly un-demonstrative?'

'But we do not mean to be undemonstrative at all,' said Masterly; 'I already feel an inward, anticipatory stirring of emotion, and, if any one is permitted to catch you, Mrs. Paragon, as you close, the privilege will be mine. It is always done by the Chief-secretary: a mere boy like Ambrose could not be trusted to do it properly, and it would be a breach of etiquette.'

'It will be into *my* arms, if into any one's,' said Chichele authoritatively, 'that Mrs. Paragon will fall. Masterly is too impassioned for such an experience. He would be thinking about it afterwards, and I should get no work out of him for a week. But I am very cross this morning. Lord Flake, who was here for a fortnight last year, has been making a speech about India in the House of Lords and has called us all Proconsuls. Why, on earth, if a man has the bad luck to be exiled to India, should people aggravate his miseries by calling him a proconsul?'

One of Mrs. Paragon's strong points was a lovely pout, with which she frequently emphasised her observations. She made use of it on the present occasion.

'A proconsul!' she cried, in tones of scorn, 'a word that—like prig, prim, prude, propriety, and a quantity more—justifies a pet theory of mine that all things that begin with PR are objectionable.'

'What do you say to Prince of Wales?' asked Ambrose.

· This was a telling stroke, for that royal personage had smiled upon Mrs. Paragon, had sent for her to be introduced to him at a Cœrulean Ball, had danced a valse with her, and taken her for a walk in the verandah. The recollection of that valse and that walk had made her supremely happy for a lifetime, and people who wished to conciliate Mrs. Paragon made a point of referring to the incident whenever occasion allowed.

'He,' she now answered with a becoming blush, 'is the brilliant exception which proves the rule, and, if it comes to that, what do you say to Sir Theophilus Prance?'

'Ha! thou hast me there!' said Chichele; 'that

thrust is a settler!   I give up the PR's.   Then there is
the prize ring we have forgotten.'

'Here is mine,' said Mrs. Paragon, showing Ambrose
the third finger of a very pretty hand, where a gold hoop
lay hid among a number of more striking ornaments,
'and by the way, my lord and master is coming up to-
morrow.'

CHAPTER XXXII

'The Gods are just, and of our pleasant vices
Make instruments to plague us.'

IF Ambrose occasionally made official blunders he had the excuse of domestic troubles, which were now gathering thick around him. Existence had begun to be something too perplexed and grievous for even his light-heartedness to bear up against with equanimity. His home life was increasingly unhappy. His efforts to make it otherwise were disastrously unsuccessful. He was conscious of a stinging sensation that his wife despised him. Camilla, on her part, was making equally strenuous and equally ineffectual struggles to crush down a growing contempt, which day by day it became less possible to ignore. So their intercourse became constrained, self-conscious, less and less pleasurable. Try as he would, Philip could not feel at ease with his wife. His mirth died away when they were together; there was no longer the easy flow of familiar chat; he found himself, sometimes, wondering how it was that once he had found her society full of the

most enjoyable repose, the most invigorating and
delightful excitement. Those happy days were as
completely gone as though they had belonged to some
other being or some former existence. Nor was his
home the only place where Philip felt uncomfortable
and ill at ease. General Rashleigh treated him with
a haughty politeness, which contrasted disagreeably
enough with the *bonhomie* of former days. Miss
Rashleigh, who seemed, at first, more likely than the
rest to be indulgent, was completely estranged. She
had told him, in so many words, that she scorned him as
a traitor. She and Camilla were the closest friends, and
Miss Rashleigh was, Ambrose knew, continually coming
to spend long days with his wife when he was away at
his office. Camilla never referred to these visits, and
Philip blushed to think what was the cause of her
silence. The two women, no doubt, compared their
experiences, and agreed in condemning the part which
he had played in each. The fact that their condem-
nation was silent made it none the less bitter. It would
have been better to be openly vituperated than thus
secretly despised. No man's fortitude is proof against
polite contempt, and Philip found very little fortitude
at his command. No one was angry with him; no one
was rude. The Rashleighs made no sort of grievance.
Miss Rashleigh met him with an unconcern that he
felt to be absolutely unfeeling. She could never then,
after all, have cared a straw about him. In every
one's demeanour alike, Philip read the damning verdict,
that he had forfeited esteem. He was a weak creature,

whose failures could excite neither surprise nor indignation.   He had behaved badly, dishonourably ; no one was interested in proclaiming his bad and dishonourable behaviour.   Consideration to his wife, perhaps even kindliness to himself, led to its being left *sub silentio;* but the horrid fact was there all the same, and was continually giving unwelcome hints of its existence.   Mr. Chichele, Philip felt positive, had come to know of what had taken place; he had dropped the pleasant familiarity of old days, and was dry, curt, and almost discourteous in his official communications.   He cut about poor Ambrose's nicely - written drafts remorselessly, and found fault with his secretariat notes with as little compunction as a critical schoolmaster with the tasks of a careless pupil.   On the other hand, his behaviour both to Camilla and Miss Rashleigh was something more than polite.   With Camilla he was on terms of friendly and confidential intimacy, and seemed for ever on the look-out for something that he could do to please her.   To Florence Rashleigh he showed a chivalrous kindness, which implied the existence of something which especially demanded consideration, and which contrasted, too markedly to escape attention, with the good-natured ease of Chichele's behaviour to most of the young ladies who enjoyed his hospitality.   Ambrose could not but suspect the cause.   Chichele considered her to have been badly treated, and his sympathy with her wrongs expressed itself in more than ordinary courtesy.   Sometimes, too, Chichele would say things that stung Philip like the lash of a whip.   One evening, for instance, by way of breaking the formality of a dull dinner, they played at children's games.

'Mineral!' some one had cried, throwing a hand-kerchief to Ambrose.

'A woman's heart!' Philip had cried—'the hardest sort of rock at present known.'

'That is why young men are so fond of trying to break them,' Chichele had observed, with sententious emphasis.

Was this an accident and unmeaning, or an intentional sneer? Philip could ask no one else, and did not dare to ask himself. Meanwhile he began to feel a disagreeable sensation of being an outsider at the gatherings in Chichele's drawing-room, and to like Chichele himself a good deal less than he had at first. Philip's conscience, aided by these subtle indications of public opinion, became distressingly self-assertive. He had generally been able to silence its upbraidings. Somehow he could do so no longer. Nor were his domestic and social grievances the only things that plagued him. His money affairs were rapidly verging to a crisis. He had plunged with half-desperate recklessness into the Muddapollium gold project. There had been brilliant reports, dazzling results of experimental crushings, and all parties concerned had imagined themselves about to become millionaires. Philip had been unable to resist the delicious chance of sudden wealth, and ignoring the official rule, which forbade his having any speculation in the province, had committed himself, in the name of one of his native creditors, to the brilliant undertaking. In various

small ways his position enabled him to smooth the way
for the promoters of the infant project. There were
questions connected with the concession from the State
and the royalty to be paid which might have been
troublesome had not a friendly hand at the Secretariat
pushed matters on, and gently put difficulties on one
side. No one of those around him had a farthing's
interest in the scheme or a suspicion of Philip's interest
in it, and his official recommendations passed. without
scrutiny or comment. The technical advisers of the
Government thought badly of the prospects of the
scheme and treated the chance of finding gold in any
paying quantities as chimerical. The ground showed
symptoms of having been carefully worked out before,
and had been abandoned probably on the search ceasing
to be remunerative. Modern appliances might possibly enable the work to be carried on again at a
profit, but it was an absolute guess. The odds were
against it. The difficulties of climate, carriage, water,
and labour were enormous; the expenditure must
in any case be most serious. On the whole the
Cœrulean authorities took a discouraging view of the
Muddapollium gold-fields, and were inclined to treat
the concessionaries with indulgence. The concessionaries, however, had grounds of confidence about which
the Government knew nothing, but of which Philip,
through his native friends, became aware. The brisk
gentleman, hailing from Australia, confident in his
vast mining experience, had again been over the
ground, and collected specimens of the quartz, which

showed that, after making every possible allowance, the undertaking could not fail to be a very Pactolus to all who had the good luck to dip their fingers in it. Then the contract was signed; in a month or two there were some public crushings of the material collected, and hope was converted into a golden certainty. There was ocular demonstration that the Muddapollium quartz was exceptionally rich in the precious ore. Everybody was convinced, except, perhaps, the Government mineralogist, who shook his head and said, *Tant pis pour les faits*. The newspapers wrote with generous enthusiasm. The probable effects of the discovery on the labour market, on general prices, on the rate of Exchange, were eagerly discussed. The news was telegraphed to London, and the Muddapollium shares rushed to a premium. A hundred per cent to-day, a hundred and fifty the next; where was it to stop?

'Suppose,' suggested Philip's native friend, 'your Highness were to sell. You have made a magnificent investment; your shares have trebled in value. At their present price they would about realise the amount which your Highness has done me the favour of making use of from his humble servant's treasury: its return just now would be a matter of convenience. I am a poor man. I crave only your Highness's favour, so often shown me. You are my protector. The market is at its top. I advise you to sell.'

'Sell!' cried Philip in indignation, 'and throw away my good luck, in a fit of cowardice, just as it is dropping into my hands. Why, Palaveram, you are not afraid, are you?'

'No,' said the native, quietly; 'I have nothing to be afraid about. I telegraphed to realise yesterday, and I have just heard of the sale at a hundred and forty. Take my advice and do the same; sell while you can.'

'You know something?' Philip cried.

'I?' said his visitor; 'God forbid; but it is a general rule of business, when you have made a good profit, to take it and clear out. Do so now.'

'Thank you for your advice,' said Philip; 'why on earth should one throw away a good thing when one has got it?'

'Your Highness is master—be it as you please,' said the native, bowing himself obsequiously from his debtor's presence. But he was evidently uneasy, and next morning came again. 'Has your Highness realised?' he asked, anxiously.

'No,' said Philip, by this time beginning to get frightened; 'do you really think I had better?'

'I told you yesterday,' said the native, with a mental ejaculation at the stolidity of his interlocutor—'I told you that I had sold my own; what more do you want? Sell, sell, without a day's delay.'

'A day's delay?' said Philip, his cheeks bloodless with a sudden apprehension; 'what is the matter?'

'Nothing is the matter,' said his visitor, with perfect composure; 'but why procrastinate?'

'Well,' said Philip, 'to please you, Palaveram, I will realise.'

The old native, despite himself, gave a sigh of relief.

'Your Highness will please himself of course,' he said, as he bowed himself out of Ambrose's study.

Philip could not make up his mind to telegraph that day. It was cruel to part with this darling project. If he sold now, indeed, he would be free of his most important creditor; but what a falling-off from the pleasant dreams, in which he had for so long been indulging, of a perennial Pactolus. So he held his hand. It was that greedy, ungrateful scoundrel's anxiety to be paid, regardless of Philip's interest. He would not be bullied or frightened. Next morning, when he opened his newspaper, the first thing that greeted his eye was a London telegram announcing that a confederacy of dissatisfied shareholders had sent out a competent inspector to Muddapollium on their own behalf; that his report was disastrous; that there had been a stormy meeting, fierce recriminations, an exposure; and that the Muddapollium gold shares were nowhere. The bubble had burst, and with it Philip's last chance of financial rehabilitation was gone. A crash was inevitable.

CHAPTER XXXIII

BROWNLOW TAKES A HOLIDAY

*'We are born to do benefits ; and what better or properer can we call
our own than the riches of our friends ?'—Timon of Athens.*

BROWNLOW had now thoroughly mastered the question
of the Hill Railway, and set about enjoying himself
with characteristic vehemence. He had all the figures
at his fingers' ends, had made up his mind as to the
terms on which his firm would undertake the contract,
and had sent down the plans and estimates to be worked
out in detail in a surveyor's office at Windipatam. In
the meantime he had nothing on his mind, and nothing
to do but to read novels and reviews, make an occasional onslaught on Chichele's weekly pile of English
papers, lounge about the garden in the mornings, ride
over the mountains with the ladies in the afternoon, and
sit up, far into the night, deep in long, pleasant chats
with Chichele over the library fire. Both men were
delighted to have finished with the railway—Brownlow,
because he had done all the thinking and asking about
it which he felt to be necessary, and saw his way clearly
to a project which promised to be interesting and pro-

fitable; Chichele, because he was heartily sick of a subject which, the more he studied it, the greater depths of puzzledom and worry did it disclose. Anyhow it was pleasant to the two men to live over some of their young times once again, and wake up, in friendly talk, recollections which had been dormant for years and were fast fading into obscurity. They were like two boys together, and lapsed into a mood of boyish fun, which the one had forgotten in officialdom and the other in hard work. They went off, by themselves, on a bear-shooting expedition, and came back, in the best of spirits, with jokes at each other's misses, and merriment, the mellow outcome of good fellowship. Brownlow declared that when he asked the head Shikaree how Chichele had been shooting, that functionary had diplomatically replied that 'the Lord sahib had shot magnificently, but God was merciful to the bears.'

'That man is a born courtier,' he said, 'and ought to have been a Lord Chamberlain. Fancy an English gamekeeper achieving such adroitness.'

Chichele was delighted once more to have a companion.

'It is such a comfort, you know,' he said to Lady Miranda, 'to have some one who does not call one "Sir," does not want an appointment or a scolding, and who has no compunction in contradicting one.'

'Ah!' said Lady Miranda, 'George is great at contradiction; he has no compunction in contradicting any one—even his wife.'

'Ungrateful woman!' said Brownlow; 'have not I

sacrificed all my most cherished convictions in political
economy on the altar of domestic love?—*Amicior veritas,
amicissima conjux.*'

'Besides,' said Chichele, 'what would life be worth
without contradiction ?

> ' " Discourse may want an animated 'No,'
>   To brush its surface and to make it flow." '

'Yes,' said Mrs. Paragon ; 'but it is one of those
tonics of which a little goes a long way, like quinine.
By the way, that is, no doubt, one of the advantages of
matrimony; you secure a never-failing supply of contradiction.'

'Yes,' said Chichele; 'and that accounts for husbands and wives being so tremendously attached.   Did
you hear of the touching answer a Cœrulean husband
sent the other day to his wife, when she proposed to
rejoin him from England?—"My love," he wrote, "I
have not yet got over the shock of our last separation."'

'That was a polite form of "an animated No," I suppose,' said Mrs. Paragon.   'For my part I consider every
form of contradiction detestable.'

'And that,' said Masterly, 'is why no one ever has
the heart to contradict Mrs. Paragon.'

'You were very good about coming here, I admit,'
said the lady with a gracious smile, 'and you have your
reward.   See how you are enjoying it.'

'Of course,' cried Masterly, throwing himself into an
attitude of mock heroics—

> ' " Without the smile from partial beauty won,
>   Oh, what were man ?   A world without its fun." '

'Is it really that?' said Mrs. Paragon, whom long experience had rendered distrustful of Masterly's quotations, 'or are you turning something with nonsense as usual?'

'Well,' said Masterly, 'it is not quite right; it should be "a child without its bun"; it's a beautiful simile, is it not? one of Campbell's finest; poor little bunless child; poor womanless humanity! Don't you feel how touching it is?'

'No,' said Mrs. Paragon; 'hot and cross are the only qualities I associate with buns; and as I am always cool and good-natured, I repudiate the insinuation.'

'Think of Bath buns!' cried Masterly, with an air of rapture; 'I used to be tremendously fond of them when I was a little boy—glazed and sticky, with a sugar plum on the top. The passion gave way before the vicissitudes of my first attachment; that is why I feel the force of the simile. I refuse to think of a bunless child or of a world without Mrs. Paragon.'

'That is all very well,' said that lady, 'but men are hard-hearted monsters. I came only yesterday on a story of an economical French gentleman who had the misfortune to lose three wives, and commemorated the virtues of all three and his own misfortunes in a single tablet, in which he described the dear departed ones as " triple source d'amer regret."'

'That reminds me,' said Montem, ' of a countryman of mine whose wife was, as he thought, needlessly protracting her last moments by various household direc-

tions. "Dinna fash yoursel', my gudewoman," he said,
"but get on with the deein'."'

Meanwhile the clouds were gathering thick about
poor Ambrose. The gold-mine project was going from
one abysmal depth to another. The English shareholders, fierce with disappointed hopes, had broken out
into vindictiveness, and were insisting on a rigorous in-
vestigation. A great deal of money had been spent in
floating the company. Into whose hands had it gone?
Who was responsible for the initiation of the scheme,
the description of the property, the reports of the gold-
testing? Ambrose was not really responsible for any
of these matters, but, somehow, the responsible people
seemed to be melting away, and he felt that he was
beginning to stand alone.

The Australian gentleman, whose prophecies graced
the infancy of the company with so golden a halo,
had disappeared, in search, no doubt, of fresh fields and
pastures new in the gullibility of his species. Philip
began to realise, with disagreeable distinctness, that,
while other things had disappeared, two solid facts stood
out, hard and cold; one, that he was the author of the
prospectus, another that he, in the person of his native
creditor, had received a round sum as one of the vendors
of the property. He had had no idea of cheating any one.
In his easy-going way he had believed in the scheme,
and in Palaveram's figures. He had made sure that all
would go right. Now, however, all was going wrong,
and Ambrose found himself confronted with a set of
angry men, vexed at their own folly in having lost their

money, and looking about, with no nice discrimination, for the guilty person, on whom vengeance might be wreaked. Philip was at a loss for a new expedient to obviate, or, at any rate, to postpone the menaced catastrophe. The old sources of supply were quite dried up. His native friends were making him feel in a hundred little ways that they understood his position, and appreciated its disagreeable aspects. Palaveram still fawned and smiled and professed eternal devotion to his patron's interests; but there was in his manner something dictatorial, insolent, menacing. His abject submissiveness barely cloaked a scornful mood and an unsparing purpose. He could ruin Philip any day he pleased, and he would so please, Philip knew, on the day when, carefully weighing the cost on either side, he resolved that, on the whole, it would pay him best to wait no longer. In the meantime he was watching, with keen, hungry eyes, how matters went, and was becoming daily more anxious to have his capital safe back in his stronghold. He gave Philip to understand, with a directness which it was no longer possible to evade, that the repayment of his loan, of a portion of it, at any rate, must no longer be delayed.

'I have obligations to meet,' he said; 'I am a poor man; I shall be ruined. Your Highness will be the cause; you must prevent it; if not, I shall be driven to desperate expedients.'

'Don't talk in that way,' said Philip, to whom interviews of this order were the black moments of existence; 'every one knows that you have been rolling up lakhs of rupees for years past, and hold the market in your hand.   My debt to you is a flea-bite.'

'To your Highness, no doubt, it would be,' said the money-lender; 'all the more reason that it should be repaid when your humble servant happens to want it. I have always been surprised at your caring to borrow on the terms on which it suits a humble person like myself to lend.   Money is scarce amongst us poor folks; my current rate is, you know, eighteen per cent.   A debt grows fast.   Yours is a large and old standing one.   Anyhow I am in need of my money.'

The evil moment had come, and Ambrose stood at bay.   He knew his opponent's meaning only too well : the day of grace had closed.

'You can do what you please,' he said; 'you know perfectly well that your money is safe, and that nothing can endanger it but your own violence and precipitancy.'

'But I am in an emergency,' said the other.   'God knows, I don't know which way to turn.   I have obligations to meet.'

'Nonsense!' cried Philip; 'you know as well as I do that it is false, and, at any rate, I can do nothing.   That cursed company of yours——'

'Of mine?' cried the money-lender; 'your Highness had far better means of knowing about it than I; and you knew more; you had more to do with starting it. Who got the concession?   Who wrote the Prospectus?'

Philip turned pale in spite of himself.   He had never realised till now that he might have to stand the chief brunt of the storm which was to break upon the promoters. The prospect was appalling. His courage rose to the occasion.

'Don't try to bully or frighten me, sir,' he said; 'what is it you want?'

'My money,' said the native, with a laconic stubbornness.

'And that,' said Ambrose, 'I have told you, I cannot, at the moment, pay you.'

'It is unfortunate,' said the other; 'your Highness's note of hand must suffice. I must make shift to do the best I can with that;' and forthwith Palaveram produced a neat piece of stamped paper, on which the sum total of Philip's indebtedness up to date was inscribed, and a promise to pay it on demand to bearer, together with interest meanwhile at eighteen per cent.

Philip hated above everything being brought to book, and this, of all bringings-to-book, was the most hateful, but there was no escape. The total had swelled to inordinate proportions. In his vexation he forgot to be polite.

'Good God!' he cried, 'you do not mean to tell me that you claim all this. It is monstrous.'

'Your Highness,' said the native—calm as fate itself —'can do the sum for yourself—it is an affair of arithmetic. If you will do me the favour to peruse this account and point out any error, I shall feel obliged.'

Ambrose knew perfectly that the account would be accurate to a farthing; but his temper was hopelessly upset.

'There,' he said, as he wrote his name across the hateful document—'take it and be damned.'

'At your Highness's pleasure,' said his imperturbable visitor, as he composedly dried the writing and restored the paper to his pocket-book; 'I may take my leave?' and so the Chetty bowed himself out.

Then, as troubles of this sort always march, not alone but in battalions, before Philip's equanimity had recovered from the shock of his disagreeable interview, there came a communication from the Board of Directors in England to say that, with a view to defraying the costs of winding up the company, all arrears on calls must be paid up forthwith, and a further call be made on all shares not paid in full. Defaulters should be sued at once. Philip's obligations, in both respects, were pretty heavy; and, heavy or light, he was utterly without the means of meeting them. At the same time delay was no longer possible. He racked his brains, and at last, in his despair, he bethought him of the expedient of having recourse to the English millionaire. Repulsive as the idea was at first, Philip gradually accustomed himself to think of it as necessary and feasible. He had become great friends with Brownlow, and had spent many hours working with him over the plans of the railway. Brownlow had been pleased with his quickness, resource, good humour, and good sense.

'You have been of great use to me,' he had said to him on one occasion, 'and I am very much obliged. You must tell me if ever I can be of use to you.' Nor was this the only ground of Philip's hope. Brownlow evidently shared Chichele's admiration of Camilla, and lost no opportunity of being polite to her. Camilla, too, had been interested in Brownlow, the only man of business she had ever known. She had been impressed with his vigorous, fertile, suggestive mind—his breadth of view, his practical, courageous way of looking at things, his varied experience. The two had often fallen to each other's lot for the afternoon ride, and both had been well content with the arrangement. Between Camilla and Lady Miranda the warmest friendship had, it was obvious, been established. Was there anything wrong or dishonourable, Philip asked himself, in applying to a friend such as Brownlow, who happened to have an indefinite supply of ready money at his disposal, to help him out of a scrape, into which any man might fall, through no fault of his, and which made a little money-help for the moment indispensable? Philip assured himself that there was not; yet he disliked and even dreaded the process of putting his design into actual execution. Once or twice, as he sat smoking with Brownlow, the occasion for doing so seemed to have arrived, and Philip had nerved himself for the task; but he had been unable to screw his courage to the sticking point, and had ignominiously deferred the disagreeable effort. 'That which we would, we should do while we would,' and Philip more and more regretted that he had not accomplished performance, while he was in the first flush of satisfaction with the new idea. At last in desperation he forced himself to speak.

'I am going,' he said, 'to take advantage of your

offer to help me sooner than you can have expected—
sooner than I expected a week or two ago. I have got
into a money trouble about a wretched company which
I was fool enough to touch, and which has gone all to
pieces. I am called upon to pay up a large sum immediately. If I do not, I shall be disgraced, and, I
suppose, lose my appointment. I am certain I can
arrange for it within the next few months, and meantime, I can pledge an insurance policy on my life. Will
you lend me £1000?   It will be the greatest favour you
could do me.'

Brownlow asked two or three questions which gave
Philip the sensation of flooding him and his affairs with
remorseless light, and putting his predicament more
clearly, and, at the same time, more disagreeably than
he would have thought possible. He was in no position, however, to decline interrogation, and his confession was frank and full.   Brownlow gave a long whistle,
and began striding up and down the room, as he did
when specially excited.

'You are in a deuce of a mess,' he said, halting
opposite Phil in the course of one of his promenades,
and confronting him with a scrutinising look which
seemed to its victim to go through and through him.

'I know,' said Philip ; 'that is why I am asking you
to help me.'

'Well,' said Brownlow, 'I must think about it : I
will tell you to-morrow.' In the meantime, as he
usually did when events became puzzling, he consulted
his wife.

'I have had the most extraordinary request from Philip Ambrose,' he told her; 'what do you think? The loan of £1000. He has got himself hopelessly embarrassed. He is a weak, blundering, confused fellow, not too scrupulous, easily misled and sure to come to grief. The worst of it is that he says that his present trouble, if he cannot get out of it, will lose him his appointment, and ruin his career.'

'And Camilla?' cried Lady Miranda, springing up with consternation written on her bloodless face.

'Ay,' said her husband, 'there is the rub, Miranda, is it not? It is a bad business. What right on earth has a man in Ambrose's position to be dabbling in companies and running into debt? It is inexcusable.'

'Of course,' said Lady Miranda, 'but that will not rescue Camilla. What must we do?'

It was at moments like this that Brownlow always found his wife completely irresistible; and on the present occasion he felt little inclined for resistance. He sat silent now, for a few seconds, watching with delight the childlike loveliness of her face, saddened now by anxiety for her friend, and quickened by a strong impulse of sympathy into that higher beauty which beautiful souls alone possess.

'What must we do, Miranda?' he said at last; 'why, rescue her and him too, if you wish it: but it will be no good. He is a bad horse, and will fall at the next fence, if we get him over this one.'

'You are the best and dearest and kindest husband in the world!' cried Miranda, with an embrace that

Brownlow, it may be believed, thought cheap at a thousand pounds ; 'it would be heartbreaking to leave Camilla in trouble, would it not ? '

'She has trouble before her, poor woman, I am afraid,' said Brownlow ; 'it is something that we can stave it off for the present.'

The next morning Ambrose got his cheque and Brownlow the policy of insurance.

' Of course you are quite free to pledge it ! ' he said, with one of his disagreeably scrutinising looks as he took the document.

' Of course,' said Philip, ' and I can never thank you enough.'

So Philip went away with his £1000 and a heavy heart. The necessity of the moment had been met ; but at what a cost, and what further troubles remained behind !

How was he to raise funds to repay Brownlow ? How was he to arrange with his native creditors ? How wipe himself clean of the contamination of this hateful company ? There was another horrid reflection, moreover, in connection with Brownlow's debt, namely, that, though the insurance policy was his, in one sense, he had, he knew, no right to pledge it. Before his marriage he had promised Sir Marmaduke to insure his life. He had put off doing so too long, but he had done it at last : no legal obligation, so far as the policy showed, restrained him from making temporary use of it : none the less it was wrong. Ambrose's conscience smote him when he thought that it was really Camilla's

property that he was pledging.   He was breaking faith
with Sir Marmaduke; he was defrauding his wife; he
had told Brownlow, to all intents and purposes, a lie;
but it was necessary.

To what horrid straits do the emergencies of life
conduct one, and what acute moral discomfort do they
entail !   Ambrose felt that Fortune, as usual, was
treating him with undeserved harshness.

Meanwhile he got a few days' leave, and pleading
an excuse to his wife, the lameness of which warned
Camilla against further inquiry, went off to Windipatam
to see what his personal presence could do towards
bringing the crisis within supportable limits.

CHAPTER XXXIV

CAMILLA IN TROUBLE

'There is a forsaking which still sits at the same board and lies on
the same couch with the forsaken soul, withering it more by
unloving proximity.'

WHEN, a few mornings afterwards, Lady Miranda went
to pay her accustomed visit to Camilla, she found her
in the depths of low spirits. The fact was that things
had being going badly with Camilla, and Philip's departure—justified by a transparently false pretext—had
produced a sort of crisis. She knew nothing about his
journey except that the true cause was, for some
reason, concealed from her. A woman's natural
jealousy suggested what the cause might be. Camilla
was shocked to find how easy it was to her to believe
that she had reason to be jealous. At one time she
would have scouted the idea as a degradation. Now,
her husband had accustomed her to the idea of a
possible infidelity,—an infidelity scarcely the less grievous, because it would not, probably, go farther than
homage paid lightly at the shrine of whoever happened
to be the favourite of the moment. But to Camilla's

serious, devoted nature, her husband's butterfly mood of hovering over every flower whose beauty caught his eye seemed a sort of profanation of the very idea of love. It shocked her moral fastidiousness to the core. It filled her with a horror, half-sad, half-contemptuous. It was a wrong and humiliation at the precise point of one's being, where nerves are most sensitive, where love feels and fears the most, where tenderness shudders at the slightest unsympathetic touch. Jealousy in such a woman's mind does not stimulate affection : more probably it strikes a mortal wound. Camilla was too proud to say a word—too conscious, perhaps, how useless, on such a subject, any spoken word must be. None the less this side of her husband's character had been a constant grievance—had helped, more perhaps than anything, to the discovery that they were fatally estranged in taste, feeling, and the theory of life. And now things had come to a critical point. Philip had gone away with a falsehood on his lips—for what, for whom ?

All a woman's fear—all a woman's jealousy, sprang to life in Camilla's mind, as little to be ignored as the flame, kindled among congenial materials, which glows and mounts, spreads and rages more fiercely as each new vantage point is carried. Camilla was more utterly wretched than ever in her life before. She had loved her husband; she loved him still; but each new step in life with him seemed only to bring her upon something that was unlovable. Lady Miranda saw at once that Camilla was perturbed.

'Something is the matter!' she said, not dropping her friend's hand; 'why do you look like that?'

'Nothing is the matter!' said Camilla, 'except the things which are always the matter, and which have to be endured as best one can. But did I look solemn? It was an accident. The truth is that I have many anxieties.'

'I know,' said Lady Miranda; 'well, the money ones are at an end, I hope?'

'The money ones!' cried Camilla in astonishment; 'what do you mean? Pray, tell me.'

Lady Miranda perceived her mistake, but too late to retract it. An explanation was inevitable.

'Did you not know?' she said; 'I am afraid I ought not to have spoken.'

'Indeed, indeed, you ought,' said the other, bitterly; 'tell me everything. You will do me good. To tell the truth, I have been making myself miserable about my husband. Something is being hidden from me, and I am frightened. It will be a relief to know the truth: tell me what anxieties you mean?'

'I have got into the most dreadful scrape I can see,' said Lady Miranda; 'but it had not occurred to me that you might not have heard of it.'

'Only tell me,' said Camilla; 'you little know what a comfort it will be to me.'

'I have alarmed you for nothing, dear Camilla,' her visitor said; 'it was nothing of the least importance. Your husband happened to be in want of a little help in the way of money. George was delighted to have it at command, and to be able to lend it to him without inconvenience. It is one of the pleasures of his being so absurdly rich that he is able to do such things for his friends; and he constantly does them. He happened to tell me, and I, chatterbox as I am, have made mischief, I see, in telling you. Let us consider it unsaid and forget all about it.'

It was in vain that Lady Miranda tried to make light of the matter. Her own heart told her that it was not to be made light of; and, if it had not told her, Camilla's grave look would have convinced her that the secret, which she had allowed to escape, was a serious one.

'I fear that I have hurt you, dear,' she said, laying her hand kindly on Miranda's, and looking at her with inquiring, tender eyes; 'tell me that I have not.'

'You could never hurt me,' said Camilla; 'but there are things in life that hurt one more perhaps than they should. As to this trouble, I should have learnt it sooner or later in any case. Philip went off in such a hurry that I suppose he had no time to tell me. Do you know why he has gone?'

'About the company, I suppose,' said Lady Miranda.

'The company?' said Camilla with a blank look, and more than ever in the dark. 'What company is that?'

Lady Miranda told her what she knew, and Camilla's face grew graver and more anxious as each new detail came to light. There had been a great deal that was disagreeable in the papers about the Muddapollium

Mines. Some high officials were hinted at as responsible for the ill-considered project, the floating of the company and the loss which the public had sustained. It had never occurred to Camilla that her husband could be personally concerned. Now the horrid possibility—probability—near at hand—was confronting her. For the first time in her life Camilla found herself face to face with danger, trouble, and humiliation. She got up without a word and walked to the window, and stood there, looking out at the clouds that were chasing each other across the mountain's brow in front. It was all that she could do to avoid a complete breakdown. Her heart was beating wildly. Lady Miranda followed her, and was shocked to see her bloodless cheek and air of despair.

'Do not look like that, you dearest creature!' she said, as she led Camilla back to the sofa; 'nothing that has happened can be bad enough for that.'

'Can it not?' said the other; 'I wish I could be sure of that. Has it ever happened to you, Lady Miranda, to feel degraded?'

'Where is the degradation?' cried Lady Miranda. 'Why should not one's friends help one? George is continually doing that sort of thing for one friend or another. Besides, there is really nothing in what he has done for your husband—not even a risk—for Mr. Ambrose has given him a policy, or something, by way of security.'

'A policy?' asked Camilla, feeling as if she was sinking from one depth to another.

'Yes,' said Lady Miranda; 'a policy of insurance. It was lying on my husband's table this morning, and he told me what it was. It makes the debt quite safe.'

'That is a comfort at any rate,' said Camilla.

She understood, however, what her husband had done, and finally dethroned him. This was the last touch. His deposition was complete. He had concealed everything from her. He had mistrusted her, deceived her, defrauded her. He had brought her close to dishonour. This was the end of her aspirations for a noble life—her dream of living above the ordinary level of human infirmity and meanness—her cravings for an ideal existence whose aims should be lofty, whose motives pure and noble, and in which the perfect confidence of a happy marriage should be merely one item in the general total of perfection. All the fair edifice lay crumbling in the dust—hopelessly, irremediably shattered. The first pang of repugnance and indignation was quickened by a dreadful suspicion that she had unwittingly been her husband's tool and had assisted in his plan. She had become very intimate with Brownlow. His liking for her had been undisguised. She had been pleased with it, and had liked him in return. The two had become great friends. It had occurred to Camilla sometimes that her husband greatly approved of this friendship, and had seemed to encourage her into greater intimacy. She had not been able to understand it. Now she understood it, and the thought was full of horror. She sat by herself when Lady Miranda had left her, blushing for very shame.

Again and again the hot tears came rushing to her eyes.
A chill despair had taken possession of her soul. What
more had life to give her? The very sanctuary of her
love had been desecrated. The place where she had
garnered up her heart, what could it be to her hereafter
but a dreadful void, peopled only by disappointment
and despair. How could she ever bear to meet the
guilty one again?

CHAPTER XXXV

THE FAKIR'S ROCK

ONE of the entertainments which figured in Mrs. Paragon's programme for the party during their sojourn at the High Ranges, was an expedition to a neighbouring waterfall, which the few who had seen it talked about with rapture. They were very few, however, for it was as nearly as possible being unapproachable. Even from Chichele's camp it involved an early start, a long ride by precipitous mountain paths, and a great deal of the commissariat management, which only the skilled proficient in camp-life can venture to attempt. The natives of India find it difficult to understand the pleasure which Englishmen derive from carrying their women and their food into Nature's wildest haunts, and extemporising a banquet on the tops of mountains, the edges of precipices, or in solemn forest solitudes, where nothing but acorns and fresh water can be obtained,

for love or money, within a hundred miles. They call
a picnic the 'madman's feast,' and regard it as one
more exhibition of the unfathomable eccentricity of
the Sahibs, whom Fate has decreed to be their rulers.
If madness it were on this occasion, it was madness
with a method in it—for Mrs. Paragon's prevision had
secured that all should go smoothly, and that when
the party arrived, tired and hot, at the foot of the falls,
they should find the servants awaiting them and preparations well advanced for an excellent repast on the
green sward beneath a large banian tree which towered
majestic above the surrounding forest, and, with its
wilderness of descending branches, seemed more like a
small natural cathedral than a tree.

Cœrulean patriotism may justly be proud of this
enchanting spot. You clamber along through a dense,
primeval jungle, where an almost imperceptible path is
all the impression that human hands and feet have
achieved upon Nature's wildness. In every direction
you see nothing but infinite depths of forest, and catch
glimpses now and then of the blue atmosphere overhead through the tangled masses of foliage. The world
is far, far away; the air is alive with the multitudinous
murmur of forest life. The soil yields with noiseless
softness beneath the tread, the *débris* of a thousand
past, autumnal falls: every cranny is crowded with
sweet sylvan growth, moss or flower or tumbling
creeper; a gentle breeze, unfelt below, is stirring the
summits of the loftier trees with a peaceful, dreamy
murmur. It is the very sanctuary of Nature's great

temple   All of a sudden the traveller emerges at the foot of a stupendous face of granite.   Far overhead a tolerable river dashes over its edge into the void, loses itself in feathery spray, and forms again in a hundred cascades on the wild rocks below.   A grand roar in the air thunders above all the gentle whispers of the forest. Everywhere the ground is alive with little rivulets which, none the worse for their late adventure, are rippling peacefully down the gorge, amidst the rocks and ferns.   A little on one side a huge boulder had fallen, ages ago, so as to form a natural cave; and here a famous Fakir passes his dreamy existence, performs his simple rites, and levies an easy toll on the passer-by, whom piety or prudence constrains to improve his chances of getting his bullocks safely through the valley by a timely offering to the local deity.   A rude gong hangs in front of his abode, whose tones ring out, now and again, amid the hurlyburly of the descending waters; a little flag flutters above a humble shrine, where scattered leaves and flowers attest the recent presence of some rustic devotee : close by some smouldering embers tell of the recluse's simple repast.   Behind are the relics of a Buddhist temple and monastery— not ruins, for they were cut in solid rock; and Nature, though she has well-nigh buried them under masses of superincumbent foliage, has still, through the long centuries, failed to efface shrine, dormitory, refectory, and monastic cell.   Still the carved roof and nicely chiselled image tell of great Buddha's myth, and of long vanished generations of pious workers who toiled

and prayed and lived a saintly life in this delicious
retreat.

Far away across the valley lay Chichele's little camp,
and the tents, clustering like a flock of white pigeons on
the mountain side.

'What a place to run excursion trains to!' cried
Brownlow, as he turned the edge of his morning's thirst
with a beaker of iced soda-water; 'my dear Chichele,
this waterfall is worth two per cent on your capital, by
itself, and I am almost certain I see a lot of copper about.'

'Copper and two per cent!' cried Miranda, running
up and putting her hand to her husband's mouth;
'really, George, you are incorrigible. Listen, listen to
the water-nymphs calling to you from their pretty
nooks. What a heavenly spot it is! How I wish
Camilla could have come.'

Camilla had pleaded fatigue, and Lady Miranda,
who knew something of the state of the case, had
managed that she should not be pressed. Chichele,
always quick to catch at other people's wishes, was
easily made to understand that Camilla was not in a
mood to join in a holiday excursion. She was longing,
above everything, for solitude; nothing seemed to her,
just then, less possible of achievement than a day of
pleasure spent in public. Chichele, with many lamen-
tations, was constrained to acquiesce. 'It is a pity,' he
said; 'because Ambrose is to meet us there. I telegraphed to him yesterday to come up that way on
purpose, and to join us to-morrow at the Falls. I
thought that his wife would like it.'

Lady Miranda had told Camilla of this; but found her firmer than ever. 'Please, please get me excused,' Camilla had said, pressing her friend's hand. Lady Miranda had fully understood her mission, and faithfully performed it. Camilla had been left in peace.

The party came to a halt under the banian tree, and were soon resting in its welcome shade. Presently Ambrose emerged from the forest on the other side of the glen, and in another minute had joined them. He had been riding since early dawn, and looked all the better, Lady Miranda thought, for being several degrees less carefully adorned than usual. He was greeted with acclamations as he rode up. 'And Camilla?' he said to Lady Miranda as he shook hands with her.

His face fell when he learnt that his wife was not of the party. 'Is she not well?' he said, 'I think I had better go on to her at once.'

'It is only a headache,' said Lady Miranda; 'she will be better for a day of perfect quiet.'

'No, Ambrose,' said Chichele, 'you must wait awhile; your ponies must be dead beat; moreover, I want you to show Mr. Brownlow the way up to the top of the Falls after lunch. It is too much of a climb for me.'

'Yes,' said Mr. Brownlow; 'will you be my guide, Ambrose?'

Philip smothered his disappointment, and accepted the proffered task with a polite show of alacrity. While they were waiting, he carried off Lady Miranda for a stroll to the Buddhist cave, and immediately began to

be confidential. 'You and Mr. Brownlow,' he said,
' have been good friends to me in my time of need ; I
can never forget that or the debt of gratitude I owe
you. Now, I must tell you what good news I found
awaiting me at Windipatam. You know what a deplorable report there was of our gold-mine. I could not
understand it, for our reports were quite the other way.
Well, it seems ours were nearer the mark of the two ;
for a great mining firm in England has sent out some
one on its own account, and thinks well enough of the
affair to buy it. All is now settled ; we are to get our
purchase-money back, and something to boot. I shall
be able to repay the money part of Mr. Brownlow's
loan in a fortnight ; the other part, the kindness, can
never be repaid.'

' I am so very, very pleased,' Lady Miranda said, with
great cordiality. Phil seemed in such a nice mood
and so inclined to be confidential that she thought
the moment opportune for a little good advice. ' I
am delighted to hear of your good luck,' she said,
' but it is good luck, all the same ; is it not? just as if
you had won it at a roulette table at Monte Carlo.
Would it not be wise, Mr. Ambrose, for a man placed as
you are, to keep out of the reach of luck ? Suppose it
had turned out the other way. Think of what your
wife would feel about it.'

Ambrose's nature always responded at once to the
monitions of a charming woman who wished to do him
good. ' I know,' he said ; ' you think I need a lecture.
But I have made a vow, and recorded it in my yester-

day's letter to Camilla, never to speculate again. I may as well make my confession complete, Lady Miranda. I have been a fool in times past; but the truth is that I was desperately anxious to set myself right about money, and to save Camilla annoyance. She took our debts to heart. Some of us are so made, you know, that it costs us no pang to be a little behindhand with our bills ; we recognise it as our normal plight, and grow accustomed to it. But it distressed her, and then it began to distress me. Now, I am glad to say, it is all over, and I have promised her to be a reformed character. Mr. Brownlow and you have helped greatly to the reformation.'

'Thank you, Mr. Ambrose,' Lady Miranda answered, 'for being so frank ; you have taken a great load from my spirits. To tell the truth, I was rather unhappy about you ; I love your wife dearly, and should grieve at any incompleteness in her happiness.'

'Ah, but you shall see !' said Philip. 'These horrid money troubles have raised a sort of cloud between us. I could not bear to tell her. It would only have given her pain. But the fact of a secret is fatal, all the same. Now all is clear again, and I mean to devote myself to making her happy, and to trying to deserve her. What else ought the husband of such a wife to think about? It is an odd thing, do you know; Nature tells us secrets about ourselves at curious moments. As I rode up the mountain this morning in the silent, solemn dawn, I got into a reverie, thinking over my past life and the time of my courtship; and there came upon me a sort of revelation about Camilla. I never knew till that moment how dearly I loved her. Now I feel a sort of passionate desire to be with her again, and tell her all, and to be forgiven. Please God she may have less in future to forgive.'

Lady Miranda had never liked Philip till now. His unworthiness to be Camilla's husband had been with her a sort of acknowledged grievance, which had to be borne as best it might. Now she began to relent, and to think that Camilla's chance of happiness was not, perhaps, desperate after all.

'You have made me very happy,' she said; 'you must always think of my husband and me as your warm friends.'

Then came the sound of voices shouting across the stream. 'Come to luncheon, good people!' cried Chichele; and to lunch, accordingly, they went; and then Mrs. Paragon's efficiency as mistress of the commissariat became apparent in a repast which their long morning's ride inclined all the party to appreciate as it deserved; all the more, perhaps, because, as was her wont on such occasions, the fair mistress of the feast, having set everything in perfect trim, retired gracefully to the background, and now figured merely as an ornamental ingredient in the party, and as the member of it who enjoyed it most heartily.

Every one, however, felt the inspiring influence of the occasion and the place. How not to enjoy existence when nature is all lovely around one, and the air full of sweet, slumberous sounds, and pleasant men and women are gathered to do honour to a sylvan feast?

Philip, all the happier for having disburthened himself to Lady Miranda, was especially joyous. 'This is the way to live!' he cried; 'quite worthy of the forest of Ardennes :

> ' " This our life, exempt from public haunt,
>   Finds tongues in trees, books in the running brooks,—
>   Sermons in stones——" '

'No,' said Chichele; 'I bar all sermons except those preached by Mrs. Paragon or the flowers.'

'And the sermon that the flowers preach,' cried Philip, 'is not to be too theological!

> ' " Take an example from the roses,
>   They live on air and light and dew;
>   They do not trouble about Moses,
>   Then why, in Heaven's name, should you ? " '

'But flowers,' Masterly said, 'have a prescriptive right to take life lightly, and not to trouble their heads about anything.'

'Not even about their dresses,' said Mrs. Paragon; 'how can indifference farther go ?'

'But it is not true, all the same,' said Chichele; 'my roses, I know, want a deal of solid, dirty food, and would trouble their pretty heads very much if they had not plenty of it, besides light, air, and dew and elegant diet of that sort. As for not caring for life, depend on it, everybody and everything cares for it intensely.'

'To be sure,' said Brownlow, extracting a small invader from his plate. 'This poor beetle, who has just taken a header into my soup, would, no doubt, feel a natural pang about dying as great as any giant's. He has tried civilisation, in the form of clear mulligatawny, and, I suspect, does not like it. He shall return to nature,—damper, and no doubt sadder, for his morning's experience.'

'Do you remember,' said Masterly, 'the poor fellow whom Browning draws, with wandering, fluttering thoughts and eyes already dim with death,—his mind all in a jumble between the row of medicine vials on the table's edge and his past recollections,—yet to whose parched lips the sweet cup of life's joys seemed sweet as ever?

> ' " What is he buzzing in my ears,
>   Now that I come to die?
>   Do I view the world as a vale of tears?
>   Ah, Reverend Sir, not I ! "

'The row of bottles grows a lane,—the sweetest, dearest, most romantic ever known ; one of them is the house, where, in the top story, the dear one lived:

> ' " She left the attic there—
> By the rim of the bottle labelled ' Ether,'—
> And stole from stair to stair ;
>
> And stood by the rose-wreathed gate—Alas !
> We loved, Sir—used to meet :
> How sad and bad and mad it was :
> But then, how it was sweet." '

'Ah!' said Chichele, 'that bottle labelled " Ether " —which awaits us all.'

'But then,' said Philip, as he got up, 'meanwhile how it is sweet! Life, in a Cœrulean forest at any rate, is a delicious affair, say what people will! Come, Mr.

Brownlow, if you are ready, let us start on our expedition.'

He looked the very impersonation of enjoyment: the cloud of anxiety which had often of late darkened his brow had passed away. There was nothing there now but a triumphant sense of health, hope, high spirits and a firm grasp on the joys of existence. He was the fitting human complement to a scene where all things around seemed revelling in a banquet of natural delights.

'And now,' said Chichele, as coffee and cigars made their appearance, 'we have arrived at the critical moment of all picnics. How on earth are we to get through the rest of the day? I wish Masterly had brought a few of his office-boxes.'

'Please do not take Mr. Masterly!' cried Lady Miranda; 'he and I are going to botanise. This valley is a little paradise of wildflowers.'

'And I,' said Mrs. Paragon, 'am going to make a sketch of this lovely glade, and to think over all the wise things I have learnt this morning.'

'Not to trouble about Moses, I hope,' said Philip. 'Meanwhile Mr. Brownlow and I are going to worship Nature on the heights. There is a lovely pool up there, where we can have a bathe, sir, if you like.'

'You may take my new pony, Ambrose,' Mr. Chichele said; 'it will do him good to have an extra march. He gets too little work, and is full of nonsense. For myself, politeness constrains me to stay behind and mend Mrs. Paragon's pencils.'

CHAPTER XXXVI

THE BROKEN THREAD

CAMILLA, as she watched the little cavalcade start on
the expedition, and go winding up the valley side, was
conscious of a great relief. She was in that state of
nervous distress in which the common intercourse of
life—the very proximity of life's ordinary companions
—becomes a burthen too grievous to be borne. The
camp-life—spent necessarily for the most part in public,
and half in picnic fashion—had tried her more than she
was aware till she experienced the comfort of its temporary cessation—the exquisite prospect of a day of
solitude. Even Lady Miranda's visits had been a
doubtful pleasure, for Camilla could not be open with
her. There were thoughts in her mind that could not
be whispered even to that sympathising ear. Camilla

almost shuddered to breathe them to herself: they were dreadful, heartrending companions; but it was something to be alone with them, to face them composedly, even though with the composure of despair.

For Camilla was in a desperate mood. A question was forcing itself upon her—the gravest, the most momentous that a woman's fate can bring to her for reply. Could she bear the burthen of her married life any longer? Could she go on with an existence which was growing every day a more and more horrid mockery—a more dismal, degrading travesty of all that married life should be — a more dreadful desecration of its sanctities, a crueller disappointment of its hopes.

She sat by the flame of waning love and watched it with eyes of terror, as it sank, flickered, sank again, and threatened to expire. That sacred fire had been life itself to her—had lit up her world with glory, radiance, hope. Now it was sinking—dying; the hearth was growing cold and black—ashes and dust where once had been the genial core of heat—the vital glow—the living light. How would life seem when the fire had finally gone out?

There are people, no doubt, who make such discoveries, and survive them. Cold, shallow, impassive natures may bear the shock of such a revelation without a mortal pang; may rally from it and live on after it, dully acquiescent in their doom. But to a nature like Camilla's—ardent, tender, sympathetic—with much to give and wanting much in return—such a discovery is a deathblow. The sort of existence which is possible

after it can at best be but a wretched compromise, which
may serve to hide from the outer world the catastrophe
that has laid the home in ruins and stripped its altars
of their sacred fire, but which, none the less, means
desolation to the inmates. Could such an existence be
borne? and, if not borne, how was it to be escaped?
This was the problem which was taking possession of
Camilla's soul with an ever-increasing intensity, crowd-
ing out every other subject from her thoughts. She was
smarting under a deep sense of disappointment, humiliation, insult. Her tender, sacred gift of love had been
misprized, profaned by a rude, careless hand. Her
husband's facile levity had made her married life one
long outrage. She had enshrined him in her heart, and
had worshipped him ardently, blindly—with the willing
blindness of a devotee. Now the illusion was destroyed;
the cruel, bitter truth had forced itself upon her, and
would no longer be ignored. Her idol was revealed in
its true colours, no longer a possible object of adoration.
A woman, it has been said, always needs to rule bene-
ficently by making the joy of another soul; but how, if
the other soul plays traitor to that kind sovereignty and
is bent on other joys than those which its gentle despot
is able or willing to afford? Camilla was looking forward now to her husband's return with absolute horror.
He had been faithless and cowardly—he had distrusted
her, deceived her, defrauded her. He had brought her
to dishonour, or near it; he had broken all the dread
moral compacts which—human laws apart—bind the
souls of husband and wife in sacred union. He had

left her, with a lie on his lips, bent on some mission of perfidy ; and he would come back—Camilla instinctively knew—bright, courteous, caressing, with an air of pleasant, easy gaiety,—with a smile—a traitor's smile—lighting up his face, and expect to be the same to her as before, and that she should be the same to him. This was more than Camilla could endure or achieve. She could not bear it ; but then, none the less, it seemed inevitable. Religion —custom—the law of God and man alike—her own sense of right, the tradition of duty and honour, the common feeling of society, barred her at every point, and, at the first thought of resistance or escape, seemed to rivet the chains which were weighing so heavily upon her. They were cutting her sensitive and finely-strung nature to the quick, but they must be worn. Turn where she would, no ray of light broke the dreariness of that sad horizon.

So Camilla sat through the still, exquisite hours, as the long day waned from the mid-day glow to the stillness of the afternoon. The valleys lay bathed in a flood of softened light; the breeze was whispering through the pine tops ; the shadows of the great fleecy clouds swept across the mountain sides, and by their noiseless motion seemed but to give a deeper intensity to the stillness of the scene; the kites, wheeling high in air, threw their shadows, too, on the bright ground below, and with their shrill scream broke, now and again, the silence which, but for them, reigned unbroken in this solemn solitude. Camilla had felt it a relief at first to be alone ; but now a sense of loneliness

began to take possession of her. Why was it, she asked
herself, that she had been longing for solitude? Why
was the sympathy of loving, tender hearts only an additional distress? Because there are troubles which
isolate us from our species; and Camilla's trouble was
one of them. Her burthen was one which no friendly
hand could lighten ; her cup of sorrow, of disappointment, of despair could be touched by no other lip. ' The
heart knoweth its own bitterness :' the grim words forced
themselves now upon her with a dreary reality. Those
pangs, no doubt, are keenest which the sufferer dares
not reveal, and to which our best friend must remain a
stranger. So the iron was entering Camilla's tender
soul : she sank backward with a groan, and hid her
face as if to shut out a world that had become to her
only a torture-house ; ' O Lord,' she cried, in bitterness
of spirit, ' have mercy upon me : I am in misery—my
strength faileth me.'

.   .   .   .   .

She started up, for a footstep fell upon her ear.
Some one was riding up to the camp by the path which
lay close beside the spot where she was sitting. She
turned to see who the newcomer was—one of the mes-
sengers, no doubt, who brought Chichele his daily batch
of letters and papers, and seemed the one slight link
which bound them to the world that they had left below.
She turned and she saw that which made her heart
stand still. Was her mind wandering ? Was she the
victim, once more, of an illusion such as had disturbed
the first weeks of her married life ? Was it the phantom

of her troubled imagination, or was it the real Sinclair who was now coming toward her? No phantom, Camilla speedily assured herself, but a living reality—the man, of all others, whom she would, if asked beforehand, have desired not to see, in this her hour of extremity; and whom yet, now that he stood there, awaiting her command, she felt powerless to turn away—powerless even to wish to do so.

His invasion of her solitude had been, it was evident, completely accidental; his surprise, when Camilla told him that Chichele and the rest were not at the camp, was obviously sincere. He had been sent for, he told her, to come to see Mr. Chichele upon business, and, he supposed, had arrived a day sooner than he was expected.

'Well,' he said, 'if Mr. Chichele has gone holiday-making, I must make holiday too. Fortune has been kind to me for once. May I stay here with you awhile?'

Camilla's first impulse had been to escape; her next to conceal from the intruder every symptom of the trouble which was weighing upon her—a trouble in which he was certain to feel so very special an interest; in which the occurrences of the voyage had given him so good a right to be interested; in which, all the more for that, Camilla revolted from the idea of allowing him any part. There are wounds so sensitive that the very approach of another's hand, however gentle, gives an apprehension of agony; some troubles in which the proffer of help seems an officious interference.

From any such meddling with her secret sorrow Camilla shrank instinctively with aversion. But even while Sinclair was speaking, this aversion began to give way before a truer, juster, more natural sentiment. There were several qualities in Sinclair which appealed to what were just now Camilla's direst wants. His strong, vehement, upright character invited confidence. Intense as his passion might be, he would never, she was certain, allow himself to abet her in departing, for an instant, by a hair's-breadth, even in thought, from that which he regarded as the highest standard of good and right—far less would he tempt her to so depart. Rather, at whatever sacrifice of less sacred considerations, he would bid her stand fast at the post of duty, and bear the worst that such steadfastness entailed. Her honour, her vow, her spotless purity of soul were, she was certain, as dear to him as to her. He had proposed to her once that which she had rejected as wrong and dishonourable; but he was prompted by an honourable passion, and he had spoken in the honest conviction that he was acting as honour bade him. He had been positive that he was right. Was it certain that he had been wrong? There was then, at any rate, room for an honest difference of opinion. There was no such ambiguity now about Camilla's position; there could be no doubt, with honourable natures, what her duty was, and there could, equally, be no doubt that Sinclair would encourage her to do it—would insist on her doing it.

This conviction made it possible to regard without

alarm another fact about Sinclair of which Camilla was
equally well assured. He loved her, she well knew,
with passionate earnestness. She had known it at first;
she had known it ever since. Ignore the fact as she
might,—as, indeed, she had,—it had, none the less, a
firm place among her most absolute convictions. His
language, his manner, his look had been alike unmistakable, and they had all told the same story. His
behaviour on the few occasions on which, since that
dreadful last interview on board ship, they had met, had
said the same thing in a manner which commanded her
regard by its chivalrous avoidance of anything that
could give her a shade of annoyance, could give scandal's
keen eye and busy tongue the barest semblance of
justification, or could seem to hint at the possibility of
reopening a forbidden topic. He had obeyed her injunction, her unspoken wishes, with the intelligent
insight of devotion,—with delicacy of taste, with fine
accuracy of judgment, with the self-abnegation which is
the choicest ingredient of worship. But, above all, he was
true and he was thorough; and truth and thoroughness
seemed just then to Camilla the two transcendent merits in
the relations of human beings to one another. Be the cause
what it might, the feeling of vexation at an unexpected
disturbance of her solitude—heightened at first by the
thought that Sinclair should be the person to disturb it—
was speedily mastered by a sense that he was a friend,
whose allegiance was firm, whose care for her would
be wise and self-restrained, whose devotion claimed
whatever recognition she could honourably make, and

who was sure to bring her help in an hour of direst need.

'Do come and sit down,' she said. 'You see I am in want of company.'

'And so am I,' said Sinclair, as he took his seat beside her; 'I have been having a solitary ride and am in a melancholy mood; but why are you not with the rest? You are not ill, I hope—but you *are* ill; your looks say so; I ought not to have come.'

'No,' said Camilla, whose bloodless cheek was by this time telling the tale of overwrought nerves and an agitated mind; 'I am not ill—not ill in body at least. I wish you to stay. My own thoughts are very bad company just now—perhaps you can help me to get rid of them.'

Camilla saw the flash of intense interest which lighted up Sinclair's face as she spoke, followed instantly by the expression of self-restraint and self-repression, which was habitual to him. There was comfort for her in both. But there was another look which Camilla could not refuse to see, and which, miserable as she was on her own account, filled her soul with pity. Sinclair's face showed symptoms of long-endured suffering; its composure bespoke less a courageous preparedness to meet the unknown blows of fate than the wretched conviction that the worst blow has fallen,—that life has no hope and no keener misery than that which is, at the moment, endured. The two looked at one another, and each read in the other's face a tragic story, the full purport of which it was only too easy to understand—a story of despair.

Camilla still struggled against a revelation. 'We had many pleasant talks on board ship,' she said; 'I feel quite in the mood for one now. Talk to me, please, as you used then.'

Sinclair perfectly understood the meaning of this invitation. It meant that the unfortunate rupture of their intimacy on the voyage to India was to be ignored, and that their relations were to be taken up at the earlier point when they were merely friends whose society was mutually pleasant. The merits of their estrangement were to be left undiscussed, undecided; but the mere fact of Camilla's readiness to renew their intimacy implied that she was less confident than before of the justice of her decision, and had, at any rate, no wish to repeat the indignant terms in which it had been expressed. They were to be friends as before: if Sinclair had been wrong, he was forgiven—if he had been wronged, he was to exercise forgiveness. Between such friends as they still were, it was unnecessary, inexpedient, to consider who had been to blame. They were to ignore all that was painful in the past; but there was something, Sinclair felt, that—keep it out of sight in act and language as one would—could never really be ignored. Camilla, too, was aware of a vital difference in their relations. She knew that she held this strong man's existence in her hand. Life was heaven or hell to him according as she smiled or turned away. And now she bade him pick up this thread of their intercourse at the point where it had been broken off, and be to her as he had been before. Camilla, if

she had had time to think, might have known that it
was an impossible request. She would have known,
too, that there was at work in the recesses of her conscience a desire to make amends to a man whom, as she
now judged her conduct, she had treated with folly and
injustice. Sinclair had warned her that she would be
miserable in her married life : he now found her in the
climax of her misery. He had tried his best to save
her, had passionately implored her to let herself be
saved. She had turned a deaf ear to his warnings—
the silly ear of inexperience and foolhardihood. She
had rejected his offers of help and rushed blindly on
her fate. She had trampled on his proposal with the
vehement decisiveness due to a dishonour and a crime.
She had tried to forget it, to forget him, to banish him
and his unholy suggestions from the confines of her
thoughts : no distant outlying region of her mind had
been allowed to harbour a thought of him. And now
bitter experience had taught her the truth in a way
which could not be gainsaid. Pride whispered a moni-
tion to conceal the humiliating reverse of all her hopes.
But pride, though a powerful factor in our lives, is not
always powerful enough to guide them wholly as it
would. Camilla's pride, at any rate, was hard pressed
by stronger impulses — her truer self — a generous
prompting to confess her mistake, to be just to the man
whom she had so fatally misjudged. The solitude of
her position was becoming too much for her to bear. She
had turned away in horror from the idea of sympathy ;
but she found now that she was longing for it at any

price. Her trouble, borne alone, was crushing her, and the possibility, suddenly disclosed, of sharing it promised a sort of exquisite relief.

Sinclair, though too wise to urge an avowal, seemed, with a fine instinct, to read her thoughts. He was a person with whom it was in vain to try to deceive, even to deceive oneself. His profound sincerity forced his companion to be sincere. 'Tell me about yourself,' he said ; 'that is the only interesting thing to talk about.'

'But,' said Camilla with a laugh, more dreary as it seemed to her companion than many sighs, 'that is what I have been talking about to myself all the morning. I do not find it edifying or interesting at all. Your arrival, I hoped, would change the conversation.'

There is probably in the small vicissitudes of human destiny no change in a man's lot so striking as when he finds himself, after months of absence or enforced silence, suddenly in the presence of a woman whom he passionately loves, alone with her, and enjoined to speak. Sinclair had ridden up the mountain that morning in a more than ordinarily gloomy mood. His work-a-day theory of dogged performance of duty being enough for mortal wants, and all that mortals have a right to ask, had completely broken down under the strain of enjoyments more delightful than any with which he had reckoned, and wants more imperative than any which he had till now experienced. His whole view of things was altered. He found that he had been used to decry the pleasant side of life simply because he knew not how great its pleasures were. The distant and occasional

sight of Camilla when they had met in the ordinary
intercourse of society had been a constant incentive
alike to his passion and his regret. He had forced both
feelings down with a determined, unsparing hand; but
he had vanquished neither, far less destroyed it. Both,
rather, had gathered secret force from the repression,
and they were now—he had been mournfully acknow-
ledging to himself as, through the long solitary hours,
he reviewed the position—his masters. Thus it was that
he judged human conduct—the forces which move it,
and the temptations that beset it—with a far different
eye, for he now knew how tremendous those forces are.
He realised that there are moral conflicts from which,
even if he emerges a victor, a man carries away with
him grievous wounds and scars, the signs of what the
victory has cost him. Sinclair had now, in a sense,
conquered himself; but the conquest had turned the
world into a desert to him; it had left him hopeless,
joyless, motiveless. He had no intention of succumbing;
but he understood how it is that many men succumb.
He had accepted the inevitable; but he had accepted it
—as the typical Mohammedan bends to the conqueror's
yoke—with silent curses, and the reservation, all the
more heartfelt for being unexpressed, that rebellion is
lawful the first moment that it becomes possible to
rebel. So he had gone on, in a sort of dumb, aimless
suffering; a previously acquired impetus still carried
him along; but the mainspring of his existence seemed
broken—or, rather, it was unshipped and passive,
though as strong as ever, if only its bearing on his life

should be restored. And now, suddenly, Camilla had restored it: she was appealing to him for help; she bade him forget all that had disturbed their relations; she asked for sympathy—for confidential intercourse. Sinclair sat for an instant looking at her in silence. There was a haggard, hungry look in his eyes, as of a thirsty man at the sight of the stream to which he may not put his famished lips. It was borne in upon Camilla that, heavy as was her load of trouble, there was some one in the world more wretched than herself.

While he hesitated, Camilla spoke again : 'I should like very much,' she said, 'to hear something about you. You are one of the people for whom I have great hopes. I have a conviction that you will do something with your life—something worth doing. It is a rare lot : few people try for it, or even wish for it—do they ? and of those who wish, how few achieve.'

'Achieve ?' said Sinclair, with bitterness ; 'it sounds ironical to human destiny to use such a word about mankind. Respectable endurance is its highest flight.'

'Well,' said Camilla, 'there are worse things than respectable endurance—are there not? It is a great achievement to be respectable. But what has brought you here ?'

'A bad business,' said Sinclair, 'I am afraid. There has been some horrid company floating, with all its usual abominations about a gold-mine at Muddapollium. The bubble has burst; all sorts of people are said to be implicated ; there will be a scandal, and I am one of the luckless victims whom Mr. Chichele has selected to have the pleasant task of exploring it. Do not you pity me now ?'

'Implicated?' said Camilla, starting up with sudden interest and disregarding the latter portion of her companion's speech; 'please tell me all you have heard about the people. Is it known who they are?'

'Not in the least,' said Sinclair. 'All that is believed about it is that some influential officials have been pulling the strings—managing the Rajah, working the Government, and so forth—and trafficking in shares, which the stockbrokers at home have been playing some nasty game with. What a business for a gentleman to have to soil his fingers in handling!'

Camilla's cup of misery had overflowed; her powers of endurance were exhausted; her vital energies seemed to be sinking; she could do, she could endure no more. She sat there cold, white, speechless. Before Sinclair's words were fully spoken, he was aware that he had unwittingly laid his finger on some sensitive nerve. 'You must help me,' was all that Camilla could force herself to say. 'You must save him.'

'Help you!' cried Sinclair, by this time as much alarmed as his companion; 'you know that I would die to do that; but tell me what you mean.'

'I mean,' said Camilla, whose stoicism had, for the moment, completely deserted her, 'that I am the most unfortunate woman in the world, and the greatest failure. Everything with me has failed. I had an intense desire to make my life something especially good, bright, and noble,—better than the common lot. The common ambitions of the world would not satisfy me. I longed for happiness, and I thought that I had found it. Now what have I come to? But you must help me. You must help my husband. That is the greatest favour you could show me. I know you are a friend, and I appeal to your friendship. Do not think from what I said just now that I have a word to say against him; but he has been unfortunate. We are embarrassed, as I daresay you know. Philip takes things lightly, and slides easily into positions which may be easily misunderstood in a bad sense. You will clear it all up, and clear him, will you not?'

'Whatever service I can do,' said Sinclair, 'is yours already. I am what I was when I spoke to you on board ship. My feelings are unchanged. I care not for life except for the chance of serving you.'

'But I must tell you one thing,' said Camilla; 'you must never think that I have repented of my answer to you or doubted that I was right. You do not doubt it —do you?'

'I doubt nothing that you tell me to believe,' said Sinclair, who perhaps cherished privately some lingering scepticism as to Philip's merits as a husband.

'I have had great happiness,' said Camilla; 'I have been very happy; some clouds of trouble come to us all. Did I say that I was unfortunate? It was wrong of me—ungrateful, weak. I gave him my heart; it is wholly his. His troubles are mine.'

Sinclair never forgot that scene, as Camilla sat looking blindly across the valley, her eyes full of tears, but with heroism in her face; the exquisite mountain range opposite; the white cascade showing like a spray through the still, blue atmosphere; the breeze whispering through the pines; the children shouting to the cattle on the hillside. Little did Camilla guess how destiny was, at that very moment, shaping her future to a new and unsuspected phase.

'Look,' she said, as a horseman came galloping over the crest of a neighbouring hill; 'who is that coming towards the camp? Mr. Chichele, surely. Go, please, and stop him. I want to be alone. If he asks for me, tell him that I am coming in directly.'

Sinclair went at once upon his mission, and awaited Chichele's arrival; but the message was not destined to be delivered. Chichele's horror-stricken face, as he came up, forbade a word. He was labouring evidently under some tremendous excitement. As he dismounted Sinclair could see that his hand was shaking; and his voice, broken and tremulous, as he asked where Mrs. Ambrose was, showed that some event of no ordinary character was taxing his powers of self-restraint to the utmost. He went away to her at once, and Sinclair sat waiting in his tent,—sick at heart with the horrid expectancy of impending disaster.

Chichele's appearance and manner as he approached Camilla announced him a herald of misfortune before a word was spoken. He took her gently by the hand; but seemed as if he could not force himself to speak. There was a moment—an eternity—of awful suspense.

Camilla could do nothing but await the blow that she felt certain was in the act of falling.

'You are a brave woman,' Chichele said at last; 'and it needs a brave man to do what I have to do now. Something awful has happened.'

Camilla by this time was as white as Chichele: her heart was beating so violently that she could not have spoken if she wished; but she had no word to say; she could only wait, as a helpless victim looks up at the coming blow. At last it fell. 'There has been a terrible accident—to your husband.' Camilla heard no more; her nerves, long overstrained, gave way; a sudden darkness had gathered round her; she was sinking— sinking; one dreadful cry Sinclair heard, as he sat, with beating heart, in the silence of his tent. Then there was a sound of hurrying feet, and in another moment he was helping Chichele to carry Camilla, unconscious and inanimate, to her tent.

Presently Lady Miranda and the rest arrived, and then Sinclair learnt the dreadful story which Mr. Chichele had to tell. Ambrose had gone off with Mr. Brownlow by the narrow mountain path which led to the top of the gorge. At a turning of the road they had come suddenly on some forest-folk, laden with huge burthens of timber, resting in a shady recess by the hillside. One of them had sprung up, as Ambrose turned the corner, and had dislodged his load from its frail balance. It fell with a crash almost at Ambrose's feet. His horse gave a start, a plunge, and sprang across the path; there was a sudden scramble at the edge; a wild cry as the falling man saw the abyss beneath him. All had happened too quickly for Brownlow to observe, far less to be able to describe it. An hour later they had clambered round by a side path, and found the dead man's body lying, far below, with his horse beside him.

It was evident that both must have been killed upon the spot. Philip's face, as they laid him that evening in his tent, showed no sign of violence. Never had poor Phil Ambrose's handsome features worn a gentler and more kindly expression. Meanwhile kind Nature had shrouded Camilla in safe oblivion from the horrid shock. Nor was it for many days that she learnt the details of the tragedy which had made her a widow.

Camilla's swoon was a long one. When she recovered consciousness, Miranda was bending tenderly over her with eyes full of pity; recollection began to revive; she felt only a frightful pang, and sank again into stupor.

CHAPTER XXXVII

INVENI PORTUM

'Inveni portum, Spes ac Fortuna, valete,
    Sat me ludistis.'

A SKILFUL analyst of human emotion has observed that the rapidity with which ideas grow old in our memories is in nicely adjusted proportion to their importance to us. 'Their apparent age,' he says, 'runs up miraculously, like the value of diamonds, as they increase in magnitude. A great calamity, for instance, is as old as the Trilobites an hour after it has happened. It stains backward through all the leaves we have turned over in the book of life, before its blot of tears or of blood is dry on the page we are turning. For this we seem to have lived; it was foreshadowed in dreams that we leaped out of in the cold sweat of terror; in the dissolving views of dark day-visions: all omens pointed to it: all paths led to it. After the tossing self-forgetfulness of the first sleep that follows such an event, it comes upon us afresh as a surprise at waking; in a few minutes it is old again—old as eternity.'

So Camilla found it with herself when, after a dark

period of prostration and obliviousness, body and mind began to rally from the shock, and she once again became sufficiently mistress of herself to review the events of her life with something more than the dimly conscious passivity of an invalid. She had regained her composure, her fortitude, the proper balance of a well-ordered nature. She seemed now to recognise that the tragedy which had just befallen her had existed all along in the predestined chronicle of her life. It was the climax of her life, and it explained it. Read in the light of it, many things about herself were clear that Camilla had never been able to understand. From the first it had been there; it had been hourly drawing nearer and nearer, creeping upon her while she, unaware of its approach, was busy with dreams of joy— the idle dreams of childhood—inexperienced in the stern realities of human lot, incredulous of disaster. The golden vision had faded,—faded and ended, at last, in a ghastly awakening. The rosy summer sky had cradled the coming thunderstorm, whose bolt had fallen upon her. It had dashed her scheme of life—her pretty scheme, rich with hope and confidence, embellished with all the materials of enjoyment—to atoms; there was nothing but a blackened ruin. For a while she lay crushed and stunned beneath the blow. Her task was now to begin, with a soberer equanimity than heretofore, with humble, reverent hands to build afresh a more substantial fabric on a humbler scheme.

Carefully tended by Lady Miranda—tender, faithful and sympathetic nurse—Camilla reached England and the roof where henceforward she would find her home. She had felt a strong desire to go to her father-in-law, and Mr. Ambrose had warmly responded to the wish. The two were, in fact, longing above everything to be together. Their souls, always in unison of taste and feeling, were bound now by the bond of a common sorrow, of which none but themselves knew the precise lineaments or had tasted the full bitterness. Life had been to each a disappointment, and the disappointment of both had centred in the same person and culminated in the same event. Their hearts were aching with the same pang, and each found in the other's companionship the best solace for their special trouble. Philip, with all his shortcomings, had given a brightness to their lives, of which the remembrance was very dear to both. His confidences to Lady Miranda, uttered while the hand of death was already closing upon him, were a last message of love, repentance, reconciliation. They robbed the dreadful story of a part—the cruellest part —of its bitterness. Father and wife could think of the lost one now only with a tender regret—with the fond, faithful partiality which blots out from the remembered picture of the past all that the loving soul would wish to have away. If Philip had failed sometimes, how much there was in him to love; how much in that bright, joyous nature—so incapable of bitterness, so ready to please and be pleased, so quick to forgive, so in love with life and life's pleasures—to claim a lenient judgment and a prompt forgiveness. Had Camilla always judged leniently and forgiven promptly? She recalled

with an aching heart some cruel speeches she had made
him, some harsh judgments, some angry moods. After
all, life would be a sombre affair if the world contained
none but the strong-minded, the unimpulsive, the firm
of purpose, the inflexible of will. Anyhow, feeble or
strong, he was lovable ; and Camilla knew now, only
too well, how dearly she had loved him.

She could not look back upon her married life without many a pang of self-reproach. What honest mortal
can ?   As for Mr. Ambrose, Philip's failings were his
own.   He read in each but the natural outcome of some
infirmity of will and purpose in himself. But neither
Camilla nor her father-in-law were in the mood for
weighing merits and apportioning blame. The past,
with its hopes, its vain attempts, its rash ambitions, its
cruel reverses—too dear, too sacred for anything but
loving retrospect,—lay behind them, dimly seen through
blinding tears. What need of judgment, for one's own
heart or another's, when one is sure of love in both ?

.   .   .   .   .

It was midwinter, and the snow lay thick on the
wide Oxfordshire pastures, when Camilla reached her
home. As they drove along, the sound of village bells
came to them through the still, clear air : the cottage
windows were stuck about with the modest honours of
Christmas-tide.   Everything was still and peaceful;
and Camilla felt a solemn sense of peace come over her.
Mr. Ambrose's gentle, pathetic air—the same that had
impressed her as a girl, sadder now and gentler than
ever—touched a responsive chord within herself. He

had grown an old man since Camilla saw him last—an old man and with a broken look, as if the burthen of life, bear it as patiently as one might, was almost too heavy. He took her hand without a word and led her in ; he pressed her to his heart : Camilla found herself sobbing like a weary child that has crept to its mother's side for aid and consolation. She was weary in spirit and body, and had come, shattered and tempest-tossed, to a harbour of peace—to 'silence and sacred rest, peace and pure joys'—best remedies for a wounded heart. We will leave her there, nor seek to disturb that *sacrum silentium* by prying eye or officious chronicle. Let us hope that those good medicaments will do their work and give her back to peace, serenity, and happiness —though happiness tempered by sad recollections and bounded by more modest hopes than heretofore :

> ' Even our failures are a prophecy,
> Even our yearnings and our bitter tears
> After that fair and true we cannot grasp.'

THE END

Printed by R. & R. CLARK, *Edinburgh.*

SOME OPINIONS OF THE PRESS ON "THE CŒRULEANS."

The *Times* says :—"This is a novel of uncommon merit. In an elegant style, and with considerable power of satire and epigram, Mr. Cunningham gives us sketch after sketch of the various Anglo-Indian types of character. . . . On the whole we should say that Cœrulean officialdom is unusually favoured in its personnel. There does not appear to be a dull day in the whole of Cœrulea. Everybody is witty, and the repartees which fly about are almost too good to be natural. . . . 'The Cœruleans' appeals to a high standard of taste and intelligence, and we shall be surprised if it does not achieve success."

The *Athenæum* says :—"Middle-aged people remember as one of the cleverest short novels they ever read a book called 'Wheat and Tares.' . . . Once only, so far as we know, until now has the writer reminded readers of fiction of his existence. But the talent, though apparently hidden, has after all been at usury. Good as was 'Wheat and Tares' twenty years ago, 'The Cœruleans' must be accounted even better. There was wit in that ; in this there is a riper wit, and abundance of wisdom as well."

The *Saturday Review* says :—"It is a joyful relief to come upon a pleasant and natural story, admirably written by a gentleman and scholar, who is at the same time blessed with a constant flow of quiet but most effective humour. Such a story is 'The Cœruleans.' . . . Mr. Cunningham's style is not only correct, but elegant—with an elegance now unhappily rare ; and all that he writes is forcible and self-contained. There is not a dull page in the book."

The *Academy* says :—"Several theories of Indian government are discussed in this brilliant book ('The Cœruleans'), and the writer has much to say on this question that is well worth consideration if it may not always command assent."

The *Guardian* says :—"'The Cœruleans' is an unusually pleasant and entertaining novel. It is clever, original, and refined, full of bright scenes and amiable conversations, as well as excellent studies of character. Above all, it contrasts favourably with the majority of clever novels of the day by the preponderance of agreeable people among its characters."

The *Morning Post* says :—"There is much that is decidedly good in this tale, the writer of which has evidently thought out the theories he puts forward in a manner that denotes intelligence and culture."

The *St. James' Gazette* says :—"This is one of the best novels that have appeared for many a long day. Interesting as a specimen of romance, the style of writing is so excellent—scholarly and at the same time easy and natural—that the two volumes are worth reading on that account alone. But there is also masterly description of persons, places, and things ; skilful analysis of character ; a constant play of wit and humour ; and a happy gift of instantaneous portraiture."

The *English Mail* says :—"Mr. Cunningham offers a feast not only to the lovers of a good story but to the students of style ; and there is scarcely a page of 'The Cœruleans' but bristles with good things well said."

The *Daily Telegraph* says :—"The story is full of incident and episodes of society and solitude, witty and wise in due season, and easily and gracefully written."

The *Literary World* says :—"The interest is very great and well sustained. 'The Cœruleans' is the kind of book we do not advise any one to begin reading late in the evening, unless he wishes to be kept out of bed till the small hours of the morning. Even a surfeited reviewer of fiction may confess to having been a victim to its seductive influence."

The *British Weekly* says :—"'The Cœruleans' is one of the wholesomest bits of reading one could spend a summer afternoon with on beach or moor."

The *Scottish Review* says :—"'The Cœruleans' has one great and, in modern novels, rare merit ; it is written in most vigorous forcible English, of which the writer has such complete mastery that his style is always easy and natural. It is also a most amusing sketch of certain phases of Indian life and character."